Book One in the **EFFIGIES** series

FATE OF
FLAMES

SARAH RAUGHLEY

Simon Pulse

New York London Toronto Sydney New Delhi

SIMON PULSE

An imprint of Simon & Schuster Children's Publishing Division

1230 Avenue of the Americas, New York, New York 10020

First Simon Pulse hardcover edition November 2016

Text copyright © 2016 by Sarah Raughley

Jacket photo-illustration copyright © 2016 by Steve Gardner

All rights reserved, including the right of reproduction in whole or in part in any form.

SIMON PULSE and colophon are registered trademarks of Simon & Schuster, Inc.

For information about special discounts for bulk purchases,

please contact Simon & Schuster Special Sales

at 1-866-506-1949 or business@simonandschuster.com.

The Simon & Schuster Speakers Bureau can bring authors to your live event.

For more information or to book an event contact the Simon & Schuster Speakers

Bureau at 1-866-248-3049 or visit our website at www.simonspeakers.com.

Jacket designed by Karina Granda

Interior designed by Mike Rosamilia

The text of this book was set in Adobe Caslon Pro.

Manufactured in the United States of America

2 4 6 8 10 9 7 5 3 1

This book has been cataloged with the Library of Congress.

ISBN 978-1-4814-6677-6 (hc)

ISBN 978-1-4814-6679-0 (eBook)

For my mom and dad

FATE OF
FLAMES

PART ONE

WHY run so fast the hurtling crowd
Adown the long streets, roaring loud?
Is Rhodes on fire?—more fast the throng,
Wedg'd close and closer, storms along.
High o'er the train, he seems to lead,
Behold a Knight on warlike Steed!
Behind is dragged a wondrous load;
Beneath what Monster groans the road?
With wide jaws like the Crocodile,
In shape a Dragon to the sight,
All eyes in wonder gaze the while—
Now on the Monster, now the Knight.

—Friedrich von Schiller, "The Fight with the Dragon"
translated by Sir Edward Bulwer Lytton, 1852

1

THE WAR SIREN WAILED.

I gaped at the windows, my eyes locked on the sky-grazing tower that stood out against the Manhattan skyline.

The Needle. Like all the others in the country, it was a tall, sleek eyesore glimmering day and night with bright streaks of the most obnoxious metallic blue running up and down its length like little live wires. It was supposed to be some kind of high frequency . . . something-something particular disrupter. Okay, I'm not great with technical terms. The *important* thing was that it was more than just a tourist attraction.

Eyesore or not, it was the only thing keeping everyone in the city from being slaughtered very messily.

Blinking lights meant we were safe.

And its lights had just blinked off.

No one in my algebra class said anything. No one could. We were screwed.

"Okay, ch-children, just remain calm," Mr. Whomsley shouted, though he tripped over his own feet trying to get around his desk.

His sunken eyes darted around the classroom as if looking for one of us to tell him what to do next. Except we were all looking at *him* now, at his gaping mouth and his greasy forehead beading with sweat. I could tell he was nervous, no, terrified—terrified because the War Siren that hadn't blown in some fifty years had just broken into short, quick pulses.

The signal for a Category Three attack.

It was all from the Hirsch-Johnson Phantom Disaster Scale. Four categories. Categories One and Two were already bad, with damage to infrastructure and physical injury expected to varying, awful degrees. But Category Three . . . large-scale destruction . . . city-wide terror . . .

And that was just the third level.

Wait. Category *Three*?

Oh god. My nails grazed my desk. *This isn't happening.*

"Don't panic!" Mr. Whomsley shuffled the papers on his desk.

"Mr. Whomsley?" Janice Gellar sounded near tears. A lot of *oh my gods* harmonized with her whimpers in the background. My own included.

"I said don't panic. Don't panic!" He started grasping his tie, wiping the sweat off his forehead with the back of his sleeve.

"What the *hell* are we supposed to *do*?" Rick Fielding roared from the back of the classroom.

Then Whomsley finally got his beady eyes to focus, probably because he knew as well as I did that another two seconds of waffling and there'd be a bloody stampede for the door. I could already hear the doors of other classrooms opening, students filing out, teachers crying out over the terrified din: "Okay, everyone, now just proceed in a calm and orderly fashion."

Calm and orderly. Like we weren't all going to die soon.

"O-okay, students, remain calm." Mr. Whomsley readjusted his toupee and sucked in a breath. "Proceed to the shelter in a . . . a calm and orderly fashion."

Right. The shelter. Just like the handbook said, going to the school's underground shelter was the first thing we were supposed to do "in the event of an emergency." 'Course, nobody really read the handbook anymore because we hadn't had to in years.

So after that . . . what were we supposed to do?

As I stood from my chair, I tried to remember what those two military guys had said at that special preparedness seminar back in September—the same one they gave every year. Bits and pieces came back to me:

In the rare case of a hostile attack, take only the essentials. Get to the shelter beneath the school within ten minutes of the first few warning pulses.

Ten minutes. Or was it *five* minutes?

Damn it, what had I been thinking, *blogging* instead of paying attention?

I slung my tote bag over my shoulder and pushed my chair in. The feet groaned against the tiles, but I could barely hear it beneath the siren's steady rhythm and my own pulse beating in my ears.

"Orderly fashion!" Mr. Whomsley cried when people started shoving. "Orderly!"

In front of me, Missy Stevenson was muttering deliriously under her breath, and I couldn't blame her. New York had one of the most efficient APDs in the world. This wasn't supposed to happen to us.

"The National Guard should be here in ten to fifteen minutes," Mr. Whomsley assured us.

True. And if there was a base nearby, the Sect could get here a bit faster. That meant there was actually a chance we could make it down to the shelter alive before the big fight scene started.

I inhaled an unsteady breath and nodded. Everything was good. Everything was going to be fine.

Except . . .

Ten to fifteen minutes would be quite enough time for a Category Three phantom to raze Manhattan to the ground.

As we flooded out of the classroom and joined the long, silent death march making its way through the labyrinthine halls, I noted the terror hollowing out the faces of students and teachers alike, even those with the good sense to at least pretend to be calm and collected. Deep down, we were all hoping for the best, praying to be saved. But what if the cavalry came too late? What if nobody came to save us?

Then *I* would end up being the city's only hope.

Oh god.

I let the thought sink in as I gazed down at my clammy hands. If people knew what I could do . . . if they knew who I was, *what* I was, especially now, then they'd ask me to save them. Beg me. And I knew I couldn't.

But if I didn't do *something* . . .

I squeezed my eyes shut, my heart rattling. What the hell was I supposed to do?

"Oh god, there it is!" Missy Stevenson shrieked, and it was like all of Ashford High erupted into chaos. She was pointing out the windows, up at the sky, its bright blue darkening by the second. Dead, gray clouds crackled with frantic energy, but nobody was expecting lightning. We knew better.

We saw *it* instead.

It was as if the clouds themselves were distended. A dark, twisting funnel slowly drooped out of the gray masses, but the farther it descended, the clearer its shape became.

I ran to the windows with everyone else, clutching the metal bars separating us from the glass. I'd never seen one before, not up close. It looked like a coiled snake detangling itself from a net, its long, thick body trying to shake itself out of the clouds. And as it slowly dipped into the stratosphere, I could see its body of gray mist hardening, an armor of black bones sprouting down its length, gripping its skin.

A phantom. A *big* one.

The metal bars bit into my palms, pinching the blood flow.

"Keep moving, students!" A teacher began shoving kids forward. "Get to the shelter. Now!"

I wasn't gaping at the sky anymore. My eyes were fixed on the chaos down below. The NYPD was doing a pretty crappy job of getting citizens off the street in a calm and orderly fashion, though a *giant freaking monster appearing from nowhere* probably made the task all the more difficult. Traffic had come to a full stop with too many cars going in too many directions. People were abandoning their vehicles altogether and fleeing on foot, though some multitasked and captured the chaos on their phones as they ran. It was bedlam down there.

Nobody seemed to notice the tiny girl who'd hidden underneath a parked Jeep.

"Keep moving, students!"

Just go to the shelter, Maia, I told myself. It was okay; the police would take care of it.

I managed to tear my eyes away from the girl, but they slid back again, helplessly. Nobody had noticed her. Where were her parents? Why wasn't anyone helping her?

"Maia," a teacher called me. Mrs. Samuelson. "Get moving!"

I clenched and unclenched my hands. No doubt they could all see me shaking.

"Get moving, Maia!"

I wanted to. God, I wanted to.

But people's lives were in danger. Neither the National Guard nor the Sect were anywhere to be found. And a horrifying monster was about to kill us all.

A deep, low cry, as haunting and pure as a whale's song, vibrated through the streets, shuddering up my bones. The tail had broken free from the clouds, sharpening to a point, coiling its way down to Earth, dangerously close to us. When this thing landed, it'd take out a good chunk of Prospect Avenue for sure. A few streets later and Ashford High would be next.

June . . . if you were me, you'd do something, wouldn't you?

A stupid question. I already knew the answer. I gritted my teeth.

Meanwhile, Missy Stevenson finally just flipped out. Clutching chunks of her hair, she tried to run in the other direction, howling like a banshee, pushing her way through students, and swinging wildly at whoever was dumb enough not to get out of her way.

It was the distraction I needed.

In that one hectic moment, I stupidly took off toward the fire exit. "Maia!"

I couldn't tell who was calling me, and it didn't matter. I was too fast.

"Maia, get back here!"

Tears stung my eyes as I sped down the steps. I wasn't ready for stuff like this: saving people, fighting things. It had only been two days, *two* days since fate crossed my name off the list of people's lives to manhandle. I needed more time.

Then again . . . technically, this *was* what I'd always wanted, in a way. This was what I'd always dreamed of, ever since I was a kid playing in the backyard with June, the two of us acting out our dumb hero fantasies with bathroom towels for capes and stuffed animals to valiantly pummel to death.

To fight like one of *them*. To save lives like one of them.

And now I *was* one of them.

An Effigy.

Careful what you wish for, I guess.

Down three flights of steps and through the ground-level fire exit, I'd just rounded a corner when a crazed, bespectacled tax accountant type almost ran me over on his way inside Ashford High. He wasn't the only one. People were rushing to find shelter; didn't matter where. Ashford security stopped trying to reason with them altogether and started barricading the entrances. That definitely meant my teachers weren't going to be following me any time soon, but the jury was still out on whether that was a good thing or not.

I stepped out onto Seventh Avenue and looked to my left. Several buildings down, beyond the street intersection, was the little girl, red hair cascading over her face in ringlets, curled up in the fetal position underneath a gaudy red Jeep. The phantom was taking its time unspooling its long torso from the sky, which gave *me* time.

Taking the thing on wasn't in the cards. I was nowhere near the level I'd need to be to fight it. But if I could just get the young girl out from underneath the car and take her somewhere safe . . .

Preferably without dying.

This was easily the dumbest thing I'd ever done. Bracing myself for the worst, I fought through the crowds, gasping in shock when a car I'd thought was parked suddenly veered into me. Luckily, I rolled off the hood with minimal injuries. An Effigy thing, no doubt. I hadn't really had much of an opportunity to test the full extent of what I could do, but now was as good a time as any.

Rubbing my left hip I slammed the hood with a fist. "What the *hell*, you jackass!" But the terrified man inside was too shocked to respond. I opened his car door. "Get out and run," I said. *"Now."*

He didn't argue. The more people ran for their lives, the clearer the street got, save for all those cars, motorcycles, and trucks. I went straight for the red Jeep, squeezing through the gaps between cars, jumping on hoods when it was faster.

"Hey, you! What the hell are you doing? You gotta get outta here!" a police officer was shouting from somewhere down the street. "Hey, moron!"

Asshole. Ignoring him, I sped to the Jeep and knelt down on the pavement.

"Hey." I kept my voice soft and nonthreatening, but still loud enough to carry over the chaos. "I'm Maia. Maia Finley. What're you doing all the way down there?"

The girl peered up at me through her red tresses, brushing strands out of her face.

"Come on, I'll take you somewhere safe, okay?"

The little girl curled her bottom lip, obviously hesitant. Unfortunately, when the sky starts crapping out giant monsters, hesitant stops being an option.

"Come on." I grabbed her hand, but the girl yanked it back. "Kid, I said *come on.*"

"I'm scared." She tearfully rubbed her dirty arms across her face.

"Yeah, I know. We're all sc—"

A crash. The street shook beneath my knees so violently I toppled over, my arm just barely cushioning my face. My head snapped up just in time for me to see it: a long, serpent-like tail of black bones disappearing behind a thicket of trees. The phantom had landed a few streets away, probably Prospect Avenue. But if it were slithering through the streets, we'd still be able to see it, wouldn't we? I couldn't. Where did it go?

"Okay, kid, enough's enough." I pulled her out from underneath the Jeep. "You like high schools? Let's go back to mine, okay?" Sweeping the girl into my arms, I started looking for a route back to Ashford. "It'll be fun. There's this really big shelter under . . ."

Underground. The phantom wasn't *on* Prospect Avenue at all.

"Hey, kid!" The same NYPD officer. He yanked my arm with fat pasty fingers. "Come on, let's go. You gotta get off the streets; there's no time."

"Wait," I sputtered. "Wait. I think it's—"

"Civilians are evacuating to the subway. Come on." He started pulling me.

"But I think it's under—I think it's under—"

Rumbling. I swiveled around. The little girl clung to my neck. Each unsteady breath scraped my throat. Officer Friendly let me go immediately and joined me in staring down the street in absolute horror.

"It's underground," I whispered.

The phantom surged out of the street, leaving a violent torrent of rubble in its wake. Its body arched in the air, knocking off a traffic light, smashing through lampposts with a long reptilian head covered in a helmet of black bones.

It was coming for us.

"Run!" yelled the officer, though I could barely hear him, what with the little girl splitting my eardrums.

Run? Where? The phantom was yards and yards away, granted, but it was coming for us. There was no way we could outrun it. There was just no way. We were dead.

My arms started shaking so violently I thought I'd drop the kid altogether. Maybe my subconscious was sending me a message: *Forget her.*

I hugged her tighter against my chest. No one could move. It was coming. It was *coming*. My brain was screaming at me: *Do something! You're an Effigy. Set it on fire! Burn it to a crisp! Just do it!*

I started crying instead, my feet cemented to the spot. We were about to die, and yet there I was, an Effigy, blubbering like a tool. We were going to die, and when we did, it would be my fault.

"Move."

A quiet, forceful word delivered through the thick mesh of a French accent. I turned just in time to catch the delicate sway of the girl's long blond hair. Those two things were all I needed to recognize her, because I was pathetically obsessed with this girl. Obsessed enough to know her by the defiant click of her boots against the pavement.

Belle Rousseau.

Oh my god, *Belle*. What was she doing in New York? The last I'd heard, she was in Moscow. I'd seen the pictures. Hell, I'd *blogged* about the pictures just last night.

Didn't matter now.

My lips trembled into a small, shell-shocked grin. The National Guard. Sect troops. NYPD.

Guess New York didn't need *them* after all.

"What's going on?" The little girl, who'd burrowed her face into the nape of my neck, shifted just enough to stare at the tall, beautiful nineteen-year-old walking down the abandoned street.

"Just watch."

By now I was half-crazed with a mixture of glee and pure relief. I was about to see with my own eyes what Belle Rousseau did best.

The phantom launched down the street toward Belle, knocking cars out of its path and sending them flying. The collision was inevitable.

The collision was glorious.

Belle dug her boots into the street to ground herself. Then she lifted her hands.

Her hands were all it took.

The phantom's body crumpled, the force of the impact propelling it upward until it crashed against a lamppost, tearing it down. I was blown to the ground, but I cushioned the little girl's head with my upper arm before rolling onto my back. Belle had been pushed back too, her knees buckling, her boots tearing the pavement as she slid across it, but she stood her ground.

Then, finally, it happened.

The air around me grew heavy and cold, so cold I could see my own haggard breaths dispersing into the atmosphere. I watched, awestruck, as frost crept from Belle's fingers, still clenched around the bones of the phantom's skull head. As she gripped them, the frost spread across the skull and down the phantom's length, continuing, relentlessly, until its body was covered entirely in thick lattices of ice.

"You're done," she said, and pushed.

Just like that, the phantom's body shattered into a blizzard of ice and snow, blown away with the wind.

In that one haunting moment, I realized that I would never have stood a chance against the creature. That despite whatever insane, heroic delusion had compelled me to stupidly risk my life during a Category Three attack, there was just no comparison between the two of us. No comparison at all between Belle Rousseau and the ridiculous Maia Finley.

Even though we were both Effigies.

2

Seven months ago
Early September
New York Fashion Week

"H-HEY, STOP PUSHING!"

The group of haute wannabes surrounding me barely let me stutter out the phrase before they pushed again, but it was every man for himself.

The back door to Lincoln Center had just opened.

I'd been waiting for what felt like hours, locked outside with everyone else whose plebeian status relegated them to the heavy, sticky air. The moment the back door opened, it was a mad push to the railings. Dropping all pretense of civility, I started elbowing my way to the front.

And above the carnage:

"Belle!"

"Belle, you look gorgeous!"

Belle had come to Manhattan for Fashion Week as a special guest of some up-and-coming designer. The paparazzi's frenzied cries pounded against my eardrums.

"Belle! Belle can you look this way, please?"

She didn't. Belle emerged from the building's exit in a haze of camera flashes and glided down the ramp with nary a glance.

The queen herself.

She strode with gallant steps, tall, regal, and proud, her long blond hair twisted into a braid over her slender shoulder—a beautiful warrior princess in a Valentino Bambolina dress destined to fly off high-end shelves the moment photos hit the net. They called it the Belle Effect.

Flanking her was a small entourage of "friends" for whom "friendship" no doubt existed for the photographic evidence alone. Leeches.

I was different.

I was different from the throng of reporters and the Fashion Week peasants who just wanted a clear shot of Belle to drive traffic to their try-hard blogs. With the pen I'd dug out of my purse and the poster I'd *earned* after winning third place in a radio contest, I knew in that moment that I was the one person who deserved to be there. A true fan.

"Belle." My voice was weak at first, quickly finding its volume. "Belle!"

At the end of the ramp awaited a black van ready to whisk Belle off to fairy-tale destinations unknown. In a few seconds, she'd be gone. I'd lose my chance.

I fought through legions of photogs and attendees, my heart racing when my hand brushed cool metal. "Belle!" I gripped the bar and pulled myself forward. Belle was coming. She was so close. What would I even say once our eyes met? *Hello, my name is Maia Finley, and I fanatically idolize you—please don't think I'm psychotic.* Or maybe: *My dead sister cosplayed as you last summer. Sign this now.*

Please . . . see me. "Belle!" I cursed underneath my breath, my slippery fingers fumbling with the pen. Belle was so close. In just a few seconds, I'd look up and there we'd both be. Just a few seconds more. *I need you to see me. . . .*

And then . . .

Present Day
Early April
Phantom Attack: Category Three

"HEY, KID!"

"Huh?"

It was strange, how easily history repeated itself. Seven months after seeing Belle at Fashion Week, and here I was again, standing dumbstruck with my sneakers frozen on the pavement, ignoring the chaos raging all around me to stare in silent awe at the Effigy whose battle stats were burned into my brain.

"Hey!" The police officer grabbed my forearm. "Come on; you need to vacate the area."

A wrecked expressway.

Overturned cars.

People screaming.

That's right. The phantom attack wasn't over. The War Siren was still wailing. How long had I been standing here, lost in my thoughts?

With great effort, I dragged myself out of my memories and the pandemonium seeped back in. The little girl was still clinging to my leg, crying. I was supposed to be doing something. Comforting her?

Protecting her? I had no clue how to do either. It didn't matter any-way. The officer quickly pried the little girl off of my flesh, scooping her into his arms as mine dangled uselessly by my sides. He was say-ing something, but I was barely listening. Belle was on her phone just a few feet away from me, flakes of snow still fresh on her blond hair. A living legend, sinfully epic even just standing there.

Belle was on the phone for only a few seconds. It was barely a conversation—maybe someone from the Sect telling her where to fight next. She'd be gone soon. It was stupid, but I couldn't let my opportunity slip away. Not again. The moment she lowered her arm, I seized my chance.

"Belle!" I stepped forward, but stopped once I noticed the way her fingers tightened around her phone. Her hands were trembling, her head bent low. Something was wrong. Belle did have the tendency to be somewhat grim, of course, but she usually carried her grimness *with* her, all business while she walked around murdering monsters. This Belle didn't move. Even from where I stood, it was obvious how tense her body had become.

"Belle?" I tried again.

Black helicopters overhead drowned out my voice as they flew in from behind, low enough for the wind from the rotor blades to thrash my hair and clothes. One paused a safe distance ahead of Belle, descending close to the earth before opening the door. A young man jumped out, his black boots striking the broken asphalt with a kind of grace that suggested he'd done this far too many times before. You'd expect that from a Sect agent.

The helicopter flew off and he started toward us. It was clear he was Sect from the dark red, full-length uniform fitted to his tall, slender body. But as far as agents went, I was expecting someone bigger, with more chin stubble and a few age lines; this guy didn't look much older than I did. A pair of high cheekbones gave his lean, clean-shaven face some rather sharp angles that weren't at all unpleasing to the eye. Actually, none of him was—unpleasing, that is. He twisted around to survey the damage; that's when I could see the muscles straining in his long neck as he craned it, and, as he drew closer, the long lashes fanning a pair of soft, dark brown eyes. He was the perfect mixture of hard and soft—handsome and delicate, but strong and capable as he stalked toward us with a businesslike quickness.

The police officer was far less impressed. "Oh great, it's the cavalry," he said once Hot Sect Agent reached us. The little girl was still quivering in his arms. "Better late than never, right?"

"This *is* somewhat of an emergency, so I'll ignore your bitchiness."

Urgency gave the agent's tenor voice enough authority to silence any debate. It was full of power for someone who looked like he should be grinning in a senior yearbook photo with the rest of his classmates. Then again, when I looked harder, I could see the thin lines of faded scars running up his arms, slashing across his neck. This "boy" had seen battle.

The slight breeze tousled his black hair against his forehead. "The other agents have already secured an emergency route down Thirteenth. Hostiles will keep appearing throughout the city until the Needle is fully operational again. You need to take every civilian you find"—his eyes flitted to me—"to a designated shelter."

"Shelter." My brain was working again. "Shelter . . . There's one under my school."

"Then go there." He shifted his broad shoulders. "Preferably now."

"Rhys?"

Belle. The young agent responded, turning to her, but Belle didn't meet his gaze. She kept her face hidden from him.

Rhys jogged up to her. "Belle, what is it?"

"Natalya."

He stopped dead and for a second it felt as if my heart would too. The expression Belle gave him sent a quiet shudder through me.

"I just got the call. Natalya has died." She said it with a lifelessness that dulled her French accent. "Rhys, you already knew, didn't you?"

Natalya's name drummed in my head, loud, terrifying, accusing. Rhys looked pretty shaken himself, like he didn't know how to answer, but I did: *Yes, Natalya is dead. Your mentor died literally just shy of forty-eight hours ago.*

She had to be dead, of course, before I could take her place.

That was how being an Effigy worked.

"She's dead." Belle was shaking. It was a Belle nobody was used to. After letting out a sharp, ragged breath, she clasped a hand against her mouth. "Oh god."

"Belle . . ." It was sheer guilt that made me speak, but what could I possibly say? "Belle, I'm sorry—"

Somewhere behind us, an explosion rattled the ground beneath our feet. I couldn't see it, but I could already hear the panic.

"Belle, I don't know who told you, but now is not the time." Rhys took her by the shoulders, letting go rather quickly when he saw her resultant death glare. "Let's go."

Whatever vulnerability Belle had shown in that moment was gone. With eyes colder than ever before, she began back down the street, striding toward me with Rhys trailing behind her.

As Belle drew near, a familiar, confusing mix of excitement and terror beat against my chest. "Belle—"

The officer grabbed my arm with his free hand. "Come on, kid."

"Wait," I cried, struggling. But what should I say? "Belle!" *Please just see me.*

It was almost elegant, the sheer indifference Belle showed me as she passed by without a word, without a glance, as if I didn't exist. Perhaps because in Belle's world, I didn't. Not seven months ago, outside Lincoln Center. Not now, either, even though we had more in common now than Belle realized. Literally nothing had changed. Nothing.

"I'm Natalya's successor. I'm an Effigy," I whispered. It was a good thing the NYPD officer wasn't listening. I let him drag me back toward the school.

Several hours passed by inside the fully stocked bomb shelter the size of a gymnasium packed with sniveling children and not-so-subtly panicking adults. I was the only one in the room with the power to do anything, and I was stuck inside, pathetically twiddling my thumbs next to a ninth grader complaining about the lack of functional bathrooms. Guess having the power to do something doesn't make you useful. My latest attempt at heroics taught me that well enough.

After those several, excruciating hours, the principal disappeared, reemerging thirty minutes later to let us know that the danger had passed. The Needle was fully operational again, its high-frequency signal obliterating any phantom left inside the city while keeping out the ones roaming outside the signal's reach, silent as nightmares. It was a wonder how the damn thing got turned off in the first place, but at least it was over. The phantoms couldn't get in anymore. We were safe, like we were supposed to be.

No thanks to me.

They finally let us go home. Stuffed inside a crowded, musty school bus, I tried calling Uncle Nathan yet again—probably for the tenth time—but the phone lines were all busy at the Municipal

Defense Control Center. He had to be okay. He was probably holed up in there with all the other brilliant young techies, clicking away at their space-age equipment to ensure the city's safety. He'd told me once that the MDCC was one of the few sites in the city fortified with all sorts of extra protection, in case of emergencies like these. He was okay. And because I wouldn't accept any other reality, I calmly left a message on his voice mail before forcing myself to think of other things.

Like where the hell did phantoms even come from?

It was pointless, but I couldn't help but think about it on the way home, ignoring the crazed chatter around me. Last year, I'd circled "1865" twice in the notes I'd taken for history class. But knowing the date of the first documented attack didn't do much to satisfy, especially when that was the only information anyone had when it came to their origins.

Same with the Effigies. There could only be four at a time. Everyone knew that. Powerful girls, monsters in their own right. But as for their origins, nobody knew. 1875—the year that the first documented Effigy was found in Beijing. A date and not much more.

Magic and monsters shrouded in mystery.

What I did know, at least, was that even phantoms had their categories: terrestrial, aquatic, aerial. Classes, too: A through E, according to size and weight. Some phantoms were smaller than an average human, while others towered over us by dozens of feet. They usually looked like serpents—really big, hellish versions anyway—especially in the sky and sea (and, apparently, underground). There was more variety on land; though most of those ones looked like huge carnivores, the consensus was that you never really knew what you were going to get—rotting flesh, usually, protruding black bones, sometimes. And then there were the ones with too many arms that were too long or too short, or with wings in places that didn't seem to work. Phantoms were like the sideshow act of some nightmare version of the animal kingdom. And yet there were aspects they all seemed to have, aspects seared into your brain: like the black smoke clinging to their black, horrible hides.

But *where* did they come from?

Everyone had their theories, from philosophers to poets, scientists, popes, and conspiracy theorists alike. Phantoms were mutants created through secret experiments gone wrong. Or maybe they were god's divine wrath made flesh to punish us. Not to mention theories about what that made Effigies. If they were experiments, then *we* were experiments. If they were god's wrath, then we were god's mercy. The possibilities were endless.

It didn't matter anyway. Phantoms existed. The entire world had found ways to deal with it, so who cared about the rest? Before today, society had operated just fine. For the most part, you could venture out into the world all you liked, as long as you used one of the secure travel routes. By following the rules like the good little citizen I was, I'd somehow managed to live sixteen years without seeing a single phantom up close. Until today.

Needless to say, I preferred them much more as pictures drawn in books, or images captured by satellite footage, or digital effects whipped up by some animation studio in a movie. Now that I'd actually seen one up close, I almost wanted to berate myself for actually having found them cool once. On family trips outside the city, me and June used to peer outside the same window, shrieking in excitement at every wisp of black smoke, every heavy footstep we could see shaking the trees, far off in the distance. I'd squeal until our frightened mother ordered us from the passenger seat to park our butts.

Mom. I shut my eyes, banishing the memory, putting it all out of my mind.

The bus ride was uncomfortable. The kid next to me was very sweaty. At least Uncle Nathan eventually called me back.

"Thank god you're okay," he said before his long, relieved sigh swallowed up the receiver.

"Yeah." Hearing his voice helped. The knots in my neck started to loosen. I rested my head back against the seat. "Good job getting the Needle running again. What even happened?"

"We think it was a glitch. I mean, it's a one-in-a-million chance, but it can happen."

"Yeah, the universe has been doing that a lot lately," I muttered.

"What?"

"Uh, nothing. Anyway, glad you're okay."

"Yeah. We have to check the systems, so I'll probably be here all night. That means you'll have to make your own dinner today."

"Cereal it is."

"Sorry." Uncle Nathan laughed. The kind of strained chuckle you spit out when your whole body's still tense from immense stress. Working at the MDCC after a phantom attack couldn't possibly be fun. "I should be back by tomorrow morning, so I'll make it up to you then. Oh, crap," he added awkwardly, because someone had just yelled his name. "Gotta go. Call me if you need anything, okay?"

Because of the traffic, it took a whole hour to get to South Slope: the unfortunate consequence of only having a handful of streets open for public use after of the attack. I returned, tired and worn, to an empty brownstone and a sink of dirty dishes I didn't feel like loading into the dishwasher. Embracing my laziness, I grabbed a bowl of cereal and went right up to my room. With clumsy precision, I stepped over the dirty clothes littering the floor, ignoring the now heartily defaced motivational posters Uncle Nathan had tacked to my wall when I'd first moved in.

Stopping at my desk, I plopped down into my chair, finding the comfortable grooves, threw my metallic blue headphones on, and shook my laptop out of hibernation with a swift click.

Doll Soldiers was in my Bookmarks page. It wasn't a great name for a forum, but it had everything an Effigy junkie needed.

Check the thread, I told myself. *Don't be nervous; just do it.* My fingers hovered over the keyboard. It would take only a few seconds to browse the thread I'd made earlier that morning before going to school. It was a dumb thread, really—no more than a rashly concocted experiment. The responses couldn't be that bad. Right? *Just check it.*

I checked the latest forum updates instead. Ah, the Belle Kill Count thread was lively as usual. And below it:

Lake Announces Debut Album Title

Was she still trying for a solo career? I rolled my eyes. Lake was like the English degree of the Effigy world. What did she even do? Where was she today, while people were dying and getting separated from loved ones? Watching it on the news from the comfort of some asshole's recording studio? A flop Effigy, and a flop pop star.

I took a breath. Lake made me crazy sometimes, crazier still because she had a cult following of "Swans" that would swiftly cut down anyone who dared speak against their "Swan Queen." Whatever.

An uncomfortable moment passed in which it dawned on me that I, too, might one day have the rare honor of inspiring irrational hatred. *Maia Finley is like the masters of fine arts degree of the Effigy world. Like, what does she even do?*

I turned up the synth-pop music pounding through my head-phones.

Apparently, Natalya's death hadn't been mentioned yet anywhere in the forum. Interesting. Then again, Natalya did only die two days ago, and Belle herself had only *just* found out about it. I probably wouldn't have known either if I weren't Natalya's successor.

Successor.

Natalya's *successor.*

My hands froze.

It'd been happening like that for the past two days, my mind oscillating between acceptance and utter disbelief. Letting my jaw slack a little, I looked down at my hands. It was curious, really, the way they trembled ever so slightly against my laptop keyboard. I loved all things Effigy. Worshipped them. Now I was one. Badass. Dream come true, right?

Growing up, I had always imagined what it would be like if I ever turned, or got called, or whatever the term was. I'd always figured that I'd go full-on town crier, running down the streets of New York with a bell in hand. And yet, in a bizarre twist of fate, as of now I was the only one in the world who knew about my secret. Almost two days of being an Effigy, and nobody knew but me.

Well, okay, no. That wasn't *entirely* true.

Check the thread, moron. Just do it. My inner voice was unusually nasty today.

Drawing in a deep sigh, I finally searched for my thread in the Rec Room subforum. Instead of using my normal account, I'd created a new one to write the post, just to make sure the thread couldn't be traced back to me. It was an experiment, after all. I just wanted to see what the responses would be. I wasn't ready for a coming-out party just yet.

I'm the Next Effigy.

I could have come up with a better title. Oh, well.

Hi, everyone.

I can't tell you my name. You probably won't believe me. I don't expect you to with the amount of trolls we've gotten here in the past, but . . . I literally swear upon my family's graves that I am seriously not lying when I say this.

Natalya's dead. I'm the next Effigy.

Seriously. I'm not lying.

. . . . cool, right?

I'm serious, though.

. . . that's it. Please don't kill me.

Needless to say, I hadn't been thinking too deeply when I wrote the contents of the post, and I wasn't surprised to see the replies, either:

[+500, -0] Go to hell.

[+ 430, - 1] Did you literally just e-kill Natalya? Wow, fuck you.

I had already suspected that they wouldn't believe me. It was stupid to start the thread in the first place.

So then why the hell did I?

Becoming an Effigy is generally a very strange thing. You can't fight it. You can't pick it. And you can't stop yourself from being picked by whatever it is that does the picking. There's no warning, no trigger. The power just fills you, strange and silent, as if you'd drawn it into your own body with a breath. And only four girls at a time could be one. What were the odds?

At first, I really had wanted to tell everyone. Then, after picturing a terrifying swarm of news cameras in my face, I'd settled on telling my uncle first, but when I tried, my entire body had seized with panic.

I still couldn't put into words why I'd reacted that way, especially since I could clearly remember that shattering need to say something to someone, anyone, as well as the frustration I'd felt when the words just wouldn't sound. Maybe that was why I'd ended up typing them instead. When it came to sharing an earth-shattering secret, anonymity was the safest option for sure.

But apparently, it was also very pointless:

[+299, - 11] LOL bye.

[+ 285, - 2] Mods lock this thread please.

[+177, -25] You know what's really sick about all the people on the internet pretending that they've been ~chosen~ and creating these elaborate fantasies with fake icons and "proof shots" and wishing so bad those fantasies were actually real? Like, you wish so bad you could be an Effigy, but do you know what that actually means? It means the last girl would have had to DIE for you to become one. Do you get that? So you actually want some girl to die so you can have your moment in the sun? Psycho.

My fingers found my keyboard right away, readying my defense, but the tirade wasn't over. I kept reading.

Like seriously, some people here act like Effigies are indestructible Super Barbies or something—but they're people. THEY DIE. THEY DIE SO FUCKING OFTEN.

My hands froze.

THEY DIE A LOT. NOBODY should be making light of that.

"I'm not . . . ," I whispered.

[+54, - 373] Hey, OP wants to be an Effigy so bad, how about we start a Death Watch Thread? Fifty bucks says OP's dead by Memorial Day.

I clicked out of the thread.

Funny, I thought it'd gone away, but it had never really left: the fear, that same fear I'd felt while helplessly watching a phantom barrel down the street toward me. It wasn't gone at all, just hiding, nestled deep into the crevices of my bones.

Dead by Memorial Day.

I wasn't Belle. I couldn't tear through monsters while looking fabulous. Hell, I couldn't even save one kid today. But I'd be expected to save them all, wouldn't I? Once the world found out. Once they knew *I* was the one chosen to succeed Natalya Filipova, one of the greatest Effigies of this age, I'd be expected to fight.

Fight, and maybe die.

Pressing my lips to keep them from trembling, I took off my

headphones just as the music's frantic beat had begun to chip away at my senses. After rubbing my temples, I checked some of the other threads because, as usual, only the internet could keep me from spiraling into the terror of my own thoughts.

Phantoms Attack New York

I clicked the title. Amid the poorly timed and painfully obvious *Why does every monster ever hate New York?* jokes was thinly veiled panic:

I'm watching CNN right now trying not to tear my goddamn hair out. Phantom attack in New York. Is nobody seriously making the connection yet? This all started with Seattle. Then four years ago Moscow happened, then Incheon, then Frankfurt, should I go on? These aren't developing areas with shoddy APDs. What the hell is happening? Isn't anyone gonna do anything about this?

It was true. New York had one of the most powerful antiphantom devices in the world. I could accept today as a freak accident, but how would that explain all the other freak accidents that had happened sporadically over the past few years?

Stupid, I berated myself. *Don't get caught up in conspiracy theories.* It was best not to dwell, best not to dwell. That was the mantra I'd been clinging to ever since my moving van had pulled up to Uncle Nathan's front door. *Just try not to think about it* was stapled to my brain like one of those pointless motivational posters on my wall.

Instead, I wrote my own comment: *I was there. Belle showed up in New York today. She saved a lot of people. As usual.*

I thought of the ghostly sheen of Belle's skin, drained white of blood as she uttered Natalya's name.

I just wish she could have looked at me. I mean, I was right there. She could have looked at me. Even if it was just once. I don't know, I just thought . . .

My gaze slipped from my laptop screen to the picture of my family on top of my disorganized bookshelf. Mom, Dad, myself, and June. June with her long, bird's-nest chestnut hair—same as mine, because she was the only person in the world who shared my face. June, smiling with the rest of us as we all stood in front of the Astro Tower at Coney Island for the last time.

I just thought it would be nice, I wrote, now acutely aware of the vast emptiness of my room, *if she would look at me just once.*

I deleted everything and exited the thread. Just in time—a new one had popped up mere seconds ago:

OH GOD, NO . . . RIP NATALYA.

3

TICK, TICK, TICK.

Natalya Filipova was dead. To every twenty-four-hour news station, the headline had fallen like manna from the heavens. The Matryoshka Princess. Russia's pride, dead at twenty-five. Why? they asked. How? What's next for the Sect as an organization, its agents, its Effigies?

Who would succeed her?

For the next week and a half, it was all the media could talk about. Why hadn't the Sect confirmed the cause of death yet? When would the family release a statement? Why hadn't they buried her? Nine days. And each day was a ticking clock, whittling down the time I had left.

I need to tell him, I thought for the thousandth time on Friday morning as I descended the stairs to the kitchen below.

Uncle Nathan's cooking weighted the air with too many sinful aromas: bacon, pancakes, scrambled eggs. Plates of them were already on the table. He even had his ASK ME ABOUT MY MASCULINITY apron on, which, along with his floppy brown hair and thick black glasses, finished off his sensitive-hipster look.

Right now, the sensitivity thing was kind of the problem.

It never took the Sect too long to find the next Effigy. And then once they found me, how long would it be before my obituary ended up on the evening news? *Maia Finley, sixteen, murdered fulfilling her duty in battle.* Uncle Nathan had already lost his brother, his sister-in-law, his niece. Hell, he'd cried more than I did at the funeral. How long would it be until I was just another dead family member?

Regardless of how Uncle Nathan discovered the truth, his reaction would be the same: terror. He knew what being an Effigy meant. Still, it was better to find out from me and not some headline. Right?

"Maia! Great, you're up on time!" He grinned with all his teeth, looking even younger than he actually was. He was so tall and scrawny that sometimes I forgot he was thirty. "Hungry?"

My lips felt dry. I turned away. To bide some time, I grabbed the remote control out from in between the cushions of our sofa, turned on the television, and there it was: Natalya's funeral, broadcast on nearly every station.

"Oh, they're doing that today?" Nathan asked. "It's been a while since she died, hasn't it?"

"The family wouldn't release the body at first," I said. "No clue why."

A long procession was already making its way through the streets of Moscow, hundreds, maybe thousands of mourners lining the barricade for one final glimpse at the world's heroine. Maybe Belle was there too, somewhere among the crowd, weeping with them. Crying over a dead loved one. An all-too-familiar scene for me.

The controller almost slipped from my hands.

"Maia?"

"I'm okay," I said quickly. I couldn't look at him. Instead I kept my eyes on the ivory horse-drawn carriage carrying Natalya's body.

Uncle Nathan stayed silent for a time. "Maia, why don't you

turn that off and eat something before you go to school? I know you were a big fan of Natalya, but . . ." He paused, trying to find the right words. "You know. The whole . . . funeral . . . *death* thing." He stopped.

I knew what he was trying to say in his own extremely clumsy way. I also knew why he was frying half the contents of our fridge, even if he wasn't consciously aware of it himself: The anniversary was coming up. It would explain how uncomfortable the wailing from Natalya's funeral had suddenly made him—the sound of televised grief blanketing him in painful memories.

Not just him.

The smell of burned pork pierced the air; Uncle Nathan had left the bacon on the pan for too long. Flicking off the heat, he hurriedly shifted the smoking pan onto the next burner.

I just watched him. "You okay over there?"

"'Course," he answered hastily before wiping the sweat from his brow. "Anyway." His face was still ruddy from the heat. "You really should turn that off. We're already going to have enough gloom tonight, don't you think?"

"Oh god," I muttered under my breath. "So we're still going to that dinner thing?"

"It's the yearly benefit." Nathan wiped his forehead again.

"And?"

"Your dad was in the company. Plus, didn't your mom help organize the last two?"

"But she didn't make me go then, and I don't want to go now. Honestly it's a bit hard to get excited at the prospect of being surrounded by stuffy people shooting pity glances at you when they think you're not looking." I slumped over the seat. "Then again, if either of us breaks down, I suppose it'll make for good gossip.

Wouldn't be surprised if that's the real reason they want us there."

"Hey, I'm not thrilled about it either." Uncle Nathan came around the counter. "Probably should have just said no in the first place. But I . . . I don't know. The head organizer called me herself and insisted. I think they're planning some kind of commemoration thing."

"Oh, great." *Shine that spotlight even brighter.* "And that made you say yes?"

"I guess they just wanted to honor them somehow. So do I."

I stayed silent as he approached.

"Look." Once he was close enough, he placed his hands on my shoulders. "It's been almost one year since . . . since it happened."

It. The "thing." It was really the only way we could mention it around each other.

"It's been hard," he continued. "There've been lots of changes, for both of us. Tonight'll probably be pretty hard too. But, hey, look at us." He pointed at the mirror at the side of the wall, where his reflection gave me a smile so forced I had to lower my eyes. "We're fine. Things are okay, right? Things have pretty much settled down."

"Settled," I repeated lifelessly.

"Right. We've survived a whole year. We'll survive another. So don't worry about tonight, okay? Or any other day for that matter. We're okay, and it's going to stay like that."

During my third night living here, I'd snuck into Uncle Nathan's room while he was sleeping to grab something for my headache. That's when I'd noticed the self-help books. The lamp was still on, so I could see each of them strewn about the floor. *Coping with Grief. Dealing with Loss.* Exactly how many would he read once I was announced as the next Effigy? Once the Sect whisked me off to one of their training facilities to learn how to avoid being torn to shreds?

How many would he read once I died in battle?

Maybe some people were just supposed to lose everything.

"Maia? Hey, are you okay?"

I couldn't tell him. I turned, hastily wiping my eyes. "I'm late; I should go." Keeping my face hidden from his, I grabbed a single pancake off a plate, pulled my bag over my shoulder, and headed out the door.

Tick, tick. It was only a matter of time.

Seven o'clock. *Just survive the night,* I told myself in front of the mirror after strapping on my short peach dress like battle armor.

My dad had worked at Seymour and Finch, one of those research and development firms. They held their benefit dinner on the fifth floor of La Charte, some swanky hotel on the Lower East Side. All I'd have to do was survive a few hours and I'd be back in my room playing my PC games in peace. I couldn't get out of it now.

"I think I left the water running," I tried anyway as we rode the elevator from the underground parking lot. "Seriously. The whole house could be flooded by now. I don't think the sofa can take it."

Uncle Nathan fidgeted with his black tie like it was a ground-dwelling ectotherm coiling lovingly around his neck, which was why a dry cough came out of his mouth instead of the laugh he'd probably intended. "It'll all be over soon."

"He said before delivering the injection."

"Truthfully?" Uncle Nathan sighed as the elevator slowed to a halt, live music muted behind the metal doors. "I think this'll be more painful."

Great. The doors opened. I kept my head down, steering clear of whatever black loafers and silk hems crossed my path. I navigated the halls, stepped over the ballroom threshold, and—

"Holy crap," said Uncle Nathan.

The closest I'd ever been to luxury was streaming *Celebrity Homes* on my laptop instead of finishing a two-page essay on Hegel. So when I stepped into a ballroom made of pure white marble, I knew I was in over my head. Patrons clinked glasses underneath the high coffered ceiling, gossiping and laughing conspiratorially near columns that glimmered red under the cast-iron skylights. In front of a wide stage and translucent podium were rows of long tables covered in white linen, each one supporting a dozen neatly set crystal dishes. On the other side of the room, a photographer snapped pictures by a set of Victorian windows, the glass only partially veiled by champagne-colored drapes. *What in the Gatsby hell?*

I gripped Uncle Nathan's arm, suddenly self-conscious enough to feel each swish of my dress against my legs. Thankfully, he chose a table near the back. I read off a card propped up on the white table-cloth. "Fourth Annual Global Orphans Foundation Benefit." Of course it was.

Near the front stage, a live band played thirties-era swing over the chatter. Maybe it was a theme. I'd stupidly left my phone at home, so I couldn't mindlessly peruse the internet. I would have been perfectly fine with spending the night quietly listening to the band from my seat, but I unfortunately ended up spending the next half hour suffering through the inanities of far too many people who, despite being at a benefit for orphans, didn't seem to have the tact required to have a functional conversation with one.

Are you okay, do you need anything, how have you been, how are you holding up, oh she's so young, oh it's such a tragedy, isn't it a tragedy?

I'd have appreciated the sympathy if it weren't for the way they all gazed at me as if I were a stray in need of feeding and bathing and maybe regular sessions with a psychiatrist.

As innocently as I could make it look, my ginger ale tumbled out of my hands and crashed against the floor. "Uncle, would it be all right if I go get another one?"

"Go ahead. Really." Uncle Nathan sounded seconds away from pulling the same line himself.

"Be right back."

I passed the bar without a glance. Folding my arms to keep my hands from shaking, I crossed the ballroom with faster and faster steps until I reached the balcony, shut away behind double glass doors. With one violent heave I shoved them open, the sounds of the streets below rushing past with the night air. After shutting the doors behind me, I draped myself over the balustrade and blew out a long, whining sigh.

"*Oh, are you okay, Maia? Are you okay?* No, I'm not okay, but by all means please feel free to do everything in your power to remind me of my family's rotting corpses, you fake assholes."

I pressed my forehead against the smooth wooden railing and moaned. Wrapping my fingers around the rail, I peered over the edge, at the parked cars, the valets, the handsomely dressed couples just entering the hotel below. "I need to get out of here."

"Even if you do, it's five stories down. Granted it's quicker, but I think far messier than an elevator."

I swiveled on my heels. I hadn't even seen the guy in the corner, but how could I have? He was lying down on the floor, practically hidden behind a fully set table. With his back propped up by a wall, his fingers were busy clicking away at a handheld game console. I could only just make out the sound whispering through his earphones because one of his buds was out.

For a minute I was too shocked to speak. "Uh, I'm sorry," I finally said. "I'll just—wait, I wasn't going to *jump*!"

"That's between you and god."

"Cute," I muttered with an incredulous huff.

If it weren't for his hair, I would have thought the most strik-ing thing about him was his lazy, sea-blue eyes, ghostly clear. But his hair—I couldn't stop looking at it. It was silver, like it'd been drained of its color, packed into a short ponytail at the back of his head. Looked good. Looked natural, though a bit jarring against his more ballroom appropriate—and, um, nicely fitting—gray vest and white dress shirt. Considering he was tucked away in a corner playing video games, I figured he was enjoying the benefit as much as I was.

"Is that next gen?" I asked, pointing at his handheld.

"Just went on sale."

"What're you playing?"

"*Metal Kolossos 3D: Reve—*"

"*Reverse Reincarnation!*" Covering my mouth, I gave myself a sec-ond to feel embarrassed before scurrying up to him. "You have that game? Oh my god, I hate you!"

He smiled. "I get that a lot."

"No, seriously, my preorder was delayed or something." I stopped at his feet. "Um . . . The graphics must be so awesome. . . ."

And I smiled at him. Taking the hint, he passed it over.

"You know I haven't even started playing that yet."

"Sorry." I sat down in the chair next to him. "I honestly just want to watch the opening video. That's all, I swear."

"Keep it as long as you like." He laid his head against the wall and shut his eyes.

He was cute. Slim, muscular build, a pretty, sculpted pale face, and full lips. He was probably only a few years older than me too. . . .

Swallowing a lump in my throat, I focused on the game, on

the lush graphics of its gorgeous yet confusing opening movie as it quickly recapped the story thus far. The Metal Kolossos series told the tale of Earth's final Effigy, Aki, who alone defended the last of humanity in a postapocalyptic underground city called Ring. The fact that she was part cyborg made everything all the more badass, but this time, apparently the series's Japanese creators had decided to tell a related side story taking place in sixties-era Seattle.

Of all settings.

"The Seven-Day Siege," said the mournful narration. "Indeed it took only seven days for humanity's bane, the phantoms, to obliterate a once-flourishing city. Seven days to reduce it to nothingness."

"God, Japanese games are so dramatic, aren't they?" he said.

"Aki time-travels back to the sixties in this one. The entire game takes place during the Seattle Siege, right?"

"Depressing, isn't it?"

On the game's thread in the Doll Soldiers forum, there were plenty of people annoyed at the fact that such a horrific moment in US history was going to be used as the backdrop to a video game. I was on there for days defending the narrative's deeper thematic possibilities to the naysayers, losing sleep over it because that's what happens when nerds fight other nerds on the internet. Dark times.

"My name is Saul, by the way." He sat up. "I thought you might like to know the name of the guy whose game you've hijacked."

"O-oh, right." My face flushed again. "Sorry." I wasn't really. I handed it back to him.

Saul laughed, and when he lifted his arm to smooth his fine hair with his long fingers, I noticed a bright ring around his right middle finger.

"Ooh, that's nice," I said, pointing at it.

"Oh, this?" He turned it over. Though the jewel's dazzling white reminded me of a pearl, heavy brushstrokes of smoky black streaked the center. "Got it off my dad."

And I suspected he'd be paying a visit to the local pawnshop after the party.

"But enough about that," he said. "You know, about that game?" He leaned back, giving me a rather mischievous sidelong glance that, truthfully, quickened my pulse. "I heard the development team wanted to make the main villain another Effigy. But not one of the regular four—a fifth one."

"A fifth Effigy?" I frowned. I hadn't heard this. Why hadn't I heard this? "Was this during the early stages or what?"

"I thought that might interest you." Saul lifted his hand. "Earth, fire, ice, wind." He counted them off with his fingers. "Everyone knows there's only four."

"So they were just going to throw in another Effigy?" I didn't know what pissed me off more: the fact that they dared consider messing with real-life canon, or the fact that I hadn't even heard about it up until now.

"Their original idea was that she'd be the one who caused it. This fifth Effigy. In this continuity, *she* was the one who destroyed Seattle."

One girl razed an entire city to the ground? I shook my head. No, what destroyed Seattle was a freak accident. Its Space Needle was the country's first antiphantom device of its size and scale, but there were too many bugs and it flaked. Simple. Having some perpetrator behind it all was pretty revisionist, even for this series.

"Okay, but why would an Effigy destroy Seattle?"

Saul smiled. "Obviously to kill people."

"O . . . oh . . ." I shifted uncomfortably.

"Or something. Who knows?" He shrugged. "I just think it's

interesting, what with all the stuff that's been going on lately. You've heard the theories, right?"

"I thought conspiracy theories were for basement-dwelling tinfoil-hat wearers."

"The arrogance." With a pretty laugh, he reached into his finely cut gray pants and drew out a cell phone. "See this?" He got up and took the chair next to me. "One of my friends has some connections of the shadowy variety. He showed me these pictures." He started flipping through them. "You know when all those APDs went offline. Moscow, Incheon, Frankfurt, Bern. Even here."

"O-oh yeah?" I nodded stiffly, trying to not think about the light brush of his model-long legs against mine. "Wait, what is that?"

As I leaned in, my narrowed eyes locked on one picture. I couldn't tell where it'd been taken, but it didn't matter. There was something grotesquely universal about the desperation to stay alive. It was there, captured in the frame, frozen on the faces of the fleeing masses. But somewhere in the midst of the dark, blurry chaos—

"Is that a mask?" I squinted. I could barely make out the person wearing it, but I could see the round, black shell clinging to his face.

"It's a 'false face,'" said Saul. "There's no mouth, but do you see those slits for eyes?"

That was the problem with conspiracy nerds: geeking out over the very thing that should terrify them. But I wouldn't let myself cross the panic threshold just yet.

"Okay. So what are you implying?"

Saul leaned against the table, his slender back tugging the cloth. "This guy isn't in all the photos, but the fact that he's in more than one? Imagine." He clicked his phone off. "So?" he asked with an unmistakably Cheshire grin. "What do you think?"

He waited. It wasn't every day I stumbled into a conversation with a good-looking guy, but this particular conversation had gotten a little too weird, even for me. I tried to form a response. Something like: *How should I know?* But the words stayed buried in me. It was the way he looked at me. His eyes pierced mine, expectant, *impatient*. Why was he looking at me like that? Why did any of this even matter? But still, he waited. He barely even blinked. His frozen smile sent a not-so-subtle shiver through me.

Instead of answering him, I rose to my feet a little too quickly. "I think a game is a game. Don't start freaking yourself out over nothing." *Don't freak* me *out over nothing.*

It'd been a while since the music had stopped playing, replaced by a long-winded speech from whoever was running the event. It would be cruel to leave Uncle Nathan there alone for any longer. As fascinating as it was bumping into an Effigy fanboy here of all places, it was time to go.

"You never told me your name, *poupée.*"

"Huh?" I turned, confused. The boy's demeanor had changed. I couldn't put my finger on how. But Saul was simply watching me.

It was *really* time to go.

With a hasty smile, as polite as I could make it, I waved good-bye and shut the glass doors behind me.

The rest of the evening should have passed by like a dull groan. The plan was to wait down the clock and then escape the premises without any more complications.

Alas:

"Holy shit!"

Twenty minutes after my conversation with Saul, I overheard the expletive from where I sat, though the young woman who'd uttered it sat at the table behind me. "Stacy totally just saw Belle Rousseau in the lobby!"

I gripped my half-filled glass tightly.

"Seriously?" said another girl. "You sure it was her?"

"I mean, it was a blond girl with a French accent who looked exactly like Belle Rousseau, so . . ."

"What's she doing *here*? Hookup?"

"Stacy said she's here looking for someone. An *Effigy*."

My hand dropped like a stone against the table.

"No way, seriously? There's one *here*?"

Tick, tick. Time was up.

4

"MAIA, WHERE ARE YOU GOING?"

"Bathroom!"

That was a lie, of course, but I didn't have time to convince Uncle Nathan to drive me home. Even if I did, who was to say there wouldn't be Sect agents waiting for me?

So where could I go? Half-baked ideas fired off one after another, none of them carefully considered because overwhelming panic tended to dull one's critical thinking skills. Maybe that was why I stupidly stuffed myself inside a crowded elevator instead of using the stairs to sneak off unnoticed. I pressed B, figuring that once I got to the basement, I'd jack a car and drive to . . . Siberia. Anywhere. *Anywhere*. I could learn how to drive after getting there.

The elevator door slid open, but to a brightly lit lobby instead of the shadowy parking lot I'd been expecting. A breath hitched in my throat. Belle wasn't there, but if Belle really had come to recruit the next Effigy, she'd probably brought some Sect agents with her. I couldn't let myself be seen.

I pushed up against the back of the elevator as a group of people lumbered out at an infuriatingly slow pace. If that weren't bad enough, a bellhop tried to push a giant, loaded luggage trolley into the elevator before I could get out. I yelled at him to back up, but when one wheel got stuck at an awkward angle, the door wouldn't close. And the longer the door stayed open, the longer I was exposed.

"I'll help," I said, and pushed the trolley as if my life depended on it.

"Miss," said the flustered bellhop, "miss, wait, that isn't help—"

"Let me give you guys a hand." A young man grabbed the trolley on the other side. "We'll lift on three, okay?"

I couldn't shake the feeling that I'd seen him before. I could see his dark eyes, bright behind a pair of black-rimmed nerd glasses just large enough to make placing his face that much more difficult.

"You ready?" he asked.

I snapped out of it long enough to help them lift and heave the trolley over the threshold, but not without a suitcase toppling over and landing right at my feet. Both the young man and the bellhop looked at me expectantly. But—

"Sorry, I have to go."

I stepped over the suitcase and slipped by them both, my heels clicking furiously against the marble floor. This was ridiculous. How did I become this paranoid mess? The guy had been wearing a polka-dot bow tie, for god's sake. Was I going to live my entire life like this? Looking over my shoulder, wondering if every pretty-boy hipster that crossed my path was secretly an expertly trained agent come to spirit me off to start my Effigy schooling?

La Charte's grandiose revolving doors were in my sights. A pair of wet children running out of the aquatics room almost toppled me over as they sped past, but a firm arm around my shoulder pulled me back in time.

The boy with the glasses.

"Yikes. That was close." I could see Nerd Glasses smile out of the corner of my eyes. "But why are you in a hurry, Maia?"

No way.

"You . . . are you . . . ?"

Strip the tie and the glasses. Strip the wicked grin and the white dress shirt with the sleeves rolled up around his elbows. Once I saw past the civilian look he was currently sporting, I realized that it was the same tousled black hair falling over his eyes, the same fine-bridged nose and full lips. Same battle scars on his arms.

The young agent from the day of the Category Three phantom attack.

"So you remember me, right?" The young man studied my face. "From the attack not too long ago? Honestly, when they showed me your face, it took me a while to place it. Shocked the hell out of me, but then . . ." And he leaned in so that only I could hear. "Who knew you'd turn out to be the next Effigy?"

I took a step back.

"I'm Aidan Rhys. Most people stick with the last name, though." He introduced himself with an all-too-casual smile and stretched out a hand. "It's gonna be okay. Don't be scared, Maia."

I ran for the doors.

"Hey, come on!"

I could hear him yelling after me, but I didn't stop, not until I realized, as I prepared to cross the street, that running was pointless.

Where was I even running to? The Sect had already found me—it was a done deal. What could I feasibly, realistically even do to avoid them for the rest of my life? It was time to stop lying to myself.

The city's usual cacophony barraged me from all sides, and a slight chill reminded me I'd fled without grabbing my coat. Biting my lip,

I stared at New York's skyline, at the bright lights scuttling up and down the Needle on the other side of the river.

Eleven days ago, just two days before the attack, that was when everything had changed. I remembered waking up in the dead of night with this tight pain in my chest, heaving as something secret and horrible seeped into me with a deep breath. I remembered the short calm, deadly silent, and then a storm of screaming. I remembered thrashing under my covers, and then watching in terror as the lightbulb screwed into my standing lamp caught fire and exploded. That I was an Effigy, the next one after the famous and heroic Natalya Filipova—it wasn't something that I had to realize. I just knew. The knowledge was just there, as calmly and as surely as I knew my own name.

And then after it happened, all I could think was that they'd gotten it so wrong. Whoever "they" were, they'd called the wrong one. It was supposed to be June. June was always the livelier one. Livelier, stronger, braver.

The one who should've lived.

"You're not running anymore."

I wiped my face with my bare arms and turned. Rhys had his hands in his pockets as he watched me from the hotel entrance.

"There isn't anywhere I can go, is there?" I said.

"Well, I didn't want to say it, but . . ."

As Rhys took a few tentative steps forward, tears trickled down my cheek, each more pitiful than the last. Ridiculous. June wouldn't have run. If she were me, she'd face everything head-on. She probably would've tested her powers by now too, instead of nearly throwing up at the thought of it like a damn coward. And then, over the years, she would've become a hero. A legend to rival Natalya.

It probably would have been June, if I'd managed to save her that day.

The tears were flowing openly now. I turned my back to the agent.

"Maia," he said, gently, carefully. "It doesn't have to be this hard. I'm not here to lock you up. I'm here to help. It's what we do. We help people."

I wiped my face one last time, but I still wouldn't look at him.

"It's been a rough few days, right? We'll help you make sense of it." He sighed. "We're not the enemy, Maia."

My tear-soaked reflection in a parked car's window stared pathetically back at me. I watched myself crying and shivering and freezing in the middle of the sidewalk. Natalya's successor.

I had to be better than this.

It took me a moment to pull myself together. Squeezing my hands into fists, I finally gave Rhys a curt nod, silently readying myself for the next step. Though my heart sank at the thought of Uncle Nathan, I had no choice but to bury it deep. He was going to find out sooner or later. Crying about it wasn't going to change anything. I had to focus on this. So I did. After sucking in a breath, I turned back toward La Charte.

Rhys was much taller than me; he must have been around six feet. Tall and slender, with broad shoulders and defined arms. I loved arms. Still didn't make this any less awkward, though.

We stood at opposite ends of the elevator, neither of us talking. I was too nervous to face him, but I could still see him in the mirror, sizing me up. At least when I did it, I was subtle about it.

He broke the silence first. "So. A benefit, huh? You . . . do benefits a lot?" It came out more awkwardly than he'd probably wanted.

I kept my arms wrapped around my chest. I wasn't surprised he knew why I was at the hotel, but it was creepy nonetheless.

"You, uh . . ." Rhys cleared his throat. "You look nice."

"Yeah, I like your getup too," I said, still peering at him through the mirror. "It's very Urkel chic. Not what I was expecting from a Sect agent."

"It was my day off." He leaned back against the metal railing and shrugged. "Besides, I was told it made me look cute."

"How *old* are you?"

"Eighteen."

"Eighteen? An eighteen-year-old Sect agent?"

"What can I say?" Rhys smiled. "They got me young."

What annoyed me most was how harmless he looked. I stared at him for a moment, silently, before nodding. "I should have run."

"It's been like three minutes. Having second thoughts already?"

I could see my reflection shaking its head in the mirror behind him. "No, I mean it. You don't know . . . I could have gotten away. I could have, I don't know, hitched a ride to Queens and got a fake ID and then hopped on a plane to the Cayman Islands or somewhere. What would you have done then, huh? Seriously, I gave up way too easy."

"I can't tell if you're joking."

I slumped back against the railing. "Yeah, I can't tell either."

Rhys only stared at me, his head cocked, his lips on their way to an infuriating grin.

I frowned. "What?"

"It's amazing, how different you guys all are."

"You 'guys'?"

Rhys closed his eyes. "You Effigies. One dies and then another one pops up like a superpowered whack-a-mole and you're always so different from the last. You and Natalya are completely different."

He gazed at me—*through* me. It was a surgical gaze that made me feel as if a photograph of my insides were on a giant projector being studied by a roomful of medical students. I turned from him, holding myself more tightly than before.

"She would have liked you," he said.

I couldn't deny that I was curious. There I was in the same elevator as someone who'd actually known the legendary Matryoshka Princess. Maybe even fought alongside her. But he didn't elaborate.

Silence stretched between us.

"I kind of want to go home," I said.

"Probably too late for that."

As if I didn't already know. But at least when he added a soft "Sorry" afterward, he sounded sincere.

The "24" finally lit up, and with a *ping*, the doors opened. Outside Room 2401 was a red-haired man in a black suit and shades. He nodded to Rhys once and stepped aside. Then, taking out his keycard, Rhys opened the door. I held my breath.

It was a suite worthy of a hotel like La Charte, its opulence no doubt designed to ensnare the greedy elite by stirring their decadent tastes. Belle sat on an elegant chaise longue at the back of the room in a dress as bloodred as her lipstick. Stunning and intimidating. Another agent in a black suit stood beside her and, unlike Rhys, he was packing heat—his left hand rested on his gun holster, his right on a black metal case reaching up to his hips. Probably Sect equipment.

The agent looked older than Rhys and was built like a rugby player. His blue eyes locked onto me the moment I walked in, but Belle never looked at me. She stayed silent, her wineglass dangling between her fingers, the luster of New York speckling the dimly lit room through the ivory curtains.

"You'll never guess who I bumped into." Rhys slapped me rather painfully on the back as we approached them. "Didn't even have to look that hard either."

"Maia Finley." The agent knew my name. Once again, my lack of surprise made it no less creepy. He lifted his square, bald head as if to scrutinize me from a higher angle. "Do you know why you're here?"

I crumpled the hem of my dress in my palms, subtly rubbing off the sweat. "I guess . . . I guess I'm here because I'm—"

"Natalya's successor."

It was the first time Belle Rousseau ever spoke to me. It changed everything. For the first time, I was looking at my hero, and my hero was looking back.

I could hear the thumping rhythm of my heart against my rib cage. It was finally happening. For days I'd wondered what would happen if this moment ever came: a handshake, a smile, a hearty *Welcome to the team*. But for too long, Belle had said nothing. And as much as I didn't want to admit it, I could see that something very important was missing in her. I could tell from the emptiness of her faraway gaze.

"Nice to meet you." I smiled shyly. "Um." I curled my toes as much as the space in my pumps would allow. "I-I'm a big fan—of you, I mean. Like, a *really* big fan."

Rein it in, Maia, I warned myself, but the dam had already broken. "I just think you're so great. *Really*." God, I was talking to Belle. *Belle Rousseau*. "Like completely amazing. Like how you save people and stuff?"

"A fan?" Rhys chuckled under his breath. "This is too good."

"I'm a platinum member of your official online fan club. Oh god," I added because I finally realized I should have stopped at *Nice to meet you*. "Do you want me to go away? I can go away. I'll just go—" But Rhys pulled me back before I could get too far.

"Fourteen," Belle said.

I gently tugged my arm out of Rhys's grasp. "What?"

"Natalya." Belle crossed her legs. "That was her number."

Rhys lowered his head with a quiet sigh. "I'm not sure I understand," I said.

"Are you aware of the Seven-Year Rule?" Belle asked. "It's a joke within the Sect. You see, an Effigy's work is quite dangerous. As you can imagine, we tend not to last very long."

I locked my fingers together to keep them from shaking.

"That's why there's the Seven-Year Rule. If you survive past seven years, you're considered to be either one of two things: a god, or a cowardly waste of human skin whose long life can be attributed only to her pathetic desire to cling to her miserable existence."

"Oh."

Belle set her wineglass down. "Natalya became an Effigy at age eleven—much earlier than most. And she was twenty-five when she died. That's fourteen: twice the number one needs to be considered a god. Fourteen years of fighting. So tell me, Maia." She tilted her head, her French braid swishing behind her. "What will your number be?"

"Belle, save the hazing, okay?" Rhys sat on the arm of one of the accent chairs near her. "You knew this was coming. Natalya's gone."

Belle's eyes shifted menacingly in his direction.

"Maia, my name is Howard Day," said the bald agent by Belle's side. "What do you know about the Sect?"

I knew what everyone else did. Effigies weren't exactly free agents. They were under the control of an international, nongovernmental organization whose operatives helped fight phantoms around the globe. Through the Sect, Effigies were trained, controlled. Maybe watched.

"I know you guys tracked me down, though I have no idea how."

"That's right." Howard was a little too calm about it.

"And apparently you're threatening global security by sneakily positioning yourselves as a neo-imperial superpower, or whatever that guy on Fox News said. You know, the guy with the crazy eyes who cries a lot."

"She jokes, too," said Rhys, amused.

"Apparently," said Howard, less amused.

"So now what?" I folded my arms. I certainly didn't look any more threatening, but at least the façade of courage made me feel less like a runny-nosed child in a room filled with adults. "What happens next? Will you . . . ? Are you going to put me to work?"

"How old are you?" asked Belle.

I blinked, taken aback. "S-sixteen."

"Sixteen. Do you have any friends, Maia?"

Friends. I lowered my head. "Y-yeah," I lied, which was better than admitting that I'd managed to scare off the few I'd had during my year of self-isolation. "Of course."

"You don't." Belle's bluntness made my insides squirm in embarrassment. "Good. It'll be easier that way. And what about family?"

I kept my eyes on the floor as I answered. "I live with my uncle."

"I see." Belle sipped from her wineglass. "And what do you think of Natalya?"

"N-Natalya?"

"What do you think of her?"

I couldn't help but notice that Rhys wouldn't look at me as I answered. "Well, I think what everyone else thinks. She was a legend."

"Actually, what everyone else thinks is that Natalya ended her own life."

"What?"

"Or rather," continued Belle, "it's what they will think once the Sect releases this statement to the public."

I stared, dumbfounded.

"Natalya's parents didn't believe it. They were so bereaved that they refused to release her body to the Sect because of it."

To do their own investigation? That would explain the funeral's delay.

"And what about you, Maia?" Belle's quiet voice was so intense I almost took a step back. "Do you think Natalya killed herself?"

"No." I didn't even hesitate. "Natalya would never do that. She just wouldn't!"

And then my mouth snapped shut. Natalya committing suicide was unthinkable to me, but *couldn't* it still be possible? Who was I to declare that it wasn't?

"N-no." I shook my head. "It's not—it can't be true."

Because if even Natalya could kill herself . . .

My hands tightened into trembling fists. "No, I don't believe it."

"I . . . didn't either." But Belle's voice had none of her earlier confidence. "At least I . . ."

Once again silence weighted the room.

Belle cleared her throat. "And what about your abilities, Maia?"

"Abilities?"

"Natalya was the *Ignis Ensis*: the Sword of Fire. The Effigy who controlled flame."

I stayed deathly still.

"So? Can you? Control flame?"

No. I'd never even attempted it. I'd done everything I could to ignore my ability to make flames out of nothing like a girl-size novelty lighter. And for eleven days, I'd just held on to my sanity for dear life. How could I admit to Belle that Natalya's successor could sooner find a cigarette on the moon than light one with her mind?

Apparently I didn't need to.

"Ah," said Belle. To my relief there wasn't a stitch of judgment in her voice, but then, there wasn't much of anything else, either. "You can't make fire. Is it because your family died in one?"

My arms fell limp at my sides.

"Belle!" Both Howard and Rhys had yelled her name, but it was Rhys who looked furious. "That's way past *enough*," he warned. "What exactly is the point of this? You've already done your research. Why put her through this?"

Belle moved her glass in gentle swirls. "Rhys, you seem oddly protective of a girl you've just met. Why is that?"

Rhys frowned. "What are you implying?"

"It's okay, you guys. I get it."

All eyes were trained on me as I spoke.

"Maia . . . ," started Rhys.

"No, I understand. It's a test, right?" The tremor in my lips was obvious only once I pried them apart. "I'm the new girl. Of course you'll grill me. I get it. Trial by . . ."

Fire. I gripped my arms. It was the heat that made you stronger, right? Forging your metal and spitting it back out again formed and ready. But to me it was thick and unbearable. That's what I remembered. The heat, the lick of flames crawling up my house as I watched from the other side of the street . . .

Once again, my lips trembled open. "Belle, to be honest, I . . ."

I remembered it too well. The fire, the sweat on my forehead, the sidewalk's asphalt grazing my legs.

And the pathetic, helpless tears of a coward.

"I want to be like you."

Belle frowned. "Excuse me?"

"I want to be like you."

"Oh?" Belle laughed, her disdain palpable.

"It's okay," I said, more to myself because Belle's expression made me feel like I was back in sixth grade, trying to hide my sweat stains in math class while the boys laughed at me. "I know I'm just some kid who might end up being one of those 'cowardly wastes of human skin.' Or dead." I searched for the words, but June was all I could see in my mind's eye. "But if you were to help me, the way Natalya helped you . . ."

"No."

"What?"

"I don't want to."

"I get it. You don't think I'm worthy. But please . . ." With my heart in my throat, I stepped forward, arms outstretched. "Make me better! *You* could do it. You can do anything! You're Belle Rousseau. You're the Twelve-Kill Rookie, right?"

I noticed Howard and Rhys freezing up at the sound of Belle's old nickname. I also noticed the strange way the wineglass dipped in Belle's grip, and the way her features had suddenly hardened like sand in a furnace. But I couldn't stop. I needed to convince her.

"Just make me better," I pleaded. "You always said in your interviews that it was Natalya who made *you* better, right?"

Without a word, Belle placed down her glass, stood, and walked over to the window. The Needle's distant electric blue speckled her hair from behind the curtains. "What does the word 'Effigy' mean to you, Maia?"

I opened and closed my mouth several times, but I couldn't respond.

"We're also called the Four Swords. Probably because we're weapons. But actually, we're much more than that." I could feel Belle watching me through the window glass. "Every new Effigy succeeds the last. Do you know what that means?"

I was too afraid to even shake my head.

"It means that once you become an Effigy, you carry the legacy of the previous girls in your line. Not just their abilities, but their regrets, their sorrows. Even their memories." Belle tapped her head with a finger. "It's all in there. All of it. I'm sure you haven't heard them yet. Or maybe they just haven't started talking to you. But once they do—that's it. You won't be allowed to be just yourself anymore." Belle pressed a hand to the window, her fingers curling against the glass. "In the end, we're all just sloppily crafted monuments to the ones who came before us. Effigies."

"But we're still human. Aren't we?" The panic in my voice surprised even me.

Belle smiled. "Maybe. Natalya used to say it didn't matter. We were what we were. Created to fight."

The air grew heavy. Gusts of cold wind cascaded out from Belle's hand, chilling until I could see the flakes of snow drifting from her palm. As Belle turned, the snow gathered, stretching its long shape until a handle formed within her fingers and a sharp point peeked through the flurry.

Once the snow dissipated, I could see it clearly: the long, thin sword clutched with pride in Belle's hand.

It was beautiful. Regal. I lost my breath as Belle raised her blade and pointed it at me alone. The glow of New York City's lights danced along the edges.

"This is proof that I've accepted what I am. A reward for committing myself to this life."

"I don't understand." I watched with barely a breath as Belle pulled the sword back, running her hand along the smooth surface.

"It's the sign of a developed Effigy. For Natalya, this was everything. The fight was everything. And just like you said, she taught me everything. But I'm not Natalya."

This time she stared at me with a glare as cold as the snow drifting past her face. "Train. Become better. Or don't. Accept your fate, or don't. Fight, or don't. To be honest, I couldn't care less what you do."

I couldn't feel anything but a dull pain in my chest.

Rhys let out a long sigh. "Right. So I guess you just decided to skip the hellos and jumped right to the soul crushing." He rubbed his temple, exasperated. "Just great."

There was a timid knock at the door, a bit jarring what with the deafening tension.

"Is it Jeff?" Rhys asked as Howard passed, probably referring to the guard outside.

"Excuse me," came a muffled voice through the door. A guy's . . . and familiar.

Rhys blinked. "That's not Jeff."

Apparently not. Howard stopped in his tracks.

"Excuse me," came the voice again. "Hello?"

"Wait a second. I think I know that voice." I combed through my memories. "Wait . . ." No way. "Saul?"

Rhys leaned sideways. "Maia, you know this guy?"

"I met him downstairs at the benefit . . . so yeah, I guess I *kind of* know him."

"The bigger problem," said Howard in a low voice, "is that we *don't*." He glared at the door. "And Jeff wouldn't abandon his post for anything. Not with the new Effigy in the room."

Silence.

Rhys stood from his chair.

"Sorry to interrupt." On the other side of the door, Saul's voice was too easy, too pleasant. "But I'd like to speak to the girl you have in there. We met earlier."

Everyone's eyes locked on me.

"This is a private meeting," Howard answered him. He nodded to Belle, who gripped her sword more tightly than before.

"Oh, I know, it's just . . ." Saul paused. "She never told me her name."

"What is this?" Belle hissed. "Who—"

At that moment, the dotted lights of New York's Needle, for the second time, shut off.

We stared at the distant tower, stunned into silence.

It was impossible. It wasn't real.

It was one of those terrible moments when time slowed to a crawl. No one could speak a word.

"My name is Saul." With a sudden heave, the door burst open and Jeff's corpse fell into the room. "And like I said, I'd like to speak to that girl over there."

Howard attacked with a swift strike of his fist, but Saul caught it and tossed him across the room with almost casual indifference. He landed near Belle. I was already screaming.

Belle pointed her sword at the intruder. "What do you want?"

Saul was too calm, almost angelic. His shining sea-blue eyes washed the ghostly paleness of his skin with color. When he saw Belle, those same eyes twinkled, bright as a child's. "Oh, it's you. Sorry, but you're not the one I'm interested in."

"I said what do you *want*?"

A muted explosion below us vibrated through my feet, up my bones. The floor shook, and dust from the ceiling fell over our heads. The vibrations had come from several floors down.

The ballroom.

Uncle Nathan.

"Right now, what I want," Saul said, his gaze never leaving me, "is for this girl to tell me her name."

5

HOWARD WAS STILL DAZED ON THE FLOOR, his body crumpled in a corner. Rhys dove for the gun still strapped at his side and aimed it at Saul, but by the time he shot, Saul had already lifted Jeff's corpse to take the bullet. Black mist wafted up from the floor at his feet, slowly hardening into torn flesh.

Phantoms.

My fingers found my hair, locking around the curls as I stumbled back, falling onto the chaise longue. This wasn't happening.

"Marian," Saul whispered.

Right in front of me.

"What?" The gasp had torn out of me so violently it hurt my throat. How had he—from across the room . . . Was I imagining it? No. I could feel his foot against mine.

"There's something I need to ask you, *poupée.*" He gripped my arm and forced me up, his wild eyes digging inside me, scraping the layers to find someone else locked deep within. "Stop wasting my time and wake up, okay?"

"Get down!" Belle yelled behind me.

With a grunt, I slammed my hands against Saul's face, sending him stumbling back. As I fell to the floor, Belle waved her hands and a rush of water rose out of the heavy air, swallowing Saul and freezing him solid within it.

"W-watch out." Howard's words slurred as he struggled to pick himself back up.

I heard growling beside me. The phantoms, three of them. They were wolflike in shape, their bones clinging precariously to wisps of black fur. As I scrambled out of the way, Belle leapt over the chaise and slashed through them with her sword.

"Rhys." Belle flipped her sword over. "Take Maia and get her out of here."

"But . . ." My lips felt alien as I moved them. "My uncle's downstairs!"

Screams from down below seeped through the windows. I ran there, peering down at the street. People were fleeing the building, but it was too far down to see if Uncle Nathan was among them.

He was probably looking for me right now.

I spun around. Saul's frozen smile beamed dreamily back at me.

"I can't leave! I have to find my uncle! I'm not going anywhere!" The words slipped out of my mouth, eager and foolish.

"Got that out of your system?" Rhys grabbed my arm. "Come on."

One crack shivered up the ice. A second. A third.

"Come on!" Rhys pulled me, but it was too late. Belle jumped back as the ice shattered on its own. Saul raised his right arm to the heavens.

And brought hell with him.

"Damn it," Rhys swore as more phantoms seeped in from the floor, twisting their necks and breaking their backs into place, ready to feast.

Howard unbuckled his black case and pulled out a giant firearm.

"You idiot," cried Rhys. "Stop!"

But Howard fired a shot anyway. I'd heard of the Sect's crazy technology, particularly the weapons they'd had to develop in order to vaporize phantoms. I'd never seen one, but I was pretty sure it wasn't meant for indoor use.

The electrical current blasted apart two phantoms, but burst against the wall, nearly taking it down and shaking the entire room. The rest attacked.

Rhys shoved me behind him. "Once you find an opening, get the hell out of here," he ordered, though his voice was drowned out by the sudden onslaught of the War Siren wailing for the second time this month. Howard tossed Rhys a short black baton he'd slipped out of his boot, and when Rhys flicked it, a long iron rod shot out of one end.

"Maia, go!" Rhys switched on an electrical charge.

But we were already surrounded.

One tore at my dress, and I kicked it off, feeling the sting of its claws in my skin. While Rhys swung his baton into the side of one beast, and then another, Howard reached inside the black case and drew out three small metal balls.

"Shield your eyes!" Rhys ordered.

Howard threw them, and white light flashed the moment they landed on the ground; I could see it through my eyelids. I opened them just in time to see the smoky black remains of phantoms dissipating into the air.

The path was clear. Belle was handling herself against her enemies—one of the phantoms was already skewered by spikes of ice shuddering through the king-size bed. And Saul—Saul was nowhere to be found. I didn't question it. I ran.

People were already fleeing down the hallway half-naked with phantoms barreling after them. A set of bone fangs sank into one poor man's leg, and the much younger woman beside him screamed in terror as blood spilled onto the carpet. I froze for a helpless second before setting my resolve and heading for the stairwell.

I had to find my uncle.

I darted down the first flight of stairs with some of the other hotel patrons. Some were clumsier than others. I had to grip the railing when someone behind me tripped and stumbled to avoid being taken down the steps with him.

The man groaned in pain on the landing. "Are you okay?" I asked, lifting him to his feet. "Come on, we gotta go!"

But we'd gotten only three steps down the next flight when the top half of the staircase exploded beneath us, launching me forward. I could just barely register the screams through the sharp ringing in my ears before I slammed into the far wall.

One side of me was numb. Shakily, I shifted onto my knees, shutting my right eye to keep out the blood dripping down my forehead.

"What . . . what's happening?" I mumbled as I felt around for something to hold on to. Everything was dull and hazy, sounds, sights. My sweaty hands slipped across a windowpane, my fingers tracing the cracks from the explosion.

"Let me help you."

Saul.

Grabbing my neck, he lifted me and shoved me against the full-length window. His other hand sealed off my screams. With wide eyes, I stared at the carnage behind him, at the people crying in the staircase as phantoms sawed through flesh. It was too much. I turned my head, my cheek pressed against the window's stinging cold. But I could still hear them screaming.

"Tell me your name."

So much screaming. I trembled in his grip, my whimpers muffled.

Saul sighed. "I thought you'd remember me on the balcony, but you're still hiding, aren't you, Marian?"

"P-please," I said once he released his hand. "Please let me go—"

"Tell me your name."

"Maia!" The word echoed in the hallway. "My name is Maia!"

He tilted his head as I dissolved into a crying mess. "You really are just going to keep hiding inside this girl, aren't you, Marian? After all this time, you still don't want to see me?"

"I don't know what you're talking about." My voice broke. Tears streamed down my cheeks. "You've got the wrong person." Why wouldn't he believe me?

"I think not. I can understand, Marian, why you wouldn't want to speak to me. But what about *him*?" Carefully, Saul tapped his temple. "He's in here as well. Screaming for you. You're going to ignore him, too?"

"Let me go." I struggled against his grip. "This is insane! Please, just let me *go*!"

Saul pressed my head against the window so hard I thought my skull would cave in. My blood thumped painfully against my brain, my head screaming in agony for relief. I just wanted it to stop.

"Yes . . . maybe *he* can jog your memory. All this time, all he's ever wanted was to hear you whisper his name again." Saul's eyes twinkled with the malicious curiosity of a boy about to pull the wings off a fly. "And to kiss you again."

I squeezed my eyes shut as he leaned in, but the moment he pressed his lips against mine, my eyes snapped back open.

The pain was gone. I couldn't see Saul at all. Scenes flashed one after another, faces and figures streaming in and out of view, but I couldn't hold on to one image. Was this what they meant by seeing your life flash before your eyes? Maybe he'd really killed me.

Then I saw the shallow stream.

Yes, a stream, white as pearl. Mist stretched out all around me as far as I could see, and through the mist, a few feet in front of me—a red door. There was a red door, a set of them blowing open with the rush of wind.

It wasn't long before my head started burning. It was hot, too hot. Images, moments, and memories blazed past like breaths of fire. None of them mine.

And then suddenly I was in a drawing room. My head wasn't burning anymore, so I could focus on everything around me—the quaintness and simplicity. I breathed in. The old curtains veiling the windows gave the air a musty smell. The floor was polished, but the dark ottomans near the eggshell sofas looked almost vintage. There was a sewing table tucked to the side, and a bust of a man's head placed near the fireplace, but it was the wooden writing desk by the center window that drew my attention. At the desk, a girl rested her head atop a pile of books, her arms cushioning her face. Her Rapunzel-gold hair draped over her chair behind her, twisting in knots as it stretched toward the floor.

But there was something off about the room, about the girl. She wore a plain-cut white nightgown with long sleeves and cuffs. The lace frills of her high collar curled up her neck. An old-fashioned look for such a young woman. Old portraits hung on the walls, portraits of people in clothes nobody would have worn in at least a century. Off in the corner ticked a grandfather clock laden with white, embroidered draperies.

The girl raised her head and turned, her pale blue eyes sparkling with mischief as she looked . . . at me.

"Ah, Marian, you came." Her lips twisted into a conspiratorial smile. "Good. I have something to show you."

Alice, whispered a voice buried deep in my mind. The memory was drawing me in, away from my own body and into the room, into this other reality.

"No, stop!" Shutting her eyes, I shook myself free, sending my consciousness spiraling back down into the stairwell. When I pried my eyes open, I was back in Saul's grip. "Get away from me," I shrieked. "Stop it! Leave me alone!"

"Guess it's no use." Saul *tsk*ed. "Marian, *poupée*, this new body of yours . . . I hate her." And then he leaned in, his breath hot against my lips. "Hurry up and find a new one."

He punched the glass. The window shattered around me, glass cascading over my head, slicing skin. Before I could register his fingers leaving my neck, he pushed me out.

6

I WAS FALLING. FALLING THROUGH THE DEAD of night. Falling twenty-three stories to certain death.

Wind whistled past my ears. My head throbbed from the pressure, limbs flailing uselessly above me. My shoe slipped off. Then the other. My mind was blank. All I could see was night and red bricks—red and black and stars and Saul's smiling face disappearing into darkness.

I was going to die.

I stopped breathing. I was going to die. I was going to die. That sole thought thrashed against my chest, pulverizing me from the inside. I was going to die. Here and now.

Die . . .

Just like that, my mind went blank. A swell of power shattered through me from my core, through my insides to my fingertips. Flames swallowed me, but I could feel some of the flickers hardening and cooling, forging themselves in my hand. My fingers twitched from the sensation of smooth iron against my palm. I closed them and found a pole there, surging with a terrifying power. The fire dissipated, and I could see it clearly: the smooth pole of a scythe clutched tightly in my hand. The symbol of death. Its massive sickle caught the moon's light.

The power of it pulled me apart from the inside. I could feel each little gasp of life slipping out of me. But there wasn't enough time to think it through, to hesitate. I plunged the edge into the brick wall. The blade crashed through brick, sending debris exploding out from every direction as it slowed my fall.

It was insane. Everything was insane. But apparently I was still alive. I finally let myself inhale, sucking in a violent gasp as I dangled one story up, alone in the filthy alleyway.

Not alone.

I could hear someone yell something beneath me. A man. He was yelling, freaking out. Because of me? Because of what he'd just seen? Did he *see* me? I couldn't tell. The air was heavy with terror. Once the ringing in my ears stopped, I could hear it all so clearly: the screaming, the War Siren, and the thundering explosions from inside the building.

Chaos.

"What the hell are you?" yelled the young man in the alleyway, but I couldn't answer. I had nothing left. The power in me fizzled. My eyelids fluttered. My fingers slackened their grip. The scythe dissipated into the air, and I fell the rest of the way down.

"Maia? Maia?" It was fuzzy at first, but the voice grew stronger, breaking through the thick fog in my head.

"Uncle . . . Nathan?"

Thank god. Uncle Nathan was staring back at me, fear graying his face to a pallid color. I wanted to smile, but all I did was blink at him, dazed. I only just barely registered the pain stinging my scraped hands, my aching back, and the rubble clinging to my legs. It was a miracle I could still move.

"Are you okay? What are you doing here?"

I . . . I didn't know. I could remember Saul pushing me and the street slamming into my bones. But everything in between was dark.

Why?

Even an Effigy couldn't survive falling from that height. How had I? I pressed my hands against my forehead. I couldn't remember.

"Come on, we've got to get out of here." He dragged me to my feet. "We'll get to a shelter. There should be one nearby."

The drumbeat pounding against my skull worsened the more I tried to move my feet, but I kept going, out of the alleyway, into the street turned bedlam by terror.

"Uncle Nathan—"

"Get in!"

Before I could gather my wits, he'd already pulled me into an abandoned luxury car, its doors wide-open. Shutting them, I peered out the window. A smoky black swarm rushed toward us from down the street, swallowing up everything in its path.

"Just what the hell is going on around here?" Uncle Nathan scrambled to the front seat of the car. With deft fingers, he started typing into the interface just below the vents.

Electromagnetic armor. Thank god Uncle Nathan had found a rich-person car to hide in.

"Do you even know the code?"

"I can bypass the security system and input my own key."

"Okay, just hurry!"

Uncle Nathan typed at lightning speed. Finally—

"*EMA activated*," came a soothing female voice from the speakers.

"The windows!" I cried. There were two still open.

Swearing, Uncle Nathan rolled them up, the glass shutting against the metal ridge just as a black swarm of phantoms swallowed the car.

I cowered in the passenger seat, watching the swarm as it flew by my window. Black wasps. I knew phantoms could take on the appearance of different beasts, but I'd never heard of *this* before. They shot past, some buzzing too close to the car before being incinerated by the electromagnetic field.

"What happened inside the hotel?" I had to scream over the whir of the EMA.

"Phantoms." Uncle Nathan's breaths came in choppy intervals. "Phantoms attacked. But how? We *just* got the damn Needle running. How did it—how could it glitch again?"

His bloodshot eyes glazed as he tried to work it out in his brain.

Another swarm arrived. This time, the force of their collision with the magnetic field pushed the car back. The tires skidded against the street, crashing into the police car behind it, throwing me off the seat.

By the time I climbed back up, the black swarm had dissipated, the last wasps slipping down the street. People were screaming. People were dead. I could see the mangled bodies staining the pavement.

No. I couldn't let this go on.

I opened the door.

"Don't even think about it!"

"I have to do something!"

Because I couldn't cut the image of their corpses out of my brain.

Because I was an Effigy.

"*Do* something? Are you insane? Don't be stupid. The police are handling it!"

Just as he said, they surrounded the front steps of La Charte, taking cover behind the body-size shields they'd used to protect themselves against the swarm. More still were pouring out of the building, stepping over the debris, carrying the injured hotel patrons, who clutched at their SWAT vests.

But people were still inside. Belle was still inside. And Rhys. And Howard. With Saul. I couldn't stay here.

"I can't—I'm sorry." I leapt out of the car.

"Maia?!"

"Stay here!"

I ran up the steps.

"Hey!" A SWAT officer tried to hold me back, but I slipped out of his grip.

Belle was wrong. Fight or don't fight. Belle said it didn't matter what I did, but I was like her now, like Rhys, like the police ushering people to safety. I could do something. I *had* to do something. I had to.

As I leapt up the steps, I tried to remember it: Saul pushing me out the window. Me landing in the alleyway. What was missing? My insides felt dry and twisted like a rotted plant, aching for something it'd lost. But I'd have to set it aside if I was going to have any chance of surviving inside the hotel.

Sure enough, carnage was there waiting for me. The floor had been split in two, blood dripped off the remains of fallen columns and rubble filled up a crater where the fountain used to be. Bodies lay strewn about the floor, some still barely alive and quivering in the corners, while others were draped over what was left of the front desk.

This is hell. I clutched my chest with a shaky hand. *This is actually hell.*

Saul presided over it all, perched in the center of the vast lobby atop a serpent-like phantom that had to fold its massive body just to stay contained beneath the high ceiling.

Time stopped as our eyes locked. He was smiling. The bastard had the audacity to smile at me while people lay dead on the floor. My blood curdled at the sight of the amusement carved into his face. Amusement, because I was still breathing. Or maybe because others weren't.

Hatred pulsed through me as I watched him hold out his hand. A dark mist filled his palm, crystallizing finally into a jagged black mask. I recognized the material.

It was made from the bones of phantoms.

The pictures. At this point I didn't really need the confirmation. "It *was* you."

With a smile, Saul wordlessly slid the mask onto his face.

Nick . . .

I covered my ears, but the sound hadn't come from anywhere else but within my own head. I'd heard the voice before . . . yes, only moments ago as Saul held me against the window. It had uttered the name with both fear and love, but did not speak again.

I didn't have time to figure it out. Saul and his phantom vanished in a storm of shadows, leaving death in their wake.

"Help!"

I heard the cry coming from the elevators. I ran toward the sound, careful not to step on bodies, careful not to *look* at bodies, as I maneuvered down the lobby. The moment I turned the corner, I jumped back. A woman crouched inside one of the elevators, her blond hair matted to her sweaty face, her broken glasses dangling askew from one ear. The cables whined as the elevator shuddered dangerously, but she was trapped—trapped behind the wall of fire that separated her from safety.

I peered through the flames, deathly still.

"Help me! Help me!" cried the woman, shrieking when the elevator shuddered.

"I will." I could barely even breathe the words. I stared at the flames and they stared back at me, mocking me, daring me to touch, to feel their heat and let it sear my skin. "This time, I will."

It was a promise to myself as I willed myself closer. But every time my muscles began to work, they'd shrink back again, keeping me locked into the same spot. Soon, I couldn't see the elevator anymore, or the woman trapped inside, but my own house on fire and the charred brick hiding my family's burning corpses from me.

No, the elevator. The elevator!

I lifted my hand. I was going to banish the flames. I was going to do it. I had to. I had to get rid of them! "I'm sorry," I sobbed, breaking down. "I'm sorry!"

"Please!" yelled the woman, but it was too late. The elevator finally gave out and tumbled down the shaft, taking the woman and her terror-filled screams with it.

I was screaming too. Holding my head, I staggered back until I lost my footing and fell. Rolling onto my knees, I gripped my hair and tugged, but the pain wouldn't give me the absolution I craved. If only I'd just die. I couldn't think of anything else. Let a new girl take over. It wasn't supposed to be me anyway!

"Maia, what are you doing?"

Rhys's voice cut through the rattle thumping against my skull. Suddenly a rough hand was lifting me to my feet.

"Maia, stop! Calm down!" He must have said it because by now I was completely incoherent, thrashing against him as he tried to hold me in place. "Calm down!"

"I killed her! I killed her!" I was wailing, my body ready to crumble in his hands. "Just kill me!"

With one swift movement, Rhys pulled me in, crushing me to his chest. The shock of it silenced my screams. I stared wide-eyed at the flames, my chest heaving against Rhys's body.

"Calm down. You have to calm down. It's okay."

I didn't believe him.

"We have to go." He grabbed my shoulders and pushed me off him. "Saul's not done. He's been spotted on the Brooklyn Bridge."

I blinked, half-dazed. "What?" But I'd just seen him. . . . On foot, from here to the bridge was at least twenty minutes.

"We need you. Come on!" Grabbing my hand, Rhys led me to the stairwell.

We were able to make our way up the seventeen flights of blood-stained stairs because the stairwell had been left mostly intact. It was only once we got to the eighteenth staircase, where Saul had attacked me, that we had to get creative.

"I guess Belle came through here," said Rhys. A ramp of ice now filled in for the part of the staircase that'd been destroyed. "Put your arms around my neck."

Once I did, he grabbed on to the railing and slowly inched up the icy path.

I squeezed his neck and stared through the now-broken window, out of which Saul had thrown me. Screams and sirens, cars crashing, police shouting orders—the sounds of a besieged city seeped into the stairwell, suffocating me.

"I can't do this," I whispered, my cheek pressed against his hair.

"Everyone says that at first," he whispered back.

Soon, Rhys stepped onto solid floor and we continued up to the roof where Belle and Howard awaited us. Howard was far more damaged than Belle; his arm was a poorly bandaged bundle of red ribbons, and his left eye was swollen twice its regular size. And yet he was still standing, his body-size firearm still strapped stubbornly to his back. A black helicopter hovered overhead, its powerful gale rippling through our hair and clothes.

"You're coming with us," said Belle over the din as the helicopter door opened and a woman in a Sect uniform threw out a rope ladder.

I bit my lip but didn't dare say a word in protest. Too terrified to remember I hated flying, I simply followed the rest of them up the ladder.

"You need to tell us everything you know about that man," said Belle as the helicopter took off, flying above the chaos toward the Brooklyn Bridge.

"What?"

"You knew his name." Rhys sat beside me. "When he came in, you said his name."

"I met him at the benefit." I thought of that handsome, well-dressed boy who'd shown me pictures of himself laying siege to various cities around the world with little more than a pleasant grin. I told them about it—about the pictures, about his obsession with Marian, whoever she was. As much as I could remember, I told them.

"Marian . . ." Belle's blond locks whipped across her face.

Rhys looked up. "That name mean anything to you?"

We all waited, hopeful, but Belle shook her head. "I . . . I'm not sure."

"Guys." Clinging to a railing above him with his good hand, Howard gestured to the window.

I stood as a fresh wave of terror ripped through me. Even from where we were I could hear the car horns shrieking into the night, see the people abandoning their vehicles altogether to slip through the stalled traffic and flee the Brooklyn Bridge on foot. A great serpent of smoke and flesh towered over them, caged by black bones already dripping in blood. Saul stood on its head with his hands in his pockets, his wicked beauty sheathed behind his dark mask.

I shook my head. "This is too much." My body teetered on the edge of passing out but never crossed that threshold into unconsciousness. It was almost cruel.

"Howard," said Rhys, "where are the reinforcements?"

"Still about five minutes from the attack site."

"Damn it." He pounded the wall with his fist.

"What are you going to do, agent?" asked the helicopter's pilot.

"What the hell do you think I'm going to do? Do you see any of my damn equipment? You think I'm hiding it in my butt crack? I've got a bow tie on, for god's sake!" He ripped it off. "Maia!"

I jumped at the sound of my name. "What?"

Rhys grabbed my shoulder harder than I'd have liked. "Are you sure that's all you know about that guy? Saul? Isn't there anything else? Anything we can use against him?"

"I . . ." My mind went blank. "I don't know."

My stomach clenched. Two cars dangled off the side of the bridge before finally plunging into the East River, taking too many people with them.

Grabbing the railing above her, Belle stood, her gorgeous face vivid with fury. "This has gone on long enough."

At first I thought, terrified, that Belle's anger was directed at me, but she aimed her steely glare instead at the bridge we were now hovering over. Once we'd gotten close enough, Belle turned to the pilot. "Open the door."

"What?" Rhys balked. "Are you insane?"

"Do it! And, Rhys: Aim Howard's gun at the mid-upper portion of the phantom's torso. Don't aim for his head. We don't want to kill Saul. This is very important. At this point, the objective should be to bring him in for questioning."

"Understood," said Howard without hesitation.

"All right," answered Rhys, far less enthusiastically.

"I'll make the opening." Belle turned back to the door. "Don't miss."

The door opened. I had to hold on to the railing to keep myself from being sucked out by the pressure. Belle stood at the threshold, one hand firm on the railing, hair whipping around her cold eyes as she watched Saul's phantom press down its warpath below.

"Belle." My voice came out hollow, lips trembling from the syllable alone. "What are you going to do?"

Belle answered by leaping out of the helicopter. I watched through the window as she flew down, her sword re-forming in her hands in a flurry of hail and snow just in time to swing at the phantom's neck.

"Watch out!" I screamed because the phantom had twisted its head just before the swing could hit. Its gaping mouth and jagged teeth awaited her, but Belle acted quickly. Before I could blink, there was a wall of ice wedged between its jaws.

The moment Belle's heels touched the surface, she skewered its face, its white, hollow eyes vivid with anger. Then, using her sword to launch herself up, she flipped over its head, landing in front of Saul. With one swift upstroke of her sword, she slashed his mask in half.

I watched, awestruck, as the pieces fell, exposing his grinning face. I wanted so badly to see Belle slash it too, but she went for his chest instead.

The sword sliced through air.

Saul had already disappeared and reappeared at her side.

"How the hell is he doing that?" Rhys took Howard's gun out of its case and set it up on a tripod.

For a split second, the two opponents just stared at each other, Saul meeting Belle's murderous glare with that same acid grin I hated. Then the phantom's massive body lurched. As if he knew what was coming next, Saul quickly grabbed one of the twisting, protruding bones sheathing the monster's body and, before Belle could react, the phantom whipped around, throwing her off its head.

"Belle!"

But my yell drowned in the phantom's deafening cry. Belle's body rocketed through the air, but she managed to grab hold of the bridge's cables, icing her hand to keep her fingers from slipping off. She was safe for now.

"Rhys, hurry up!" barked Howard. Wincing, he grabbed his bandaged arm as Rhys locked the gun into the tripod and flicked a series of switches. The gun moaned, lights flashing red then blue then green as it charged. Rhys knelt, balancing part of the gun on his shoulder, closing one eye as he peered through the scope.

At Saul's urging, the phantom flung itself at the screaming masses below.

"Rhys," I shrieked, "do it!"

Three swift clicks. Rhys aimed and fired, incinerating the top half of the phantom's torso. He fired again, this time at its head as it tumbled down with Saul. The electrical stream vaporized the phantom's skull before it could crash onto the bridge below, but Saul had vanished. He reappeared midair, slamming atop an abandoned truck. I was expecting a smoother getaway; the attack must have rattled him.

"Good," said Howard. "Now if we can just take him alive . . ."

As Belle slid down the bridge's cables, Saul struggled to his feet and raised his arms. A groundswell of black mist rose up from the river, toward the bridge and the already terrified mess of civilians struggling to hold on to what little life and sanity they had left. I covered my ears. This had to end. This had to *end*. I shut my eyes.

More screams. I couldn't take it. Grabbing the railing above me, I stood at the foot of the helicopter's open door, my hair whipping around my face. "Nick!" I cried. "Stop!"

What?

But Saul stopped.

My heart battered against my rib cage. Nick. Why "Nick"?

Somehow, the name had been ready on my lips, slipping from them without hesitation as if I'd known it intimately.

And then he was looking at me. Saul, his arms dangling at his sides, staring, just staring.

"What just happened?" Rhys was looking at me too, as if expecting me to have some semblance of a clue. I didn't. I didn't know why Saul was gaping at me, suddenly lost, as if in that moment he'd changed into a different person. What mattered was that it was a distraction that gave Belle time.

Without warning, Saul doubled over, grabbing his head just as Belle jumped from the roof of the van next to him. She readied herself for the takedown, but it was too late to catch him. Still clutching his head, Saul vanished, this time for good.

7

RHYS CLICKED OFF HIS PHONE. "MAIA, SORRY, but we've got to go."

"Huh? Where?"

He jogged up to the helicopter. It had been less than half an hour since we'd touched down in Brooklyn Bridge Park, staying out of the way while Howard got hauled off to the hospital and Belle helped with rescue operations on the bridge. For twenty minutes, I'd been waiting for something, anything to happen. As soon as Rhys spoke, I'd jumped to my feet, my eyes alert and my nerves shot to hell.

"Are you taking me home?" I asked eagerly.

Rhys hopped inside the helicopter, grabbing hold of the cabin railing to steady himself. "You're still in school, right?"

"What?"

He lifted his phone. "One of my superiors just called: We've got to be at JFK Airport in ten minutes."

"*What?*" I shifted out of the way as he headed for the cockpit, but grabbed the back of his shirt before he could get too far. "Why? How come you're not taking me home? For god's sake, I don't even have any damn shoes on!" Not even Effigy speed-healing could cure my feet at this point.

Rhys's eyes were sunken, his face sallow as he stared back at me. He looked as drained as I felt, but he managed a half smile anyway.

"Looks like you just got your very first mission." He patted my shoulder. "Better take your homework with you. And we'll get you some shoes."

"Wait." I grabbed his wrist this time, my feet cold against the metal floor. "My uncle. What about my uncle? He was at the benefit with me. . . ."

Rhys hid his face, probably so I wouldn't notice how grim his expression got. "Nathan Finley, right? Since he's related to you, he's in our database. Don't worry, I'll get some agents to confirm his where-abouts."

But I'm not making any promises. He'd all but said it. My hand loos-ened its grip and slipped back to my side.

My lips pressed into a thin line. Since my cell phone was currently useless on top of my bedroom dresser, I couldn't call to see if he was safe. But I'd left him in a car protected by electromagnetic armor. He was a smart guy; he'd stay inside. Or get behind the platoon of police officers with all the other rescued civilians. He had to be okay. I made myself believe it.

We flew straight to the airport. I stepped barefoot onto the helipad at JFK in my battered peach dress, freezing, sore, and barely cognizant of what was happening around me. For a hot second my eyes started rolling to the back of my head, my eyelids fluttering, and I could feel the warmth of my bedcovers snuggling me into sweet dreams.

"Agent Rhys."

My eyes snapped open just as I started to sway on my feet. A young agent in black came up from behind us and handed Rhys a duffel bag. "Your go bag, sir."

"Ah, thanks, Phil." He took it from him happily.

That was when an agent approached me. "Ma'am," he said, and shoved another duffel into my hands.

I couldn't believe what I found inside. "You were at my house. . . ."

"I had them raid your closet." Rhys flashed a wry smile as I rummaged through the clothes. "They got a few other things too, I think."

Sneakers! I put them on. My laptop. Not a scratch on it. And, thank god, my *phone*.

"You were at my house." I looked at the agent. "My uncle."

"What?"

"My uncle! Was my uncle there? Is he okay? Did you find him?"

"Nathan Finley? He's okay," answered Phil. Those two words made all the difference. My stomach flopped as if the gravity around me had suddenly changed. "He was outside the hotel with the other civilians, so it didn't take us too long to confirm his safety."

Good, good. Sucking in a breath, I plucked my phone out of my bag, ready to dial.

"Good, you're all here."

Belle approached us from her own parked helicopter, her gorgeous dress veiled by a sleek black coat. Always fashionable even in the middle of a nightmare. Normally, I would have been gushing.

"What's going on?" I rounded on her instead. "Why did you guys bring me here? Why aren't you taking me home?"

Belle pulled down the silver scarf covering her lips. "While the city worked on getting the Needle back online, agents and police officers patrolled the boroughs."

"Was it—I mean, did everything go okay?" I instantly dreaded the answer.

"Nobody else was hurt," replied Belle. "There were no phantoms to hurt them. During the crisis, no other phantoms appeared. *Anywhere* in the city."

Belle wasn't lying. The deadly serious look on her face ruled out the possibility. I clutched my bag tighter.

"That's the report." Rhys pulled a long jean jacket out of his duffel. "The only attack sites were the hotel and the bridge. Once Saul left, the phantoms didn't attack again."

"What does that mean? Who *is* this guy?"

My words hitched in my throat as Rhys's jacket hurtled toward me. I caught it awkwardly by the crook of my fingers.

"Good question," Rhys said. "Nobody can do what he's done. It's impossible. *He's* impossible."

Vanishing into thin air, reappearing at will. Treating phantoms like his own personal winged monkeys. It didn't make sense. Phantoms were forces of nature, without consciousness, drive, or direction. They roamed outside the margins of our society, killing whichever poor bastard had the exceptional misfortune of straying from the protection of our technology. When they killed us, their violence was random and indiscriminate, but not this time. This time, somehow, Saul had managed to bend them to his will—weaponized them.

"He's controlling them," I concluded, without a single inflection in my voice, because my brain couldn't process the information. My fingers bit into the denim. "That's—"

"Against the rules," finished Rhys. "Right? Reality's not supposed to work like that."

My thoughts were swirling. Saul's existence contradicted everything I knew about the monsters of the world. But for someone so powerful to freeze at the very sound of a name—well, it was about as ridiculous as everything else about him.

"Nick," I said. "When I yelled that name, during the fight I mean, it was like I'd hit him with something."

"There are a lot of things we don't know about him, which is why we need to bring him in." Belle beckoned to one of the agents, who promptly produced a steel-gray computer tablet. "More than a threat, he's a valuable asset to the Sect. The information we learn from studying him might give us more insight into the phantoms themselves. But it should be obvious by now that the three of us aren't enough to take him down."

With a few swift taps upon the tablet's surface, Belle brought up the image of two faces, each taking up half the screen. I gulped. Neither needed introducing.

Belle's sharp eyes fixed on me. "You know who they are, don't you?"

I couldn't be a premium-level member on the Doll Soldiers forum if I didn't. Victoria "Lake" Soyinka and Chae Rin Kim stared back at me from the soft glow of the screen. Two final names to round out the current roster of girls who'd won—or lost—the cosmic lottery that bestowed upon us the title of Effigy.

"Orders from above," Belle said. "Finding and capturing Saul will take an extensive operation that'll require the involvement of many operatives."

"Yeah," chimed Rhys. "Which means we're going to need all the firepower we can get."

I could barely muster an "okay." Information bombarded me from all sides, and my head just kept spinning and spinning.

"Right." Rhys started dialing a number on his cell phone. "So Chae Rin and Lake are back in the game. I'll call some agents to pick them up."

"No." Belle put up a hand to stop him. "We're to pick them up ourselves. They're Effigies." And this time, Belle's gaze shifted to me. "If they're going to be called onto the battlefield, it should be by another Effigy."

I clutched the jacket close to my chest, hoping Belle wouldn't notice the slight tremor in my arms.

Belle turned to Rhys. "According to the reports, Chae Rin still works at *Le Cirque de Minuit.*"

"Maia and I'll take that one." Rhys rubbed the back of his neck. "Since I think Chae Rin might hate you."

I tried to interject, but my lips felt like clay.

"Then I'll go to Lake," Belle said.

"You know where she is?"

It took only a couple of clicks to bring up Lake's entire social media catalog; her pending *Seventeen* magazine fan signing in Glendale, California, was splashed across every site with as many exclamation points the character limit would allow.

Laughing, Rhys shook his head. "Finding her shouldn't be hard."

"Regardless." Belle handed the tablet back to the agent as two shuttle buses arrived on the helipad. "Phil," she said to the agent, "we should be leaving soon. Make sure everything's arranged."

"Just wait a damn second!" I'd yelled it louder than I'd meant to. It did the trick, but now that all eyes were on me and I hadn't the faintest clue what to say next. "U-um," I stuttered, wringing Rhys's jacket. "Belle, can I talk to you alone for a second?"

After shooting Rhys an indecipherable glance, Belle motioned for the other agents to go ahead and enter the shuttle. I stared down at the denim as Belle stalked past me without a word. I followed.

When we were far enough away, Belle swiveled around. "We don't have a lot of time."

"I know." Belle and intimidation just went hand in hand. I was too scared to even look her in the eyes.

"Well, then? What do you want?"

I thought carefully before speaking next. "It's about the name I said back there. The one that stalled Saul: Nick."

"What about it? Why that name?"

I shook my head. "I don't know. It just came to me. When Saul kissed me back at the hotel, I saw something . . . like a memory. After that I started hearing a girl's voice. And names: Alice, Nick." I pressed a hand against my forehead, squeezing my eyes shut. "For a second, it was like there was someone else living in here."

"Memories." Belle's sharp gaze wandered past me, seeing something I couldn't. "*Les portes rouge . . .*"

"*Le* what?" Something told me I was going to regret choosing Spanish as my second-language credit. Which I barely passed.

"Did you see Natalya?"

The question stunned me into silence. "No. Why . . . would I?"

Belle considered me for a long moment. I could see the riddles twisting and knotting behind the blue sheen of her eyes, but before I could prod further, she looked away. "It's something I'll have to think about further. For now, just focus on your mission." With a newfound sense of urgency, she started back to the shuttles. But a few steps into her stride, she stopped. "Maia."

I jumped. "Y-yes?"

She turned. "Do your best."

It was a curious phenomenon. Belle's words weren't so special; there were only three of them, and they probably weren't even the best she could have come up with. And yet, just like that, I suddenly remembered, down to my bones, what it felt like to see her at Fashion Week, gliding down the ramp at Lincoln Center—as if she had a right to own the world she'd shed blood to protect. The awe and heartache.

Don't let me down. That was what she was really saying. I was sure of it. And I wouldn't. It was obvious that I couldn't. We were finally on the same team.

Slipping my arms inside Rhys's jacket, I readied myself for the work ahead.

8

THERE IS, GENERALLY, SOMETHING INFINITELY disturbing about being able to see monsters outside of your window, even if they're so far away you can barely see them. Car rides were fine. I was used to it then. But when you already hate flying . . .

The first thing I did after boarding the Sect's private jet was shut my window blinds. Ten minutes into the flight, I was still cowering in the corner.

"You okay?" said Rhys from his seat opposite mine.

"'Course," I lied with a resolute nod. "I'm ready."

"I can see that."

"So, let's do this. Where do we start?"

Rhys had switched his dork glasses for some contact lenses, which, as he'd told me in the airport, were far more suited to battle. He brought out his tablet and stared at the screen. "It's going to take us only an hour to get to Montreal, so I'm going to have to bring you up to speed pretty quick."

"Right, right." I nodded again, very resolutely, my bloodshot eyes straining.

Rhys's quizzical gaze stayed on me for a moment more before he reached into his bag again. Then a candy bar flew at my face.

"*Ow*," I complained after it bounced off my nose.

"Sorry, didn't mean to throw it that hard."

I picked it off the table. "What's this?"

"You've never seen chocolate?"

I flipped it over. "Why are you giving it to me?"

"Would you prefer to starve?"

"This jet doesn't serve *real* food?"

"Fine, give it back." Rhys reached for it.

Quickly, I clutched it to my chest. "So you said there was information I needed to know?"

Rhys's lips quirked into a little grin.

"Chae Rin Kim," he said as I quietly began tearing the wrapper. "Stop me if you've heard this. Eighteen. Born in Daegu, raised in the suburbs of Burnaby, Vancouver. Youngest of two daughters." He handed me his tablet.

Chae Rin looked particularly disinterested in the picture next to her stats, though the stats themselves were nothing to shrug at: high number of missions, high number of kills. I bit off a piece of chocolate. "Her parents own a restaurant too. It's pretty famous."

The pathetic truth, of course, was that June had almost convinced me to save up for a cheap plane ticket. If June had had her way, we both would have been part of the customer boom Daegu Grill experienced once the news finally leaked that the owner's youngest daughter was an Effigy.

The plane shook. Just the slight jolt almost made me choke. Swallowing my candy before it could go down the wrong pipe, I shrank even deeper into my sad little corner.

Rhys sat back, sliding his coffee toward him. "Well, since I'm at least mostly sure you're one of those weird Effigy fanatics—which, by the way, I still find endlessly ironic—you probably already know she works near Montreal."

I nodded. "At a circus. But as far as I know, she hasn't been in the field for, like, months."

"It was that last mission. Happened just outside a little fishing village near Hong Kong." Rhys's index finger linked around the handle of his coffee mug. "Didn't go well. Some villages in certain parts of the world have weak APDs, so attacks are inevitable. Even though agents managed to evacuate the village, it was a hard fight; the damage Chae Rin caused was massive."

"I remember hearing about that, but I didn't know she was involved. I just thought phantoms wrecked the place."

"The Sect suppressed that information from the media," Rhys continued. "But dealing with governments is another matter. Of course, a certain amount of damage is unavoidable during missions like this, but as an international organization, it's crucial that the Sect maintains its political relationships and takes responsibility for situations like these. Because of what happened, Chae Rin's been suspended for the time being."

"Suspended." I cocked a brow. "Didn't know you could be suspended from a cosmic duty."

"Cosmic duty or no, there are rules," said Rhys. "Usually when an Effigy screws up, there's an investigation—not only of the incident, but also of the Effigy herself." Rhys sipped his coffee. "They look at everything: past training scores, psych evaluations, mission proficiency, and so on. They even interview people in her life. Then a council assesses her potential and figures out what to do with her. Depending on the results, they could order the Effigy to be retrained, jailed, or put to use in other ways. But while that's going on, the Effigy has to leave the field."

"Okay, but isn't the Sect scared she'll cause some damage while she's on hiatus?"

Rhys took the tablet back into his possession. "In extreme circumstances, an Effigy can be taken into custody during the investigation. But Chae Rin's saved a lot of lives. I've met her a few times myself. Despite her temper, she's usually proficient in the field. Plus she had a couple of agents vouch for her, so she was given some leeway."

Another jolt. Wrapping my arms around myself, I pressed my shoulder firmly against the window for support.

"Scared of flying?"

My eyes snapped open. I hadn't even realized I'd shut them. "No."

"It's just turbulence."

"I said no."

"Or don't tell me. . . ." Rhys tilted his head. "Are you scared something out there might be *causing* the turbulence?"

"Something *always* causes turbulence." I avoided his eyes, but couldn't look at the window either. "Air pressure and velocity and—I don't know, clouds and other sciencey stuff."

Rhys moved to open the blinds, but with lightning-fast reflexes, I grabbed the handle and kept them shut. Even after he started laughing, I held firm, though my cheeks burned.

"You do know there are antiphantom signals inside airplanes, right?"

"Obviously." I didn't know the science behind it, except they worked like Needles. Their range wasn't nearly as vast, but they helped create clear pathways for flight.

He leaned in. "And they have EMA. You know that, too, yeah?"

Yes, yes, in case the signal didn't work and the plane needed to be protected via electromagnetic armor. I could tell this one had it because of the pulse vibrating through my skin from the cabin wall.

"And this is a *Sect* jet. Trust me, you're safe."

"I *know* that."

"Just a bad flier?"

"Why do you *care?*"

Apparently, this caught Rhys off guard. Blinking, he sat back. "Should I not?"

We were silent for too long.

Then, out of the blue: "Your uncle's okay."

"What?"

"In case you were still worried, I mean. He's fine."

"I know."

"Some agents even gave him a lift to the control center in Manhattan. He works there, right?"

My hands felt cold. Without saying a word, I pulled my legs up onto the seat, wrapping my arms around my knees. "Did they tell him about me?"

I never thought I'd be so happy to see someone shake his head. "No, not yet. They gave him some excuse about needing you as a witness or something."

"Creative."

I wanted to wait for the right moment. That was the official excuse. But it made sense, didn't it? I *wanted* to tell Uncle Nathan, but not now, not from an airplane in the middle of a dangerous mission to take down a mass murderer.

"I'm curious, though." Rhys lowered his eyes to his mug, turning it around by the handle. "You've had over a week to tell him the truth about you. Why didn't you?"

"Excuse me?" I squeezed the candy bar in my hand until chocolate oozed out the other end. "That's . . ." I fidgeted in my seat. "That's private."

"It'll be hard, though. The longer you wait, the harder it'll be on both of you." Rhys kept his eyes low as he quietly added, "If you're not careful, you might end up getting hurt."

An uncomfortable heat rose up my neck as I stared at him. "Why do you care?"

"Why shouldn't I?"

The second I caught his eyes, I wished I hadn't. My body stiffened. My heart thumped against my chest, but the sound of the beat made my fingers curl against my lap. It was his expression: pity, or concern, or whatever else. The shocking tenderness pried me open, and in that one moment, I felt cruelly exposed. Helpless.

He didn't even *know* me. And I was vulnerable. This wasn't fair.

I placed my candy bar on the table and wordlessly slipped off Rhys's jacket.

"What are you doing?" he asked, but I didn't answer.

It's not that I didn't appreciate his kindness. But Belle had already warned me about what it meant to be the next so soon after the last. The struggle to remain yourself, to draw that line. Apparently mine would begin with his jacket, since he probably hadn't given it to *me* at all. Folding it in my hands, I stretched out my arm, presenting it to him.

"Take it."

"What? Weren't you cold?"

"I'm fine. Thank you. Just take it, please."

"But—"

"Natalya's dead." I was expressionless as I said it. "She isn't here anymore."

I could see Rhys's hands twitch. "That's—"

"I'm not her." And I looked at him. "I'm me. You don't know me, so don't . . ." I sighed. "I don't need you to worry about me. It just makes me feel . . . all awkward." I shifted my shoulders uncomfortably. "Please. I'll be okay. Let's just . . . work. I want to work."

By the time he spoke again, whatever awkward warmth flushing his skin had already dissipated. Taking back the jacket, he straightened up in his seat. "Okay, then. Back to Chae Rin."

We touched down at eleven. Because I wouldn't let up about it, Rhys got a couple of hotel rooms so we could finally clean up and change clothes before heading off in the Sect car waiting for us outside.

Montreal was a really pretty city with a nighttime skyline. And unlike New York, it wasn't ruined by a giant blinking monster-repelling tower. I didn't know much about Canada and its antiphantom tech, except that they apparently used a rail system in the parts of the country where the population was concentrated. I guess being flashy was an American thing.

Somewhere beyond the rails protecting Montreal was Le Cirque de Minuit, hidden deep in the boreal forest.

Sitting in the backseat, I thumbed through a brochure of the circus I'd picked up from the hotel's front desk. Apparently, Mastigouche Reserve had to be abandoned in the late nineteenth century once the phantoms appeared. That made it one of the many areas around the world that we ended up having to leave to them: a Dead Zone. According to the pamphlet, a private investor spent millions in the forties buying up some of the area, paving a single, fortified road and setting up one of the most successful circuses in the country.

I shook my head. Turning a Dead Zone into an attraction. It was just crazy enough to work. People do love the thrill of danger. But over the years, countries began passing laws that regulated people's access to those sorts of areas, so even with the circus's permit and strict security measures, their business started to suffer. These days, they toured the world for most of the year as a troupe, but for a few special weeks out of the year, they put on the ridiculously spectacular shows they were famous for in Mastigouche. June had always wanted us to go to one together. Would have been nice.

After a few minutes, we'd arrived at the first tollgate at the city limits. In America, you had to pay a small fee to use the officially sanctioned highways. Canada had them too, except apparently they were so cheap here the driver might as well have paid with Monopoly money.

Of course, tollgates were also used to mark official, government-sanctioned entries into Dead Zones. It took almost an extra two hours of highway travel to get to the one marking off Mastigouche Reserve. Rhys showed the officers a bunch of papers, and then, after inspecting our identification, the officers lumbered out of their tollbooths for a meticulous—and lengthy—inspection of the vehicle.

"Aren't any bodies in the trunk, boys," Rhys mumbled in the front seat.

"There's been a lot of illegal activity in this province's Dead Zones lately," explained the driver when we were finally allowed to leave. "Traffickers. They're being extra vigilant."

"Isn't that something you guys take care of?" I asked from the backseat.

"Nope." Rhys turned to the window. "We fight *things*. Not people."

"Sure about that?" I sank into my seat as I pictured Saul's grinning face.

We drove on a narrow, two-lane road. A large part of Mastigouche Reserve was still technically a Dead Zone, but of course, you can't have customers getting eaten on their way to the circus. The protective rails alongside the road did their job just fine, but the antiphantom technology wasn't quite strong enough to keep phantoms at a comfortable distance.

The sight beyond the window stole my breath before I could make a sound. It had all happened so fast. Black bones stretching out of smoke camouflaged by the night. A roar, the gaping jaws of a serpent barreling at the car. But coming too close to the rails was its mistake—in a blink of an eye, it exploded into black mist, fading back into darkness.

I covered my ears. "I hate this."

"Ha! I love this!" Rhys said at the very same time, his eyes glued to the window like a wide-eyed child. "God, this place never disappoints."

I dropped my hands. "You've been here before?"

"Yeah, once. My mom took me here for my twelfth birthday." He laughed. "But I haven't been here since. Can't believe this place still—"

I screamed for real this time when another phantom approached from the left and promptly evaporated. "What if we go over the rails?"

"Relax, the car can't swerve," explained Rhys. "There's an electro-magnetic current going down the rails and up the bars." He pointed at the row of bars jutting up out of the rails. Each one curved in ninety degrees over the road, forming a row of frames to pass beneath. "It's supposed to keep the car in place *and* atomize the phantoms."

"How thoughtful."

Rhys took in the chaos with all the giddiness of the schoolboy he would have been if he weren't already an agent. I bent over, wrapping my arms around my stomach.

"Oh, come on, don't be like that!" Rhys turned in his seat. "The phantoms are part of the attraction. It's badass! Like *Jurassic Park* or something—actually, wait, I think I have the sound track on my phone."

"Can you please *stop* him?" I begged the driver before a piercing roar had me ducking for cover.

But Rhys was right. There were more phantoms drifting between the trees, more serpents. They arched their bodies over the tree-tops, long and twisting like magnificent dragons of legend, a bright sheen blanketing their black bodies as they caught the light of the stars. Maybe it was the cheap thrill of being so close to something so dangerous, but there was actually something hauntingly beautiful about their lithe forms, their graceful movements—like the creatures written about in ancient legends. Fairy-tale monsters dreamed up by storytellers who never could have imagined that they would one day become as real as flesh.

It didn't take long to get there. We drove through a white gate, and at the end of a wide road paved in red brick was the massive Le Cirque de Minuit. A string of lights hung from the pointed tips of the building, twisting around the towering fir trees.

The driver, having met Chae Rin on one particularly unfavorable occasion, decided to wait in the lobby. There were only about fifteen minutes left in the two-hour midnight show. Rhys's Sect ID badge sufficed as a ticket.

"We're here for Chae Rin," he told security before dragging me away from the adorable baby tiger in the lobby and into the massive arena.

Streams of colorful lights broke the darkness—soft hues of primary colors washing over the sea of heads all enraptured by the center stage. And I couldn't blame them. The moment I stepped inside, my knees nearly gave out from under me.

"Christ," Rhys said in a breathless whisper. Even in the darkness I could see his hands shaking. A giant, clear tank took up most of the center stage . . . just big enough for the phantom within it.

I staggered forward to the edge of the staircase, clutching the railing. A serpent—the same type of phantom as the ones in the forest. Lazily, it drifted in the fluid-filled tank, a sea dragon circling its own tail. It was impossible. Unthinkable.

A phantom in a cage.

The audience whispered excitedly, craning their heads for a better look. And then there was the ringmaster standing in front of the tank, his red ringlets of hair tumbling over his face from beneath his top hat. He worked them into a frenzy, throwing his sparkling lavender jacket around—dramatic and cheesy in proper ringmaster fashion: "Have you ever seen such a sight? Have you ever imagined the power of a monster tamed by one man?"

"Apparently it's all the rage these days," Rhys said, eyes narrowed.

I turned to him. "What do we do?"

The ringmaster spread out his arms. "But tonight," he bellowed, "tonight, you'll see!"

She came out of nowhere. Tumbling out of the sky, emerging out of the darkness. Though her flips were wild, the young woman's feet touched down on the high wire above the stage in a perfect landing she ended in an elegant bow. A golden Venetian mask covered half of her pale face. Adornments laced her black ponytail. The silver body paint sliding up her tall, slender body made it impossible to tell where the leotard began and ended. And yet, despite the getup, I knew.

"It's her," I whispered as the ringmaster lifted up a gloved hand.

"Tonight you'll believe! Ladies and gentlemen: the power of phantoms!"

As he brought his arm down, the phantom burst from the top of its cage.

9

THE TANK'S FLUID CASCADED ONTO THE STAGE
as the phantom hurtled toward the shrieking audience. While
Rhys moved in front of me, I ducked for cover, but I didn't need
to. The phantom skirted above the countless heads—close enough
for the scare alone—before scaling the wall back up to the ceiling.
I drew my hands from my face just in time to see the phantom arch
its sleek body over the young performer standing calmly upon the
high wire.

Chae Rin.

Spurred on by the shuddering gasps and wild cheers from the
audience, the ringmaster cried out, waving his arm forward. On cue,
Chae Rin jumped right as the phantom circled underneath the wire.
The timing was perfect. She landed on its head without so much
as a quiver. Steady on the beast, Chae Rin rode it around the arena,
scaring and thrilling.

An Effigy-phantom circus act. If I hadn't seen it, I'd never have
believed it.

Chae Rin kept perfect balance, waving at the crowd. Ethereal music beat in the background as more performers in masks flipped and danced onto the stage.

I looked down at the aisle seat one row below. A woman's bag lay open on the floor, her tablet exposed. Thankfully, she was too dazzled by the magical act to notice me stealing it.

I typed fast and then, climbing back to my spot, held up the screen as Chae Rin passed.

BELLE SENT US. Big yellow letters set against a black screen. It was impossible to miss, what with me jumping wildly at the top of the staircase. For a split second, my eyes met the brown pair framed by the elaborate mask. Then Chae Rin was gone, flying back over the stage to the crowd on the other side.

The show ended with a musical flourish, a curtain call, and the phantom back in its tank, docile. Even as the audience began to shuffle out of the arena, the tank stayed onstage, an eerie reminder of an even eerier performance. I followed Rhys down the stairs, but when we got close to the stage, security stopped us.

"At least tell her to meet us here," Rhys demanded. "This is urgent."

One man nodded to another and left the arena, but Chae Rin didn't come right away. Soon it was just me and Rhys alone with a host of security guarding a phantom in a tank. My life couldn't get any weirder. Eventually, Rhys grabbed a seat, flinging his leg over the armrest.

"A phantom in a cage," I heard him grumble.

The phantom's white, glassy eyes never blinked. Endlessly deep, they fixed on me, just as I stood there fixed by them. If phantoms could think—and who knows, maybe they could—what was it thinking right now? What did it think of me, the Effigy staring at it from the other side of its prison? Did it know, deep down, who I was? What I was?

"Maia," called Rhys, because I was walking toward it. Security blocked my path before I could get too close, but my eyes never left it.

In the past few days I'd seen more phantoms than I'd ever wanted to. I'd seen firsthand the death they caused, the horror they left in their wake. And now here I was, standing mere feet away from one, separated only by a wall of uniforms. Perfectly safe. The very creature I'd been taught to fear was now close enough to touch, *safe* enough to touch. A powerless, powerful thing. I couldn't quite articulate the sudden recklessness swelling in my chest, but maybe this very feeling was why Le Cirque de Minuit was successful. It was a genius and dangerous invention.

When the forklift arrived to drag the tank out of the arena, I knew it was getting late. I'd been awake for far too long; the seemingly constant bursts of adrenaline would keep me standing for only about an hour or so more, which meant the clock was ticking.

"Hey!"

The word sent a shock through my chest. I jumped and turned, almost tripping over my own feet. The girl at the staircase a few rows up from Rhys still had a towel dangling over her long, wet hair. I expected the attitude, the sneer, the piercing dark eyes. Like every picture of Chae Rin Kim gracing the internet.

The bunny slippers and sweats, though—I didn't expect those.

"I was brushing my teeth. What the hell do you want?"

Chae Rin's youthful face was long and lean, a perfect oval shape with a healthy red flush behind her pale skin. A beauty unmarred even by a scowl.

"Want? Uh . . . I . . ." I gulped, hating myself for being so pathetic.

"Hey, kid." Chae Rin descended the stairs with the slow intensity of a jungle predator considering which limb to tear off first. I had to remember to breathe. "Were you serious before?"

Be calm and confident, Maia. This was what I'd told myself back at the hotel when I'd pictured this moment happening. *Calm and* confident, *damn it!*

"S-serious about . . . ?"

"You wrote 'Belle sent us.'" Chae Rin came closer. "Did she really? Or are you just some sort of psycho fangirl angling for an autograph?"

Usually? Yes. "Well, a-actually—"

"You *are* a fangirl, aren't you?" She glared at security. "Jesus, you guys literally dragged me out of the bathroom for *this*?" Chae Rin whipped off her towel and threw it at a security guard, who silently let it slide off his chest. The girl had good aim. "What the hell?"

Finally, Rhys stood. "Chae Rin."

Chae Rin whipped around, her frown deepening when she found him waving his fingers at her. "Oh, it's you."

"Nice seeing you again too," he said with a smile.

"Aidan Rhys. Guess Belle really did send you. Well, in that case." Chae Rin flashed me a bright grin. "Since I'm no longer obligated to give a rat's ass what that stuck-up bitch thinks about anything anymore, feel free to show yourselves out."

I blinked. "Huh?"

"That's right!" she sang, stretching out her back. "I got sacked by the Sect. So, if you'll excuse me." Chae Rin started back up the stairs. "Oh, and tell Belle that if she wants to give me a message, she can do it her damn self. Who the hell does she think she is?"

"Wait!" I rushed forward, only to be cut off by Rhys.

"Hey, Kim," he said coolly, hands in his pocket. "What's up with the phantom in a box?"

Chae Rin stopped. The forklift carefully loaded the tank, the sounds of its engine and signals cutting the silence among the three of us.

"I'm pretty sure if the Sect knew you were surfing on phantoms instead of killing them, it would have been included in the reports. Which means this is obviously a recent development."

"A new act, in fact." And though Chae Rin glared at Rhys defiantly, it was hard not to notice the slight waver in her tone. "Though we've been practicing it for a while now. Three months, if you were wondering. And look at me now. I'm already a star. Seems like being an Effigy is part of the draw."

Rhys frowned. "Why?"

"Why *what*? I'm sorry, is there something you're taking issue with here?" Chae Rin wasn't as tall as he was, but her intensity made up the difference. "This isn't against any Sect rule. My scheduled check-in isn't for another three weeks, and most important, I'm not doing anything illegal. So? You're, what, mad I didn't kill it?" She laughed. "I don't do that anymore, remember? You guys fired *me*."

"The Sect didn't fire you, Chae Rin."

"Oh, I'm sorry, I'm on 'indefinite leave for further assessment.'" Chae Rin rolled her eyes. "As if we don't already know how that's going to end."

"We don't," said Rhys. "You've been an asset to the Sect so far."

"Asset," Chae Rin repeated with an exasperated laugh.

"I'm sure whatever they decide, it'll be fair."

Chae Rin shook her head. "I didn't ask to be anyone's *asset*. Paid my dues anyway, though. I trained. I went on missions. I did what I was told. Then after one screwup, the Sect just goes, *Fuck all your hard work and sacrifice. Turns out you're nothing but a problem we need to deal with, so we'll just go ahead and treat you accordingly.*"

"It was a bit more than a screwup, Chae Rin," said Rhys.

"You weren't there."

"But I read the reports. You were *reckless*." Rhys swept his hand, motioning to the stage behind him. "Besides, considering all the leeway they're clearly giving you, right now, if I were you, I'd be grateful."

"Grateful? You know what it's like to be *summoned* to Internal Court like you're a damn criminal? To be stared down by a group of strangers like you're a murderer? Belle and Natalya get to be heroes. Meanwhile, I've never once been thanked or appreciated for anything I've done, but when I mess up, they treat me like an 'issue.' And then, when they need me again, they *beckon* me like I'm some call girl." She turned. "To hell with that. I'm done with you guys."

"Can I just ask one question?" I asked before Chae Rin could start back up the stairs. "Do you have any idea what's been going on these past few months?"

It was like Chae Rin had forgotten I was there. She gave me a sidelong glance. "Who's this, Rhys? Your partner? Looks like she could use a bit more time in the oven."

I swallowed. "Just answer the question."

"Sorry, I haven't had much time for TV lately. But let me guess: phantoms? And other shit that happens, like, every day, so who cares?"

I sucked in a shaky breath. "Natalya's dead."

That got her. Chae Rin's face softened. She looked away, awkward and silent as the forklift slowly wheeled the phantom tank away.

"Take five, guys," she told security. "We need a moment."

Once they left, Chae Rin straightened back up, wiping black strands of hair from her face with a steady hand. "Yeah." She shifted her weight to the other foot. "I know. It's . . ." Wetting her lips, she stared resolutely at the stage. "It's too bad. And?"

"And . . . ?" I paused. "And there's someone out there who can control phantoms." Chae Rin cocked an eyebrow. "Someone else, I mean."

"Didn't you think it was strange?" Rhys asked. "When your manager told you about the new act? When he told you it was possible to make a phantom compliant enough to let you ride it around like a show pony?"

Chae Rin tilted her head, gathering her dripping hair into her hands. "Maybe." She wrung it, water spilling onto the steps at her feet.

"Why didn't you report it?"

"Report what?" She whipped her hair back. "It's not a big deal. This whole area is protected from phantoms from the outside. It's just in here. My boss said he's drugging it with some kind of fluid: the fluid in the tank. It's like . . . I don't know. He said it leaves the damn thing open to suggestion or something."

"So you can, what? Teach them tricks?" Rhys shook his head. "You believed that tripe?"

"Why not?" Chae Rin wiped her damp hands on her gray sweatshirt. "Look, I don't know how it works. I just ride the damn thing. At any rate, what do we *really* know about the phantoms anyway? Who's to say it isn't possible?"

"If that's the case," I said, "then what about Saul? What's he been using? Because I sure don't think he's hiding a tank anywhere."

"Who?"

I frowned. "Rhys, give me your phone."

Rhys looked taken aback by my expectant hand waiting for it, but he obediently gave it over regardless. I didn't have to search too long for the video I wanted. Someone had captured and already uploaded footage from the battle on the Brooklyn Bridge. The terror. The screaming. People running for their lives as Saul's phantom barreled through traffic, sending cars over the edge. And . . .

I couldn't look at it. It was all I could do to listen to the frenzied sounds, recorded on a device woefully insufficient to capture the true horror of that night. I didn't even dare to blink, because I knew the second I shut my eyes I'd be back there, walking across the hotel lobby, seeing with my own two eyes the remains of human life.

Instead, I watched Chae Rin, watched as her lips thinned, watched as that healthy red flush drained from her skin. I watched her with tears in my eyes. And when Chae Rin's eyes met mine, I didn't look away.

"You're an Effigy," I whispered. "Tell me you don't feel anything."

Blinking the growing wetness from her eyes, Chae Rin looked at me now like she hadn't before. "Who are you?" she asked after a time.

My voice shook as I answered. "I'm . . . Natalya's—"

"You're an Effigy." Chae Rin's chest heaved. "You're Natalya's successor, aren't you? The next Effigy of Fire."

The muscles in Chae Rin's jaw hardened and set. I tried to think of something to say, some kind of introduction, but there wasn't anything stronger than this silent moment passing between us like an electric current.

"Ah," Chae Rin said, once she'd composed herself. "This must be how Natalya felt when she met me for the first time. We pop up so quickly, don't we?"

Chae Rin descended the staircase until we were level with each other. I braced myself for the inspection I knew would come next. Now that it was Effigy to Effigy, I tried my best to hide any weakness that could be picked apart and scrutinized.

Very unfortunately, I didn't react quickly enough to block Chae Rin's quite unexpected, *quite* hard finger flick to my forehead.

And it was really hard.

"Ah!" The shock of pain split through my head, just from one flick. For a second I thought my skull would shatter. Chae Rin's abnormal strength was as painful as advertised.

"You okay?" Rhys gripped my shoulder once I began to double over.

"Y-yeah." Shaking, I pressed a hand against my forehead.

"Slow reflexes." Chae Rin leaned against one of the seats. "Look at her. I didn't even put my back into it."

A terrifying thought.

"This kid's not even half of what Natalya was. Probably never will be. Oh, well." She turned. "Anyway, I appreciate you coming all the way up here to meet me, and I'm sympathetic, I really am, but I've already been suspended. Whatever's going on out there isn't any of my concern. The Sect can't just throw me away and pick me up whenever they want. They're the ones who wanted me off the field. They made their bed." She stretched her long arms over her head and yawned. "Anyway, just tell Belle to fix it."

"This is insane." Still wincing, I balled my hands into fists. "You saw the video. You saw what's going on and you don't care because you're pissed off at the Sect? No. I refuse to believe that this is all *just* because of your pride."

Chae Rin started to walk off.

"You're an Effigy, for god's sake!" I thought of June poring over books, telling me facts upon facts about the heroes who protected us from the monsters outside our city. "You're an Effigy! What the hell is wrong with you? Hey! Are you listening to me?"

I rushed up the steps, but the second I was in grabbing distance, Chae Rin stomped her foot. Immediately, I felt the steps quake beneath my feet. Before I could figure out what was going on, the ground opened up, just enough to swallow me whole.

Down I fell through the debris of cement and stone, too shocked to even scream, until I crashed onto a mound of earth. Only after rubbing the dirt from my eyes could I peek up through the dust to see Chae Rin's expressionless face staring back down at me.

"Shit," Chae Rin said. "Guess I'll have to fix that later."

10

UNDERNEATH MY WARM BEDCOVERS, I WATCHED the footage on my phone for the fifth time since waking up this morning: Chae Rin outside a coffee shop in Thunder Bay, Ontario, beating the ever-living crap out of a group of pink-faced frat boys. She'd only been fifteen then, just started her training. I had to dig deep in the Doll Soldiers archive to find the historic post: Breaking: CHAE RIN KIM LOSES HER SHIT (AGAIN)! One hundred pages before it got locked by mods.

In the grainy video, you could just hear Chae Rin yell, "The *hell* did you just call me? I said *come back here*," before kicking down a lamppost with the amount of effort comparable to passing a soccer ball to a two-year-old. Cell Phone Guy ran for his life just as his feed cut.

"Only one year into training! Can the Sect control their new Effigy?" Cable news television had eaten it up, and from that point on Chae Rin's temper became her narrative. It made people understandably nervous.

One thing I'd learned about Effigies during my years as a lowly fan was that they were stronger than regular humans. They had to be; they were built to fight monsters.

We. I shifted uncomfortably in my bed.

It was the sort of deal where you get stronger as you go along. Strength with experience, or something like that. Except Chae Rin was the strongest Effigy by far, even before she started training. The dark purple bruise on my innocent, unsuspecting forehead could attest to that. If anything, it only highlighted just how little the world still knew about the Effigies, despite all the research. Just like the phantoms. So little information out there about the monsters of the world.

One thing was for sure: I'd have to be very careful the next time we talked. Hopefully Rhys had packed a helmet.

With an oafish grumble, I dragged myself out of bed, ready to execute plan B. Last night, we'd found a hotel in a quaint, rustic little town a stone's throw away. Rhys had been checking in when a staff member told me about the fair happening today.

"It's a promotional event in town," he'd explained. "The circus does it whenever they debut shows. Should be going on all day tomorrow!"

I had to give it a shot. After getting directions, I dumped my phone into my sweater pocket and headed to the fair. It wasn't a guarantee that I would find Chae Rin in town with the other performers, but if I did, something told me I'd do better on my own. Rhys was an agent of the organization Chae Rin was currently pissed off at, but I was an Effigy like her. Maybe she'd drop some of her guard if we could talk one-on-one.

Why the hell did Effigies have to be so damn hard to deal with?

Crossing my arms, I trudged through the town.

The fair was in full swing. Tons of people packed the streets, delighted by the juggling clowns, the makeshift acts, the rogue balloons, and the stands upon stands of food and merchandise. It was distracting, to say the least. I tried to focus on finding Chae Rin, but after two hours of searching and asking around, it became clear that she wasn't here. Plan B was a bust.

"Jolie fille!" said one of the vendors as I approached. *"Puis-je vous intéresser à un collier?"*

"Sorry, I can't understand you," I told him absently, because I was still a bit distracted by the llama pen I'd just passed.

The vendor promptly switched to English. "A pretty necklace for a pretty girl?"

I never understood why some salesmen thought creepiness was the way to rake in profits. A polite "no" was ready on the tip of my tongue, but I stopped once I noticed the row of dolls on the wall behind him.

The vendor followed my gaze, grinning with all his teeth. "Ah yes, our matryoshka dolls. The finest quality, imported from Russia, carved by the country's finest craftsmen."

Please. I knew better than to believe that nonsense, but the dolls held me nonetheless. Little black-inked faces, red scarves, and flowery dresses painted with fine strokes onto delicate wood. The vendor took one off the shelf and popped off the top. One girl after another after another, each tinier than the last, until the vendor placed the final doll at the end of the row. As it was too small for any loving detail, the painter had opted to give her only a simple stroke that might have been a smile.

"Do you like them? They are very pretty, no?"

They fascinated me, the dolls. They drew me to them with their silent siren call. But their beady eyes and painted smiles felt twisted somehow, as if they were hiding secrets from me.

My skin was crawling. Why? Why were my fingers twitching? My mouth dried, and even still I couldn't articulate why.

"Matryoshka," I repeated.

It was Natalya who was the Matryoshka Princess, not me. Never once did it seem like a fitting nickname, but it was one Natalya had held on to with pride when she was alive. Matryoshka.

One girl after another after another . . . locked endlessly . . . helplessly . . .

A flash of pain shot across my head. I doubled over, my hand pressed against my left temple.

"Are you okay, little miss?"

I nodded, but then winced again. The pain beat against my skull, too loud for me to make out the voices now whispering beneath the dull rhythm.

"Miss?"

"Thanks," I said quickly. "I should go now."

I stumbled forward, but the pain kept pounding against my head, relentless. I shut my eyes to block it out, but by the time I pried them open again, I wasn't at the fair anymore.

Scenes passed by like a torrent of wind, rushed and bewildering. Disoriented, I stumbled along, but I couldn't feel the cobbled street beneath my sneakers.

It was wet. I looked down. No street. I was standing in a shallow white stream. Hot. And in front of me—a red door, deep in the mist. Grand and imperial. Magnificent. But fleeting. It vanished as soon as it'd entered my vision.

What the hell was going on? I held my head, every part of me trembling. I'd felt this before. At La Charte. In Brooklyn. After Saul's diseased lips had violated mine.

Last time, I saw a girl sleeping in her study. This time I was in a beautiful penthouse, sleek and modern with its white settees and trendy pop art. A stylish and glamorous apartment. The very same one featured on an entertainment news show about three months ago.

That is, when Natalya had given them the tour.

I was in Natalya's apartment in Madrid. And there was Chae Rin by the fireplace, leaning against the wall. Her arms fiddled with something behind her back.

"Anyway, don't see it as something to feel embarrassed about."

It was Natalya's voice, her Russian accent.

Except they were passing through my lips.

I could panic only on the inside; my hands were moving without my say so, as if they weren't mine at all. They took the top off of a crystal decanter on the shelf and poured scotch into a tiny glass. I couldn't even stand the taste of alcohol.

"Like I said earlier, Chae Rin, just think of it as a learning experience."

"Uh, y-yeah, okay. Thanks, Natalya."

I'd never seen Chae Rin look this nervous before. And the guilt in her eyes—naked guilt. It was hard to ignore.

The ring . . . The whisper came from deep within me. This had happened before too, during Saul's attack. A voice whispering *to* me from *inside* me. But this voice was distinctly different. It was Natalya's. This time, it was Natalya whispering to me. . . .

"Chae Rin?" Natalya's voice was beyond my ability to control. "Is anything wrong?"

At this, Chae Rin jumped.

Fire suddenly enveloped the memory in an unforgiving inferno. Grabbing my throbbing head, I stumbled backward, out of Natalya's body, out of the apartment, out of Madrid, until I felt my feet splash back into the white stream.

No, this was all wrong. I didn't want this. I had to get back home.

I shut my eyes. It took every bit of strength I had, but I managed to forcibly detangle myself from the trap of my own mind, dragging myself back into reality step by painful step. I collapsed, gasping for air as I finally forced my eyelids apart, dizzy and disoriented.

Thank god. I was back at the fair, crumpled on the ground in front of a pretty shocked circus performer. It was a little weird how she was tied flat against a brightly painted wooden target, but I didn't question it. Not at first.

I saw the glint of the blade in the knife thrower's hand before I realized I should be screaming.

"*Bougez!*" he screeched behind me.

People probably didn't stumble in front of his target often, but I still hoped his circus instincts would be sharp enough to keep him from letting a knife fly while I was in his line of fire, a sitting duck. Thankfully, the knife stayed in his raised grip.

But he'd had help. There was a guy standing next to him, his hand wrapped around the knife thrower's trembling wrist. The guy was perfectly calm, but the performer definitely wasn't, and judging by his panicked eyes, I could guess that if the young man hadn't grabbed him in time, I'd have gotten a brand-new hole in my head. It was only when the performer's shock wore off and his arm slackened that he was let go.

As for the guy, he was really tall and thin, his chic, angled face, long, frail limbs, and shaggy hair reminding me of one of those Eurotrash models who always looked like an industry party away from rehab. The tight-fitting jeans and plain white shirt secured the look.

This was the guy who'd just saved me from an accidental skewering.

"Are you okay?" he asked in an accent I couldn't recognize. There was a bit of Russian in it, but unlike Natalya's it sounded as if it'd been sanded down and scratched away over the years, blending with too many things that made it now indecipherable.

"My head," I whispered, but even whispering was painful. I still couldn't speak. My throat now felt alien to me, hoarse from the sensation of carrying someone else's words. I could only look up at the young man, at his delicate face framed by pale gold hair.

"Move!" said the female circus performer behind me, still tied to the target. That was when I finally noticed the knives sticking out of the wood, inches away from her skintight leotard.

"Yes, move!" It was the knife thrower this time. "You should not be here. We are in the middle of an act!"

Evidently. Crowds of people were gawking at me. My chic rescuer, on the other hand, looked seconds away from bursting into laughter. He was probably just some kid who'd passed by the right place at the right time. Luckily for me.

I looked around. Perhaps it was because of the crowd, but I couldn't see the doll vendor. I couldn't even remember leaving his stand. How did I get all the way here? It was like I'd been sleep-walking. . . .

"It's time to get up," said my rescuer, but my legs refused to cooperate. I flopped uselessly on the ground.

"Miss," the knife thrower prodded, but the young man's chilling stare stopped him dead. I wasn't even sure if I'd seen it correctly. Its joyously murderous glint, in one moment dangerously clear, vanished the very next second, leaving a cold void in his catlike eyes.

This guy wasn't normal.

The knife thrower must have felt it too, because his arm seized at his side.

"This young lady seems to be having some trouble." I could smell the blood off his pleasant smile. "Please be kind and give us a moment."

Leave, in other words. The knife thrower was too quick to oblige, turning to the audience and apologizing in French and English. He was probably too shaken to notice the knife slipping from his hand and landing on the soft earth at his feet.

"I'm sorry." I slurred my own apology as the crowd began to dissipate. The female performer slipped out of her binds pretty easily and joined her partner in scurrying away to explain the situation to one of their colleagues.

"Never mind that." The young man shifted the scarf around his neck. "Are you okay? Let me help you up."

"No, it's okay," I said as urgently as I could. Gently batting his hand away, I'd just started to crawl off when he grabbed me by both arms and lifted me. I managed to stay on my feet this time, but the grip that kept me steady was the same one I was trying to get away from.

"Growing up, I was told never to reject help when it's freely given," he said in a friendly enough tone. "Or you may not be as lucky the next time around."

His grip tightened.

"But then," he continued, his thin lips red with Cheshire mischief, "Natalya never believed in luck."

Wincing, I looked up at him, too shocked to speak.

With a long finger, he trailed a line down his sunken cheek. I was close enough to hear the scratch of his nail. "Do you?"

The knife thrower's last blade flew, digging its point deep into the wood behind us. The golden strands falling from Creepy Guy's head were the only physical proof of just how close he'd come to death.

Apparently, that amused him.

"Aidan," he said.

Rhys stood where the knife thrower had been, his hard gaze fixed on the mysterious boy.

"Maia, get away from him."

I didn't need telling twice. I'd already taken advantage of the distraction, pushing myself away from him.

The boy laughed as I stumbled back. "This is curious. Where did you come from, Aidan?"

Rhys jerked his head toward me. "Tracked her phone."

My hands found my cell phone in my pocket.

"Aidan, come on, don't look at me like that," the boy said. "You know I'd never do anything to her." He tilted his head. "Unless I was ordered to. But that's just the job, right?"

I swallowed.

Rhys stuck his hands into his pockets, but even then I could tell that they were balled into fists. "Vasily."

The young man leaned forward. "Yes?"

"I'm really not a fan of clichés. But touch her again and I will kill you. I'm serious."

At this, somehow, Vasily looked positively gleeful. "You can't. You don't have any more knives."

"I always have more knives."

When Rhys took a step forward, Vasily raised his hands in defeat. "Okay, okay. I was only helping her out." And he laughed again. "Why always so dramatic?"

I inched closer to Rhys's side. "Rhys, who is he?"

"An old friend," Vasily answered at the same time Rhys replied, "An agent."

Agent? I blamed the depiction of Sect agents on prime-time television for my utter disbelief: strong and strapping men and women, young but not *too* young, cool in black suits and shades, or in their red combat-ready flak jackets. Howard had fit the bill better than either Vasily *or* Rhys, the latter too geeky and the former too heroin chic in his jeans and coat to set off any authority bells. At the end of the day, it just showed how little I knew about the Sect, an organization that shared almost nothing with the world whose safety they were supposed to ensure.

I looked between the two of them, at Rhys's anger quietly simmering as Vasily held his hands coyly behind his back.

"What are you doing here, Vasily?" It was more of a demand than a question.

"I was in the neighborhood, doing a few things here and there."

"For Blackwell? You still his personal errand boy?"

The insult didn't seem to register or, at the very least, Vasily didn't seem to care. He considered his nails with a particularly pleasant expression. "Since I heard you were coming here, I thought I'd see how you were doing with the mission."

"We're doing fine," Rhys answered shortly.

"Then where's Chae Rin?"

Rhys frowned. I knew he couldn't very well answer, *Bathroom*, without looking like a moron.

"You were sent the update too, weren't you, Aidan?" Vasily hid his hand inside his pocket and moments later drew out a phone. "The update on the pending operation?"

Rhys nodded stiffly. I sucked in a breath and waited.

"I'm assuming that's why you rushed out to find this girl." He jerked his head toward me. "Things are moving along, but the situation is more time sensitive than ever before. To meet the Sect's schedule, you'll need to recruit Chae Rin within the next hour."

One hour to find *and* placate a pissed-off Effigy. Should be easy.

"There's something else," said Rhys. "There's another reason why you're here, isn't there?"

"Don't be so paranoid, Aidan. I just follow my orders like everyone else." Closing his eyes, Vasily lifted his head and breathed in the fresh air. "And who knows? Maybe I'll catch a show while I'm in the area. What do you think?"

Rhys's eyes narrowed, but it was obvious that Vasily was already done with him.

"It was nice meeting you, Maia Finley."

I shivered at the sound of my name on his tongue.

"Oh," he added, stroking the faded stubble on his chin. "One more thing—about the new circus act that debuted yesterday . . ."

Rhys must have reported it earlier, which meant by now the information was already circulating throughout the organization. Would Chae Rin get in trouble? I bit my lip.

"I heard a rumor from a particularly interested party. You could call it a lead." He plucked a balloon out of a passing clown's hand, twisting the string around his finger. "When you talk to the manager, remember to check for a white jewel."

"White jewel?" said Rhys.

"I'm almost certain he'll have it on his person."

But Rhys didn't look convinced. "Why are you telling me this?"

"Truthfully, I have other things to attend to. Otherwise, I'd check it out myself. Now that I've told you this, I'm counting on you to handle things quickly and professionally, as always."

His smirk held a deeper meaning. A secret. Rhys must have known what it was, because his body stiffened at the sight of it, but it was a secret neither boy would tell.

"Of course," Vasily continued, "since time is of the essence, if you're not able to get things done, then I have orders to take matters into my own hands. And nobody wants that."

It looked to be the case, because Rhys's expression became colder and harder than ever before. I shuddered.

Vasily turned. "Quickly now."

"Wait," said Rhys, but Vasily had already disappeared into the crowd.

11

"SECT." RHYS FLASHED HIS BADGE. "WE'RE HERE to talk to the manager. Tell Chae Rin to meet us at his office."

The circus dorms were tucked behind the main venue. Rhys and I made our way through the first floor until we reached the manager's office.

Rhys knocked on the door. "Henry Guillaume? We're from the Sect. We need to discuss something with you urgently."

I leaned against the wall. "You really think we should bother with the manager?"

"Vasily's a lot of things, but he's still an agent. If he thinks we should check him out, I'm willing to do it." He knocked again. "Besides, if this is the guy behind Chae Rin's me-and-my-pet-monster act, then I'd like to have a little chat with him anyway."

His expression darkened.

Just when he lifted his arm to knock again, the door swung open.

I gaped. "It's you."

The ringmaster. Apparently, he doubled as the manager, but today he looked much less extravagant than his theatrical persona, what with the beach shorts stretching down to his knees. I couldn't stop staring at his hairy legs.

"What do you want?" He peered down at me from behind a pair of dark shades.

"We . . . uh . . . need to talk . . . to you. . . ." I had to force myself to focus on his face, which did not go unnoticed by a very amused Rhys.

"Book an appointment."

Rhys's hand found the door before it could slam shut. "We could, but then we'd have to come back with a whole lot of people." He smiled. "And handcuffs."

The ringmaster stepped aside, glaring at us as we entered, but he quickly gathered himself, straightening his purple dress shirt and popping the collar of his blazer with professional gusto. Neither act did anything to counter the ridiculousness of his shorts.

"You're Henry Guillaume? General manager?" Rhys walked up to the front desk, tilting the name plaque on his desk.

"Yes," he said, his red hair tied not-so-neatly behind his head. "And I can guess why you're here. I knew the Sect would show up sooner or later. But this circus is privately owned. You don't have the right to infringe upon any private matters here."

"Even when you throw in a giant monster or two for your final act?" Rhys tossed up the plaque, catching its other end. "You couldn't afford an elephant?"

Guillaume grabbed it out of his hands. "It's our business. Not yours."

"Somehow you found some way to control phantoms, the very thing that's been terrorizing all of mankind for more than a century, and you didn't think it was something you should mention to the authorities?"

"What of it, boy?"

Lightning fast, Rhys grabbed the collar of his shirt, drawing him close. "Do you have any idea how many people have died because of phantoms in the past week alone? Let me give you an estimate."

Guillaume stuttered something, but I wasn't listening. I'd just noticed the ring on his finger, tiny and inconspicuous but for the white stone framed at the center of it. It looked so familiar. . . .

Oh my god.

"Where did you get that?" I demanded, my heart rate rising by the second. "That ring? *Where* did you get it?"

Black strokes buried deep in the pool of blinding white. It was the same ring as Saul's. The same ring he'd shown me on the balcony before commanding an army of phantoms to slaughter the hotel.

I told Rhys and instantly regretted it. Without missing a beat, he flipped Guillaume onto the table, pinning the flailing man down onto the wood.

"Rhys!"

"You heard her: Where did you get it?"

"This, this is illegal!" The ringmaster coughed and sputtered like a struggling jalopy.

"I said where did you get the ring?"

"What the hell do you two bozos think you're doing?"

Chae Rin stood at the door in a pair of jogging-ready leggings, wild-eyed and furious.

"This isn't what it looks like," I said pointlessly. It was exactly what it looked like.

"Kim!" Guillaume tried and failed to pry Rhys's fingers off his shirt. "Kim! Get these mad people away from me!"

Chae Rin shook her head. "I cannot freaking *believe* this!"

Once Chae Rin began striding toward us, Rhys let the ringmaster go. "Chae Rin—"

"Don't 'Chae Rin' me. Come on, you idiots!" Grabbing the two of us by the wrists, she single-handedly dragged us both out of the office.

"We need to get that ring," I said once Chae Rin let us go, Guillaume's promises to press charges muffled behind the shut door. "He's using that ring to control the phantom!"

"Oh, yeah? And how the hell do you know that?" she demanded.

I explained everything as quickly as I could, but Chae Rin still wasn't convinced. "Rhys, you should know better than to harass a private citizen over complete guesswork," she said. "Especially guesswork dreamed up by an overly excited rookie."

"But—"

"*Stop.*" She looked exhausted with the two of us, exhausted by the whole ordeal. "Can you guys just . . . *please*. Don't do this. Not today." Sticking her earbuds in, Chae Rin zipped up her white wind jacket. "Today's really important for me and I don't need the distraction. Let's talk tomorrow, okay? Come with an army of Sect bureaucrats if you need to. Just do it tomorrow."

Chae Rin took off for her run at a furious pace, but I wasn't letting her go that easily. By the time Rhys called after me, I was already chasing her. She was finally in my sights. I wasn't about to screw up again.

Chae Rin was athletic and fast, and the music she blasted was probably too loud for my desperate cries to cut through, but I forced my legs to keep working nevertheless.

The dorms overlooked a tiny but majestic lake, sparkling beneath the heat of the sun. When Chae Rin looked back and saw I wasn't going away, she sprinted even harder.

"Wait!" I was panting. I did pretty well at track in school, but Chae Rin was on another level. "You friggin' jerk!" I'd screamed it at the top of my lungs. "I said wait!"

Chae Rin spun around. I nearly tripped over my own feet as I dug my heels into the soft earth to stop my own momentum.

"What did you call me?" Chae Rin ripped the buds out of her ears.

Propping myself up against my knees, I let out a nervous chuckle, which was definitely hard to manage with my chest heaving. "Oh, so you could hear me?"

"So I'm a jerk, huh?"

Staring down Chae Rin was the stuff of nightmares, but I finally found my courage and stood my ground. "It's true, isn't it? I told you everything that's going on and what, you just don't care?"

"Didn't I say we can talk later?"

"Now!" I straightened up, stomach hot as the anger bubbled inside me. "We need to talk now. We need that ring *now*. And you need to come with us *now*. There *is* no later."

"You presumptuous little shit. You think you can order me around?"

"Why not?" My tongue was loosening at an alarming rate, about as fast as my anger rose. "I mean, who are you? An Effigy?" I scoffed. "More like a poor excuse for one. You know, every time I hear about you in the news it's about one of your failures."

Chae Rin stayed silent.

"You have the chance to make up for all of that. There is a *terrorist* on the loose, and we *need* you. Why is this so difficult? If Natalya were here, she'd—"

"She'd what? Save the day?"

The cold breeze wafting over the lake carried Chae Rin's frigid laughter. "You have no idea, do you? What she was really like. No, you're just another wide-eyed fangirl."

Chae Rin started toward me. Her lips remained frozen in a grin, but it was her eyes that told me everything. Even when she was burying me under a pit of earth yesterday, her eyes weren't even close to being this cold.

"Let me guess. You think Effigies are just the *bestest*, don't you? And you've got posters of Natalya pinned to your wall next to your limited-edition action figures?"

"No." My one poster was in my closet somewhere.

"So do you want to hear about the real Natalya? The raging alcoholic with a psychotic need to throw herself into danger at every turn? 'The Sect' this and 'the Sect' that. Duty, honor. I always figured she'd get herself killed, but who knew she'd end up killing herself instead?"

"Stop." My nails dug into my palms. "Stop it. Don't talk about her like that!"

"Why not?" Chae Rin spread her arms wide. "Welcome to reality, newbie. Welcome to the life. Effigies? We die. We get killed or we kill ourselves. Natalya? She killed *herself*."

Water blurred my vision. "She didn't."

"Everyone's saying she did. That sound super cool to you, fangirl?"

"Stop!"

"Me, I'm taking the third option: living out the rest of my pathetic life in shame. But it's not so bad." Chae Rin gestured around herself. "Living my dream. It was either this or gymnast . . . that is, before fate came a-knocking. And you know what? I may not be saving lives anymore like your precious Princess Natalya, but I'm making people happy. I'm happy. Don't I have the right to choose that for myself?"

Chae Rin didn't stop until we were face-to-face, staring each other down. "If you're so pathetic and broken that you need magic powers to validate your meaningless life, then feel free to follow in your hero's footsteps, right into a casket. But leave me out of it."

I stared at the ground, rage blinding me. I'd heard the stories. I knew how Chae Rin was, but she wasn't supposed to be *this*. She was an Effigy. Effigies were supposed to be . . .

I closed my eyes. June grinned happily at me in the darkness.

"Strong. You're supposed to be strong. A hero." I trembled. "Natalya was. But you . . . You're nothing compared to her!" And now it was my turn to wear a cruel grin. "You're scared, aren't you? That's what this is about. All this talk about the Sect humiliating you or whatever, it's all crap."

"Oh, yeah?"

"Yeah. You messed up at your job and you can't even take accountability for it. You're mad that the Sect treats you like an issue? Is it the Sect's fault you're more famous for your crap attitude and messy tantrums than you are your battle stats? Hell, even your own parents are ashamed of you! Wonder why."

Chae Rin went deathly still. I knew it was an awful, low blow. I knew I'd crossed the line. I was insulting her blindly now. But I just couldn't stop myself, even when everything inside me was screaming at me to.

"So you don't want to help? Fine, good. Stay gone. Who needs you? You couldn't even make it through your first mission! Ended up on a stretcher—"

I could feel my stomach caving in. Chae Rin's punch sent my body smashing into the ground.

"Don't worry," Chae Rin said in a low, terrifying tone as she lifted me back up by the collar. "Effigies heal fast."

And she tossed me into the lake. I thrashed about in the gentle waves, prying my eyelids open just in time to see Chae Rin lifting me out of the water.

"How fucking dare you?" Chae Rin shook me. "How *dare* you say that to me?"

I wanted to believe that the wetness in Chae Rin's eyes was simply part of the lake water dripping down her face. I knew it wasn't.

"You have no idea. You don't know me at all." Dragging me behind her by the collar, she pinned me down onto the shore. "You want to know what it's like? To have your body broken? To see someone's guts spewed out over the sidewalk? To see hell?" Chae Rin shook. "And then to *still* be the screwup? You think I don't know what my family thinks of me?"

The tears spilled from her eyes, dripping onto my face. I didn't even know when my own had begun falling.

"Who are you?" Chae Rin's voice broke. "Who are *you* to say that to me?"

"I'm no one." My lips trembled as I said it, my body bruised and tender. "Not like you. Or Natalya or Belle."

All those people. On the bridge. At the La Charte hotel. The woman in the elevator.

My own family.

"I can't save anyone." I looked up at the other Effigy, tears still streaming down my cheeks. "But you have all this strength, all this power. You can save them. I know you can. Why won't you?"

Wiping the tears from her face, Chae Rin let me go and trudged past me, her labored steps drawing a trail in the sand. She took a moment to flip the hair from her face, breathing deeply. Then, finally, she bowed her head.

"My family's coming today." She was so quiet. I could barely hear her. "To the first afternoon show. My sister, my dad. My . . ." She choked up. "My mom. You know, this whole Effigy thing? It's hardest on the families. My mom . . . once she found out I was chosen, she . . ."

She stopped. Something must have happened, something not even the public knew. I know Chae Rin's parents owned a restaurant in Vancouver, but the internet never told me anything else.

"But she's okay now." Chae Rin turned, her eyes bright and once again filled with youthful innocence. "They're coming here to see me. I've paid my dues. And now my family doesn't have to worry about me. I'm done." She bit her lip. "I'm . . . I'm sorry."

The surprising thing was that she truly looked it.

Effigies really did heal fast. Chae Rin had done some damage, but nothing too serious. After few hours of rest in the Sect's car, I bounced back with a few—or more—bruises to remind me of what Chae Rin could do when she was angry. Not like I didn't deserve them.

"We're running out of options," Rhys said. Rather than shuttle back to the town, we stayed in the massive circus parking lot. It was already filled up with the audience for the first show of the day. "I tried to get back into the manager's office, but he'd already called security. This is ridiculous."

I sat up in the backseat, thankful for the ice pack Rhys had given me. Gingerly, I lowered it from my throbbing temple. Even as my body ached, I still couldn't forget Chae Rin's tears. We'd both exchanged some pretty vicious words, but I knew all too well that I'd gone too far.

Don't I have the right to choose that for myself?

Chae Rin's own words. I should have noticed the desperation behind them.

Everything had always seemed so much cooler from behind my laptop screen.

"Not only do we need to find a way to convince Chae Rin to come with us, but we also need to get that ring," Rhys said from the front seat as the ice pack dripped in my hands. "The question is how." He rubbed his forehead. "I already broke protocol back there with the assault and all, so I can't just bust in and grab it. But getting a team down here would take too damn long."

His phone buzzed, and he stared at it. "Vasily . . . ?" he whispered.

"What is it?" I leaned to look over his shoulder.

The text was just three simple words:

Time's up. Sorry.

And a smiley face.

The two of us stared at the glowing screen in silence.

I threw down the ice pack. "I'm going to see Chae Rin again."

"Right now?"

"Something tells me I don't want to see that guy taking things into his own hands. I can reach her. I have to try."

I leapt out of the car and took off back to the circus tent. Rhys followed close behind.

As we approached, I could hear the audience screaming from the lobby.

"What's going on?" This wasn't the kind of delighted terror I'd heard yesterday.

Rhys sped into the arena first, but held out his arm to stop me the moment I'd entered the darkness after him.

"Vasily," he hissed.

A flush of heat emptied from my skin. Vasily stood behind the terrified ringmaster, holding a knife to his throat.

"Vasily!" Rhys started down the steps. "What are you doing?"

It didn't seem like Vasily could hear his name being called out over the pandemonium. Perhaps he simply sensed us, because he looked up and saw us barreling down the steps. He mouthed two words. His grin stretched, sharp as his knife. Then off came Guillaume's ring.

Along with Guillaume's finger.

"Oh god!" I steadied myself on the railing as the ringmaster screeched in pain.

Smoke shot out of the spigots along the center stage, pre-programmed to liven the performance with bright hues. Each stream lit the phantom's tank a different color.

Vasily slipped the ring off the bloody finger, tossing the latter behind him with a troubling lack of concern.

"Vasily!" Rhys went for him but stopped, his eyes fixed on the tank.

Vasily didn't say a word. He didn't have to. With his remorseless gaze still on us, he stepped back, his hands in his pockets, just as a fresh stream of smoke fired from the spigots, enveloping the stage. His grin vanished last into the thick mist.

Rhys spun around. "Get everyone out!"

But why? Vasily would come back. He had the ring now. He'd come back.

Vasily was a Sect agent, and he'd just succeeded in taking the ring into Sect custody. That was good for us. He had to come back. He wouldn't just . . .

My legs felt weak. He wouldn't just . . .

Leave.

The phantom stirred violently in its tank.

"Get *out*!" Rhys ran to the ringmaster just as the phantom's long body crashed out of its cage, splitting through funnels of steam as it began its rampage.

Too many bodies made for the exit at once. To avoid the stampede, I climbed onto an empty seat just as the phantom blitzed past. As patrons dove to the ground, I shielded my head, but peeked up out of some morbid sense of curiosity; the phantom's torso slithered overhead, bone and smoke and flesh close enough to whip the curls from my face from the sheer force alone.

"Rhys," I shouted, but I couldn't see him anymore. "Rhys!" I staggered off the chair and into the stairway.

The phantom shot through the ceiling, crashing through to the open air. I screamed as debris from the rafters began plummeting to the ground.

A wooden beam had been shaken loose. Falling backward onto the hard ground, I watched it hurtle toward me before shutting my eyes.

I heard the collision before I felt the pressure reverberating through the floor.

Chae Rin had one foot firm on the step behind her to keep her steady, and though she held the beam in place, the impact had clearly broken one of her hands. She cried out in pain, grunting as she threw the beam off to the side.

"Chae Rin!" I scrambled to my feet. "Where did you—are you okay?"

Soot tarnished the silver of Chae Rin's leotard and only half of her face was done up in the heavy makeup meant for her performance. Too shocked to respond, she turned, her cloudy eyes wandering across the turmoil in a befuddled haze.

"Dad? Mom?" I could hear her speak beneath the din. *"Eomma?!"*

I grabbed her arm. "Chae Rin, I—"

"Get people out!" Chae Rin looked frantic. "Go!"

I didn't need telling twice. As Chae Rin ran off to look for her family, I did whatever I could to get people out of the arena, hauling them off the ground and helping those who couldn't move on their own, like the old man whose brittle limbs stopped him from hobbling up the stairs as quickly as I would have liked.

"Oh god, help! Someone help!" a voice cried down below.

I grabbed a guy who was shuttling past and pulled him to me. "Help him," I ordered, and as he took the old man's arm, I ran toward the voice.

In the middle of a row of seats, a teenage boy was trying to lift debris that had fallen on a woman's legs. But the phantom had just burst back into the crumbling arena. They were both running out of time.

Chae Rin reached them first. Flipping the broken rafter off with ease, she crouched down next to the screaming, crying woman.

I hopped over the row of seats to get to them. "Is she okay?"

Clenching her teeth to silence her cries, the woman shook her head. Her right leg was broken, but she was alive.

As she whimpered, the boy stared up at Chae Rin through his square glasses. "You," he breathed. "You're an Effigy!"

It amazed me to see him possessed by awe despite the horror and chaos around him. That was the effect Effigies were supposed to have.

Chae Rin had noticed too. Her fingers clinched around the seat behind her, parted lips frozen as she stood fixed by it: his naked, unflinching faith.

"It's coming," the woman cried, screaming as the phantom made for us.

Without missing a beat, Chae Rin raised her hands; a wall of stone rose with them. It sloped upward, forcing the phantom to follow its curve back around, away from the group.

She'd bought us time.

"Help her up," she ordered me.

Slinging the woman's arm around my neck, I dragged her to the stairway with the boy following close behind. I whipped around just in time to see the phantom make for Chae Rin. It was as if it recognized her, the girl who'd ridden it like a mechanical bull for profit. It rushed toward her, jaws gaping.

"Yeah, come get it." Chae Rin jumped onto a seat and, with a flip that could only be executed by an expert high-wire artist, grabbed hold of her former partner by grasping one of the exposed bones with her good hand.

It went wild, jerking violently and trying unsuccessfully to fling her off until finally changing course with a devastating roar.

I held my breath. It was coming for *us*.

The floor groaned, shifted, and then finally cracked apart as a pillar of stone exploded out from underneath the chairs. With the single thrust, the jagged edge pierced the phantom's neck, stopping it brutally in its tracks.

Chae Rin let out a heavy sigh and slid off its twitching body with a dull thud.

The phantom was dead.

A brigade of ambulances were parked outside Le Cirque de Minuit, their personnel tending to the damage. Chae Rin sat on the hood of a police car in her running jacket, batting away an EMT's hand when he tried to tend to the bloody tear on her forehead.

"He's just trying to help," I said with an exhausted, halfhearted chuckle.

"I'm fine." Chae Rin let her long hair out of its bun, shaking it loose with a hand. "Effigies heal fast, remember," she added with a sly glance meant for me.

Shaking my head, I took a seat next to her, pleasantly surprised when Chae Rin shifted to give me room. But for a long time, I couldn't speak. Maybe I'd never get used to it: the stretchers, the destruction, the mess of injured innocents still too shocked to comprehend what was happening around them.

It had to end.

"I know," Chae Rin spoke up before I could say a word. "I already know. You still want me to come with, don't you?"

She picked at the bandage wrapped around her broken hand.

"Where are your parents?" I asked. "Are they okay?"

Chae Rin laughed. "Didn't come. I just got their text." She pulled her phone out of her jacket pocket, flipping it over. "Good thing. I don't know how I would have explained all that."

As she dumped her phone back into her pocket with a nonchalant smirk, I thought of the childlike terror in her eyes while she searched for her family in the arena.

"You know that ring." Chae Rin gripped her knees. "It was Natalya's."

I wasn't surprised. Natalya herself had tried to tell me that, in her memory. That's what it was, right? Slowly, it was starting to come together, but it was so surreal, too surreal to even comprehend. That I'd seen into the consciousness of the legendary Effigy . . . that a dead girl could communicate with me from inside me. It shook me more than I dared to let on.

"I took it from her the last time I saw her. And, uh . . . a bunch of other stuff."

"Why?"

"I don't know! It was stupid!" Chae Rin rested her head against her good hand. "I was pissed off and I needed money, so I pawned some of her stuff, but the ring . . . I knew there was something off about it, but like an idiot, I ended up giving it to the manager."

"He wanted the ring specifically?"

"I don't think he knew what it did. He probably figured it out afterward. But he's a greedy bastard, and anyone can tell it's worth a lot. He said he'd let me be part of the troupe if I gave it to him. I know it's messed up. I wasn't thinking. I just . . . ugh." She went quiet.

I just nodded. As far as mistakes went, I knew too well that there were worse ones she could have committed. What concerned me more was the ring itself, which was now in the hands of a psycho agent who maybe never was on our side to begin with. Natalya's ring—but where had *Natalya* gotten it?

"From one screwup to another, we could really use your help," I said. "Just one mission. And once it's all done—"

"If we survive—"

"—you can go back to the circus—"

"If it reopens." Chae Rin sighed. "But I guess I don't really have a leg to stand on here." She gazed out over the crowds. "No sense in letting someone else clean up my mess."

I straightened up as Chae Rin hopped off the car. "What are you saying?"

"I'm saying give me a second to pack." Without turning, she waved her hand in a temporary farewell before disappearing into the crowd.

Sweet relief. I stepped onto the ground trying very hard not to pump my fists in the air in front of a crowd of overworked EMTs and injured audience members who most likely would have found it incredibly inappropriate. I'd completed my first mission. Maybe it could have gone a little more smoothly and with a little less carnage, but at least I wouldn't go back to Belle empty-handed. That was worth the bruises.

"Rhys!" I'd just seen him slip out from behind a group of EMTs. At first he didn't notice me. He lowered his phone from his ear, frustration still fresh on his face. After I called out again, he finally saw me standing there and came forward. Once he reached me, he grabbed my arms and pulled me forward, checking for wounds.

"You all right? Wait." He stopped. "Are you laughing? At me?"

At the very least I was giggling. "You remind me of my *grandma*."

"Oh, yeah?"

"Just without the Jamaican accent."

Still, there was something kind of deeply pleasant about the sheepish smile playing on his lips as the tenseness in his features slowly eased away. The way he was looking at me, the easy way his eyes held mine ... 'Course, that wasn't something I could exactly admit.

Quickly, I looked down, shuffling my feet. "Chae Rin's coming along."

"I thought she would. Good job."

"Well, the phantom did all the work. What about Vasily?"

"Gone."

"Shouldn't we go after him?"

"That's what I thought, but I've been told not to." Rhys's features darkened. "*Everything's under control*, they said. He's on his way back to the European Division headquarters in London with the ring. He's even reported in."

"*Reported in*," I repeated incredulously. "Oh well, great to know he hasn't gone rogue or something. So did he also tell the Sect about how he almost got us all killed?"

"I'm sure it wouldn't make a difference if he did. Vasily's not exactly a regular agent. He doesn't answer to the official channels of authority."

"What do you mean?"

Rhys didn't elaborate. He'd become silent, grim, but it all vanished with a deep sigh as he shoved his phone back into his pocket. "Anyway, we have other orders. Once Chae Rin's ready, we'll leave for Argentina."

I blinked, stupefied as he pulled out his car keys. "Argentina?"

"That's right." Rhys spun them around his finger. "Pack your sunscreen."

12

CHAE RIN GRABBED A MAGAZINE OFF THE rack at one of the airport convenience stores and tossed it to me. Blinking, I drew it to my face.

The painfully gorgeous girl on the cover beamed at the camera, her lips frozen in a soundless laugh, her dewy, exquisite skin coated in fresh makeup. It was honestly unreal how pretty she was.

I lowered the magazine. "Have you . . . ever met her?"

"Lake?" As we stepped onto one of the moving sidewalks, Chae Rin pushed her rather large identity-veiling shades up her nose. "'Course not. What, you think all us Effigies meet twice a week for book club or something?"

I didn't even want to imagine what kind of horror that would entail.

Behind us, Rhys leaned against the railing, thumbing through one of those Spanish dictionaries for tourists. "One Effigy's a singer-model; the other's a circus performer." He flipped a page. "Mild-mannered high school student sounds a bit dull in comparison, doesn't it?"

The term "singer" might have been pushing it for Lake. I personally never thought she was that impressive, even back when she was on that British talent show years ago, but I would never say that on the internet. Not anymore. Lake's psychotic fans were always watching.

"Not a fan of her?" Lowering his book, Rhys peered at me quizzically. "I thought you were a general-purpose Effigy fangirl."

I hadn't realized I'd been sneering at the cover. As Chae Rin snorted, I relaxed my face and shifted awkwardly. Even as a fangirl, I had standards. Chae Rin had at least tried to fulfill her duties. Lake barely finished training and rarely went on missions. Health reasons or something. Didn't stop the photo shoots. "Swans," of course, made up all kinds of excuses, as crazy fans do.

"Listen to this: 'From Girl Group Outcast to Solo Supergirl!!!'" I read the cover with all the fake enthusiasm the number of exclamation marks implied, and then flipped through the magazine until I reached the full-page spread. Lake posed cheerfully in a vibrant pastel dress showing off her gloriously long, pencil-stick legs. But what I noticed first was the red superhero mask strapped to her face. Her brown eyes gleamed shamelessly from the eyeholes.

I pointed to it. "Doesn't this bother you?"

Chae Rin took the magazine for a closer look. "What, you mean how she's using being an Effigy as a marketing concept?" She shrugged. "Wouldn't be the first. Hell, even my Effigy-ness helped boost ticket sales at the circus."

"Okay." I tried again. "But doesn't it bother you that she gets to flake on missions? I mean, I get that Effigies can live their lives in between missions, but does she ever do *anything* Effigy-oriented? The only time I hear about her is when she's promoting herself or hanging out with some soulless reality TV star."

"Depends on how many missions you get called for and how

frequently," replied Chae Rin. "I never had much time until I got suspended, but from what I know, Lake isn't exactly your go-to Effigy. Last I heard, she had some kind of a breakdown in Milan a while back, so the Sect put her on temporary hiatus."

Rhys flipped a page of his book. "Her parents got involved. And lawyers. The whole deal."

Chae Rin laughed. "Guess not everyone's cut out for monsters, blood, and death. At least she's making the most of her time off."

I frowned. A breakdown? This was my first time hearing about it.

"Anyway, what's it to you?" After Chae Rin tossed the magazine back to me, I distinctly heard her add under her breath: "So damn judgey, god."

Since exhaustion was really the only thing keeping my flight terror at bay, I welcomed it. We all had plenty of time to sleep on the nearly fifteen-hour nonstop jet flight to Sierra de la Ventana. The Sect had built the headquarters for their South American Division somewhere along the foot of the looming mountain range.

Argentina was unbearably hot, as expected. I already had my sweatshirt tied around my waist as I sat at the back of the black van with Chae Rin, my clammy, sweaty skin roasting beneath the heat of the early-morning sun.

I peered out my window at the rugged Argentinean terrain.

This was crazy. The farthest I'd ever traveled was Kingston to visit family. Now here I was in a whole other part of the world, breathing in the clear air, snapping pictures of the golden sunflower fields with my phone. I'd have enjoyed it a lot more if not for the dull whisper of dread reminding me that this wasn't a vacation.

Rhys told us a little about the facility on the way there. Like all the ones situated outside urban areas, this one came equipped with a powerful enough APD to fortify the miles' worth of land sur-rounding it—which is why I didn't quite get the high guard towers on the other side of the gated entrance, but then I guess it never hurt to be vigilant. Two armed guards in red Sect combat uniforms occu-pied each tower—no. There was a *third* one in the rightmost tower: a young woman in regular clothes. A pair of binoculars hid her face.

Shielding my eyes from the sun, I peered through the window for a better look as our van passed, but the towers were too high and too far from the road. Maybe it was better I couldn't see their faces. I could tell they were staring at me too—a fact that made me deeply uncomfortable.

The underground parking lot wasn't too far. A team of agents was already waiting for us.

"Agent Rhys," said the man standing at the front. "It's nice to meet you. I am Agent Ortega."

In his very agent-like black suit and tie, Ortega held himself as if he were six inches taller than he really was and not at all ashamed of his messy man-bun.

"Good to meet you too." Rhys shook Ortega's hand with a serious, businesslike nod that didn't at all fit his varsity jacket glee club look, but he still pulled it off. "And these two are—"

"The Effigies."

Almost as if it were a nervous tic, I averted my eyes when Ortega turned to us.

"Chae Rin Kim and Maia Finley, I presume?" After sizing us up, he nodded. "Good. Belle Rousseau arrived a few hours ago with Victoria Soyinka." I still wasn't used to hearing Lake's real name. "Once all four of you are gathered, we can debrief you on our current situation."

"Sounds good," Rhys said. "Take us to Communications."

Just as we reached the elevator, I patted my jeans pockets and then the sweatshirt around my waist. "Crap! I think I forgot my phone in the car."

"Of course you did." Chae Rin rolled her eyes. "She's battle ready, this one."

Heat flushed my face at the precise moment my stomach squeezed at the word "battle." "Give me the keys? I'll be quick!"

The driver tossed them to me, and I ran back down the sloped pavement to the van. *Damn it, Maia.* Forgetting my phone on the eve of a giant operation? As if I needed the sucker punch to my self-esteem.

Once I reached the van, I swung open the door, but before I could dive in, a glint of light caught my eye. It was coming from farther back in the garage, several rows behind me.

A motorcycle.

It was off to the side, shadowed by the low, ruddy brick wall behind it, and sandwiched between vans. It wouldn't have interested me at all if it weren't for the motorcyclist still on the bike, hunched over with his hands on the handlebars and the key in the ignition. He stayed like that, frozen, even after I started quietly approaching.

"Hello?"

At the sound of my voice, the motorcyclist's whole body twitched like a child who'd just been found in the bathroom sneaking ice cream before dinner. I heard a nearly indecipherable "Crap."

A distinctly feminine voice.

That was when I noticed just how slender the brown hands on the handles were—with little stars drawn on each brightly painted nail.

"Are you okay?" I asked. The motorcyclist was shaking. Even though I couldn't see the face behind the helmet, it was very possible that this person was having some kind of a panic attack.

"Please," came the voice: young, delicate. British. "Um . . . can you please move? If that's okay?" Her words sounded extra timid while being carried by her breathy tone.

"Excuse me?"

"Hey, kid!" I could hear Chae Rin's barking from there. "The hell are you doing?"

"Give me a second," I yelled back, squeezing the keys in my hand.

"Um." The motorcyclist tried again. "Move . . . out of the way . . . please?" Her long legs twitched on the pedal as if her skinny jeans were too tight and consequently messing with her nervous system.

The moment I stepped closer to check on her, my feet lifted off the ground. It was a gentle gust, clean and swift, but with enough power to sweep me into the air and deposit me carefully atop the trunk of the Jeep behind me.

It took me a disorienting second to realize what had just happened. "Oh, you've got to be kidding me."

The girl gave an awkward shrug. "Sorry!"

The motorcycle revved and she was off.

I ran back to the van. Chae Rin was there, gaping at the motorcycle with my phone in her hand.

"It's her!" I shook her. "She's getting away!"

"Huh?"

"Lake! Dude, that was *Lake*!"

"Trying to ditch, eh?" Chae Rin narrowed her eyes. "You got the keys?"

We didn't wait for agent approval. After tossing Chae Rin the keys, I leapt into the passenger seat and braced myself as Chae Rin drove off.

As I buckled my seat belt, I could see Rhys and the other agents through the rearview mirror, dumbfounded and frozen by the elevators.

We chased Lake through the underground garage and up the ramp into the daylight. Since when did a dainty pop princess double as a seasoned *biker*?

I rolled down the window and stuck my head into the open air, but at the speed we were going, there was no way we'd be able to communicate. Lake drove with the determination to flee the devil.

We were getting close to the main entrance. The gate remained determinedly shut, but Lake wasn't slowing down. She must have been crazy if she thought they'd open it for her.

Unless she was planning to blow it open.

My phone rang. Probably not the best time, but I answered it anyway. "Hello?"

"Give the phone to Chae Rin," said the cool voice on the other end.

The phone nearly slipped from my hands. "I-it's for you," I said, handing it over.

Chae Rin snatched it. "Huh? Where the hell are you?" She leaned forward so she could peer up at the guard towers through the windshield. "Well, shit."

I saw her too. Belle. She was the third "officer" at the rightmost tower, her foot planted on the ledge as she spoke into her cell phone. Because her binoculars now hung around her neck, they no longer masked her aloof gaze.

"What? Yeah, I see her," Chae Rin said into the phone. After a second or two, she rolled her eyes. "You really just *love* telling people what to do, don't you? Whatever."

Chae Rin tossed the phone behind her. "Hold on to something, kid."

"What?"

Without warning, she stomped on the brakes. The seat belt bit hard into my chest while the van skidded to a halt. Then Chae Rin hopped out.

"What's going on?" Unlike the van, my head hadn't stopped spinning. With fumbling hands, I unfastened myself. "What about Lake?"

Instead of answering, Chae Rin watched the motorcycle draw closer to the gate. Then, with a sharp movement, she raised her newly healed arm. The muscles tensed in the slender limb as Chae Rin balled her hand into a fist, and the moment she brought it down, a hole opened up beneath the motorcycle. I'd seen the trick before, but this was different. The sandy ground glooped and gelled together as it sank deeper and deeper, pulling Lake's motorcycle with it.

Sand, clay, and water. Two Effigies working together.

Lake cried out; the mud was like a vortex, dragging her in.

"Stop!" I cried, but Chae Rin put up a hand to calm me. She must have known what Lake would do next.

Abandoning the bike, the girl jumped—no, it was too high and graceful to be called a jump. Gently swept up by the breeze at her command, she touched down lightly upon the solid ground, perfectly safe, but incredibly pissed.

"Oi!" Lake threw off her helmet, strands of her short hair flying everywhere. "Have you gone absolutely *mental?*"

Chae Rin clearly had a quip ready, but she wouldn't have time to use it. Long, twisted spikes of ice shuddered up off the ground's surface, locking Lake into a jagged, cone-shaped cage too small to throw a fit in.

Up on the tower, Belle threw off her binoculars.

"Gotcha," gloated Chae Rin. Lake gripped one of the frigid bars, slumping in defeat.

"Runaway pop star." Once again Rhys shook his head. He'd been doing that a lot since we'd dragged Lake back to the facility. "I don't even know where to start."

It was not the epic meeting I'd imagined. We four Effigies walked in silence as Rhys, Ortega, and the other agents led us through the twisting corridors of the facility. With Belle and Chae Rin at the front, I was left at the back of the party with the beautiful seventeen-year-old pop princess wannabe whose nervous gaze kept flitting to me. As the two of us eased into our discomfort, Rhys continued his tirade.

"What I don't quite understand is how a facility with a perfectly functioning surveillance system almost let one of our secret weapons drive straight out the front door."

Seemed like Rhys was trying to keep his tone somewhat neutral, but Ortega had clearly registered the serrated tip hiding in his criticism.

"It's something I'm just hearing about," he answered grimly. "Right now we've got troops on standby, an administrative liaison dealing with the Argentinean government, not to mention we're dealing with the temporary replacement for Director Aleandro."

"Oh, right, he was in charge here."

"Yes, he was in charge here; now he's stuck in a bed, sick and delirious. It all happened too suddenly, and with all the preparations under way, it's not hard to see how they might have overlooked one little factor."

"Little factor?" Chae Rin scoffed. "If we're that 'little,' then why the hell did you drag our asses out here in the first place?"

The agent responded with a slight bow of his head. "My apologies."

"So she got away because nobody was looking for her," Rhys said.

"I at least noticed." Even the slight shift of Belle's head made Lake jump. "Rather than distract the base, I looked for her myself. Anyway, it's over. Let's not belabor the point."

Belle turned to her, but Lake couldn't meet her gaze. The recent escapee kept her head low, not at all befitting the image of a girl who'd just finished up a fan signing in Los Angeles. *This* Lake deflated with each step she took, small despite her giant, willowy frame. Her obvious misery only made me that much more uncomfortable.

"Um."

Lake's little voice snapped me out of my thoughts. I looked up, immediately shaken by the sight of the very tall Lake looking down at me.

"Um . . . hi," she said.

Well, at least it was straight to the point.

"Hi . . ."

I was incredibly, mysteriously aware of myself. Rhys, Belle, and the other agents walked a little faster than the rest of us as they discussed Ortega's latest progress report on the coming operation. Chae Rin slowed down, meandering between both groups—excited, no doubt, to hear the impending awkwardness behind her. I wasn't quite terrible enough to scurry ahead while Lake was trying to make conversation, but . . . yeah. Awkward. I could still remember most of the bitchy comments I'd left on a Lake appreciation thread last week. Comments I'd written just to piss off the forum's neighborhood Swans.

I held on to the sleeves of my sweatshirt still tied around my waist. Lake ran her fingers through her straightened, shoulder-length black hair.

"I'm Victoria—oh, I mean. Lake. Well . . ." She paused as if she couldn't decide. "What's your name?"

In front of us, Chae Rin snorted but didn't turn around.

"Oh no, I hope you don't mind if I ask. It's just . . ." Lake nervous and cringing at her own ridiculousness was also not something I was familiar with. "I know *them*, all right." She pointed at Chae Rin and Belle. "I mean, I've heard of them, at least. Haven't met them. But you

I haven't even heard of. N-not that you're not worth hearing about, of course . . . I didn't . . ." She cut off her own rambling with a sheepish smile. "What's your name?"

I let my fingers trail the wall as I walked. "Maia."

"Maia?"

"Finley."

"Oh, that's cute!" Lake literally had soft gooey Bambi eyes that may or may not have sparkled a little as she perked up, delighted at the apparent progress of the conversation. "I met Natalya once. She was really nice—a bit intense, you know? But I guess that's just how some people are."

"Yeah."

"I bet you're probably feeling a bit like, um, like it's big shoes. Right? I mean, Natalya was no joke."

"Why did you run?"

What else could I even say to the girl whose fans I'd spent far too many cumulative hours arguing with online? Fans who'd probably *still* blindly defend her even if they knew about her attempted escape.

Whatever life had returned to Lake's face during that short conversation simply vanished. She stayed silent for a time, her heels clicking against the ground, her long fingers opening and closing at her sides. I noted her sharp intake of breath, but waited for her answer all the same.

Finally it came: "Aren't you scared too?" And with a little sad smile, Lake added, "Honestly? It'd be weirder if you weren't."

She'd whispered it, as if afraid to let anyone but me hear.

Aren't you scared too?

I couldn't lie, but the truth disturbed me too much for me to admit. I opted for silence instead.

We rounded a corner into a tiny corridor. Ortega stopped in

front of a door with a small screen and keypad at its center, together rimmed in black. With deft fingers, he punched in the security code. The screen scanned his eyes, its faded blue light streaming into his face before vanishing in an instant.

"Retina pattern confirmed," came the computer in a feminine, dulcet tone as Ortega's image appeared on the screen.

"This is some *Star Trek* shit," Chae Rin muttered without a hint of discretion.

Star Trek indeed.

After a series of loud clicks, the door slid open, revealing what literally looked like the bridge of the *Enterprise*. Communications was an enormous enclave with two stories of Sect employees working at computer terminals. The din enveloped me—chattering, ringing, the whir of sophisticated software, soft little *ping*s each time a finger tapped the wide, translucent touch screens. On the second floor, agents rushed along walkways from the other side of long, clear windows. Everyone was too busy to even spare a glance for us.

Belle walked up to one of the monitors in the back row, motioning us to follow her. "Maia," she said. "Before we talk about the operation, there's something you need to see."

Curious, I sidled up to her.

"This is her," Belle told the woman at the monitor. "Can you bring up the file?"

It was a video of an alley in the night. A stray dog poked its nose through the pile of trash against the graffitied brick wall. Nothing really interesting, except for the sounds of utter chaos in the background. The guy holding the cell phone stumbled back and fell onto the concrete with a crash, his terrified whimpers barely audible underneath the clamor of shrieks and explosions. Something about this felt familiar.

Steadily, the video panned up the side of the building. Up and up.

And then there was a girl falling off the top floor of the building, flames enveloping her body, bricks bursting out into the air as the newly created weapon in her hands crashed into them.

A scythe.

An honest-to-god scythe.

"No way." My hands went bone cold. The camera followed the girl all the way down until she crashed, flesh and bone, against the alleyway.

"That was . . ." I could barely form words. "That was—"

"You."

It wasn't Belle who'd spoken. A woman was descending the staircase from the second floor, her hawk eyes already latched on to me. Hawk eyes, aquiline nose. High cheekbones, angles everywhere. The pale gray pantsuit was like milk splashed against her dark skin, clean-cut and professional. Everything about her was sharp enough to draw blood. It was a look that perfectly matched the confidence of her stride.

"Sibyl Langley." As the woman introduced herself, she stripped off her sleek black gloves and handed them to the mousy assistant scrambling behind her. "Director of the European Division."

I instinctively stepped back as she approached. "European Division?" I never would have guessed since our accents were identical.

"A temporary replacement for Director Aleandro," Belle explained. "For this mission at least."

I didn't need to be told she was the one in charge. I sucked in a breath as Sibyl towered over me.

"Was that . . . ?" I swallowed, focusing on the floor. "Was that really me?"

"It was," Sibyl said, quick and blunt. "And trust me, it wasn't easy to pull that off the internet before it could go viral. Maia, I want you to come with me. And the other Effigies too. You should all hear this."

"What is this about?" My heart was beating rapidly now. "What does any of this have to do with the operation?"

"Quite a bit," answered Sibyl. "Since you're the key to the whole mission."

13

SIBYL AND HER ASSISTANT CHERYL WERE THE
only Sect personnel that came with us into the tactical operations
room, which was freezing. The air-conditioning must have been running on overdrive. I slipped my sweatshirt back on, but still didn't feel
comfortable.

As I took a seat at the long oval table, my hands started to shake. I
felt like I'd just been dumped into a dangerous parallel universe with
nothing to fend for myself but a spoon and some hair bands.

This was it. The real mission. The blood was already pumping fast
through my veins.

Sibyl stood at the front of the room. "Cheryl, play the video again,
please."

There it was again. I couldn't believe it, but I couldn't look away,
either. It was actually weirdly badass: me plummeting through the air,
a swell of power, a miraculous escape from certain death at the last
minute. Surreal. If it were another Effigy, I would almost certainly
have tried to steal the video so I could edit it, set it to some awesome
rock music, and put it up online.

Cheryl played the video one more time. Just as the long weapon began forming in my hands, Sibyl told her to pause it.

"This," Sibyl said, with one hand clasping the chair in front of her, "is a result of your psychic abilities. The same all Effigies have."

Sibyl, despite her youth, bore a faint resemblance to my philosophy teacher—not at all in appearance, since Mr. Strom was a rather bloated elderly white male with a comb-over. It was the no-nonsense, rapid delivery, the rigid posture and humorless glare, as if I'd get a ruler over the hands if I was caught daydreaming.

"The creation and manipulation of a classical element is just one of three psychic techniques Effigies possess. The second . . ." Sibyl pointed at the screen. "Summoning."

"I showed you once," Belle said from across the table. "At the hotel."

That felt like lifetimes ago. I remembered the icy breeze prickling the hairs on my skin as Belle called forth that glorious sword. The kind that could have belonged to an honor-bound eighteenth-century aristocrat. How could I forget its beauty, the moonlight and snowflakes dancing across the blade? Or how awesome Belle looked as she turned it against Saul?

It's the sign of a fully developed Effigy, Belle had told me back then. *For Natalya, this was everything. . . .*

"There's a reason you're called the Four Swords," Sibyl said. "Over the years, we've found that technically every Effigy is capable of it—"

Chae Rin lifted her hand. "I can't."

"—given extensive psychological training and mental discipline."

"Oh." She went back to filing her nails.

"Probably why I can't either," Lake mumbled. "Which kind of sucks. I want a sword too."

Chae Rin scoffed. "You barely even finished training."

"S-so?" Lake shot back, scandalized.

"So you're kind of useless."

"Excuse me!" Needless to say, her voice was not so mumbly anymore. "I *can* do *some* things, you know. Loads of things, actually."

"Huh. Too bad holding a note isn't one of them."

"Wow," I said, but I covered my mouth the second Lake trained her doe eyes on me.

Sibyl cleared her throat. "That means 'stop,'" she clarified. We did.

"I have one question." I swiped my hair off my forehead. "If this is something you can do only after extensive training, then why could I do it?"

"'Cause you're special," sang Chae Rin, just barely audible.

"Maia, you told Belle something before leaving New York, didn't you?" Sibyl was the only one who'd left her seat empty. Maybe she thought better on her feet. "You told her that after Saul kissed you, you saw a memory."

Memory. Like the one I'd seen in Quebec. But as I thought back to that terrifying scene in Brooklyn, as I revisited the dream Saul had forced on me as he held me against the hotel window, I knew right away that the memory wasn't Natalya's. The girl in the vision, the décor . . . Everything had seemed as if it was from another century.

"You told me that after the memory, you heard a girl's voice," Belle continued. "And names. Can you recall them now?"

I could. "Alice." The girl in the study. "And . . . Nick." The name Saul fell to.

"Even after an Effigy dies," Sibyl said, "she never really leaves. A part of her psyche lingers on inside the mind of the next in her line."

Not just Natalya. Marian. It was the name Saul kept calling me, as if I were a mere vessel for a girl who'd lived long ago.

As per usual, it was a lot to take in. You'd think I'd get used to that by now. I propped my elbows up against the desk and laid my head in my hands. "How do you even know all this?"

Cheryl the assistant perked up like that one eager kid in class endlessly searching for ways to prove her critical acuity. "It's actually something we've discovered over the years based on personal accounts of the Effigies we've worked with," she explained. "Given the data we've gathered, we've found that each new Effigy *should* have the ability to search through echoes of the memories passed on by all the previous in her line. Think of it as having several past lives. Of course, the memories of the last Effigy would be the freshest."

Like Natalya.

I stifled a shudder as Cheryl adjusted her tiny rectangle glasses over her sharp-pointed nose and continued.

"We've also found that an Effigy's ability to enter this state is somehow related to their summoning aptitude, though there isn't enough evidence yet to hypothesize possible reasons."

I shook my head. "I don't get it."

"She's saying that the memory thing and the weapon thing are connected, and they don't know why yet," Lake clarified, adding, "What?" when she found both me and Chae Rin staring at her with raised eyebrows. "So I'm a celebrity—doesn't mean I'm *entirely* daft, yeah?"

"Usually it takes years." Belle closed her eyes. "Years to achieve the discipline necessary to hear the voices. To open that first door and enter the first memory. Your intimate contact with Saul might have triggered something, forcing you across the threshold. Perhaps it's made passage through the psyches easier."

Forced by a kiss. Gross.

"But it wasn't Natalya's memory I saw," I said. "It was someone else's. I think it was a girl named Marian. When the girl in the memory looked up, she called me that name. The same name Saul kept calling me."

It was the same in both Marian and Natalya's memories: Both times it was as if my mind had slipped into their bodies. Both times I could only see through their eyes as they moved.

Being imprisoned inside someone else's flesh wasn't a pleasant feeling, to say the least.

"Marian." As Sibyl tilted her head to think, her long black ponytail brushed her peplum lapel. "Truthfully, we don't have records of all the Effigies to have ever existed, but, as you've suggested, it's more than likely that this *Saul* has some kind of a connection with her. This is the conclusion we came to based on Belle's reports on the Brooklyn attack, and this is exactly why we need you involved in this operation."

At Sibyl's wordless request, Cheryl clicked the remote, bringing up a map of a city.

"There's been an abnormal increase recently in the illegal trafficking activity through the Dead Zones of northeastern Argentina," said Sibyl. "It's forced the government to fortify security along each route, including all suspected urban checkpoints. This includes the Chacarita district of Buenos Aires."

Cheryl zoomed into the neighborhood. "If it weren't for the increased surveillance over the past five years, we may never have noticed."

An impatient Chae Rin tapped her file against the tips of her nails. "Noticed *what?*"

Cheryl clicked through surveillance photos. Despite the different dates, each picture captured the same basic scene: a hooded young man in a cemetery, hands in his trench coat pockets, alone in front of a grave.

"The photos go back five years," said Sibyl. "Every year on the same day in January, always at nine in the morning."

I leaned forward. Some of the photos were at different angles, and some of those angles revealed the silver locks of hair peeking out from underneath the hood. "That's him?"

"Yes. At Chacarita's British Cemetery, always at the same grave: Louis Hudson, born 1850 and died 1883."

"And do we know what the connection to Saul is?" Belle asked.

"No, but that doesn't mean we can't use it against him. That's where you come in, Maia."

The sound of my name was like hammer against steel. I knew I couldn't avoid asking. "What do you need me to do?"

Sibyl finally sat down, drawing her face close to her clasped fingers. "About six months before she died, Natalya expressed concern that she was being stalked."

I thought I saw Belle go rigid at the opposite side of the table, but I kept my eyes on Sibyl.

"But we could never find him. She tried to confront him in Frankfurt four months ago, but according to her, he vanished right when she'd cornered him. The phantom attack on the city started later that afternoon."

"Saul." I imagined him smirking as he followed Natalya through the narrow streets. "Then you've known about him?"

"We knew almost nothing about a shadow Natalya wasn't even sure she'd seen." Sibyl shifted in her seat to cross her legs. "Certainly not enough to go on."

"She never told me about any of this. . . ." Belle's whisper, though soft, still demanded an answer, but Sibyl didn't give it.

"It isn't just you, Maia," Sibyl continued. "If Saul approached both you and Natalya, we have enough reason to believe that it's the Effigy in your line he's truly after. The one whose memories you have access to."

Lowering my head, I swallowed the lump in my throat. "He said he needed to ask me a question. He was desperate to talk to Marian."

"And we'll use that. Maia, in one hour you'll record a video asking Saul to meet at the cemetery, at the 'usual time,'" said Sibyl. "The key is to say enough to make him think you've recovered enough of Marian's memories that you'll be useful to him. Using what we know about the grave might help in that regard."

"The thing is, Maia," Cheryl added, "we can't know where Saul is right now. The message you record will have to be broadcast around the world. The only way we make sure it'll be picked up by international news sources—"

"Is if you announce yourself as the next Effigy."

Sibyl had said it so simply. No flourish, no drama. Not a single indication that she realized just how thoroughly this one act would change my life. Sibyl looked at me with the arrogant calm of a high-ranking agent who knew her word was law.

It was *always* going to come to this. Sooner or later. I'd had several chances to tell Uncle Nathan, and I'd run away each and every single time. Now he was going to see my confession played across every major news station in the world.

"Oh, come on," scoffed Chae Rin. "Do you know how many girls have been putting videos online claiming to be the next Effigy? No one's even paying attention anymore. And from what I can tell, Maia can barely spark a flame, so how are we going to convince international media to take her video seriously?"

"Oh, they'll take it seriously," Sibyl said. "Because *we'll* be the ones giving it to them. An official gift from the Sect. Only the public can't know that. We'll tell our contacts to say that the video was sent anonymously so Saul thinks that Maia's acting on her own. He won't expect us. Once you draw Saul to the mission site, our troops will strike. You girls will need to be prepared, too."

I felt Lake's tentative hand on my shoulder. A considerate gesture, and I welcomed it, but it still didn't stop my head from spinning. This was it. It was do or die. Only problem was the latter was more likely.

I bit my lip. I could do this. I could, right?

After a deep breath, I turned to Sibyl. "What if he doesn't even come?"

"He'll come," Sibyl said. "Who knows how long he's been after Marian? He'll come and you'll be there."

I waited in a cold, dark room. I'd already called Uncle Nathan a few times to try to make things right, but it was no use. He wasn't answering. That was it, then. My big, deep dark secret, and he wasn't going to hear it from me. It wasn't anyone's fault but my own.

They'd powdered my face, changed my clothes, and combed my bird's nest of a hair mane as well as they could to get me ready for the world. I *wasn't* ready, of course, but no way was I going to admit that.

June'd been born my older sister by a difference of only three minutes, so how was it that we'd turned out so different? We were both nerds, but while I kept my geekery well hidden within the labyrinthine secrecy of my laptop, June never hid. She'd had this pair of goggles she'd wear, even at school, until she got dinged for dress code violations. She'd go to conventions, dye her hair pink, and dress up in pseudo-Victorian outfits. She'd make fake laser guns out of bottles and show them off at the mall to her friends. She'd hold her head high, higher at the sound of vicious mocking.

She was strong. Fearless. More than me. Even though we had the same face.

Under the lonely light of a hanging lamp, I laid my head back

against my chair and shut my eyes. Bright speckles broke the monot-
ony of darkness behind my lids, and out of the interplay of light and
dark came June's face, full of life and defiance just as I remembered it.

Back in New York there were so many people I couldn't save.
Even right now, I could still hear that woman pleading for help in the
elevator as it collapsed, plummeting down the shoot, taking her frail
body down with it along with her screams. . . .

The beginnings of a sob scraped my throat, but I banished it
through sheer will alone, rubbing my eyes dry. Back at the hotel, I'd
asked Belle to make me better. This mission was my chance. My
chance to save people. To make something of myself. To make up for
everything.

"So don't be scared," I whispered to myself, willing my pulse to
slow to its regular rhythm.

I could do this. I could be an Effigy. Uncle Nathan, the kids in
school, the whole world. Soon they'd know it too.

The whole world.

The door creaked open and Rhys walked in. I hastily stood from
my seat, straightening the sleeves of the white blouse Sibyl had
brought in for me to wear. It was a bit simple, but Sibyl had insisted
on neutrality. This was my global debut as an Effigy. Couldn't give the
wrong impression. Jokingly, I'd asked if I could write my own theme
song and have it play in the background during the video. Nobody
had laughed.

"Rhys." I rested a hand on the chair's smooth metal. "Are they
finally ready?"

"Yeah." He ran his fingers through his messy hair. "They're done
setting up. Looks like you're set for your worldwide debut. Sadly, I
couldn't get anyone on that theme song, though."

My laughter was a little too high-pitched for what was essentially a B-level joke. "Yeah, the theme song! Right, right." I turned. "Well, the Sect can only do so much, I guess."

If I hadn't turned away from him, I probably would have seen a very confused Rhys staring back at me.

"Maia?"

"Sorry." I shook my head. "I'm okay." I flashed a smile too obviously fake to be convincing. "I'm okay. Really. I mean, I'm not scared or any-thing," I added quickly. "I mean . . . if that's what you're thinking."

Silence. I gripped the chair. I wasn't scared. I wasn't.

Rhys stuffed his hands into his pockets. "You know . . . even if there were no crisis," he said, "there's a protocol for finding new Effigies. They're usually taken for at least two years and trained for duty. They can't really hide. A media circus is pretty inevitable."

The secret would have come out sooner or later, was what he was try-ing to say.

"I know," I said.

"So?" With measured steps, Rhys walked up to me. "Are you *really* okay?"

His expression was soft and sweet with kindness. I soaked it in, in spite of myself. One by one, the knots in my chest loosened. I could breathe.

"Maia . . . I can't imagine how you feel right now. I was raised in this. You weren't." He reached out to touch my shoulder before paus-ing. "Honestly, I wish you had more of a choice. I'm sorry you don't."

A choice. The universe had a choice. It picked me. *Me*, after Natalya Filipova. Me over June. And now everyone would know. They'd know who I was, what I was, where I lived, what kind of grades I had in school, how my family had died. They'd expect me to save them, and if I didn't? Public skewering in the media. Hate threads in forums.

"No, it's fine. It's okay," I said, surprising even myself. I straightened up and peered into his dark eyes until I was sure I looked as defiant as June would have been. "I told you before. I'm . . . I'm not scared. I can do this. I know I can."

Rhys considered me for a moment. "You sure?" He asked it as if he was testing me. "No turning back."

"But that was always obvious, wasn't it?" And I gave him a real smile this time, one that matched the determination in my steady voice. "So. Let's do this, Agent Rhys. Make me a star."

Lights. Cameras.

"Hello. My name is Maia Finley." I followed the script to the letter, keeping my face soft and natural, but determined, just like they told me. "And I'm the new fire Effigy. The next after Natalya Filipova."

I swallowed, thinking of Uncle Nathan.

"It's okay if you don't believe me, because this message isn't for you. It's for Saul. Saul." I breathed. "I know. I did what you told me and I remembered. About Marian, the girl I was. About Nick . . . who loved her," I added, remembering Saul's mocking words at the hotel. "About Alice. And the answer to the question you wanted to ask me. I'm ready to talk. So meet me at Louis's grave. Tomorrow, Monday. At the usual time. Let's meet, so we can finally finish this. Please."

14

"MAIA, STAY ALERT." RHYS'S VOICE WAS SCRATCHY through my earpiece. "It's already past the meeting time. Saul can show up any minute."

For security purposes, I was never told where Rhys, the rest of the troops, or even the other Effigies were, just in case my eyes flitted to their positions and gave them away. With a rose in hand, I focused instead on the gravestone in front of me: the mysterious Louis Hudson's. Whoever this guy was, his existence had given us the leverage we needed to launch our trap.

Thanks, buddy. Rest in peace, I guess.

I wiped my forehead. The cloudless sky left me at the mercy of the Argentinean sun, the muggy air sluggish as it slopped into my lungs. What if Saul was to see me sweating like this and thought it was because of nerves? Would it tip him off?

"You're doing fine," Rhys reminded me for perhaps the thousandth time. "Just relax."

I was relaxed. Yes. Fully relaxed. I was actually doing pretty well for my first real mission; granted, being bait for a psychotic mass murderer didn't require much physical effort.

I patted my hands on my shorts. Civilians milled about, visiting the graves of their loved ones. Some knelt before headstones while others scattered the soil with white lilies and other flowers I couldn't identify. Mourning families weren't exactly fun to see. The bigger problem, though, would be clearing them all out once Saul showed up. Who knew what that psycho was planning? These people were in danger. You'd think an international organization would have considered that by now.

Might as well bring it up. "Hey, Rhys," I whispered.

"Don't talk into the mic."

Oh, yeah.

"But—"

"Shh."

Hopefully he hadn't heard my sigh.

Rhys was a field agent. This meant he spent his days as one of a handful of agents stationed in towns with weak APDs, protecting the locals whenever phantoms appeared. Still, there were times when even field agents were recalled and mobilized to disaster sites with the Sect's organized troops. After Brooklyn, he could have chosen to go back to his post in rural New York.

Instead, he was here with me.

I wanted to thank him, but I didn't feel like getting shushed again. Maybe later . . . if we were both still alive.

More waiting. It was already ten minutes past the meeting time. Even though I was told not to, I started panicking. Last night my face had been splashed across every newspaper, online article, and television station—plus a brand-new, seventy-page thread on the Doll Soldiers forum. Bookmarked, naturally.

SIXTEEN-YEAR-OLD MAIA FINLEY: THE NEXT EFFIGY?
IS MAIA FINLEY REALLY WHO SHE SAYS SHE IS?

Saul *had* to have seen my message, but what if he hadn't? Worse: What if he didn't care?

"What?" Rhys sounded frantic. "What did you just say?"

I frowned. "I didn't say anything. You told me not to."

"No, not you, Maia—stand by." A few heart-pounding seconds later: "Saul's just been spotted five miles east of here."

Even in the stifling heat, my hands numbed from the chill surging through me. What happened next was a chaotic blur: The other visitors at the cemetery ran toward me, shouting into their communication devices. Sect agents. Rhys was among them. Before I could fully wrap my head around what was happening, they'd already swept me into a white van.

"El Ateneo bookshop." Rhys showed me the map on his phone as we drove through the busy streets. "He has hostages, but it's you he wants, Maia."

"Yay," I said without a hint of mirth. Hostages at a bookshop. Saul was nothing if not dramatic.

Apparently, it had taken Sibyl all of half a minute to come up with a plan B from headquarters. I listened as they explained what I'd have to do, and before long, we'd arrived at the bookstore. News vans, city police, and Sect personnel crowded the street. Police had their guns, but they wouldn't be enough; a black cloud closed off the entrance.

Phantoms. Wasplike, same as the ones that had swarmed us outside La Charte. But these ones didn't attack. They simply hovered and watched, a poisonous barrier of flickering black smoke. It was as if they were following an order.

At the window was the one who'd given it. Saul slid up to the glass, a sly, nightmarish grin on his ghost-pale, fine-boned face.

"Just shoot him!" Chae Rin. She'd just hopped out of one of the Sect vans with Lake and Belle, and her hand had already found Rhys's collar. "What are you doing?"

"We can't!" He shrugged her off.

"Why not?" Lake and I had asked at the same time.

"The building's full of phantoms," he fired back. "And as he made damn sure to let us know, they'll slaughter people at the slightest provocation."

"I can't believe this!" Chae Rin looked like she wanted to punch something, which was probably why Rhys shifted away from her. "Phantoms. But isn't this place protected?"

It was. So was Brooklyn. And Moscow and Bern and all the other cities whose antiphantom devices Saul had managed to scramble.

"Maia." Belle gripped my shoulder and forced me around, but I was on her before she could even speak.

"What the hell is happening?" I didn't care who could hear me. "I thought you guys had this under control!"

"We do," Belle said. "Nothing's changed. We have him here. Now you have to do your job. Consider this your first solo mission as an Effigy."

My face hardened. "I already did."

Belle reiterated Sibyl's plan. My knees twitched, but there was no time to indulge any fear. The longer I freaked, the more time Saul had to hurt someone, and there was no way I was going to let that happen. Not again.

Both of the tools I needed for the mission were small enough to fit in my back jeans pocket. The agents said I'd have to be discreet when it came time to reach for them. Saul would be watching.

I retied the sweatshirt around my waist to hide them.

"Wait!" Lake grabbed my arms. "You're seriously going in there? Alone?"

"It's okay," I said with a smile. "Stay here."

I made for the phantom horde, the reporters who'd refused to be evacuated crowding me as I approached. The new Effigy striding into battle, her heroics caught on camera.

From the window, Saul's gaze trailed every step I took until he was out of my line of vision. The phantoms parted to let me through the glass doors.

How courteous.

I'd heard of El Ateneo before, seen pictures. For a bookstore, it was shamelessly ornate. Several floors spanned up in rings, each lined with bright lights, and beyond the metal railings, rows and rows of bookshelves in place of the theater seats from the bookstore's earlier days as an amphitheater.

Now, books littered the floors, probably scattered in the pandemonium of fleeing customers. I moved beyond the tall columns and up the steps, my eyes wandering across the gorgeous frescoed ceiling before spotting a heavy set of crimson curtains framing the far front stage.

The curtains were already drawn.

Phantoms. At the center of the stage, massive wolves of shadow and smoke encircled a small group of terrified customers. The stage must have doubled as a coffee shop; tables and chairs lay in pieces, white mugs bleeding coffee all over the finished floor.

One of the customers saw me and shouted something in Spanish, only for a phantom to threaten him into silence with a snap of its rotting, unhinged jaw.

"So, *poupée*," came Saul's voice from above. "You wanted to talk?"

Saul leaned over the railing of the third floor, his arms dangling leisurely as if he were simply enjoying the view. He hadn't yet wiped off the streaks of blood on his hands.

Stay cool, Maia, I told myself. That's right. This time, *I* was the badass Effigy come to save the day. I stood firm on my unsteady feet.

"Is this really necessary?" I forced my tone to be as casual as possible. "Can't we just talk *without* the live audience?" I figured Belle or Natalya would have said something snappy like that.

Saul's white locks flowed loose over his shoulders. With one smooth movement, he linked his fingers into his hair and swept them back. "They were just to get your attention." He propped his head up with a hand. "Plus, I thought I'd need the insurance. A lot of people outside want me dead."

"And whose fault is that?"

Saul raised a hand and the phantoms began snarling, white frothing saliva dripping from their twisted teeth. The customers held in their screams, gripping each other tight.

"You don't need them, because you have me," I said quickly. "Nobody'll shoot as long as I'm in here. I mean, that's just obvious."

"You sure about that?" He examined his nails. "That's the thing about Effigies. Each girl is just one dismal link in an obnoxiously long chain." He smirked. "And every once in a while, a worthless little girl like you appears. Last time we met, you couldn't even defend yourself against me. It's a miracle you're still alive."

He sounded so annoyingly, punchably, sure of himself. I balled my hands into fists. "Exactly," I said, thinking quickly. "Okay, I'm worthless as an Effigy. You got me. I can barely light a match. But if you kill me, the Sect'll have to waste time trying to find the next one all over again. *You'll* have to waste time finding the next one. I'm right here. I have Marian in my head and all the answers you want.

If you let these guys go and just keep me . . . I mean, it's not like I'll be a threat to you, right?"

As Saul considered it, I watched the cowering customers from the corner of my eye.

Finally, he shrugged. "Fine."

With a snap of his fingers, the wolves backed off, leaving just enough room for the customers to scurry down the steps in shock, grateful to still have their lives.

As soon as the doors opened, the customers were swallowed up by police and reporters, but nobody else came inside the building. I heard Rhys's voice through the earpiece.

"Good job. Great, Maia. Now remember the rest of the plan. It's okay, you can do it."

His voice was like a lifeline—gentle, strong, and sure. It was what I needed right now more than ever.

"What are you waiting for?" Saul waved for me to come join him.

Staring at him was like staring down the barrel of a gun, but there was no turning back now. With a silent but deep inhale, I started off, acutely and painfully aware of the phantoms loping behind me. It was almost kind of funny, the way they entered the elevator with me. I would have asked which floor they wanted if they hadn't forced me into a corner, locking me into place with their murderous gaze and threatening teeth. They wouldn't have appreciated the joke anyway.

They backed off once the doors opened, just enough to let me step carefully out of the elevator. Behind the bookshelves in one of the old theater booths, Saul sat in an armchair. Just to his right was the window I'd first seen him through. If I peered through the glass I'd see them all: the agents, the police, the reporters, and the other girls, all watching for some sort of signal.

But I couldn't give it to them. Not yet. There would come a time for that, but for now I had to follow the plan exactly. For now I had to stay out of sight, like him.

Saul had a book between his fingers, and when he noticed me staring at it, he showed me the cover: *The Picture of Dorian Gray.* Oscar Wilde.

"And here I thought you were just a video game junkie." I didn't even bother to hide my contempt. "How nice that you read, too."

"Well, I've had decades to do both. Not that I haven't been busy."

Decades? I couldn't show my confusion; it would give me away. Instead I nodded, my features creased into a frown. "It's been a long time, hasn't it?" I asked as he placed the book gingerly on the table beside him. "Since you've talked to Marian, I mean."

"Well, you should know." Saul leaned in. "Since you've remembered everything."

I swallowed. "Yeah."

"Or were you lying?"

"What?" I moved my leg back, stopping abruptly when I remembered the snarling phantoms nipping at my heels. "No. That's why I'm here. To talk."

Saul was on his feet. "About?"

"Everything."

He wasn't convinced. It was obvious. He studied me as he approached, a slit of a smile across his face, watching for even the faintest hint of dishonesty.

This was not the plan.

"Relax." Rhys. It was like I could breathe again at the sound of his voice. "This is *your* interrogation."

True. The plan was to get as much information as possible from Saul before striking. If I was going to get those answers, I'd have to turn the tables, and fast.

"Is that why you've been attacking all those cities?" I gripped the reins of the conversation for dear life, shifting my weight to my leg and folding my arms to show at least the illusion of confidence. "Just to see Marian?"

"Of course not. I told you before. I did it to kill people." I flinched at his touch, his fingers trailing down my cheek. I jerked my head away, holding in a shudder. "But then, even killing people is a part of the game."

"Game?"

"Of which Marian is a key part, so if you wouldn't mind . . . ?"

My hands trembled. "You murdered people. You think that qualifies as a goddamn game? You—"

"Let me talk to Marian now, or I'll have them eat you."

I went rigid, willing my knees not to buckle despite the brush of the phantom's breath against them. "Oh yeah, I forgot," I said as coolly as I could. "They're basically your winged monkeys, aren't they? Controlling phantoms. Never seen that before. But . . . I wonder if that pretty piece of jewelry you have on your finger has anything to do with it?"

On his right-hand middle finger: a ring. *The* ring. Saul let his silent grin speak for him, but its murderous thirst gave me a reason to change focus.

"Okay, I'll let you talk to Marian," I said, "but you're going to have to tell me how to do it."

"How to bring forth Marian, you must mean. Interesting." Saul studied me. "Okay. But would you humor me? I need to explain a few things first."

Slipping his hands into his pockets, Saul walked past me to the bookshelf. "You see, Effigies are sad little things," he said. "There's no peace after whatever gruesome death awaits them. No light at the end of the tunnel. They're bound to the next Effigy." He laughed. "So many girls crammed inside one frail human body. Strange, isn't it?"

I said nothing.

"Links in a chain." Saul repeated the phrase with a derisive laugh. "Only one mind can have dominance at any time—like yours, in this case. But searching through the scattered memories leaves your own mind vulnerable."

I was well aware. Going into Natalya's memories just once had disoriented me so badly I nearly got myself skewered in a circus act.

"I figured," I said through gritted teeth.

"Then you should also know this." Saul placed his book back into an empty slot on the shelf and turned. "That very same vulnerability makes it possible for another mind to take over."

My jaw set. *No. No, I didn't know that.*

"Do you know why I'm saying this?" He seemed pleased at the sight of my grim face. "As weak as you are." He stepped toward me. "As fresh, as untrained." Another step. And another. "If you really did recall *all* of Marian's memories, there's no way you would have been able to retain your own self." He tapped his temple. "She would have taken over."

Saul had me pinned between himself and his phantom beasts. It wasn't possible anymore to keep my breathing quiet, but I met his mocking eyes head-on. Lifting my trembling chin, I shrugged. "Maybe she's not the type. Maybe she didn't want to take over someone else's body, *Nick*," I added viciously, and waited for the hit to land. Nothing. It didn't work. The name hadn't affected him at all. And I was running out of options.

Saul's grin turned truly wicked. "But who wouldn't?" He grabbed my throat and lifted me off my feet. "If you were hoping to get me again with that name, don't worry: I made sure to send Nick far, *far* away. He gets a bit annoying when he starts picking at the locks, so I buried the whole cage." He grinned. "He won't hear you again. Promise."

I could barely hear any of it. The blood pulsed in my ears as Saul squeezed my throat.

"Maia, is it? I know you lied. I know it was all just to get me here, but still, before I kill you, there's something I need to know."

I clutched at his hands, kicking my feet to set myself free. The phantoms nipped at my heels as my legs dangled in the air.

"Is what I'm doing really so bad?" Saul seemed only half-sincere as he squeezed the air out of my lungs. "You called it 'murder.' Okay, yes, I know it's wrong. But isn't there something you'd give anything for? Isn't there a wish you have?"

I was wheezing and coughing my own air away. But it was okay. My hands were still free. . . .

"A secret wish. A wish you'd sacrifice anything or anyone for."

Once again I was flat against the window. Saul relished the familiar scene, peeking through the window at the officers below. "Don't judge me, Maia. I'm not the only one. Nick has his wish too, even if he won't admit it. What about you, *poupée*?"

He leaned in, his sweet breath brushing my cheek.

I had to stay calm. No matter what. Just stay calm. I slipped a hand underneath my sweatshirt.

"Maia, isn't there something you want more than anything?"

I pried my lips open with a gasp and forced words up my hoarse throat.

"What?" Saul leaned in. "What did you say?"

"I said . . ." I glared at him. "I want you to shut the hell up."

My hands found my back pocket. The little metal tracking device was the size and shape of a button—small enough to fit into the gaping hole of Saul's mouth. I shoved it in, clamping his jaw shut. The sight of his Adam's apple bobbing made me nearly delirious with success. He stumbled back, obviously too shocked to command his phantoms to pounce.

In case he got away. Sibyl's contingency plan.

A flood of adrenaline flushed my system as I dug the inoculation gun out of my other pocket. Long, thick, and red—I'd thought it was a pen the first time I'd seen it.

Don't let the design throw you off. It's like any other pressurized inoculation device.

This is what Rhys had told me earlier. The agents had gone over the specs of the device with me in meticulous detail on the way to the bookstore, but I could remember only pieces of it.

It injects specially engineered enzymes that'll momentarily disrupt—
Huh?

All you need to know is that if our hunch about Saul is true, this might be your only chance to stop him from using his abilities.

And if it's not?

I didn't have time to think about it. Grabbing him by his collar, I heaved him against the window, flicked off the safety, and jammed the device into his neck. Saul's wild eyes dulled, his lips twitching as he let out a soundless gasp.

"It's done!" I screamed.

"Now get out of the way!" Rhys ordered through my earpiece.

I dove. The gunshots blasted through the window, piercing Saul's kneecaps. The objective was to capture, not kill. Saul's mouth slacked open, too stunned to talk. His delicate features creased into a grimace, wrinkling his face. I could tell he was trying to vanish again, the same sideshow act he'd shown off in Brooklyn, but he couldn't. He stayed right there, right in front of me, perfectly corporeal. Helpless.

Not helpless.

His malicious gaze shifted to his monsters, still on standby behind me. At his wordless command, they thundered out a crazed growl and leapt for me, but I'd already launched myself forward. With as much force as I could muster, I pushed Saul out of the cracked window, soaring into the air with him. As the wind whipped against my face, I held my breath.

"I got you!"

Lake. Charioted by the wind, she caught me before I could fall too far, grunting from the sudden shock of my weight. Her feet lightly tapped the brick and then, with one powerful leap, she boosted us both upward. After executing a wobbly landing on the balcony ledge beneath her, she dumped me onto the floor and tended to her arms.

Saul, on the other hand, continued to fall, but he wasn't out of tricks just yet.

The streets rumbled and groaned.

"Move out of the way," I heard someone yell below, but it was too late. A phantom burst out of the street's asphalt, black smoke clinging to its fleshy worm body. It was massive.

"Jesus!" Lake swore, falling backward off the ledge from the shock alone. I kept her steady.

The timing was perfect. The phantom's jaws snapped open and swallowed Saul whole before arching its body and tearing back inside the earth.

I gaped as the last bit of the phantom disappeared underneath the street with Saul's body inside it. "It . . . it ate him." I gripped the ledge. "It freaking *ate* him. I-is he dead?"

More phantoms rocketed out of the ground, debris exploding off in different directions as reporters scrambled for cover.

The police were in charge of getting the civilians to safety. The

Sect agents had already assembled their arsenal and begun their assault. On the ceilings of adjacent buildings, agents mounted guns, aiming the barrels at phantoms too big to dispatch with ground tactics alone.

"Rhys?" I peered through the chaotic battle, but I couldn't find him. "Rhys?" My heart rattled against my chest. Where had he gone? Was he okay?

I thought of his soft voice comforting me through the earpiece, of the wry smile he always wore whenever I made fun of his clothes. "Rhys," I said again, though this time it was nothing more than a timid, fearful whisper. He was okay. He had to be okay.

"Maia! Lake! Get down here!"

Belle. She'd just finished dragging a barely conscious Chae Rin onto the hood of an abandoned news van. What the hell happened? Chae Rin was holding on to her head, her eyelids fluttering as she winced in pain.

"Hurry!" Belle commanded.

The street shifted, rocking the news van. Belle laid her back against the windshield to steady herself, keeping a tight hold on Chae Rin.

Gripping the balcony ledge, I peered over it with bloodshot eyes. "Lake," I said, "we have to—"

"Go down there." Lake was trembling; her words were barely the faintest of breaths. "But there are phantoms down there." She backed away.

Crouching in the corner, she buried her head in her knees. But the balcony was creaking, groaning. Too many phantoms crashing into the building, too much shuddering beneath the streets. I could see the steady stream of debris flowing down the bricks next to us.

"Maia! Lake!" Belle's frantic voice rose above the chaos. "Hurry!"

If Lake was having a breakdown I couldn't blame her, but I was so past the point of fear that the idea of leaping over bludgeoned bodies, bloodied blades, and terrifying monsters seemed like the obvious thing to do. Better than staying trapped on a precariously quivering balcony.

I lifted Lake onto her feet and dragged her to the balcony railing. She fought the entire way, but despite her height, her waif frame and blank state of mind made the battle futile.

"Come on!" I said. "We're jumping!"

Lake's eyes welled with tears. She clung to me, refusing to look at the chaos below. "This is terrible. This is mad. I can't!" Her fingers dug into my flesh. "I . . ." She inhaled a shaky breath. "I hate them," she whispered.

I thought of the phantoms in Brooklyn. The death they'd left in their wake. My own hands began to shake.

"Me too," I whispered back.

I jumped, pulling Lake with me. I was right to believe in her: As if by basic instinct alone, the long-legged beauty ran across the sky, the wind caressing her cheeks, catching the tears as they fell. Carefully, we descended, lower and lower, toward the van, but that only took us closer to the phantoms below. One leapt for us, and Lake launched us up, just barely avoiding its sinkhole mouth.

I gasped from each sharp tug of gravity hooking my stomach and throwing it up and down, but just when I thought I'd hurl on the street, Lake banished the wind and let us both fall. We landed painfully, but safely, next to the van.

"Get inside the car," ordered Belle as she sliced a phantom's jaw with her sword and dragged Chae Rin inside with her.

Lake went for the passenger door just as one of Saul's wolves leapt at her. Screaming wildly, she kicked it, catching its nostril with her heel while my clammy hands fumbled the door open.

"Get in, get in!" I cried.

Lake dove inside and slammed the door behind her.

I pulled her onto the bench. "Lake, you okay?"

She wasn't, and not just because of the bloody strips running down her leg. Unable to move, Lake responded only in belabored breaths, her beautiful face frozen in shock.

"Goddamn it, this hurts." Chae Rin was crumpled in the passenger seat, groaning and swearing as she kept a hand pressed against her temple. There wasn't any blood, so she must have gotten bludgeoned by something amid the confusion.

Belle dug something out of her jeans, cell phone–like, except for the metallic blue schematics bright on the screen.

"The tracking device you forced into Saul. Look: He's traveling underground. Inside the phantom." Belle pointed at the blinking red dot moving through the diagram. "Sibyl's orders." She tapped her own earpiece. "We'll catch him."

There were no windows in the back of the van. I twisted around anyway as if I could see Rhys fighting through the pounds of metal.

Belle grabbed the keys abandoned in the ignition and started the van just as a massive force crashed into it, nearly lifting it off its wheels.

"Allons-y!" Belle slammed on the gas and we were off down the ruined streets. "Wake up!" She jolted Chae Rin alert with a violent shake before tossing me the tracking device. "I can't drive and watch it at the same time," she said. "You tell me where to go."

I could barely handle the GPS in Uncle Nathan's car, but with Chae Rin only semiconscious and Lake experiencing some form of post-traumatic stress, I tried my best. Following the blinking red on the screen, I directed Belle's frenzied driving through the back roads instead.

"Turn right," I said as we swerved onto a barren street, but the earsplitting screech of ripping metal silenced my next words. A phantom crashed through the top of the van, tearing the ceiling off. The tracking device shot out of my hands, hit the back of the driver's seat, and rattled on the floor. I couldn't tell which of us were screaming—maybe it was just me. We ducked for cover, but Belle kept hold of the steering wheel while the car spun out of control.

"Get lost!" Chae Rin sharpened the earth into several terrible spikes that skewered the beast just as Belle reined the car back under her control.

I peered into the open sky. A helicopter was chasing us from a safe distance above, the red logo of a news station painted across the side.

Effigy car chase. News at eleven.

"Maia!"

I jumped at the sound of Belle's voice. "R-right!" As the wind whipped my hair, I slid off the bench and frantically felt around the floor until I found the tracking device. "Keep going straight ahead!"

Cordoba Avenue. Then Bouchard Street. We were getting near the waterfront. What was Saul planning? Would he burrow deeper underground? Burst into the neighborhood? Or escape underwater?

"Chae Rin." I was amazed at how calm Belle sounded. "Still with us?"

"I just kebabbed a phantom not more than two minutes ago."

Despite Chae Rin's indignation, her breathing was haggard, and her head dangled at an odd angle against the headrest. She was clearly struggling hard just to stay conscious.

"We'll lose the signal if he makes it to the river."

Chae Rin twisted in her chair. "So split the sea, Moses."

"I can't. Not without flooding the place. We'll have to get him before then."

There were docked boats, restaurants, and shops along the board-walk, none of which were guaranteed to be empty. If we were going to stop Saul, Chae Rin would have to do something big, but it would also have to be as precise as possible.

I watched the red dot draw closer to our position. Either Saul's phantom was losing steam, or we were gaining on him. Whichever it was, it didn't matter. "We're almost right over him!"

"Okay." Chae Rin closed her eyes as if feeling the phantom slith-ering through the earth.

"Just end it." Lake held on to my arm for dear life. "Please, just finish it!"

Yelling, Chae Rin raised both her arms. Belle slammed on the brakes. The phantom exploded out of the ground as if the earth, under Chae Rin's command, were ridding itself of a toxin. It soared into the air toward the river, but its body found a jagged bed of ice instead. Belle made sure the edges were sharp enough to cut the phantom's head clean off, stopping it dead.

I stared into the deep hole where its head used to be: hollow, but for some flesh and bone lining the neck. Out of the phantom's carcass climbed Saul, his hand clasping bone to pull himself out, his mouth rasping in the fresh air. He couldn't disappear. Once he'd crawled all the way out, he collapsed onto the ice bed, resting there for a moment before pulling himself into sitting position. I saw no strength in his wicked face, but his eyes . . . his eyes stayed on me. And only me.

After taking a moment to catch our breath, Belle and I got out of the car. Painfully, I dragged myself behind her along a freshly made ice walkway. Despite trying to look everywhere but Saul, inevitably my eyes would slide back to him. His gaze kept me fixed.

"Am I under arrest?" he asked once we reached him. Even with his broken body propped against the phantom's carcass, he still managed an evil little grin.

Belle stood tall despite the strain and fatigue obvious on her face. "You'll be taken in for questioning."

"Good. Question me. Search me. Dig as deeply as you wish. But Maia . . ." With an unsteady hand, he reached for me. "Will you be ready for what you'll find?"

Suddenly, he leaned over and gripped my ankle. Maybe it was because I just had nothing left, but the shock from his touch alone rocketed through my body. Even after Belle kicked his hand away, I continued to shudder.

I gasped. My head was suddenly searing with pain like it'd just caught fire. I knew this feeling. I'd felt it before, in Brooklyn, in Quebec.

Memories. So many memories.

They tore through me like bloody talons; I couldn't make sense of them all.

I pressed my hands against my eyes, mind swirling, but the next time I opened them I was somewhere else entirely.

It had become too dark too quickly. My eyes couldn't adjust. But I knew that I was sitting in an armchair.

Armchair?

The art on the wall felt familiar even while cloaked in darkness. The scotch-filled decanter on the table. The red lipstick staining the rims of glasses. The bottles of alcohol.

Natalya.

I reached for it, but my hand found my throat instead.

No. It wasn't *my* hand at all.

I couldn't speak. I couldn't breathe. Why couldn't I breathe? Where was I? If this was Natalya's memory, then which memory was this?

I tried calling out a name, but I sputtered and coughed instead.

Help me. It was Natalya desperately begging from the deep recesses of my mind. *Please help me. . . .*

Pain sliced apart my chest from the inside as I toppled over the chair. I clawed at the rug because I couldn't use my legs anymore. With the single goal of staying alive, I clung to a pair of feet standing by the table, but they didn't budge, didn't move to help me. Why? Please. *Please!*

I would have cried out if I'd found my voice. I would have asked him why. Why was he just standing there letting me cling to him? Why was he calmly watching me die?

But Natalya would die without ever knowing the answer.

15

NATALYA FILIPOVA WAS MURDERED.

It was more than a hypothesis. However fleeting and confusing the memory had been, it had given me something no one else could: insight into Natalya's last moments.

Natalya was murdered.

Or was she?

Groaning, I buried my head in my hands. It'd already been half a day since Sect agents dragged Saul off to the Division headquarters. Good. Mission accomplished. For a second I thought they'd finally let me go back to Brooklyn, but then Sibyl forced all four of us—me, Belle, Lake, and Chae Rin—to stick around. Why? She wouldn't say. I wasn't even allowed to call Uncle Nathan. Even stranger, Uncle Nathan wasn't trying to call me.

The Sect facility here wasn't equipped for four emotionally and physically exhausted Effigies. After a battle like that? We needed R & R. We needed beds and showers and food that wasn't bad coffee. After a lengthy bout of passionate lobbying led by Lake, the Sect had finally caved and put us up in a nice hotel on the edge of the city, far from the battle site. I'd managed to get four good hours of sleep before waking up to the sounds of helicopters outside my window. Helicopters. Reporters on the ground. Hollering locals. Maybe Effigy fans. Hell, I probably would have been right there with them, back in the day.

Luckily, the Sect, anticipating the deluge of international reporters, had booked the entire eleventh floor of the hotel just for us, but while it helped with security, the media frenzy still found its way inside my comfy hotel room through various means.

Meet Maia Finley: Natalya's Successor. This was the title of a post on an online gossip site, which, to my endless delight, featured interviews from my classmates at Ashford High—like gymnastics queen Missy Stevenson, who didn't waste a second telling the world about every embarrassing thing she'd ever seen me do. I wished I could say they were all lies.

Can Finley Fill Filipova's Shoes? From the *Washington Post.* Should have gone for "flippers," what with the alliteration they already had going.

The battle with Saul had already been dragged into the bloodthirsty arena of twenty-four-hour news television. Pundits cynically picked at the story from every angle. Some of the footage was online already: of me walking inside the bookstore, of Saul's phantom leaping up to swallow him.

"The Department of Defense is issuing an emergency assessment of every Needle and antiphantom device in the country," said a CNN news anchor. Her face was split-screened with a chubby, gross-looking man who blustered from his side of the TV. "According to a statement issued by the Sect press secretary, they have a suspect in custody. But, John, they've given no details on the nature of this suspect or the recent international phantom attacks."

"Wendy, what are you expecting? The Sect has proved time and time again that they are not only incapable of handling matters of international security, but utterly unwilling to fulfill their promises of transparency." John's bloated face reddened by the second. "What are they even good for nowadays? Aside from a few agents who aren't nearly as well trained as our proud American military officers, they've got little girls with godlike abilities running around without any kind of supervision. I mean, should we *really* feel safe with that kind of power in the hands of a bunch of hormonal teens? Does anyone *really* believe they're capable of protecting us?"

Douche bag.

"To be fair, John, they were *instrumental* in apprehending the suspected terrorist."

"Today. Think about it. If you were a young woman with incredible power at your fingertips, would you have the emotional stability to handle it?" He scoffed. "Even Natalya Filipova ended up killing herself."

I shut my eyes, trying to forget the sensation of Natalya's rug in my fingernails.

"And what's stopping the Sect from using the Effigies against us?" John continued. "All this secrecy—what exactly are they trying to hide, Wendy?"

"The hell are you watching?"

I hadn't even heard Chae Rin come in.

I shut my laptop and I fluffed the pillow on my lap. "Feeling better?"

"My head doesn't feel like an omelet anymore, so I guess so." After sitting on the bed next to me, Chae Rin pointed at the windows. "Distracting, isn't it?"

She was referring, of course, to the commotion beyond my shut blinds.

"Chae Rin, what are you doing here?"

"Just came to give you the update," she answered before rummaging around in my minifridge. "They're transporting Saul to the London headquarters."

London headquarters: as in the headquarters for the Sect's European Division.

"Why?"

"Wouldn't say."

Maybe John had a point about that whole transparency part of his rant.

I squeezed the pillow against my chest. "Is it even safe?"

"Don't worry." Chae Rin dug out a can of beer. "They probably froze him up in carbonite or something. They *better* have his ass on lock after all the crap we went through catching him."

As Chae Rin checked the beer brand, I cleared my throat. "Aren't you . . . underage?"

Chae Rin raised a skeptical eyebrow. "Seriously? After I nearly *died* in battle? Well, aren't you a good girl." She took a swig. "Wonder how long they're gonna keep us here."

"I don't know. They told me I couldn't even contact my uncle." Suddenly restless, I buried myself back into the world of my laptop.

The Doll Soldiers forum was in utter chaos with threads being created and locked every other second. I'd steadily avoided all the ones about me, but there was one thread, freshly created, that I couldn't ignore: *Victoria Fail-yinka's Mission Flop in Buenos Aires.*

My stomach sank. The thread had footage of Lake cowering in our van as we chased Saul through the streets of the city, courtesy of the helicopter that'd been chasing *us.*

[+980, - 318] I cannot with this dumb bitch wtf why is she even an Effigy? SMH

[+912, - 310] Flop singer, flop Effigy

"What's that?" Chae Rin leaned in. "Wow. Rough."

Yeah, especially since apparently nobody had gotten the footage of Lake running up a freaking building to save me from splatting all over the street. Thankfully, Lake's Swans refused to stay silent.

[+ 589, - 299] Sorry not everyone is a f*ing warrior princess but what the f does it even matter? She's not even a fully trained Effigy but she still did her best STFU.

[+ 598, - 256] Lol oh look it's the armchair brigade gracing the internet with opinions no one asked for on shit they know NOTHING about. Have YOU ever been in a battle for your life against phantoms? No? THEN STFU

[+ 501, - 273] Wtf is everyone's deal? What is with this bare-bones, commercialized, overly simplistic faux-feminist perception of gurl power? Like a girl has to be able to murder giants without batting an eye before anyone can see her as strong?

The thread was an utter war zone. But then, not too long ago, I would have been a part of it, ignorantly and arrogantly slinging mud with the rest of Lake's attackers.

"Ooh, someone linked a video!" Chae Rin clicked it before I could stop her. That grating assemblage of noises was the debut song of Girls by Day, a tween girl group formed in the bowels of British reality TV and cynically marketed to the Disney crowd. Lake was never the strongest vocally, but at the tender age of fourteen had already earned the title of the cutest. Unfortunately, her cuteness didn't save her from her own nerves or the embarrassment of flubbing their first live performance as an official group.

"What does this even have to do with anything?" I swallowed a spark of anger. "Ugh, why are people so—"

"Terrible! God, she's *terrible*," laughed Chae Rin at the same time. Just as the door creaked open.

Lake stood in the doorway carrying a box of donuts.

"Oh." Chae Rin promptly cleared her throat. A moment of silence passed before she shrugged. "Yes, we're making fun of you, Sandy," she said.

"*She* is!" I clarified, pointing at Chae Rin. "Not me!" As if it made things better.

"Oh, I remember that." Lake giggled. "It was rubbish, wasn't it? Watch me hit those high notes with all the subtlety of a drunken cat. Still, I looked good, yeah?"

She set the donuts down on the table before jumping onto the bed next to us. "Anyway, don't worry about all that," she said as I centered myself atop the bouncing bed. "Online comments and that, I'm used to it. Even *I* could show you worse videos than this one."

I wondered if Lake had noticed the strain in her own laughter. A sudden, strange feeling started corroding my insides. I couldn't put a name to it if I tried, but it wasn't pleasant. And I couldn't look Lake in the eye.

A knock on the door and in came Belle, though not alone. I couldn't believe my eyes when she stepped aside and a man and woman entered the room behind her. Though they were middle-aged, they shouldn't have looked so old, so tired and worn; the kiss of youth must have left them the moment they'd heard their daughter committed suicide.

The wife clung to her husband, her fair hair wrapped in a scarf brushing his thick beard as she buried her face in his neck. It was seeing me that started her waterworks. Tears fell from her clear blue eyes—Natalya's eyes.

Natalya's father held his wife sturdily, his wrinkled hands gripping her around the waist. I turned to Belle wordlessly, because what could I say in the presence of Natalya's parents?

"Maria Filipova and Aleksei Filipov." Belle gave her perfunctory introduction with the barest of emotion. "They came to see you, Maia."

She turned to leave.

"Oh!" Natalya's mother caught Belle by the sleeve. "Belle, please," she said, her deep Russian accent fraught with desperation. "You too. Please, stay and talk with us. . . ."

I never thought I'd see fear, so plain, in Belle's eyes. It flickered for a moment, but left an unmistakable trace. Gently, she pulled her arm from the grieving mother's grip and shut the door behind her.

"That would be our cue too." Chae Rin stood, pulling Lake with her.

I wished she hadn't. I focused on my pillow tight against my chest, flinching when the door shut softly, leaving me alone with Natalya's parents.

"We will not stay long," Mrs. Filipova said. Natalya's father only nodded. The collar of his lavender dress shirt lay perfectly over his vest, fully buttoned despite the hot weather. Even such a small detail reminded me of Natalya, who never let a strand of her hair out of place.

"My husband, he struggles with English," the woman said. "But we don't have much to say."

Mrs. Filipova took in the sight of the girl whose picture she'd probably seen countless times since her worldwide media debut. I planted my feet on the ground, but I didn't know whether to stand or to stay seated, to fold my arms or to keep them neat on my lap.

"My daughter, she . . ." Mrs. Filipova's breath hitched. The tears began budding again in her eyes, but she dotted them away. Her husband held her hand tight as if willing her to stay right by his side. "She believes—*believed* that every life is precious. She worked hard to fulfill her duty to protect. Noble and proud. That was the kind of woman she was."

And the kind of woman I had to live up to. "I'll . . . try my best." It was a promise devoid of courage.

"I'm sure you will, but that is not why I am here." Natalya's mother began to shake. Her husband held her tighter. "Natalya told us once that even after death, she'll remain in the next. Her memories . . . her feelings . . ."

I knew what was coming next, and I wished to my bones that Natalya's mother wouldn't ask what she was clearly about to.

"Natalya . . . They said she killed herself. But she would never . . ." Mrs. Filipova shook her head. "We hired lawyers, did our own investigations, but still everyone said it was suicide. I can't—"

"I don't know." My lips thinned into a trembling line. "I . . . haven't seen Natalya's memories," I lied. "I don't know how."

As Natalya's mother began to cry, my world grew dim and pointless. I wanted to run away, as far from the grieving couple as I could, because I knew I couldn't give them what they wanted. They'd lost someone they loved. All they wanted were answers. Turning to me was a desperate, last-ditch attempt. I could still vividly remember the pain of suffocation . . . but I just didn't know if I could trust myself, trust the memory. Was Natalya really murdered? Or had she done it to herself? How accurate were memories, really?

And if Natalya really was murdered, why would the Sect announce it as a suicide?

At this point, until I was sure of anything, I knew it would just be plain irresponsible to tell Natalya's parents about the memory. Especially now that they were so fragile. I had to make sure.

"I'm sorry," I whispered.

"No." Natalya's mother shook her head, untangling herself from her husband's arms. "It's okay. It's okay. I had to try." As she calmed herself with unsteady breaths, she reached into her beaten purse and pulled out a skeleton key attached to a thin string. "Please, take this."

I frowned. "What . . . what is it?" The stone key looked from another century. Though confused, I allowed Natalya's mother to press it into my palm.

"A week before she died, Natalya told me to give this to the next girl, should anything happen to her. I'm fulfilling that promise now."

I didn't understand, but I thanked her anyway. With a sad bow of her head, Mrs. Filipova turned from me.

"Sect." Natalya's father. A nasty sneer followed the word. "Don't trust them." He looked me square in the eyes as he said it.

After Natalya's parents left, Sibyl summoned me to Belle's suite. Everyone was waiting. Clad in yet another fabulous pantsuit, Sibyl had taken the sofa for herself. Cheryl stood behind her, her long ginger braid laid over her chest. Belle sat in one of the comfy chairs by the porcelain vase with Chae Rin and Lake on the opposite side of the table. And—

"Rhys." My heart calmed at the sight of him standing in front of the billowing curtains of the grand windows, his dark hair thick and tousled over his face. Under other circumstances, I might have made a snide comment about the geeky, thin suspenders holding up his jeans, but I couldn't see past the bandages around his forehead: a souvenir from the battle, no doubt.

It could have been worse.

"How's your head?" I hadn't meant for it to come out so timidly.

"Still attached to the rest of me." His grin was infectious. I hated being gooey, but I couldn't help but smile too, shuffling my feet awkwardly like an insecure kid as I brushed the thick curls from my face.

"You two want to be alone when we're done here?" Chae Rin slid her chair's pillow out from under her. "Plenty of rooms."

"Maia." Sibyl said my name loudly enough to signal an end to the conversation. "Sit. Please."

"Since you asked so nicely." I took the chair next to Belle, whose disinterested gaze was fixed on a piece of art on the wall.

"I've discussed it with the Council." Sibyl crossed her legs.

Congrats on a mission well-done, Maia! So grateful you nearly died several times so we could kidnap Saul! I knew better than to expect any of these things to pass from Sibyls lips, but it pissed me off nonetheless.

"Maia," Sibyl continued, "you're to be taken to England. After your inaugural assessment with the Council, you'll be taken to the London headquarters to begin your formal training—*if* you pass your assessment, that is." Her frigid tone was like a gavel on wood.

"Right," I said lifelessly. Not like I hadn't been expecting this.

Chae Rin laughed. "Guess it's your turn now, kid. But, ugh, that assessment thing is *brutal*. I seriously hate that Blackwell guy."

"You'll be coming too, Chae Rin," Sibyl clarified. "Each of you. You'll be helping to train her."

"What?" Chae Rin's back went straight as a board. "Why?"

"It's the Council's decision."

"That's informative," I mumbled.

"Um?" Lake raised a hand. "Doesn't the Sect already have people that specifically train Effigies? Like, an instructor? Can't you just get one for Maia?"

Chae Rin nodded. "I remember my old instructor. Knocked her out by accident once."

Sibyl leaned back into her sofa. "I agree with their decision. You each have experience. Share it. Train her. And while you're training her, you'll be training yourselves, and maybe even one another."

Lake lurched, silent like the rest. Sibyl's tone made it clear that this was not a debate.

"You're not telling us everything, are you?" Plucking a rose from the vase next to her, Belle considered it as she spoke. "The reason you want us together . . . you're planning something."

"If this is a plan, then you're one of the most important factors." The shade from the wide brim of Sibyl's hat cast shadows over her eyes. "You'll be teaching Maia how to scry."

Belle bent the rose stem with her grip. And Rhys: Though he'd been listening calmly, at the sound of the word "scry," he took a jerky step forward, forgetting himself.

"Scry?" I asked.

"You've been doing it already." Cheryl spoke this time. "Seeing into the memories of the other Effigies. Like Natalya's, I'm sure."

Rhys froze. "Natalya?" Slowly, he looked at me, his lips open in a part. "You've been . . . you've been seeing Natalya? Already?"

"Just bits and pieces of her memories." I turned away. "N-nothing . . . serious."

"If you're trained you'll be able to do it more consistently," Cheryl said. "The memories will come more clearly and, what's more, you'll be able to control the process, perhaps even target specific Effigies in your line. I gather you'll experience less pain, too."

Rhys's face darkened. "Agent Langley," he said quietly. "What are you planning?"

Sibyl gestured toward Cheryl, who promptly produced from her bag the same inoculation pen I'd jammed into Saul's neck.

"Maia." Sibyl regarded the device in her hands. "Do you know what fuels an Effigy's power?"

"Cylithium," Lake answered before I could even wrap my mind around the question. "What?" she added, once again, when she found me and Chae Rin staring at her.

"What sets an Effigy apart from the rest of us is the presence of a rare chemical element," Cheryl explained. "The Sect first discovered its existence in the fifties during the Cambridge Experiments. It's found in a chemical by-product formed in your pituitary."

I nodded as if I understood, but I doubted I was convincing anyone.

"Back at the bookstore, you inoculated Saul with enzymes designed to disrupt the chemical's formation. It worked. For a time, Saul couldn't use his abilities."

"So what you're saying"—my fingers fastened together in a vise grip—"is that Saul is an Effigy."

The room went quiet.

"Possibly," Sibyl answered. "Of course, cylithium is also an element commonly found in the remains of phantoms."

I gripped the armrests on either side of me. A fifth Effigy? A phantom? What the hell was he?

"I know it's confusing. That's why we need you," Sibyl said. "We know Saul's connection to an undocumented Effigy named Marian. We know he visits the grave of a man who died in the nineteenth century."

"Decades." I recalled Saul's taunting. "Back in the bookstore, he said he's had decades to read books. But the guy looks like a college undergrad."

"Vampire?" Chae Rin shrugged, skillfully avoiding Sibyl's sharp glare.

"That's why, with Belle's help, Maia, you'll learn all you can about Marian. Peer into her memories. We might find Saul there. This is not a democratic decision," she added the second Rhys opened his mouth to speak. I could see his hands tighten into fists.

My hand found the skeleton key I'd hidden underneath my blouse. Learning how to scry meant I'd also have the opportunity to delve deeper into Natalya's life.

And, more important, her death.

If Natalya really had been murdered, then who had killed her? And why? When I closed my eyes, I could still see Natalya's hand reaching for the loafers of a man who had simply stood by and watched her die. Natalya's parents so desperately wanted answers.

So did I.

Did the Sect have them?

I watched Sibyl tap her perfectly manicured nails against her knee. Then the tapping stopped. "Is there something else, Maia?"

I could just tell her. I'd told them about the other memories. But I couldn't forget Mr. Filipov's bitter face before telling me not to trust the Sect. I already tried denying it. It was easier to. But in my heart, I knew. In that excruciating, heartbreaking moment, Natalya hadn't wanted to die. She hadn't been expecting it, and she'd fought so hard against it.

Just a few days ago, the Sect had confidently told the world about Natalya's suicide. The Sect . . . How much did I really know about them?

"Well?" Sibyl asked again.

I tried to speak, but the words wouldn't form. "No," I said at last. I shrank back, taking my secrets with me. "Nothing."

I had time to figure things out. For now, I would do as I was told. Not like I had much of a choice.

"Okay," I said. "I'm in."

It relieved me to see the other girls nodding as well, to have them with me as I took the elevator down to the lobby overcrowded with reporters.

At the very least, I wouldn't be alone. It was a comforting thought.

Steeling myself for the mission to come, I drew in a breath and dove blindly into the dizzying, flashing lights.

PART TWO

There have always been dolls
as long as there have been people.
In the trash heaps and abandoned temples,
the dolls pile up;
the sea is filling with them.

What causes them?
Or are they gods, causeless,
something to talk to
when you have to talk,
something to throw against the wall?

A doll is a witness
who cannot die,
with a doll you are never alone.

—Margaret Atwood, "Five Poems for Dolls"

16

"HANG ON, NO ONE CALLED THE PRESS?" Sliding off her shades, Lake glanced around Heathrow Airport, utterly scandalized. "No free publicity? I'm still working on that record, you know."

Chae Rin wheeled her suitcase with the energy of a sloth. "You sound chipper."

"Of course I am! I'm home!" Lifting her face, Lake breathed in the airport air. "Last time they locked me in some facility in Finland. It was awful! But this time I'm training right here in London! By the way, do you guys want to pop on over to my mum and dad's for dinner tonight? We always have room for guests!"

"Let's get to the facility first before we start making dinner plans, okay?" Chae Rin rubbed the sleep from her eyes. "And what's with *you*?"

I felt Chae Rin's sharp poke just as I finished listening to Uncle Nathan's voice mail again. I answered her with an amicable enough smile, but the phone still trembled in my hands while I stuffed it back into my pocket. He was probably busy. I'd just have to try again later.

The graying clouds threatened a sunless day. I was getting used to being picked up at airport terminals by Sect vans. I reached for the door handle.

"Maia." Belle stopped me. "You'll be going with them."

Behind the van, agents waited by a small black car.

"Hey, wait," I said as they grabbed my go bag and threw it into the trunk. "Where exactly am I going?"

"Cambridgeshire," Belle replied, before shutting my door. The knowing faces of the other girls passed by my window as the driver took off down the crowded London streets.

What the hell? Why did I have to spend an additional two hours cramped in a car while the other girls got to relax in the facility dorms? Sullen, I pressed my cheek up against the cold window, lazily watching Britain's antiphantom nets threading through telephone poles along the inter-city highway.

The little town of Ely in Cambridgeshire hadn't woken up yet. The agents drove me through the empty streets to a stunning cathedral rising from the flat land of the countryside, mired in the mist. It was a creepy kind of beautiful: Its stone towers and turrets seemed drawn out of a Gothic fairy tale, cold and forbidding beneath the dark gloom of the sky.

"Why did you bring me here?" I stepped out of the car onto the cobbled road.

"You'll have to go inside on your own," said the driver. "We'll wait."

They probably wouldn't make all this fuss about me being key to their investigations just to ambush and murder me later in some obscure British church. I'd just have to trust them.

This *wasn't* just some obscure church. The inside took my breath away. I walked the long stretch of its ghostly hall, each step reverberating off the stone and marble. I wasn't particularly religious, so I couldn't recognize the Christian references painted into the magnificent vaulted ceiling, but its beauty still wrung shivers from me. Ely Cathedral.

I'd been too distracted by the interiors to notice that I wasn't alone. This was a church, but there were only two worshippers beneath the octagonal stone lantern. One sat in the empty choir aisle, and the moment I saw his face clearly, my mouth dried.

Vasily: the guy who'd left us to die in Quebec. The guy who'd taken a man's finger with little more than a grin. It was him.

That grin turned wicked the moment he saw me.

Maybe this *was* an ambush.

I stepped back. The other "worshipper" was a man I'd never seen before. Vasily's partner? He sat in the presbytery in a chair at the high altar. Well, if he was about to spring an attack, he'd have to stand up, which worked in my favor because he looked way too comfortable sitting there with his long black hair curling in ringlets over his broad shoulders.

His thick black brows arched in amusement as he peered at me through the flickering candle flame. "Maia Finley." His voice was a booming, arrogant British baritone. "So you've finally come. Good." He tilted his head. "Come closer."

"No, thanks."

I didn't know what to make of him. He looked rich, what with the finely cut suit and the huge, fancy ring on his left middle finger. The ring's silver engravings caught the light from the stained glass windows behind him, but maybe that was the point. He didn't seem like the subtle type. As he sat there with his arms on the rests he looked almost like a riddling Sphinx, his wild mane of hair a headdress draped over his shoulders, his treacherous grin sharp as if cut into his face with a blade.

Needless to say, I was ready to run in the other direction.

With a soft chuckle, he closed his eyes. "Unfortunately, my dear girl, you have no choice."

A ghost breeze swept through the room, soft and cold against my bare skin.

Reaching into his left sleeve, he pulled out a gold coin. "My name is Bartholomäus Blackwell," he told me. "Representative of the seven houses that compose the Sect's High Council. Consider this the beginning of your inaugural assessment."

Assessment. Sibyl had mentioned it in Argentina, but this wasn't exactly what I'd been expecting.

I kept still.

"Do you know this cathedral, Maia?" He swept his hand over the presbytery. "In the late nineteenth century, when the Sect was formed, this was the original meeting place of the founders. They gather here still . . . that is, when it comes time to meet the new Effigies."

Perhaps ghosts really did live in the old walls; I could hear soft chattering in them.

"I don't like the look of her."

I spun around.

"She hasn't any confidence, really. Look at her. It's troubling."

I checked the arches, the pillars, but I couldn't find a source. Mumbling voices with different accents surrounded me—some older, some younger, some male, some female, all faceless.

My blood ran cold in my veins, but I couldn't take a single step to save my own life. My feet froze against the marble floor.

"The file says she's sixteen."

"Natalya was much younger when she was called to duty."

"The younger they're called, the more potential they have—isn't that the case?"

The last voice, old and sniveling, let out a series of hacks that reverberated throughout the hall. The voices surrounded me. Taking another step back, I wrapped my arms around my chest.

"Don't be scared, love." Blackwell pointed to the arches. "Cameras. They can see you."

But I couldn't see them—the Council. How nice of them to hide, leaving me exposed in a den of strangers.

"The members of the Council are secret, you see, for their own protection. That, of course, is why they need me to act as their representative. I am the face of the Sect." Blackwell cheesily stroked his chin without a hint of shame. "But don't worry. All Effigies must go through an assessment before the Council can sanction their official training. It's tradition." He flipped his coin, catching it between his fingers. "We'll ask just a few questions. That's all we'll need to figure out what to do with you."

I eyed Vasily by the choir aisle. "What . . . to do with me?"

Blackwell stretched out his hand and Vasily came to him. Gingerly, he placed a thin, black book in Blackwell's hand. "It was 1957. Jasper, Texas: the little town that Mary Lou Russell called home."

My stomach lurched at the sound of her name.

"I'm sure you've heard of her. Quite an infamous Effigy, not in the least because of the blow she'd dealt to the image of the Sect. It didn't start out that way, of course." He didn't have to explain but continued anyway. "Quite the opposite. She had the most beautiful blond hair. Magnificent blue eyes. The first ever Effigy born in America. You could say she was the first to bridge the gap between duty and celebrity. A very beautiful girl, right, Vasily?"

Vasily answered Blackwell by leaning against the side of his extravagant chair.

"Perhaps that was why nobody wanted to believe, at first, that she'd been using her *talents* to help her father and brother burn down churches and schools on the other side of town."

I bent over, my breaths weighted by the sudden realization that the girl was inside me somewhere: Mary Lou Russell, the beautiful fifteen-year-old Effigy raised by white supremacists. She was in me. I couldn't put words to the horror of it.

"An embarrassment," cried a voice, male, high and shrill. "The horrid child called the press and announced she wouldn't stop killing until she'd cleansed her country."

"A very dark day for the Sect. It was exactly what detractors needed to bolster their narrative of the Sect as a neo-imperial threat."

"Utterly ridiculous."

I could imagine the Council nodding from the comfort of their shadowy offices while they watched me sweat and squirm from their monitors. "Why are you telling me this?"

Blackwell gave me a sidelong look. "Each Effigy we indoctrinate is a potential liability. This isn't a personal bias; it's reality. With that in mind, I'd like to ask you some questions."

"To see if I'm a potential liability?"

"The Council simply wishes to get to you know a little bit better, my dear."

"And if I check off all the wrong boxes?"

Blackwell lifted the bound bookmark from between the pages of his book. "Well, of course, then we may have to cut our losses and start anew."

Funny, the stone walls hadn't seemed this close when I'd walked in. A chill ran up my bare legs, wrenching a shiver from my core.

"Maia Finley: age sixteen. Born in Buffalo, New York. But not alone." I bit the inside of my cheek as he flipped a page. "Father from Buffalo and mother from Kingston—ah, my most beloved of island parishes."

"Does any of this really matter?"

"No, love," Blackwell answered. "What matters is that they all died in a house fire last year."

All my bones locked into place. Something painful and heavy slid down my throat, but my mind was too blank to figure out what it was.

"David Finley, Samantha Finley, June Finley—your twin sister." Blackwell's voice tainted each name. "April of last year, faulty wiring started a fire in your home in Buffalo. . . ."

No. I couldn't feel my arms. "Please stop."

"—you had snuck out in the dead of night after fighting with your sister—"

"Stop!" My desperate cry reverberated across the hollow ceiling. A thousand Maias screaming.

Blackwell shut his book, placing it delicately atop his lap. "According to police reports."

"So what?" I concentrated so hard on the carvings on the floor, though I couldn't really see them at all. "You gonna tell me my favorite color? Or the brand of my underwear?"

"So disrespectful," sniveled one of the voices.

"Well, yes," said another, "but Belle was much worse, wasn't she?"

"The Council is concerned," said Blackwell, "that such a tragedy may eventually manifest itself in unsettling ways."

"You think I'm going to go crazy?" I felt sick. Enraged. My face burned in anger.

"Being an Effigy is not some gift," rasped an old woman from beyond the walls, as if I would ever see it that way. "We want to hear from your own lips, Maia Finley. Why should we trust you?"

"I don't know," I answered. It was the truth. But, as expected, it wasn't good enough.

"What of your skills?" The man sniffed so loudly I imagined his hairy nostrils vibrating from the inhale. "*Terrae Ensis. Aquae Ensis. Ventus Ensis. You*, my dear, are the *Ignis Ensis*: the Sword of Fire. However, according to the reports so far, you have yet to engage in any conscious form of elemental creation *or* manipulation."

"It's also troubling to think you were able to unknowingly summon a weapon in a moment of turmoil," said another faceless man. "Such instability could have easily turned deadly in other circumstances."

"Tell me, Maia, why should we trust you?"

"Why should we allow you to be the focal point in such an important investigation when your psychological stability may be in doubt?"

"After such a horrible tragedy."

"Why should mankind put their faith in you, as an Effigy—"

"How the *hell* should I know?" I squeezed my hands so tightly I thought they may draw blood. "You assholes are acting like I asked for any of this, acting tough while hiding your damn faces! And you call this glorified hazing an *assessment*! *Tradition?* Screw *all* of you!"

I gasped. My vision blurred. The cathedral fizzled and spun around me, and for one fleeting second I could see Natalya. Tall and willowy, the fallen soldier stood before me, reaching out to me, mouthing a name I couldn't hear. But with a blink, she was gone.

Gripping my throbbing head, I fell to my knees, my body burning from the inside. I didn't want to cry, not now when there were a bunch of cowards waiting for an excuse to dismiss me as a defective product so they could melt me down for parts. But the tears budded anyway.

"Leave her." It was voice I hadn't heard yet—young, elegant, and feminine. The woman spoke softly. "She's young, and she's already done so well. Let her prove herself. Every Effigy should be allowed to have that chance."

The voice was the air my chest had been aching for. I drew in a sharp breath, my shoulders loosening.

Blackwell's laughter broke the silence.

"Very well, then," said a member of the Council. "Blackwell, bring the book."

It was Vasily who moved, reaching across the altar behind him. The tome had remained hidden behind Blackwell, but now, as Vasily handed it to him, the magnificent leather-bound book held my gaze. Blackwell's grip buckled slightly under its weight.

"The Sect is an organization of millions." Blackwell rose to his feet. He was much taller than he'd originally looked, his rigid back giving him a sense of majesty. "Warriors, scientists, even businessmen. Each member of our Order has sworn to protect its aims." He took the steps one by one, his eyes never leaving me. "And you, Maia . . . you are an Effigy. Sworn to protect mankind. And so you must swear to us."

I was still on my knees when Blackwell stopped in front of me.

"One knee," he told me.

Both of mine were on the floor. Kneeling while Blackwell loomed above me stripped me of confidence in ways I hadn't thought possible. I felt small. Powerless. And that was probably the point. But here, with the Council watching, I didn't have a choice. I had to comply.

Begrudgingly, I lifted my right knee.

"Good," Blackwell said. "This codex *is* the Sect. It is our history, our present, our future. It contains our rules, our goals. And now you must swear on it." He stretched out his arms. "That you will be loyal to us. To the Sect. That you will protect this organization as passionately and as dutifully as you will protect mankind. Swear yourself to us, Maia Finley, Effigy of Fire."

I placed my hand on the book. I was shaking. "I—I s-swear."

It was quiet, feeble. Certainly not the kind of response to engender confidence in the Council members watching, but apparently, it was enough. Blackwell withdrew the codex.

"Maia Finley," said a member of the Council. "We give you leave to proceed with your duties as an Effigy. But you'll be monitored closely."

"We also hereby require that you undergo monthly psychological assessments in order to be assured of your continuing ability to perform to the utmost of your abilities."

Monthly assessments. Well, I already had about a year of therapy under my belt. It was certainly better than the nuclear option they were originally itching for.

I rose to my feet, my legs numb. "Is that it? Is . . . is there anything else?"

Blackwell grinned as he turned from me. "You may go, little Maia Finley. You may go."

It was raining outside. Of course it was. But my heart lifted when I saw Rhys waiting by the car under an umbrella.

"I heard you'd already gone to Ely." Droplets of water rolled off the tips of the umbrella and splashed at his feet. "Figured you might want to see a familiar face."

At first I was surprised to hear he'd be coming to England to help me. Now I didn't even want to imagine an alternate reality where he hadn't. He met me halfway, grabbing my hand and drawing me under the umbrella with him. "Are you okay?"

I didn't know how to answer. Luckily, I didn't have to.

"Come on." He reached for the car door.

"Aidan Rhys. So we meet again." Blackwell exited the cathedral with his elongated hands in his pockets. Vasily held a pearl-white umbrella over his head. "How's your mother?"

Rhys met the lighthearted greeting with a cold glare, colder still when it found Vasily.

"Oh." Blackwell looked from one to the other. "Oh yes, I heard there was some kind of misunderstanding between the two of you in Canada."

"You would have," said Rhys, "since you were the one who sent him there in the first place."

"And why would you think that?"

"Why wouldn't I? You're the only one he answers to."

Rain dribbled freely down Vasily's cat grin. I felt Rhys's rough hand snake around my wrist. He drew me closer.

Blackwell laughed. "Yes, well, do forgive him for any mishaps. Vasily's still a little rough around the edges, you see. You should know that better than anyone, having trained with him—Greenland, was it? Horrid place."

"Rhys," I whispered, because his grip had tightened suddenly.

"Don't worry," Blackwell continued. "The ring is already being processed at the London headquarters, along with the other one you confiscated in South America."

Rhys's frown deepened. "What I want to know is how you knew about its existence when nobody else did. He had to have gotten the lead from somewhere, after all."

"Rhys!" I wrenched my sore wrist from his grip, rubbing it as he stared back at me. Judging from the look of slight shock on the face, he probably hadn't even realized he was hurting me.

"The poor girl has been through so much this morning." Blackwell tilted his head in a suspect show of empathy. "Take her home, Aidan."

A white vintage luxury car was there waiting for the strange pair. I stepped aside, my hand going absently to Rhys's chest as they passed. Surprised at myself, I quickly drew it away.

"Let's go," he said.

"Yeah."

Don't trust them. Natalya's father had warned me, and for a second it seemed like Natalya's ghost had too, appearing in the ancient chapel just to make sure I wouldn't forget.

I wouldn't.

And I definitely wasn't going to forgive those assholes for the not-so-old wounds they'd torn open, all in the name of "assessing" me. Limp in the backseat of the Sect car, I pressed my hand against the growing pain in my chest. It couldn't get any worse.

I dialed Uncle Nathan again. And again.

"Maia," Rhys said, after I'd left my seventh message. "Sorry, Maia." He sighed. "You won't be able to contact your family during your training period. It's a new rule. They say it'll help with training." He sounded skeptical. "I'm really sorry, but your uncle's been told too. He . . . won't be calling you back."

I stared blankly at the black screen of my phone.

From: Maia F. neoqueenmaia@gomail.com
To: Nathan Finley finleyn@gomail.com
Date: Thursday, April 23 at 2:37 AM
Subject: hi (Draft)

Hey Uncle Nathan,

It's late here, so I'm just sending a quick e-mail to let you know I'm okay. Landed in London and now I'm safely inside my bedcovers with some hot chocolate and my laptop, which is all I ever wanted in life anyway. So all is good.

Everything's set up. They put my stuff in this housing complex in the east wing (because this place is huge enough to have an east wing). Seriously, it's pretty sweet. London HQ is in Epping Forest, so there's lots of trees around. The dorm's a couple of floors, so there's plenty of space. We've got a kitchen, a terrace, a jumbo TV screwed into the wall, and a closet full of new clothes I didn't even buy myself. I feel like I'm being fattened up for the slaughter . . . heh.

The girls are here too. Still can't believe Belle Rousseau is breathing the same air as me. Chae Rin is terrifying but weirdly okay. I'm rooming with Lake. She's got way too much stuff and her beauty products have annexed the bathroom, but she's actually really nice . . . except she's also really depressed. She can't see her parents even though they live in town. Chae Rin's depressed too. I can tell, though she'd probably rather die than admit it. I know her relationship with her parents is a bit complicated. . . .

I can't see you either. I can't even e-mail you. You'll never read this. Why am I writing it?

Uncle, you said everything would be okay. You meant it, right?

The truth is I can't sleep. I can't sleep can't sleep can't sleep. I wish I could call you. I don't want to be alone. I wish you were here. I wish June were here. I wish wish wishwishwish.

I know we haven't always seen eye to eye, but you're my uncle, and if you say everything's going to be okay, if you say it, then I'll believe you. Okay?

Please just tell me everything's going to be okay. . . .

There's no point to this.

17

THE YOGA PANTS I FOUND IN MY DRESSER CUT
off awkwardly at the bottom. It was chilly outside too. I pulled the
strings of my hoodie, rubbing my legs so feverishly Lake suggested I
use "the loo" before we started with the lesson.

Sibyl's orders. We had a schedule to follow, and apparently it
involved a lack of sleep.

We'd gone to a field on the west end of the facility. Though
the sun was barely up, Lake was chatting excitedly about an old
boyfriend—Carlos, a hot male model—though she was sharing
quite a bit more detail than I was comfortable with. "Talk, Maia,"
Lake said. "Trust me, the more we talk, the more heat we generate."
She nudged me in the ribs. "How about you? Any boyfriend? Girlfriend?"

I shuffled my feet. "Nope. Forever alone." The memory of being
under Rhys's umbrella slithered wickedly into my thoughts. I chased
it away.

"Single? Really?" Lake bent down; she had to in order to reach my eye level. "You're so cute. Clean your skin up a bit, and you could definitely get it."

"You sound like you're trying to sell me face cream by preying on my insecurities."

"Ooh, face cream! I have loads of it. You can just have it if you want. I got it all free anyway. Though a lot of it's still back home."

She went quiet.

I straightened out my back, eager to change the subject. "Well . . . since we're here . . ."

"Yes, training. Hmm, I thought Belle would be here too. I guess she'll only be helping with your scrying thing. I thought she'd help out with the other stuff too, though."

So had I.

"Chae Rin, you ready?"

Chae Rin, who'd plunked herself down on a bench the moment she got here, answered Lake with the kind of noise a vicious animal might make if it were attempting to intimidate its prey while lying there bloated and dying. Her eyes sagged with dark circles. I couldn't blame her. The coffee hadn't even finished boiling by the time we were dragged out of the dorm by agents. Chae Rin had to leave her flask on the kitchen counter.

"Okay, well, let's start. Welcome to your first lesson in elemental training." Lake grabbed the duffel bag by Chae Rin's bench and took out a heart monitor. "Put this on. It's a standard part of the training. It's just to make sure you don't overexert yourself."

I strapped it to my wrists and clicked it on. Once the LCD screen lit up, a small digital heart began beating steadily on the monitor. "You think I might overexert myself?"

"It happens. I mean, the whole process of elemental training . . . it can definitely cause a little stress, you know? Especially when you're just starting."

I turned my wrist over. "So . . . what is it like? Making fire or ice out of nothing?"

"What is it like?" Lake placed her hands on her hips. "It's kind of like . . . er, what *is* it like, Chae Rin?" She turned. "Hey!"

Lake kicked the bench just as Chae Rin had begun to snore.

"What? How should I know?" Chae Rin rolled onto her back, legs dangling off the edge of the bench.

"You're supposed to be helping Maia too, you know."

"But I'm cranky and tired." She sat up, propping her arm over one knee. "Plus she's probably too slow to get it anyway, so who cares?"

"Hey!"

"It's Sibyl's orders, remember? We train her." Lake flicked strands of hair out of her eyes. "Besides, you could use a little training yourself, or so I hear. Didn't you nearly level, like, an entire city once?"

Chae Rin opened and closed her mouth several times, her cheeks flaring red. "Completely, totally exaggerated. Besides, what about you, *Victoria*? You barely passed your training. Didn't you try to fake an injury so you could bolt?"

Lake huffed. "So? Who cares? Anyway, I definitely did a good job with my elemental training. I worked bloody hard on that, you know."

I didn't doubt her. After all, we were both alive today because of it. "Guess we could all use some work," I said. "Except Belle. Can you believe she killed *twelve* phantoms her first mission alone?"

Wrong thing to say. They were on me in a flash.

"So you're basically saying Belle's better than us, eh?" Chae Rin tilted her head. "But then, you *are* Princess Belle's personal fangirl, aren't you? Don't know why I'm surprised."

"No." I waved my hands in lieu of a white flag. "I didn't mean—"

"Geez, Maia, that's kind of mean." Lake kicked the grass. "It probably does help her that she has more experience than us, you know."

"I didn't mean—"

"Anyway," Lake said rather loudly, "back to training. Your job today is to try to create fire. There's no real science to it, though. You just have to feel it. Think of it like . . ." Lake paused. "Like the power is actually *outside* of you. It's not, but just pretend it is. Close your eyes and picture yourself pulling it into your body."

Shutting her eyes, Lake drew in a deep, serene breath. "Trap and release. That's what I was taught. Trap the power, release the power as fire."

I frowned. "But . . . how do I trap? How do I release? Release it where?"

"Like I said," said Lake, a little sharply, "you have to feel it. Just relax." She lifted a hand, the palm upturned. "And bring it in."

The chilled air began to move around me, gaining momentum by the second until, in a flash, the breeze became a powerful gust that knocked me off my feet. The duffel bag tumbled over the side of the bench. Chae Rin grabbed the edges of the wood to keep herself from following suit, but she ended up losing her grip and falling anyway.

An instant later, the wind died down, and the air was calm again. "Sorry 'bout that," said Lake with a cute shrug.

Chae Rin moaned.

Brushing myself off, I got back to my feet. "So, uh, just concentrate, huh, Lake?"

"Yep. Bring on the flames."

Lake winked and stepped back several paces, maybe to protect herself. But she needn't have. I concentrated. Nothing happened. For almost an hour, Lake tried to coach me through the block, but nothing she suggested worked. Meditation, visualization, even a few laps around the field. I was a hell of a lot sweatier, but aside from that, nothing. Not even a spark.

"This is ridiculous," I said, panting facedown on the grass.

"*You're* ridiculous." Chae Rin yanked weeds out of the dirt. "It's really not that hard."

"You're new at this." Lake knelt down next to me. "Don't be so hard on yourself. It's okay if you don't get it on the first try."

"You know what the problem is." Chae Rin got to her feet. "Not enough adrenaline."

"I've been running around for the past ten minutes." I sat up and rubbed my thighs.

"Not the right kind of adrenaline. You need a good fight." Chae Rin grabbed my arm rather painfully and heaved me back to my feet. "Fight me."

The two words leached the warmth from my skin. I could already feel the imminent breaking of my rib cage. The heart rate number on my monitor climbed accordingly.

"No, thanks."

"That wasn't a request."

Chae Rin shoved me—just one push—and I flew black.

"*Ow!* What the hell are you doing?"

"Running won't do it, but fighting will. That adrenaline you feel when you're inches away from death, like your foot might not touch that high wire . . ." She relished the thought. "Fight me and you'll bring that fire out real quick. Well, you'll have to if you want to live."

My jaw dropped. "You're crazy!"

"No . . . no, she might have a point." Lake giggled as I shot her an incredulous look. "Let's just see where this goes."

"Consider it a demonstration," Chae Rin said very sweetly before launching at me.

I barely had time to scramble to my feet before Chae Rin kneed me in the stomach and sent me crashing back to the ground.

Chae Rin rolled her eyes. "Oh, come on, get *up!*"

I did, but to run. Chae Rin was insane. The lack of sleep and caffeine had finally whittled down her senses until she was nothing more than a raging girl beast. I managed to make it past the bench when the ground rose below me, bursting out and sending me soaring. After a rough landing, I rolled over on the ground, rubbing my sides, but it wasn't over. I blanched at the sight of the jagged pulpit of dirt and soil jutting out of the grass.

"Trap and release," Chae Rin said with a cute finger wave before stomping the ground. A wet mass of soil launched up at her feet. Catching it, she lobbed it at me. I ducked, gasping when I saw the missile dent a tree a few feet away.

"This is not training!" I swiped the hair from my eyes. "This is *attempted murder!*"

"Feel the adrenaline," said Lake, from behind a tree. "Bring it out! Come on!"

But I couldn't. Finding my footing, I backed away. "This is stupid! You know what? I'm . . . I'm telling Sibyl!"

Chae Rin doubled over laughing. "Savior of Earth, ladies and gentlemen. Well done!"

"Oh, yeah?" I wasn't thinking when I yelled, "Then I'm telling Belle!"

I honestly didn't know why I'd said it. Maybe because I knew it'd piss her off, which made it all the more stupid. Chae Rin stopped laughing, her lips sinking into a scowl.

"*Belle?* Oh, you're telling *Belle?*"

I threw my hands up in an apologetic plea. "I was kidding."

"And what authority does *Belle* have?" I could practically see steam rising out of her ears. "Where's she, anyway? How come the agents didn't drag *her* ass out here? Like she's too good to *bother* with the rest of us? Is *that* it? Ugh!"

Chae Rin punched the ground and it cracked immediately. The trembling earth split at my feet, sliding my legs apart. Before I could fall into the fissure, I jumped to the side, rolling in the grass. Lake clung to her tree like a raft in the middle of the ocean.

"God, she is so *infuriating.*" Chae Rin huffed, blowing her hair out of her eyes as the ground stopped shaking. "You know what? Screw this. I'm going back to bed."

With her hands in her pockets, she walked away, leaving me and Lake to stare at the brand-new fault she'd made.

"Light."

Alone in my dark room, I sat by the window with a brass candlestick in my hands, my middle finger linked through the handle.

"Light *now!*" I waited for the candle wick to erupt in flame. "Come on!"

Still nothing. After slamming the candlestick down upon the window ledge, I buried my face in my hands.

I was an Effigy, and I couldn't even use my power. Lake and Chae Rin's careers may have had a few hiccups along the way, but they could deliver. I, on the other hand? I was a defective product waiting for recall, and judging by the mood at the Cathedral, it wouldn't be surprising if the Sect's High Council decided to cut their losses and start over with another girl. One who could actually do her job.

Cut their losses . . .

I thought of Natalya reaching out to me, a ghost of a memory hidden from the Council's unforgiving gaze.

Had they cut their losses with Natalya, too?

I couldn't shake away the memory of Mrs. Filipova's grief, or the disdain on Natalya's father's face as he spat out his warning. Natalya was arguably one of the best Effigies in history: a legend. I didn't want to even imagine it, but the seed of dread sprouting in the pit of my stomach was impossible to quash.

I pressed a hand against the skeleton key around my neck, the old pewter cold against my chest. I'd watched Natalya die. There had to be more to the story, but without any kind of guidance, scraps and ghosts were all I had. I needed reliable, structured access to Natalya's memories. Scrying would give me that, but Belle had barely said a word to me since we'd arrived in London.

I'd just have to take matters into my own hands.

Lake was fast asleep, and quiet, but she was a slight sleeper, so I'd have to be quieter. Tiptoeing past her in the fuzzy, cute slippers she'd lent me, I creaked open the door and started toward Belle's room. Our "dorm" was more like a round, two-story apartment with all the bedrooms located on the second level, along with a set of glass doors that led to a terrace outside. The floor up here was a wide strip of polished wood that went all the way around the curved walls, separated from the center space by an iron railing. Beyond the railings, I could see the front door, the living room, and the kitchen below in one open area on the main floor. It was a nice place, kept clean because of Lake's nagging.

"Belle?"

Before I could reach her room, I saw her through the glass doors of the terrace. She was painting. Or rather, she'd just begun to paint. Serenely, Belle considered the canvas on the easel in front of her as if she didn't know where her brush should strike first. A gentle breeze ruffled through her long, plain white dress.

I pushed open the doors carefully, almost reverently. "Um, Belle?" When she didn't answer, I bit my lip. "Do . . . do you always paint at night?"

Belle didn't look up. "Only when it's cold."

And cold it was. Even in my thick, cotton pajamas, I could feel the chill snaking up my arms. Silently, I watched Belle paint her first stroke. I still couldn't believe it; I was living in a dorm with Belle Rousseau. *Belle Rosseau*: the girl whose action figure I'd have dozens of if they actually existed. I sucked in a breath, gathering my courage.

"Belle," I said, "wh-when do you think you'll start . . . um . . . teaching me how to . . . um . . ." I forgot the word.

"Scry."

"Yeah." I rubbed the back of my head sheepishly. "Remember, Sibyl wants me to find out about Saul through this Marian person."

"I know."

Belle continued painting.

"Well . . ." I shuffled from one foot to another, not surprised, but still kind of discouraged, to see that Belle still hadn't glanced at me once. "When do we start?"

"Scrying is a very unwieldy art. I'm still considering the best way to teach you."

So never. I tried to keep from being buried under my own pessimism, but it was clear that, for some reason, Belle didn't see the matter as urgently as I did.

"Well, I do have a question, since you're here." After taking Belle's lack of response as an invitation, I leaned against the glass doors and continued. "I have been 'scrying' a bit on my own. I mean, I've been seeing things. Memories. Mostly Natalya's."

Belle's hand froze in midair. "Is that so?" She lowered her arm.

"Yeah." I couldn't help but notice the brush tremble, just slightly, in Belle's grip. "I've been getting bits and pieces of her memories."

"Natalya's memories will always be the freshest, since she was the last Effigy before you. The others before her will be more difficult to discern—like tangled yarn."

"But most of the time when I'm in Natalya's memories, it's like . . . like I'm her. And she's me." I touched my chest as I remembered my own lungs fighting for air while Natalya lay dying on the carpet. I shook my head. "I hate it."

"Because you don't have control yet."

That was probably true. Then again, it was my lack of control that had given me such speedy access to Natalya's memories in the first place—and insight into her death.

"Belle . . . there's something else."

I stopped. Voicing my theory on Natalya's death meant openly accusing the Sect of something very serious. If I told Belle, and Belle reported me to Sibyl—or worse, the Council—how fast would the next Effigy pop up to take my place?

But then, back at La Charte, Belle hadn't seemed so sure about their suicide claim either. It was worth a try. Even if Belle was super loyal to the Sect, she wouldn't turn on me. Belle wasn't like that.

"Belle, when we first met," I continued, "I mean, when we first talked, at the hotel in Brooklyn, you said you didn't believe Natalya could commit suicide." When Belle said nothing, I inhaled deeply and continued. "Like I said, I've been seeing some of her memories."

Belle's hand squeezed her paintbrush more tightly than before. "Yes, you said."

"Well . . . about Natalya's death . . ."

"I don't want to know."

"What?" I frowned. She couldn't be serious. "What do you mean—"

"What I mean is that I don't want to know." Belle's voice was quiet. "I'm not interested. At all. So please don't say another word."

"But why—"

"I said, please *don't say another word.*"

The rough edge of Belle's voice spooked me into silence. Belle let her arms dangle uselessly at her sides for a moment before finally placing her brush down with a sigh. "Maia," she said after some time. "Don't . . . don't focus on Natalya's memories. Leave them alone. I know you might think that it matters, but it doesn't. Chae Rin, Victoria, you, and I—we're each here for a specific purpose. A duty to fulfill. Your duty is to find Marian, to access *her* memories. *That* is your only goal. Don't be distracted by anything else."

It sounded almost like a plea.

"Focus on the mission at hand," Belle continued. "It's what . . . it's what Natalya would have done."

The words were calm enough, but because Belle had turned her back to me, I couldn't see her expression. My imagination filled in the blanks, forcing me to picture the same devastated eyes I'd seen during our first real meeting at La Charte.

Belle's first meeting, that is, with Natalya's pathetic replacement.

I lowered my head. "It must be weird, right? Me being here? Instead of her?"

"It's just the way things are." With light barefoot steps on the mahogany flooring, Belle walked over to the lavender settee.

Silence stretched between us.

"I was the oldest girl in the foster home," Belle said, surprising me. "Just thirteen. Wayward. Angry. Natalya found me and gave me a new purpose." Her loose blond hair shielded her face.

Belle never spoke publicly about her pre-Sect childhood. Her foster mother, Madame Bisette, had given plenty of interviews to French media about their supposedly wonderful life, but given that Belle had yet to publicly acknowledge her existence, I'd always suspected that Bisette's tales were more fiction than fact.

Natalya, on the other hand—Belle had talked about her plenty of times in interviews: a mentor who'd become like blood. And I of all people understood how important having a family was.

"My sister used to be such a fan of her," I said with a soft chuckle.

"Did she?"

For Belle Rousseau to ask even the simplest question about June, even if it was out of boredom alone . . . I couldn't believe it. My heart soared.

"Yes!" I replied, taking an excited step forward. "June—my sister—she totally worshipped both of you! She knew everything about you! All the stats!" I wanted to tell her everything. If only by some miracle June could see me do it, see me standing in front of Belle, uttering her name. "You guys . . . you and Natalya. You guys were like her heroes."

"That's her mistake, then."

Quick and efficient. Belle's sudden frigidness crushed my euphoria before it could sweep me away. And yet, as devastated as I was, I might have taken it a whole lot worse if Belle weren't so obviously trying to avoid my eyes. Belle let her body sink into the settee, twisting so she could peer over the edge of the railing and into the field. What did she see when she cast her gaze over the

thicket of trees silhouetted in the night? What was she was looking for with those eyes that had suddenly lost what little life they
had left in them?

"You should know too," Belle said, quiet as a grave. "None of us are
really heroes."

18

IT WAS A SUNNY AFTERNOON, PERFECT FOR A stroll, so stroll I did. I walked through the museum, peacefully, dreamily, like I was floating with the breeze. Squeezing through the other tourists, I passed the glass cases of butterflies and the magnificent displays of dinosaur bones with a sense of purpose. I knew exactly where I needed to go: a small shadowed archway in a forgotten corner of the building, blocked off by yellow tape. After one quick look over my shoulder, I ducked underneath it and entered the long, dark hallway.

Fear began drumming against my rib cage. I had to finish this as quickly as I could; I didn't know how much time I had left, after all, before someone eventually came for me. Once I reached the end of the hall, I punched the code into the security pad. The door dragged open with a deep groan.

"Good."

Natalya's voice. It was Natalya's voice.

Which meant that once again, I was inside one of Natalya's memories, experiencing it from inside her body.

The moment I realized it, the memory fizzled as if a fuse had shorted somewhere. Seconds later I was standing in a secret room hidden away in this nameless museum. Thick books spanned its two stories, but the fossilized exoskeleton was what drew my attention first.

Long, twisting, and serpent-like—a phantom. Its sharp wings fanned out as if prepared for flight, fastened to the ceiling with sturdy, metal wires. A phantom's skin was usually a nightmare mix of ghost and rotted flesh and skin spread too thinly over bone, but what I saw here was different. Its body was hard as crystal—no, it *was* crystal. It pricked my skin as I touched it, light dancing across its diamond-like surface. Creepy. Strange. And beautiful.

I could have stayed, entranced by it forever, but I had work to do. I moved on.

Odd-colored lamps hung from the vaulted ceiling on thin chains: massive, glowing pendants of every odd shape, dangling above my head. There were old globes strewn about the floor in between paintings that hadn't been hung yet—except one. Directly over the fireplace hung the portrait of a bearded man in a dapper frock. On his head: an arrogantly extravagant silk hat, fastened over the familiar dark curls spilling down his neck. Wild but elegant. I read the plaque beneath the portrait.

Bartholomäus Blackwell II: 1849–1910

Blackwell. From deep inside Natalya's body, I heard her chuckles, quiet in the musty air. "I should have known," Natalya whispered. I would never get used to the feeling of my own lips pushing out someone else's sounds. "They look exactly the same."

It didn't matter. I moved on to a row of books on the first floor. There were twelve of them, identical in shape and color, each bound in velvet and engraved in silver.

"The Castor Volumes," whispered Natalya. I pulled out just one, my fingers tracing the Roman numeral on the cover.

This would have to do. Looking over my shoulder, I slipped a bit of paper from my pocket. Such a silly plan, but by now I was desperate. I just hoped that Belle would understand the message.

Le maison de merde
Floorboards

I had just slipped it between the sheets when I heard the wooden floor creak behind me. With a gasp, I dropped the book, turned—

The dream ended.

I woke up, sweaty and hot beneath my covers, the end of Natalya's memory still a question.

"Rhys!"

Unlike the Effigies' dorms, the agent dorms on the west wing were dull and colorless, narrow doors cloned in rows like an assembly line. Somewhat unfair, but then so was destiny.

"Rhys?" I knocked again, more urgently. "Rhys! It's me! I need—"

The door swung open.

"Maia?"

My lips trembled shut. For maybe a good minute, I just let myself stare at him, at his thin, unbuttoned shirt open and fluttering, granting my eyes the cruel gift of his hard stomach, still wet and glistening. Oh god. A damp towel hung around his scarred neck, all askew as if he'd slung it there in a hurry.

Did he notice? He definitely noticed.

"Come on in." With a playful grin, he stepped aside to let me through. It was a painfully plain room: bed, table, chair, closet. Well, it *was* a temporary place for him; he'd decided to stay in London until the Saul thing was over. Made me wonder how he normally lived at his field post. Or at home, wherever his home was. If he even had one.

Now that I thought of it, I didn't know much about him at all. Maybe that was why I hadn't told him about Natalya's death yet.

Rhys adjusted the towel so it hung over his shoulder. The soft patter of the shower seeped in from the bathroom. "Something wrong?"

Yes. I couldn't stop staring at the black sweatpants clinging to his hips. I shook my head. "I wanted to ask something." It took me a minute to remember what.

His Adam's apple bobbed in his throat. "What about?"

Rhys was still an agent of the Sect. As much as I liked him, at the end of the day, I didn't know how he would react once I told him my doubts about Natalya's "suicide."

And yet . . .

Biting my lip, I remembered the way his hand felt, rough against my wrist as he drew me to him while Vasily and Blackwell approached. He'd done it to *protect* me. This was a guy who'd temporarily abandoned his field post in New York to look out for me—well, at least I wanted to believe it was for me and not the girl inside me.

I mean, he'd known her. Probably worked with her. Maybe they'd been close. But even if Rhys's kindness to me was rooted in his attachment to her, whatever their relationship had been, that alone only strengthened my gut feeling: I could trust him. He'd want to know if someone had killed Natalya, wouldn't he? He wouldn't spill my secrets to the wrong people; I had to believe that.

I just couldn't handle this alone. I had to trust someone.

Nervously, I drew in a breath. "It's about Natalya," I said. "I . . . I think something happened to her."

"Well, we all know that."

"No." I shut the door behind me. "I've been seeing some of her memories, even while I'm sleeping. And I—I think maybe she didn't commit suicide."

A trail of water trickled down his forearm as he squeezed the white towel in his hands. "Maia." Sighing, he sat on the desk by the wall, folding his arms. "Scrying can be unreliable, especially when you haven't been trained."

"I know, I know. I'm only seeing bits and pieces right now, but I'm serious! I think something could be really happening here."

Rhys didn't seem convinced. Sliding the towel off his shoulder, he went back to drying his hair.

"Fine," I said impatiently. "Then let me ask you this." I thought of the dream I'd just had, the secret room where Natalya had left her urgent note. "Rhys, do you know what the Castor Volumes are?"

Rhys cocked his head, water dribbling from his soaking black hair down to his chin. "The Castor Volumes? Yeah, sure I do—every agent would. Thomas Castor." He rubbed his hair. "He was one of the first Sect agents. Former employee of the East India Company. He traveled around recruiting other agents. He even found two of the first documented Effigies. Then . . . well, I guess he wrote a bunch of stuff about it." He paused. "Why?"

"And his books . . . they're in a museum, right?"

"Why?"

"Which museum?"

"*Why?* Or have you always been interested in nineteenth-century travel literature?"

I didn't like the way he was staring at me. All of the brightness usually there on his face seemed noticeably, painfully absent. Now he just looked tired and agitated, and the thought that I'd somehow caused it made me more self-conscious than it should have.

"Just curious," I said. "I'm trying to figure out what Natalya would want with them."

"Is that what you saw in your memory?" Wearily, Rhys swept the matted locks out of his face. "Don't. Your job isn't to snoop around in Natalya's memories, but to figure out what you can about 'Marian.' Don't forget that."

"I haven't!" I watched him dry his hair through narrowed eyes. "But don't you think there's something a little off about—"

"No, I don't," said Rhys shortly. "The Sect investigated and ruled Natalya's death a suicide. That's what they told us. That's what they told *me*." He shook his head. "And you're saying something else might have happened. Do you realize that you're accusing the Sect of lying? It's just ridiculous."

"But it's possible."

"It's *not*." I could tell from the growing tension in his face that he was rapidly losing his patience. "That's not the way the Sect works."

"That's not how the Sect works?" I turned to the door, my hand resting on the knob. "Is that a fact or a wish?" I mumbled.

"What do you mean by *that*?"

I faced him. "You've been with the Sect for how many years?"

Rhys narrowed his eyes. "Almost all my life."

"Exactly. All your life is a long time to be loyal to a place. I guess it's a hard habit to break." I shook my head. "I should have known."

"That's not—"

"And wasn't Natalya your friend?"

"Yes." He gritted his teeth.

"Then if there's even just the smallest chance that something could have happened to her, wouldn't you want to get to the bottom of it? Or are you so loyal to the Sect that you'd rather just toe the company line?"

"Maia!"

I'd heard him yell my name plenty of times before, but not like that. He whipped the towel from his head, and though he looked wild in his desperation for a second, it vanished with his next breath. His shoulders slumped with the exhale.

"I'm sorry." The towel loosened in his grip. "It's just . . . This is a very dangerous game you're playing, Maia, and not *just* because you, a brand-new Effigy, are accusing an international organization of covering up a murder with unreliable evidence. Scrying *itself* is dangerous. If you're not careful, you can lose yourself in the memories. And you can lose a lot more than that."

"I know that! But I can't control the memories, and the more I see, the more I—"

"Then don't see." Dropping the towel, Rhys walked up to me. His hands were large and hot against my arms. "Just forget about it," he said. "Let Belle teach you. Find Marian. But leave Natalya's memories alone. Okay?"

Leave Natalya alone. It was the second time I'd heard that plea.

I looked at him. "What are you so afraid of?"

"What?"

Carefully, I removed his hands—one, then the other. "You and Belle. You both told me to leave this alone. Why?" I searched his wickedly handsome face. "Are you afraid of what I'll see?"

Rhys's face remained unreadable even as he planted his hand on the door just above my head. The fine hair of his wet arm brushed my face. I could smell his bath soap, thick and sweet, curling from him with the heat. "Drop it. I mean it," he said, the bluntness of his words was undercut by the pleading softness in his voice.

Under any other circumstances, I might have ended up giving in, melting into him, helpless. Not today. I was tired of being jerked around. With an impatient huff, I placed a hand on his chest and pushed him away. "Fine. Whatever. Thanks for nothing."

"Wait," Rhys said, just as I gripped the doorknob.

"What is it?"

Rhys hesitated before speaking. "No matter what you think about me, I hope you know something." There was no fight in his voice as he spoke. He could barely even meet my eyes. "I'm still going to do my best to look after you. That's what I promised myself when I first met you. For Natalya's sake."

His cell phone rang. We looked at each other, frozen by the sudden buzzing from the table. Then, silently, he pulled himself away.

"Hello?"

Sighing, I left Rhys's room and started down the hall.

"Maia." Rhys swung open the door, his phone still in his hands.

"What?" I spun around. "What is it now?"

"Saul." His face turned grave. "They're ready for the first interrogation. And they want you there."

19

RHYS AND I PROMPTLY ARRIVED AT THE Research and Development department in the north wing. It was packed and busy; technicians in white lab coats whirled around, tinkering with monitors, sorting out wires, and handling medical equipment I couldn't name if I tried.

"Good, you're here," said one tech after noticing us approach. "They're just about ready to interrogate the suspect. Everyone else is already inside the observation room."

He pointed at the pristine white door at the far left side of the room. We made our way there, stepping over long tubes coiled around the floor like metal vines.

The observation room was dark, but I could see them all clearly: the men and women lined up at the back, observing the window with stern faces. Sibyl stood at the front, hovering over the technicians at the monitor. And at the center of the room . . .

My lips curled. "Vasily?" He waved at me as I approached. "What are *you* doing here?"

"I'm here to observe the interrogation on behalf of Mr.

Blackwell, who, unfortunately, is otherwise disposed. Besides," he added, "you shouldn't be too surprised to see me around these days. The Council *did* let you know that you'll be monitored closely, isn't that right?"

I shuddered at his grin. Luckily, Rhys tapped my shoulder to draw my attention away from him.

"Saul," he said, pointing at the observation window.

Through the window was a dark, domed room. Saul was caged inside some sort of chamber. Dozens of cables connected to it from machinery lining the walls, streams of metallic blue crawling up and down their lengths. Though his eyelids fluttered, they stayed mostly shut, and yet he was standing, his shoulders slumped over as if some invisible force kept him upright. They'd probably drugged him. It would make sense to keep him sedated, given what he was capable of. But it was weird. Inside the chamber he looked helpless, almost frail. Mass murderers came in all shapes and sizes, of course, but it was the vulnerability that caught me off guard.

"Maia, you're here," said Sibyl. "Good."

I couldn't tear my eyes away from the window. "Why did you want me here?"

"I want you with me during the interrogation," said Sibyl. "While his mental defenses are down, he might tell us something. Anderson, is he ready?"

"Almost," answered one of the technicians at the monitors. "He's sedated, and his abilities are being suppressed. We just have to wait for his readings to return to a steady state. Then we'll be able to wake him up."

"Abilities," said Rhys. "You mean his disappearing act?"

"Yes. It's amazing." The technician shook his head. "To think that there could be other Effigies out there . . . and with abilities extending beyond the classical elements."

"So it's true?" I stepped forward. "Saul really is an Effigy?"

"Yes, it would seem so." Sibyl folded her arms. "The technician used a dye to track his cylithium production to the pituitary gland—the same place you four produce yours. He's an Effigy. No question."

A fifth Effigy. And there could be more out there. The very idea made me ill.

"So what happens now?" asked Rhys.

"We noticed something strange during our first day of experiments," answered another technician. "He was mumbling to himself. Actually, it was more like he was *fighting* with himself."

"His accent kept switching between British and American," said another. "And there were times when we couldn't read his spectrographic signature at all."

Rhys frowned. "Spectrographic signature?"

"Cylithium is a very strange element. It's a mineral, but even though the normal human body can't produce it, it's found naturally in an Effigy's pituitary gland . . . and in phantom remains. On top of that, even though it's a solid at room temperature, we've discovered cylithium vapor existing in nature. Phantoms typically spring out of these cylithium-rich areas."

"Like ghosts." Vasily winked at me. It wasn't something I wanted to see again.

The technician nodded. "Ghosts that suddenly grow bones and flesh and skin from seemingly nothing but black smoke. There are cylithium-rich areas around the globe; human populations are typically concentrated in areas where there's a cylithium deficit, and antiphantom devices do the rest. But like I said, cylithium exists in Effigies, too—you produce your own. That's where your abilities come from."

I nodded stiffly, though I was shifting from foot to foot restlessly.

"Okay, and?" I said, impatient. "What does that have to do with any of this?"

"Regardless of the state, cylithium gives off a frequency signal like other elements: its spectrographic signature. And when it transitions into other states, it gives off a *stronger* frequency. That's what the Communications department uses to track both Effigies and phantoms."

I cocked my head, trying to process it all. "So then . . . if Saul is an Effigy, why haven't you been able to track him?"

"Exactly." Sibyl walked up to the monitors, her hawk eyes fixed on Saul. "That's the problem. Saul's been using his powers, appearing in and out of the cities he attacks. The Sect should have been able to track him. So why haven't we?"

"Perhaps he can mask his frequency," Vasily suggested.

Rhys frowned. "Is that possible?"

"At this point we have to assume that anything's possible, as uncertain as that makes me." Sibyl kept her tone level. "But his frequency comes and goes."

"Like his accent," chimed a technician. "While you interrogate him, we'll be monitoring his spectrographic signature and his brain wave activity concurrently. We might be able to figure out what's happening after we see the results."

"Two minutes until he reaches steady state," called a technician. "Keep in mind he'll still be a bit disoriented."

"Hey, Aidan." Vasily sidled up to Rhys with his hands in his pockets. "Remember the little 'waiting game' we used to play?"

Rhys didn't respond.

"Come on, you remember—during our training days in Greenland?" His flicked his head at Saul, thin lips quirked into a lopsided grin. "If you had to kill him, where would you start?"

He'd whispered it, his voice low enough to keep the conversation private, but I still heard him. I snapped my head up, shocked, watching as Rhys ignored the both of us.

"Jugular? Or would you go for one of the major arteries? I seem to recall it was one of your favorite go-to answers." When Rhys made a disgusted noise, Vasily smirked. "What? Not like we haven't had these conversations before."

"Yeah," replied Rhys. "Well, we were fucked-up twelve-year-olds then, weren't we?"

"But those were the best times."

"Stop."

Vasily chuckled, backing off just as the technicians nodded to Sibyl.

"Maia," Sibyl said, "come with me."

Gently, Rhys gripped my wrist, but his touch suddenly felt more alien than usual. "Remember, we're all right here," he told me.

"That's right, Maia." Though I didn't look to him, I could feel Vasily's eyes on me as he spoke. "We're all here."

As Rhys shot him a dark look, I slipped from his grasp without a word and followed Sibyl into the interrogation room. A wave of cold hit me the moment I walked in, and I wrapped my arms around myself. My breath dissipated into the frigid air, but Sibyl didn't seem bothered by the polar temperatures. Not now, when Saul's eyes were already fluttering open.

Here we go.

Cautioning me to stay back, Sibyl walked up to the chamber with measured steps, her heels echoing off the walls. "Saul."

It looked as if Saul would raise his head, but it flopped back down again, his chin pressed against his chest.

"Saul," Sibyl tried again.

"Wh . . . o . . ." Saul's dry, cracked lips twitched syllables I couldn't understand. The effort seemed to drain him. He stopped, breathing heavily.

"Saul!"

He twitched. "Who . . . who is that? Saul? Who is that?"

Finally I could see the blue of his eyes, but they were far less cold than the last time I'd seen them. And confused. And *scared*. As they darted from me to Sibyl, his body confined to its glass prison, he looked as helpless as if he'd been buried alive.

"Tell me your name," Sibyl asked.

"Where . . . am I? What . . . year . . . ?" Saul swallowed, peering through the glass. "Why?"

His British accent came through clearer now. It was unreal. The attitude, the *evil* was just gone. Despite having the same face, he was a completely different person.

"Your name," demanded Sibyl, more forcefully.

"Nick."

"What?"

His lips wobbled with each breath. "Nick. Hudson. I . . ." He gasped for air and gave up, letting his head hang as he gathered himself. He probably would have collapsed, but there wasn't enough room in his little prison.

Nick Hudson? I turned to the window behind us. Though I couldn't see anything but darkness on the other side, I knew everyone in the observation room could hear every word.

Sibyl crossed her arms. "Hudson. Do you have any relation to Louis Hudson?"

Louis Hudson. The man whose Argentinean grave I'd practically memorized during those excruciating minutes I'd waited for Saul.

But he was a man who'd never seen the twentieth century.

At the sound of his name, Nick lifted his head, eyes wide. "Louis. Louis? Is he here? I need to speak to him."

"Why?"

"Louis." With great effort, Nick shook his head. "No, no, I can't. He's already gone to the Americas. The railroad. No!"

I never would have imagined I'd ever see those eyes well up with tears. Despite the stringy, unwashed silver hair spilling over his face and the deep creases lining his eyes, somehow, as Nick struggled with himself, he looked every bit the boy he should have been.

"No, I can't do this alone. Not against her. She won't let me rest. God, she won't let me rest. I try to be strong, but . . ." He let out a strangled moan.

"Why are you alone, Nick?" Sibyl cocked her head. "What happened to Louis?"

"If Louis were here, it wouldn't be so hard. I wouldn't be alone . . . ," he moaned. "Brother . . ."

"Brother?" I clasped a hand over my mouth, but it was too late. Nick noticed me.

"Marian?" Even in this chill, warmth flooded Nick's face. "Marian . . . is it you? God, I've missed you." One by one the tears leaked from his eyes. "Marian . . . Marian . . ."

"What? No, my name is—"

Sibyl put up a hand to silence me. "I'll let you talk to Marian, but you need to talk to me first. Where are you from?"

"Yorkshire. But, Marian . . ." He looked at me urgently now, blinking away his tears. "She hasn't stopped looking for you. She needs something from you. She won't stop—"

Sibyl snapped her fingers to draw his focus back to her. "Who won't stop? Nick, *who* won't stop? And what does she want with Marian?"

"She needs to know where the other ones are." He pressed his hands against the glass, desperate to reach me.

"Other what?" I asked, ignoring Sibyl's glare. "She needs to know where *what* is?"

"It's why she's been murdering for so long. Sacrifice. They demand sacrifice."

"Other *what*?" I stepped forward, and though Sibyl held me back, I'd already won the battle for Nick's attention. "I don't understand. What does 'she' need Marian for? Who is 'she'? Why are you so scared of her?" My hands trembled. "What has she been killing all those people for? Why?"

"My dear *poupée*, I told you before, didn't I?" He grinned. "Isn't there something you want more than anything? Something you'd give anything for?"

His voice had changed. His accent was gone. His body no longer quivered, and his eyes were no longer wet. Despite the exhaustion in his body, despite the wear etched deep in his handsome face, graying his skin, the arrogance in his grin had returned.

"You're not Nick." Sibyl pushed me back before peering up at him. "Who am I talking to now?"

Saul tilted his head. "Not telling," he said, his voice light and teasing.

"How childish."

"Well, I am quite young." He looked down at his hands. "Did you take my ring?"

"It's safe."

"Safe?" Saul smirked. "Well, I suppose that depends on who has it now."

Sibyl's expression remained inscrutable, but one thing was certain: She wasn't at all interested in playing the games Saul so clearly loved.

"Moscow," she said. "Incheon, Bern, Brooklyn." She listed them off with her fingers.

"And others as test runs. Though Seattle did get out of hand, I admit. I certainly didn't plan on destroying the entire city. Oops."

Saul's laughter, though restrained from the effect of the drugs, still hit its mark. Sibyl's eyes narrowed to slits. "Why?"

"I could tell you that, but the question you should be asking is, *How?* All those cities. Plenty of security. How could it happen? That was the question Natalya had asked, not so long ago. But where is she now?"

Saul stared past us, at the window where members of the Sect stood and watched unseen. He sounded almost spiteful as he turned his gaze on me, lips twisted into a cruel smirk. "Tell me: Where is she now, *poupée?*"

He said nothing more.

20

"MAIA!" I'D PLUCKED THE PHONE STRAIGHT out of Lake's hand. As I clicked it off, Lake hopped off her bed. "Are you mental? That was my manager!"

I tossed the phone back to her. "I need your help."

"Yes, I can see that," Lake said as she watched me pace back and forth. She smoothed her skirt over her long legs. "Well, I could use a bit of help too—thanks for asking. This bloody training is totally screwing up with my comeback attempts. Already I've had to cancel two mall appearances, a fan signing, and a promotional guest spot on that awful American version of *Britain's Too Talented*." Sighing, Lake checked her messages. "Actually can't complain about that one—"

"Lake!" I stopped pacing. After pushing out a short, exasperated huff, I paused, pointedly, before taking the plunge. "I think someone killed Natalya."

The phone slipped from Lake's hands. "Pardon?"

"I think . . . someone killed Natalya." I watched Lake's expression carefully. "And I think it has something to do with Saul and his attacks."

Slowly, Lake slid off her bed. "Why . . . why would anyone kill Natalya? Over *Saul*?"

"Saul's an Effigy. He's a terrorist, but he's an Effigy. He's an Effigy terrorist." I tried to grasp the thoughts as they popped into my mind, but it was a bit like playing whack-a-mole. "But it's like he's got a split personality. One of them had to have been born sometime in the nineteenth century, because his brother died in the 1800s; I saw his grave in Argentina. And the other one . . . I don't know. I think that's the one that's been attacking everyone. Like, the evil one. It's like there are two people living in his head and one is super afraid of the other."

It sounded even crazier out loud. I pressed a hand against my forehead. Natalya. Marian. Each living Effigy came equipped with their entire Effigy line already programmed into their brain. Did that mean there were more dead Effigies milling about inside his consciousness?

"Maia? Oi!" Lake grabbed my shoulders and gave me a much-needed shake. "You need to relax and tell me what the bloody hell is going on in plain English!"

Though it took a lot of effort, I calmed down and explained everything as thoroughly as I could: my unstable scrying into Natalya's memories, Saul's interrogation. I told Lake as much as I could remember.

"Brilliant. Well, it's all very Jekyll and Hyde, isn't it?" Lake cocked her head. "You think they fight, the two personalities? Like over day-to-day things, like who gets to watch what on the telly and when?"

"Is that all you got from this?" I plopped down onto Lake's bed with a groan.

"It's just so *mental*."

"Tell me about it." I remembered what the technicians had told us after the interrogation had ended. "The techs explained it this way," I said. "When we use our powers, we send out these radio frequencies that the Sect can pick up on. Saul can hide his, but only when one of his personalities is dominant—the mean one." I thought back to his vicious grin and shuddered. "He said something about Natalya, too. Like he knew something about her. But what do they have to do with each other? I can only get bits and pieces from her memories. . . ."

"I don't know about you scrying right now, Maia. I think you should be careful." Lake pulled up a stool at our dresser and crossed her legs. "I mean, I personally wouldn't know; I don't scry usually . . . or, well, ever. But isn't scrying pretty dangerous to do while you're not, you know, trained up to handle it?"

"It's hard to control. I can't really help it." With my head on the pillow, I grabbed Lake's kitty alarm clock off of the night table and raised it above my head. "Last night I saw a memory while I was asleep. Natalya went to some secret room somewhere in a museum."

"Ooh, was it hidden behind a bookshelf?"

"*No*," I answered shortly, annoyed. "But there was a bookshelf involved. Natalya hid a note for Belle in one of the books. She looked really anxious, like she thought someone might be following her."

"And you think the Sect might have been involved?"

Above me, the kitty clock's beady black eyes stared at me incredulously as the second hand ticked away. "I know it sounds stupid. The Sect told everyone Natalya committed suicide, but I clearly saw her die, and she definitely didn't do it herself."

"You see who did?"

I lowered my arms. "No. But during the interrogation, Saul said

Natalya was investigating him before she died. And . . ." I shook my head. "I don't know. Why would the Sect lie about her suicide?"

"If she was killed, the murderer could have made it look like a suicide and fooled the Sect. But you said Natalya's own dad warned you not to trust them." Sighing, Lake tapped her rainbow-colored nails on the dresser table. "Oh!" She flapped her hands. "The note!"

I sat up. "What?"

"The note! You said Natalya put a note for Belle in a book in a secret museum room, which was regrettably not hidden behind a bookshelf. You remember what it said?"

Pulling my knees up to my chest, I buried my head in them and thought. "Something French." I squeezed my eyes shut. *"Morte? Merde. Merde . . ."*

La maison du merde

Floorboards

"La maison du merde!"

Lake cocked an eyebrow. "The house . . . of shit?"

"Is that what it means?" I gripped my knees. "It sounds familiar, but . . ."

"This can be easily solved."

Lake whipped out her phone and started typing. *"La maison du merde,"* she repeated as she swiftly clicked the letters. "Another key word or words: Belle Rousseau? Let's see what we get."

I hopped off the bed to see the screen. One of the first hits was a short clip of an interview Belle had done four years ago, when she was barely fifteen years old. It looked familiar, but then I'd seen so much Belle-related media throughout my years as a shameless fangirl I could barely keep it all straight anymore.

Lake clicked the link. It was a press conference the Sect had called to announce that Belle would be part of the opening ceremonies of the Olympic Games in France—a mind-blowing personal request from the country's own president.

"Belle," said one very eager reporter in the room, "tell me: What do you think your family would say if they could see you now?"

Belle frowned. Even as a kid, her glare could freeze hell. "Family?" In her mouth it sounded like a swear word.

"U-uh. Yes." I couldn't blame the guy for looking nervous. "At your foster home?"

Belle scoffed. "Ah, *la maison du merde*. I don't live there anymore, so luckily I don't have to care what they'd say."

"Ouch," said Lake.

"That's right. I almost forgot!" I slapped my forehead. "She made a few headlines in France with that one. I read about it a long time ago."

"She was adopted or something, wasn't she? Sounds like she's got some major issues about it."

Clearly. "Floorboards . . . Natalya must have put something underneath the floorboards of Belle's old foster home. She grew up near Paris, didn't she? I mean, where else, right?"

After crossing the room, I reached into my drawer, under a pile of loose papers, and pulled out the skeleton key. As the string dangled from my middle finger, I gave Lake a deadly serious look. "We need to get into that foster home. We need to get to the bottom of this."

"Looks like." Lake tapped her bottom lip with her index finger. "And lucky for you, I might have a way to do it."

"A field trip?" Cheryl looked up from Lake's detailed proposal, unimpressed, if her bespectacled scowl was any indication. "Maia's in the middle of training."

"We know that, right, Maia?"

After a nudge from Lake, I nodded very quickly.

Cheryl leaned back in her office chair. "And we're in the middle of dealing with an international terrorist, which will likely require some kind of involvement from, again, Maia."

"We know that, too." Lake patted my shoulder. "Quite the little star, isn't she?"

"And you want us to travel all the way to Paris for a photoshoot?"

"I already got my agent to set it all up. I've worked with *Teen Vogue* before. They're positively *salivating* at the opportunity to get all four of us. All four Effigies!"

"You've already set it up? You should have checked with us first!" Cheryl gave a very disapproving cluck of her tongue—very school-marmy despite being relatively young-ish. "I just don't know if it's appropriate."

Lake leaned over Cheryl's desk and plucked the multipage, hastily stapled, typo-ridden document out of her hands. "See these quotes?" She tapped the page. "CNN, BBC, CBC—all these news sources have been talking about the Sect recently. Here, let me read one." She cleared her throat. "'At the heart of the growing public anxiety surrounding international security lies the Sect, which, despite its nearly two centuries of existence, has yet to solve its issues with transparency.' Hear that?"

"Yes, yes, I hear you." Cheryl rubbed her brow wearily.

"And there's more. 'At stake for the Sect is trust. Bringing in a suspected terrorist, but being unwilling to share information with the rest of the world, has left many uneasy.'"

Cheryl sighed. "This has always been the issue for the Sect. We're an organization sworn to protect the world from phantoms. Other countries have caught up in terms of antiphantom technology, but what they don't have is you." She pointed at the two of us. "Walking, talking biological warheads. It's always freaked them out, especially during the Great War, with all the different countries trying to recruit Effigies."

Yeah, I remembered that from my World History class. "I thought the Sect swore never to involve themselves in nonphantom conflicts?"

"Which frustrated them even more. There was always a worry that the Sect could one day turn against the world, especially as the organization went international. That's why the Council signed the Greenwich Accords as a promise to the nations. Unfortunately, people don't pay attention in history class, and these pundits"—Cheryl took Lake's proposal—"their entire careers depend on people's laughably short memories. There's zero point in indulging any of them."

Lake and I exchanged nervous glances as Cheryl tossed the proposal aside, next to a very scarily large pile of paperwork. So this was what she did when she wasn't following Sibyl around.

Lake tried again. "Thing is, you might say there's no point in indulging in them, but right now they've got the public by the nose. It's just the way it is. Trust me, I know what it's like. . . . Fighting the tide of public opinion isn't exactly a battle you can win by shrugging your shoulders. Who knows where it can all lead?"

"And you think parading yourself around like some girl group is going to change things?"

"Well, I mean, it depends on the type of girl group. I was in one, so I should know." Winking, Lake propped herself up on Cheryl's desk, her smile sly. "People want the sparkly, the cool . . . the girls you can kind of relate to even though they're so pretty and posh. PR's all about the face you show to the public. Which face would *you* want the Sect to show the world? I mean, right now they've got a shadowy council no one ever sees."

"Blackwell's their representative," said Cheryl.

"But people barely see him, either, except in diplomatic meetings or whatever. But we—me, Maia, Belle, Chae Rin." Straightening up, she linked arms with me, pulling me close. "We're young! We're pretty! Me and Belle already have lovely fans, and Maia and Chae Rin, well . . ." She glanced at me. I grinned with my teeth. "We can work on it. Think of what you can do for the Sect's public image just by putting us out there. It's bulletproof!"

Lake sounded like a greasy snake oil salesman pitching a crappy movie to some cigar-smoking, money-hungry Hollywood exec, and it might have been working.

"I understand what you're saying, but the Sect went through something like that before with the Effigies who fought during the Seattle Siege. Didn't turn out too well."

The "Seattle Siege Dolls." Back in the sixties, when people still used "dolls" as a patronizing nickname for Effigies. Back when Seattle had spent seven days under siege by phantoms. A siege I now knew had been Saul's "test run."

The Effigies had done their best, fighting battered and broken in a never-ending nightmare. Munich's Heidi Krantz, Allison Whitney from upper-class Detroit, Roselyn Alvarez from Mexico City, and Abena Owusu from Accra, Ghana. She was the youngest. She fought the hardest.

Though Seattle had to be given up to the phantoms, the girls had done all they could and survived the fight together. It was the first time Effigies had ever fought as a team instead of as singular agents—the moment when the image of four girls battling together side by side became part of our public memory as a potent symbol.

The power of it even ended up launching a short-lived pop cultural phenomenon.

And yet it was Allison who cashed in the most, despite having done the least. PTSD took Heidi and Roselyn, and both girls eventually shut themselves away from the living. Abena shunned the spotlight, struggling through her commitments as an Effigy for the rest of her short life. Allison's ghost-pale face and fairy-tale dark hair made her an American favorite, but her reign as a public darling ended fast when Abena revealed to the whole world that Allison had spent most of the siege looking for new places to hide, even when it meant leaving people to die.

"People wanted heroes, and they got four broken dolls instead." Cheryl tightened the band around her auburn braid. "In a way, it ended up *damaging* the Sect's image."

"But we can be different! We just need to start small and smart! A little interview and a pretty photoshoot can be just what the Sect needs to start repairing some of the damage. Come on, please?" Lake clasped her hands together. "You'll talk to Sibyl, right? Please, please?"

"But Maia's training—"

"I'll train her on the plane!"

Cheryl deflated. She knew this wasn't a battle she could win. "Fine."

Lake and I decided against a high five, but grinned devilishly nonetheless.

"Oh my god, are you playing *Metal Kolossos II*?" The heat rushed to my head once I recognized the familiar characters.

"The Lost Colony." Chae Rin shifted her toothpick to the other side of her mouth as she clicked away at her keyboard.

Lake and I had found her sitting on the floor at the foot of her bed underneath a blanket pulled up just enough so she could see what she was doing. *MKII* was an old game—well, three years, so old by video game standards. Despite not having played it in a while, I knew it inside and out on account of having shut myself in with June for several days to finish it.

All the lights in Chae Rin's room were off except for one standing lamp in the corner, but its weak light didn't do much by way of illumination. Certainly not as much as the constant barrage of flashes from Chae Rin's laptop screen.

"Looks like you're already halfway through," I said. "Did you find the Old Sage yet? Which emulator are you using?" I squatted down next to her. "Oh, I'm super good at this level. Do you need help? Because I can—" Chae Rin batted my hand away the second it strayed too close to her keyboard.

After flicking on the main light, Lake stepped tentatively inside the room, closing the door behind her. With a grimace, she looked around at the takeout containers strewn about the floor and the dirty laundry hanging off the table fan.

"Lovely setup you have here," she said, carefully avoiding the dirty spoons on the floor. "Anyway, Chae Rin, we've got something to tell you. We're going to need your help on this."

"Oh?"

I tore my eyes away from the pretty HD graphics and focused on the task at hand. The plan was simple. The first step was convincing Cheryl to convince Sibyl to let us go to France. Assuming that worked, after getting to the hotel, we'd make up an excuse and check out Belle's old foster home. Then we'd create a diversion, sneak off to find Belle's room, and look underneath the floorboards. Since a crowbar made for a pretty conspicuous accessory, bringing Chae Rin made sense . . . as long as she didn't put a hole in the floor.

Luckily, telling Chae Rin about the plan didn't take as long as we thought it would.

"Yeah, I can see someone killing Natalya." She shrugged, still focused on her laptop screen as Lake and I exchanged incredulous looks. "You know, sometimes, when I was in Quebec, it felt like there was something watching me . . . or stalking me, or something."

"Stalking?"

With a sigh, Chae Rin finally paused her game and slid the covers off of her head. "I never saw him," she said, stretching out her back before standing. "At first I thought it was a fanboy or something, but maybe it was an Informer—you know, those specialized agents who shadow sketchy Effigies and bring the info back to the Sect. Not that *I'm* sketchy." She stopped. "Okay, I'm a bit sketchy, obviously. I'm not surprised that the Sect would order an Informer to watch me while I'm suspended, but then, my phantom whispering wasn't in any of the reports, so that's sketchy in and of itself. If I really was being watched, then either that Informer didn't do his job, or he had another agenda."

I sat on her bed, though not before brushing away the empty protein bar wrappers. "Do you think someone from the Sect might have been following Natalya around?"

Chae Rin nodded. "You said she looked scared in the memory you saw, right? Kept looking over her shoulder? Plus she had that creepy ring in her jewelry box— the one I gave to Guillaume."

Lake frowned. "Who?"

"Chae Rin's old circus boss," I answered. The one currently missing a finger. "I don't think Natalya knew what the ring could do. If she did, she wouldn't have left it in such a stealable place."

"But she got it somehow." Chae Rin grabbed a can of soda off her dresser and took a sip. "Which means she probably *was* investigating Saul. If her death has anything to do with it, then we have to find out why." Chae Rin looked down at the can in her hand. "I owe her that."

A wave of relief washed over me. Natalya's death wasn't easy to bear, but now, finally, I was starting to feel the burden chip away, bit by bit. Lake and Chae Rin—I should have trusted them earlier, gone to them earlier. It was a mistake I wouldn't make again.

The longer the interrogations with Saul went on, the louder the grumbling was from international media. A few days after Lake's impromptu presentation, Sibyl finally gave us the go-ahead. The shoot was set for the end of the week, though my mind was so preoccupied with the plan that I barely had room to feel amazed over my impending modeling debut. Seeing Belle agree to go amazed me more.

"It's fine," Belle told us without the slightest inflection in her voice. "I don't care one way or the other."

Chae Rin and Lake exchanged glances from the kitchen table as Belle left the dorm.

"Enthusiastic as always." Chae Rin went on buttering her croissant.

Lake waited for Belle to shut the door before leaning in. "So, about Belle," she said in a low voice as if Belle could be listening on the other side of the door. "Shouldn't we tell her about the whole Natalya thing? The message is for her, after all."

I swirled the spoon in my cereal before letting it drop against the bowl with a *clang*. "No," I decided with a sigh. "Not yet. The last time I tried to bring it up, Belle flipped out. She didn't even let me get a word out. She just did not want to know about any of it. Natalya's death is still really fresh for her. Painful. I know . . ." I stopped. I knew what it was like to flinch at the very sound of the name of a lost loved one. "I'm worried that if we tell her everything now, if we tell her what this whole trip is about, then she'll refuse to go with us. And if she refuses to go, it'll be that much harder to get into her old house."

"Let's be real here. It's way more serious than that." Chae Rin swallowed her mouthful of bread before elaborating. "Natalya and Belle both dedicated their lives to the Sect. If Belle finds out that Natalya was killed and the Sect is covering it up or, worse, had something to do with the murder, who knows how she'll react? Like, what if she freaks out and just slaughters the shit out of everyone?" She shuddered. "Let's tread carefully on this one. We figure out what's going on first. Then we can decide what we're going to do about it."

A knock on the dorm door. We looked at each other.

I got up. "Stay there. I'll get it." Setting aside my orange juice, I rushed to the door.

"Rhys?"

"Uh, hi." Rhys leaned against the door frame, the definition of his arms and hardened abs well hidden inside his ridiculous fuzzy sweater. "Can . . . we talk?"

My heart gave an awkward thump in my chest when I said yes. I hadn't spoken to him since Saul's first interrogation, and I still couldn't forget his particularly disturbing conversation with Vasily.

"The door's real thin," said Chae Rin as they left the kitchen and started upstairs, her mouth full of bread, "so if you make out we'll know."

After tossing her the side eye, I shut the door behind me and cleared my throat. "What do you want?"

"Your trip to Paris on Friday . . ." He shifted. "I guess I'm just letting you know that I'm coming with you." Rhys avoided my eyes as he told me.

Ignoring the nervous jolt in my heart, I wrapped my thin sweater tighter around myself. "Why?"

"They asked me to come along. Maybe they see me as your personal guard or something." He laughed. "I feel so typecast."

After everything, I still liked the sound of his laugh. But Rhys wasn't exactly ready to jump on the Natalya-Sect conspiracy train. He'd been with the Sect his entire life. Of course he was loyal to them—fearful of them. Doing this with him on my back would only make things more difficult, and yet something in me wouldn't let me refuse. I didn't think I could anyway.

Rhys looked as if he was gathering his courage. Stuffing his hands inside his pants pockets he finally met my eyes. "Maia," he started, "about before: I'm really sorry—"

"You don't have to say anything," I told him. "It's okay. You don't have to talk about what you don't want to talk about."

"Right." Rhys smiled at me. There was something dangerously alluring about Rhys's eyes, dark and boyish at the same time. I wasn't naïve. I knew I was looking into something heavy, something potentially dangerous. I could understand why Rhys would try to steer me off that path, but there must have been more to it than that. He was hiding something.

"You know, there's a lot you don't know about me," he said.

"Well, obviously. I just met you."

Rhys chuckled. "Yeah. Well, I just wanted you to know, in case you got the wrong idea, that I'm not like him," he said. "Like Vasily."

Vasily. No, I could never think of Rhys that way. They were completely different. Then again, it was also true that I knew very little about him—about his past in the Sect, about his training side by side with a guy who'd grow up to one day joyfully slice off a man's finger.

"Everything's all good. Just make sure you pack plenty of bow ties for Paris." Playfully, I punched his arm—which, admittedly, was cheesy, but it was the only thing I could think of to ease the tension between us. "I hear the French love that sort of thing."

"Oh, I've sworn them off."

As he gave me a gentle smile, I sincerely hoped my hunch about Natalya's death—and the Sect—turned out to be wrong after all.

21

"AH, PARIS." BELLE WINCED AT LAKE'S AFFECTED French accent, wincing again when Lake twirled, her double-breasted red coat and polka-dot skirt swirling with her. "How I've missed you!"

I couldn't blame Lake for the enthusiasm. It was probably all in my excitable little tourist head, but even the air was different in France. The moment we touched down, I felt it, relishing the foreign air that slipped down my throat as we traveled through the chilled airport terminal.

A van took us through the narrow, twisting streets of Paris. I rolled down my window, the late-afternoon sun a delight on my face. There was a different energy here. A nervous kind of excitement settled in my bones despite the lingering jet lag. I could hear wisps of French spoken by the women and children strolling down the sidewalks, by the waiters scribbling new menus on the chalkboards outside their cafés, and by the men who threw smoking cigar butts into the gutters outside bars.

The narrow street emptied into the wider avenues of central Paris, tall buildings zipping in and out of our view. Taking out my cell phone, I leaned through my window and snapped a shot of the rolling river sparkling under the sun: La Seine, or so my guidebook told me. As we passed, a white ferry pulled at least a hundred tourists underneath a magnificent bridge carved in gaping arches.

My lips parted. The bridge. The bridge itself was an antiphantom device. It must have been Paris's equivalent of a Needle. Though the design was very different, I could tell it was an APD by the engine core cutting through the center. Electrical sparks flew from the motor's heart, gliding down the tracks along the bridge as the core's clockwork gears clinked and shifted.

I checked my guidebook. The Pont Saint-Michel was outfitted as an antiphantom device in the early sixties, shortly after the Paris massacre of 1961. Maybe it was more a cathartic move than anything else—turning a site that had seen so much death into a monument to the protection of life.

"Pretty, isn't it?" whispered Lake next to me. "Ugh, wouldn't it just be the perfect place to have the photo shoot?"

Chae Rin scoffed behind her. "The shoot's tomorrow, right? Personally, I don't really care where they take the pictures, just as long as they don't put me in anything stupid."

Said the circus performer.

We reached the hotel and went up to the seventh floor, once again bought out by the Sect for privacy. Thankfully, no one knew we were in town, and our hotel, being one frequented by the international elite, was well versed in the principles of discretion, so we didn't need to worry about getting mobbed by the press.

At any rate, now that we were in France, we were a step closer to fulfilling the plan, but there was one key part that still needed to be sorted: Belle. Steeling our nerves, Chae Rin, Lake, and I traveled down the hall and knocked on her door.

"Belle?"

Belle opened the door and let us in. In a white tank top and yoga pants, she looked ready to hit the gym, which probably explained the pair of little weights on the table next to the television.

"What is it?" Belle flipped her ponytail out of her shirt and headed to the windows.

Chae Rin pushed me forward a little too hard; I hopped three steps and nearly crashed into the bedpost.

"Oh, I was just wondering." I shifted my back painfully. "You grew up near Paris, didn't you?"

Without looking back, Belle stretched out her neck. "Why?"

I darted a quick glance to Lake, who not-so-discreetly spurred me on. Damn, why was I the one who had to do it? "Since we're close by," I said, "I thought it might be . . . uh, k-kind of nice to visit your old foster home!"

I giggled nervously as Belle stared at me. Clearly, this was going to be a tough sell, but I also knew it'd be much easier to get into a stranger's home if we could use the old *I used to live here, and I was just wondering if I could have a look around again* con.

"Visit my old home," Belle repeated in a toneless voice. "All four of us."

I glanced at the other girls again before nodding. "Why not? We're close by."

Belle rolled her eyes with a quiet sigh before turning her back to us.

"Might be a good opportunity for a bit of Effigy bonding," Lake tried as Belle began stretching her arms above her head. "I mean, since we're all here?"

Belle went very quiet, which meant that she was either really pissed off or lost in thought. Hopefully, it wasn't the former. "And you're all just so interested in my childhood."

"Not really," Chae Rin mumbled under her breath before getting a sharp nudge in the ribs from Lake.

"Maia wanting to go, I would have bought, but you two? Please." Belle's hands found her hips as she turned and leaned back against the eggshell-white curtains veiling her window. "You three should have thought this through a bit more, yes?"

I deflated. She was right, of course, but the lie was worth a shot. So plan A was a bust. The alternative was definitely riskier, but we didn't really have a choice now. We needed to get inside that house.

I'd have to word this very carefully.

"Look," I said. "I know you didn't want to hear about . . . about Natalya's memories."

Belle's hands slowly slid off her hips.

"But," I continued quickly, "we think she left something for you in your old foster home. I dreamed about it. We just want to know what it is. It seemed really important."

"She . . . she left something for me?" Confusion passed over Belle's flushed face.

I nodded. "In secret. Trust me, she really wanted you to find it."

Belle lowered her head but didn't say a word.

"Come on, Belle," said Chae Rin. "I get that the whole Natalya thing is a sore spot for you, but do you really think you should ignore this?"

Belle looked up and locked eyes with me. "Tell me the whole dream."

I did, explaining it in as much detail as I could recall. By the end, Belle was sitting at the foot of the bed, hunched over with her arms propped up against her knees.

"The Castor Volumes," she whispered.

Lake cocked her head. "What?"

"One of the last conversations I had with Natalya before she . . ." With a sharp gasp, Belle swallowed the next word. "A month ago, I planned on visiting the National Museum in Prague. It's where the original Castor Volumes are kept. I know what's in them, for the most part, but I've never had a chance to actually read them. There was one volume in particular I was interested in. I told Natalya I was planning to go during the last three days of March, but I never ended up doing it."

"So Natalya hid that message for you thinking you'd be there," said Chae Rin.

"Why not just meet me and tell me in person?"

I remembered rushing through the museum in Natalya's body, navigating the halls with a single focus. I remembered the rush of relief after leaving the note for Belle in the book, the kind of relief you got after crossing an item off of a very long, very important to-do list. And through it all, Natalya had known she was being followed.

"It's not that she didn't want to," I said quietly. "Maybe she couldn't."

I hesitated. Chae Rin was right: We still had no idea how Belle would react if we told her about Natalya's death. Belle's pain was still too raw; it was there clear as day, darkening the confusion creasing her beautiful face. For now we had to focus on getting inside Belle's old room, but convincing her was easier said than done.

"I just don't understand," Belle said. "Why that house? Why *there*?" It was hard not to notice the slight tremor of Belle's hand as she ran her fingers through her hair. "Why would she want me to go back there knowing . . . ?"

Belle's lips snapped shut. She shook her head and said nothing more.

"Belle." With cautious steps, I walked up to her. "I know there are a lot of questions right now. Let's just go there first, and we can figure it out later."

"Who knows," Lake added with a calming, sweet smile. "It could turn out to be nothing. But it's worth a quick look, isn't it?"

Belle looked at the three of us for a long time. Finally, she straightened up. "Yes." Sucking in a deep breath, she nodded. "It's . . . it's worth a look."

I would have felt a bit easier if I'd heard even the slightest bit of conviction in her voice. But maybe it didn't matter. Now that we had Belle's consent, all the pieces were in place.

The plan was a go.

The sun was already dying. With the photo shoot scheduled for tomorrow morning, the clock was ticking. We had to go now, but Rhys wouldn't be left behind.

"Sorry, but Agent Langley asked me to look after you guys." He zipped up his coat before shutting the door to his room. "Or did you guys think you could give me the slip?"

"Never," mumbled Chae Rin.

"Hey, I'm giving up a decent night alone with my pay-per-view for this," he said as he passed her. He sighed. "Why is it that every time I have a chance to watch *Godzilla vs. Hedorah* in French, it slips away? Am I cursed?"

"*Godzilla vs. Hedorah*?" I whipped around. "Oh my god, I love that movie!"

"Really?"

"It's literally a masterpiece!"

"Right?" Rhys's full lips quirked into a silly, boyish grin. "And people say it's one of the worst ones!"

"Fools."

"Excuse me, geek squad?" Chae Rin waved a hand to get our attention. "Save it for the car ride."

As Rhys turned around with a chuckle and left for the elevators, Chae Rin poked me.

"Sect Boy coming along makes things a bit dicey," she whispered. "We're gonna have to keep him distracted somehow. Remember, we still don't know where this is all gonna lead. The fewer people who know about this, especially *Sect* personnel, the better."

My smile disappeared. Not like I forgot my first disastrous attempt to broach the Natalya topic with Rhys. I knew he didn't mean any ill, but I had to see where this went first before going to Rhys again . . . if I did at all.

I responded with a solemn nod.

We drove over to Gisors, a satellite town of Paris protected by the bridge. The Pont's antiphantom signal wasn't as strong out here. The town probably had a lower-level APD picking up the slack, not to mention a few Sect field agents living in town just in case.

Belle's foster home was one of the many town houses at the center of the community. I didn't know what to expect when Belle knocked on the door, but I *had* assumed that Belle would at the very least *say* something once it opened to the emotional face of a middle-aged woman.

"Belle?" The woman reached for Belle's face, tears budding on her lashes.

"Madame Duval." Flinching at her touch, Belle said a few more words I couldn't understand, but then I didn't really need to; even in French, her greeting felt cold and emotionless. The woman smiled nonetheless.

"These are my colleagues," Belle said in English, gesturing to the rest of the group.

Colleague. I hid a smile. Definitely an upgrade from internet stalker.

Luckily, the woman's enthusiasm extended to us, too. She stepped back with a welcoming sweep of her arms. "Please, please come in!"

The house carried the faint smell of mildew. I could see its age in the worn plaster. Duval obviously hadn't been expecting company—there were still filthy dinner plates in the sink, a dirty kitchen table, and a floor littered with broken toys.

"I'm so sorry about the mess." She dried her hands on the apron tied around her long waist. Her skirt swished as she scurried through the kitchen in old slippers. "And the noise," she added because the television was blaring from the living room.

"Madame Duval," Belle started, but Duval was too excited to let her finish.

"I cannot believe you've come back, Belle." She cleared the kitchen table. "It has been so long. Please, all of you sit down. Let me make you something to eat."

As Belle stepped carefully across the rug, her gaze followed the framed pictures on the wall, all of them of children. I scanned them too, looking for Belle, but I didn't find her.

"Where is Madame Bisette?" Belle asked, her voice strained.

In the living room, an old man watched television from his wheelchair. At the sound of the name, he gave a quick grunt, but didn't turn. Duval, on the other hand, dropped the cloth in her hand and looked up, shocked. "You didn't know? Belle, she died almost two years ago."

"Who's that?" Lake asked as she unbuttoned her coat.

"A friend of mine. She used to take care of the children here." After stooping down to pick up the cloth she'd dropped, Duval went to the cupboards for plates. "Years ago, when I was still living in Paris, I would visit from time to time. When she died, Papa and I moved here. Oh, Belle, it would have been so wonderful if you could have seen her one last time. She always spoke so fondly of you!"

Belle's lips curled, and for a second I thought she might snarl a response. Anyone who could refer to her old foster home as "shit" probably wouldn't have nice things to say about the lady who used to run things. Luckily, Belle followed the old dictum and said nothing at all, but she couldn't disguise her anger; her stone grimace had already given it away.

I heard soft footsteps coming down a flight of steps behind the wall. Three small children rounded the corner. As soon as they saw Belle, they latched on to Duval's long skirt, speaking excitedly in French. Duval laughed brightly.

"Ah, this is Charlotte, Claudine, and Jean. They've heard so much about you, Belle!"

One of the two girls ran up to Belle and, grabbing her hand, began babbling in French. I didn't have to know the language to understand that the girl was utterly starstruck. Her little body looked as if it would burst from the excitement.

I grinned. The girl's bright eyes spoke volumes.

"Claudine is just saying that she sleeps in Belle's room now," said Duval. Chae Rin nudged me. "She collects everything about Belle! She is very happy to see her."

Despite the little girl's zeal, Belle stood there awkwardly, listening but responding only with curt nods. She must have made a point to spend her entire life steering clear of the presence of children, because she seemed thoroughly unable to relate to the one in front of her.

"This is a tad awkward," Rhys said. He really didn't have to. He checked his watch before tapping my shoulder. "How long are you guys planning on staying again?"

The sun was swiftly retreating. We needed to get up to Belle's room fast.

"Madame Duval," Belle said.

"*Oui?*" Duval asked slowly, her voice vexed with apprehension. "Belle?"

Belle stayed silent for too long. Then, finally: "Are you hurting this girl?"

A sudden silence followed Belle's shocking question. Duval almost dropped her cup.

"*Pardon?*" sputtered the woman.

Belle didn't have to ask again.

"I am *not!*" Duval looked utterly gutted. "I would never!"

Belle knelt in front of the girl and asked her something in French. When the girl shook her head, Belle repeated the question to Charlotte and Jean, who responded the same. Each child looked genuinely surprised and confused, which made Belle and Duval's elderly father, wholly uninterested in the world outside his TV, the only ones inside the house who weren't.

"Belle," said Duval, frozen in shock. "Why? Why would you—"

"Why wouldn't I?" Belle faced her. "Madame Duval, do you really not know? But then, Bisette never missed a chance to sell her lies. . . . I suppose you simply bought them."

Duval carefully set her cup down on the counter. "Belle, what . . . what do you mean?"

Despite every interview Bisette had given the French media, Belle had never even mentioned the woman, even when asked. Her silence spoke volumes, but I never imagined it would be this bad. And Belle still had so much anger stored up inside her. She shook with it.

"Wayward," "angry"—the words Belle had used to describe her pre-Effigy self. And now that she was here in this house again, she could barely stand the sight of the pictures on the wall: pictures of children happier than she ever was.

Belle shut her eyes and turned from us. "I'm sorry. I . . . It was a mistake coming here." Without a second glance to the children, she started toward the door.

"Belle, wait!" I tried to grab her shoulder, but she evaded me with a quick shift of her body.

"I'm sorry," Belle repeated, more softly this time. "Whatever you need to do, I'm sure you can do it without me."

"That's not what I . . ."

"Need to do?" Rhys repeated.

Chae Rin, Lake, and I exchanged a glance. We'd already made it inside the house. We couldn't make our grand exit now, not before checking Belle's old floorboards. As concerned as I was for her, I couldn't get caught up in her pain right now.

"We still want to have a look around, if that's okay with you," said Lake quickly.

Rhys raised an eyebrow but said nothing.

Belle lowered her head. "I'll . . . be in town. Call me when you're finished."

And then, to Duval and the children's utter devastation, she strode out the door.

As they stood there, stunned into silence, Rhys nudged me. "You really want to stay?"

I thought fast. "We can't just leave them like this." Then, to Duval, "I'm sorry about Belle." I walked up to her. "I guess she's still working stuff out. It has nothing to do with you."

The woman nodded, but shakily.

"We'll stay for dinner!" Lake turned to me and Chae Rin. "Right?"

"Absolutely," I said.

Rhys looked baffled when Chae Rin nodded too. "I'm game."

"Also . . ." Lake bent over as she spoke to Claudine, her hands on her knees. "It would be really cool if you guys could show us around. You said you sleep in Belle's old room, right?"

Claudine blinked.

Claudine, like the little fangirl-in-training she was, absolutely jumped at the chance to give a group of Effigies a tour of her house while Duval cooked dinner. Belle's old room was behind the staircase at the end of the hall, third door on the left. I eyed the wooden floorboards as we walked in.

"Claudine?" Lake bent over again, smiling. "Why don't you come into the kitchen with me?"

Claudine couldn't understand, so Lake offered the little girl her hand instead. She took it. "I can buy you two some time," Lake told me and Chae Rin, "but you'll have to hurry."

I nodded. "Thanks. But what about Rhys?" He'd chosen to stay with Duval to smooth things over, and before he knew it, he was helping her cook.

"Don't worry. I'll keep them all busy. Didn't I ever tell you about that time I was positively *assaulted* by French paparazzi? It's quite a long story." Winking, Lake pulled Claudine along.

"Okay, let's do this," said Chae Rin.

But just as I started to close the door, I stopped and looked around the door frame. It was quiet, but I was sure I'd heard it: a soft, almost indecipherable *thump* coming from the next room. Jean and Charlotte were with Duval in the kitchen. Were there more kids in there?

"What are you doing?" Chae Rin waved me over. "Come on. Let's just get this over with."

Hesitantly, I shut the door. "I feel so dirty doing this."

"No point getting cold feet now." Chae Rin knelt on the ground and put her ear close to the floor. "Besides, we'll put everything back the way it was." She began tapping the wood. "If Natalya really did put something in the floor, that spot should be hollow. Quit standing around like a moron and get down here."

Stifling a few choice insults, I followed suit, getting on my knees. "Ugh, I feel like I'm in an old spy movie."

Chae Rin looked me up and down. "Not in that basic-ass sweat-shirt, you don't."

"What's wrong with my sweatshirt?"

"Just keep looking."

Chae Rin and I moved along the floorboards, tapping and listening.

"Man," I complained, "where is it?"

"I don't know. Why don't you go ask—wait!" By the window, on the other side of Claudine's bed, Chae Rin lifted the rug and tapped again. Hollow.

"Be careful," I warned. "At the end of this we have to put it all back."

Chae Rin rolled her eyes. "I know, I know."

It was one of those rare moments I was actually thankful for Chae Rin's violent strength. She had to restrain herself to keep from ruining the floor, but she managed to yank out two boards cleanly, setting them aside behind her.

"Holy crap," Chae Rin said, peering inside. "You were totally right."

Nestled deep in a hollow hole was what looked like a cigar box.

"It looks like an antique," I said. Handcrafted, too, as evidenced by the beautiful carvings. But it was also dirty. Soil clung to the dark wood, trickling off when I turned it on its side. I ran my hand along the top over the engraving of a serpent curled in a circle, long enough to eat its own tail. But I couldn't open it. The box was fastened by a brass keyhole.

Keyhole.

"I can't believe it." I reached inside my sweatshirt and lifted the necklace over my head to reveal the skeleton key. "No way."

It was a perfect fit. My heart raced as I lifted the box's lid, but the moment it came off I yelped; a beetle crawled out of the box, scurrying across my fingers until I flung it off. Chae Rin squashed it with her hand.

"Let's not infest the poor girl's room," she said before grabbing a tissue off of Claudine's desk and wiping her hand. "So . . ." She leaned over. "What's in the box?"

A lot of things, and unfortunately, none of them made any sense. An old pocket watch, its rusted chain long since broken. A pair of dice. Some silk ribbons and pearl buttons. Just random stuff.

"Wait, is that a doll?" Chae Rin plucked it out of the box and grimaced.

Dry mud caked its face so thoroughly that I wouldn't have been surprised if it had been done on purpose. Threads stuck out of its simple maid dress at odd angles, its black hair of yarn ravaged and disheveled. Its eyes had been torn out of the fabric, but stranger still were its arms, both tied behind its back with black string.

"Creepy." Chae Rin shook her head.

Definitely. I couldn't even begin to fathom why Natalya would have wanted Belle to find this. There had to be more to it.

It was finally dark out. The rustling trees outside the sliding glass door veiled parts of the sky. The smell of roast beef wafted through the ventilation. That was our ticking clock. We didn't have to understand everything now. We had the box. Now we just had to take it back to the hotel and figure it out from there.

"Wait."

Chae Rin drew her face closer to the box, squinting as she spied something beneath all the strange paraphernalia. It was an old sheet of paper, perfectly folded. Because of the dirt covering it, I'd almost missed it entirely. Chae Rin dusted it off and unfolded it.

"It's a letter!" she said.

"Let me see." Setting the box down, I took the letter. Thankfully, it was in English. Long, looping handwriting scrawled across the brittle, off-white paper. After sharing an uneasy glance with Chae Rin, I read the contents:

"March the first, 1872

My Dear Poupée:"

I stopped. "*Poupée . . .*"

Chae Rin nudged me. "If you're going to read, then read. We're running out of time here."

"Okay, okay."

"My Dear Poupée:

I am writing this letter knowing that you shall never read it. Indeed it pains me greatly to know that we will never converse again until I join you in hell, though I'm afraid you will have to wait longer than even I had initially expected.

Two years, my dear friend, my sister, since you passed away, and I find my thoughts are still attached to you, to Patricia, to Emilia, and yes, even Abigail. Perhaps it is guilt.

You would say, I suppose, that I should feel guilty. It was I who showed the gift to you, who began the game. It was I who started

you all down your accursed paths. I'm sure you regret it. I'm sure
you regret having ever come to my estate, but you see, that is why I
am writing this letter.

I do not feel guilty. I regret none of it.

This is the freedom I have longed for. I will not turn away from
this opportunity for the sake of appeasing whatever ghost of yours
still walks these lands, troubling my sleep night after night with
your judging eyes. I alone will use the power that has been given to
me to its fullest. I will achieve what even you could not. This is the
promise I make to you, that I give unto your grave with the hopes
that your soul will finally let me go.

I will do wondrous things, Marian, together with Nicholas. I will
fulfill all my dirty wishes. I will reshape the world.

I hope you'll watch me fondly.

Yours for the last time,
Alice"

I lowered the letter. "Alice . . ." My lips parted in a half gasp.
"Marian . . . and Nicholas . . . ?"

There was a knock on the door behind us. Chae Rin dropped the
doll and straightened up. "Hurry and put the damn letter back in the
box. Hey, what are you doing?"

I couldn't move. The letter trembled in my grip. "Alice . . . Alice
wrote this to Marian. *That* Marian. Saul's Marian."

Another knock.

"*Poupée*. Saul kept calling me that, right from the beginning. Even during the investigation, but only when he wasn't Nick anymore."

I thought back to the first time I'd scried, back to Marian's memory of a girl alone in her study, her long blond hair spiraling to the floor as she rested her head on a pile of books, like a fairy tale immortalized in painting.

"Saul's two personalities." My lips went dry. "Nick . . . and Alice. I think Alice is the other personality. But this was dated 1872."

"*Maia!*"

"Saul's—no, Nick's brother died in the late 1800s." I got to my feet. "What if—"

Someone kicked the door open. I turned just in time to see Chae Rin crumple to the ground. A hard rock had hit its mark, right at the back of her head, knocking her out cold before she'd even seen who'd thrown it.

The man's face was hidden behind a ski mask. A robber? Where had he come from? Where were the others? I could still hear the television, undercut occasionally by Lake's bright laughter. They didn't know. And they weren't going to. The man shut the door and stopped it with a chair.

Frantic, I stuffed the letter back into the box and slid it underneath the bed with my foot. I prepared a scream, but fear snatched it as the assailant launched at me, grabbing my arm.

In his other hand was a device like the one I'd used on Saul in Argentina. Pushing me against the window, he tried to stab me in the neck with it, but I blocked his arm with mine. After a short struggle, I grabbed at his face and, with a feral tug, wrenched off his mask.

No.

"Vasily?"

He grinned.

I tried to pass him, but he grabbed me and shoved me back against the sliding glass door. That was when I found my voice again, loud and screeching, but I couldn't wait for help, and I didn't have time to think. Pushing him away, I slid open the door and ran out into the night.

I was in a tiny backyard lined by a fence too tall to scale. I'd have to go around to the front. My adrenaline wouldn't let my feet stop, but Vasily was faster than I was. I felt his hand around my sweatshirt collar, yanking me back before pushing me to the grass. The moment I turned onto my back, he was on top of me.

"Get off me!" I fought against him as he climbed on top of me. "What are you doing?

"I could ask the same thing to you." Vasily's ice-blond hair slipped its bond and fell over his face, strands of it clinging to the blood on his cheek from a wound I must have given him. "I was told to keep an eye on you, but to think you were digging into something like this . . . It's too bad. I really liked you."

He gripped my neck.

"No, don't!" I sputtered, my right palm planted on his face as I tried to push him back.

My hand was too sweaty. He flung it off with a jerk of his head.

"Sorry," he said, "but it's just easier if I get rid of you. Don't worry, it'll be quick." Blowing his hair out of his face, Vasily leaned in close. "Some things really should stay buried. Natalya made the same mistake."

The pain in my chest was almost too much to bear. It was a pain I'd never felt before. The world grew dimmer with each frantic beat of my heart, but my eyes were still wide-open, staring blankly at the night sky.

Was this what it felt like? For Mom, Dad, and June? Did it hurt this much when they felt their last breaths being torn from their bodies? No, I didn't want to think about it. I didn't want to think about them dying, and I didn't want to die.

But I was. I *was* dying. I could feel myself dying.

Mom . . . Dad . . . June . . . Tears leaked from my eyes, but I couldn't feel them at all against my skin. *No . . . no, no, no! No!*

With a guttural yell, Rhys threw Vasily off me. I flopped onto my stomach, clawing the ground, soil clumping in my fingernails.

"What the hell are you doing?" Rhys. "I'm gonna *fucking kill you!*"

I heard Rhys's scream, but I couldn't see them. I could only see the blades of grass, the chunks of dirt I'd ripped from the ground. I could see my dirty hands shaking.

Vasily laughed. "Would you really kill me for her?"

They were struggling, I could tell, but my mind was blank. As my heart thrashed against my chest, something pure and terrible began to shudder inside me. Anger? No. I didn't know, but it hurt, it burned, it tore me from the inside. Shutting my eyes, I pressed my forehead against the ground, tears leaking as I pictured their faces: Mom, Dad, June. Since their deaths, I'd refused to think about it: what it must have been like to burn up in flames, the skin peeling off your flesh, the breath squeezing out of your throat for the last time. But now I couldn't stop. Over and over again I saw them dying in my mind's eye. I couldn't stop.

"I'm following *orders*, Aidan!"

"You're out of control!" Rhys must have punched him, because Vasily grunted. "You always have been!"

"I learned to survive just like you. Wasn't that the whole point of the Devil's Hole?"

"No! I'm not like that anymore!"

"Yes, you are. If you weren't, then why did y—"

More punches. More noises deep from the gut. Off in the distance, I could hear children screaming . . . or was it June? I couldn't tell anymore. I closed my eyes.

The pure and terrible thing stirring inside me rumbled louder the faster the world spun. If I was safe, my body didn't know it; I could still feel myself dying. I was still gasping for air. I could still see my parents, still imagine them suffocating and crying out for me. And Natalya—I could see her, too, clutching the rug, struggling to stay alive. It was too much. It was *too much*.

The dam broke. I screamed and screamed. And when I opened my eyes—

Fire. There was fire everywhere. Fire sprawling across the grass, crawling up the trees, licking the house.

The house. The house was in flames. My house was on fire again.

"Stop." I gripped my head. "Stop! Please! Mom! Daddy!"

I was incoherent now, between the screaming, crying, and pleading. Somewhere, deep within the hell I'd created, I heard Rhys's voice.

"Maia! Maia, stop! You can stop it!"

I couldn't hear him. I could only hear my family crying the way I'd always imagined they had when the fire took them.

"Maia, please! Calm down! Breathe! You can do it!"

"I can't." I covered my mouth against my meager, ragged breaths. "I can't. I can't!"

It happened quickly. An ice-cold torrent of wind with the fury of a tornado swept through the backyard, taking the fire with it. The trees, the grass, the side of the house. By the time I had lowered my hands, all of it was covered in sleet and snow. The ashes turned to wintry flakes caught in the fine hairs of my skin. It was the last thing I saw before passing out.

22

A CIGARETTE HAD CAUSED THE FIRE. RHYS and Belle told the police that lie because the truth would have caused a media frenzy: Maia Finley, successor to the great Natalya Filipova, freaks out and almost burns down a foster home filled with kids. The new face of the Sect indeed.

I'd been alone in my sterile, private hospital room for at least an hour, staring blankly at the window, my latest failure replaying over and over again in my mind.

When Rhys walked in and shut the door behind him, I pulled the covers over my face.

"They're okay, you know." He sat in the chair next to me. "The fire didn't spread as much as you probably think it did. Belle and Lake took care of it, though it did take a while to haul away some of the broken tree branches."

I already knew. Lake had called not too long ago. No one had gotten hurt, but that was only a fleeting relief from the misery. After gathering just enough of my senses to tell her about the box beneath Claudine's bed, I'd ended the conversation there.

"I could have killed them." I clenched my bedcovers. "It's all my fault."

"It's Vasily's fault." Gently, Rhys untangled the sheet from my fingers. "Not yours. His."

Wiping the wetness from my eyes, I sat up. "Where is he?"

"He escaped." Rhys's features grew cold. "While everyone was distracted by the fire. I put some field agents in town on the alert, but they haven't seen him. He's probably long gone by now."

I thought of Vasily's remorseless smirk as he tried to choke the life from me. There was no other explanation: "He killed Natalya."

"What?"

I looked at Rhys. "He killed her. He practically admitted it when he tried to kill me."

Rhys's face shut like a door, like it had before when I'd brought up the possibility of Natalya's murder. But this time was different. He leaned over, propping himself up on his legs, his fingers twined between his knees. "If anyone's capable of it . . . it's him."

"Tell me about him." I shifted to my side, pushing off my covers. "Who is he? He works for Blackwell, right? Could Blackwell have ordered Natalya's death?"

"I started training as an agent when I was ten years old," he said suddenly. "A lot of us are like that." His eyes were fixed on my bedspread. "The Sect likes to take in kids. Orphans, street kids, and so on. Kids can be molded more easily, I guess."

It was a rare opportunity, hearing Rhys speak about himself. "Are you an orphan?"

"No," he said. "There are some families out there that have sworn themselves to the Sect. Some have been with the Sect for decades. Like mine." He smirked. "Fighting monsters as a family tradition."

I could see the muscles in his face and neck work as he swallowed, each tiny movement displaying the defined edges of his jaw.

"I come from one of those families," he said. "My dad fought. My brother, too."

I blinked. "You have a brother?"

I must have sounded a little too baffled, because Rhys smiled. "He's more into the administrative side of things now."

"Oh."

He grew solemn. "I met Vasily at one of the Sect's training facilities. In Greenland. Some training facilities are a little tougher than others."

I waited for him to elaborate. He never did.

"When Vasily graduated and became an agent, he was scouted by Blackwell to be his personal operative. It happens sometimes. But what happened in Greenland . . ." Rhys shook his head. "I guess it changed him."

"Did it change you?"

Rhys wouldn't look at me. "Experiences always change people. But at the end of the day, he's a Sect agent. He follows his orders. That's what agents do. The Sect is absolute."

I stiffened on my bed. Of course Rhys would feel that way. He'd been trained too, by his family and by the same Sect that had forced me to swear allegiance to them.

"But Natalya was learning about Saul," I said. "About Nick and Alice. Vasily may have been ordered by the Sect to watch me, but when he realized I was learning too much, he tried to *kill* me. You said Vasily follows orders. Doesn't that mean there's someone in the Sect who knows more about Saul than they're letting on? Isn't it possible they killed Natalya to keep it all quiet?"

Silently, Rhys stood and crossed the room to the window. I waited.

"I didn't know Natalya for that long," he finally said, "but I liked her. She was so . . ." He leaned over, planting his hand on the windowpane. "Noble. Just. And I could see it was killing her. The burden she had to bear . . . I wouldn't wish it on anyone."

He turned to me. My cheeks flushed, but I kept myself steady, even as he closed the distance between us. "When I first met you in that Brooklyn hotel, I saw this innocent kid who'd suddenly had the weight of the world dumped onto her shoulders. The weight of Natalya's legacy. And . . ." He pressed his lips. "I just wanted to help you."

The dimness of his eyes worried me. It was like the light had been stolen from them.

"Rhys . . . why are you telling me this?"

He sat next to me on the bed, a respectable distance away. When he brushed back his tangled black hair, for the first time I noticed how tired he looked—the bags under his eyes, his faded pallor, his lips aching for moisture.

I wished someone would tell me how to react as his fingers squeezed mine, so tightly and desperately I wondered what he was really clinging to. What would June have done in my place if she'd seen the silent tears running down his cheeks?

Rhys couldn't look at me, even as he gripped my hand tight. "Maia . . . Natalya . . . she . . ."

"It's okay." Something hardened in me as I watched him. "I'll find him." I was more determined than ever. "I won't let Vasily get away with murdering Natalya. I promise."

Rhys lifted his head, but a rustling at the door kept the words from forming. My body went rigid. Silence stretched between the three of us—Rhys and me on the bed, and Belle standing bewildered at the door.

"Belle . . ." I withdrew my hand, but the rest of me was frozen. "I—"

"It's okay. It's . . ." Belle shut her eyes, her hands slipping off the knob. "No, this is good. Maia, come with me. I've decided." By the time she'd opened her eyes again, they'd hardened to steel. "I'm going to teach you how to scry."

It was pitch-black outside. Even with my coat and sweatshirt, the cold night seeped into my skin. Belle had taken me to a place called "Le Lavoir," overlooking the Epte River. I couldn't believe it was a tourist attraction: It looked like a long sidewalk of cobbled stone, sheltered by an equally long rusted roof. Definitely different. But I could tell that it was also very old: a monument, perhaps, to the town's early days, before the phantoms came.

On the way there I'd told Belle about Natalya's death, the memories I'd seen, and the cigar box hidden underneath her floorboards. It was a bit worrying, the way Belle stayed silent throughout the explanation. She didn't speak at all until she walked up to the stone balustrade separating us from the river.

"Do you know what our job is, Maia?" Belle placed her hands on the ridge. "As Effigies?"

I nodded, very sure of myself as I pulled up my jacket hood for warmth. "To protect people."

"Our job is to destroy phantoms," she said, turning. I shifted uncomfortably. "But Natalya . . . She always did more than she needed to. Always an idealist."

Her tone turned flat and lifeless as she said the word, her shoulders slumping as she looked off into the distance.

"And you're not?"

Belle's silent response unnerved me. Natalya's drive to protect life made her a hero. Didn't it?

I thought of Natalya's apartment: the decanter filled with

scotch, the empty bottles of wine and vodka decorating the tables like ornaments.

I shook my head. Natalya was a hero. Belle, too. Fighting phantoms and protecting people went hand in hand. That was what Belle had probably meant.

It was just the look on her face that made me so uncomfortable.

Belle turned back to the river. "Scrying is very simple. Natalya once used a matryoshka doll to explain the concept to me. The Effigies." She tapped her head with a finger. "Each time one dies, a piece of her mind remains in the next. You know this. You also know that the consciousness of the last Effigy to die will be the strongest, the freshest. Yes?"

I nodded.

"There is a barrier separating your mind from the shards of consciousness remaining from Natalya, but it's penetrable. Achieving a state of pure calm and peace allows your psyche to cross into hers comfortably. Once you do, you'll see it. Perhaps you already have: the red door."

"Red door?"

"And a white stream. I haven't been there in a long time, but I can still remember." Shutting her eyes, Belle lifted her head. "The frigid white waters rippling around my ankles. The fog, so thick you can see nothing else but the red door in the distance. It is the gateway to the mind of the one who died before me. This is what you'll see if you scry the correct way."

Like striding through the front door with pride instead of being dragged in, screaming and blindfolded, through the back window.

I kicked my foot across the stone floor. "I don't know if you've noticed, but I haven't exactly been the poster child of 'pure calm' lately."

"I told you in Argentina. It was Saul who prematurely forced you over the first threshold. Now, if your mind becomes disturbed, even while asleep, parts of your psyche can potentially cross over into hers. But the reverse is also true." Belle peered into the rippling waters. "While scrying, your mind is more vulnerable than ever before. If, in that state, you become too deeply unsettled, the psyche of the previous Effigies can slip into yours. In extreme cases, one can take control of your physical form for a short time."

Saul had told me that once too. I hugged myself to keep from shuddering too violently. "If that's the case, then shouldn't you have taught me proper scrying a little earlier?"

I could see Belle deflating.

"Natalya committed suicide." Belle's hair whipped gently over her face as she spoke. "I never believed it. I couldn't. But if it turned out . . . that she really did . . . that she . . ."

She looked away.

For me, the best and worst aspect about losing my family was knowing, deep inside, that they weren't really gone. They're never really gone—a point belabored ad nauseam by all the priests and counselors and therapists. I'd resented it then, but it was true. Some days, I would have rested easier if they'd simply been eradicated from the world. But the dead left traces: pictures, old messages on answering machines. Memories. Pain. Bits and pieces of each lost life remained on Earth, trapped here and there, comforting and haunting their loved ones in equal measure. And part of Natalya remained in me, along with the truth of her death. I couldn't blame Belle for being scared.

"But now we know. No, I *want* to know." Something quiet and frightening passed across Belle's features as she looked at me. "Scry, Maia. Find Natalya."

I tried. I followed Belle's every instruction, staring at the river, letting its peaceful, rippling rhythm ease my nerves. Each time I lost focus, Belle urged me to try again in a soft tone only thinly hiding the urgency belying it.

I kept trying.

Shut out the cold. I repeated Belle's words like a dutiful student. *Count each breath. Don't think. Don't feel. Just let your mind fall into the waters and search for her.*

But when I gazed into the river, I saw my own face, June's face, staring back at me. June, who would never smile at me again. And suddenly, I was thinking of what June's face would have looked like after the fire . . . what my own face would transform into after being ravaged by flames.

I could only imagine it; I never saw June's remains. Uncle Nathan was the one who'd identified the bodies. And Uncle Nathan . . . Was he okay? No, of course not. How could he be, after losing his family, and then losing me to the Sect? I just wanted to talk to him. Why wouldn't they let me *talk* to him?

As the tears blurred my vision, a sharp burning pain scorched my skull. Grimacing, I gripped my head and dropped to my knees. I could see stars behind my eyelids, flashes of light in the black. The next time I opened them, Belle was kneeling on the ground in front of me.

Or was it Belle? It couldn't have been. The girl *looked* like her, but she was suddenly so much younger. Blood and sweat matted her blond hair wildly to her face. She was screaming with her bloodshot eyes, but when her lips fluttered, bits of French and broken English passed through them in hoarse whispers. Her little body was bent over, fingers hidden in the sand she gripped.

"Belle?"

It was Natalya's voice. Belle didn't respond to it. She only trembled, rasping for air.

"I saved them." Belle nodded quickly, planting her dirty hand on her dirtier face. "I saved them. I killed the phantoms. Twelve. I killed twelve. I killed twelve. Are you proud of me, Natalya?"

That was when I saw it: the bodies draped across the sandy field. Bodies of Sect troops interspersed between the remains of phantoms rotting in the sinking sun.

"Kill me," Belle cried and grabbed her hair. "Kill me! I want to die. I can't do this! Kill me!"

With a violent shudder, I awoke from Natalya's memory, only to find the present Belle gripping her shoulders.

"What did you see?" Belle demanded. "Did you see Natalya's killer?"

Belle, the Twelve-Kill Rookie. It should have been a moniker of pride for the girl who'd managed to take down twelve phantoms during one of her first missions. But that memory . . . that horror I'd just witnessed . . . how could I even put it into words? I tried to push them out, but they wouldn't go.

Belle just kept shaking me, her nails digging into my skin. "Tell me what you saw. Tell me! *Who killed Natalya?*"

"Please stop!"

The moment I let out the desperate plea, Belle finally got hold of herself. But it was a tenuous grasp.

"That's enough," Belle said, stumbling back. "That's . . . that's enough for today."

23

BELLE WAS A BADASS FIGHTER. IT WAS PART OF why I was such a fan. Back in my Paris hotel room, I watched an old video feed of the Effigy battling in South Carolina. Sect troops had sent tanks in, not knowing that the phantoms were burrowing underground.

I gasped as the monsters' wormlike bodies ripped through the ground, flipping a tank in the air. As the tank crashed to the ground, Belle jumped atop another, yelling at them to fire as it swiveled around. Then she launched herself into the air, grabbing hold of one of the phantoms while it was still reeling. Belle. The Legendary Effigy. The Twelve-Kill Rookie.

Kill me! I want to die. I can't do this! Kill me!

Shivering, I shut out the memory by clicking open another video. Natalya Filipova. She stood in the streets of Moscow, a white Russian fur hat covering what I knew was a raven-black pixie cut underneath. A few strands from her black bangs peeked out from beneath the white material, falling over one of her brown eyes. The wind blew snow across her long mauve coat and past her high, black boots, getting caught on the buckles.

She stood in the streets of Moscow back-to-back with Belle as the War Siren blew, Saint Basil's Cathedral just barely visible behind a blizzard.

Natalya tugged her red gloves taut over her fingers and stretched her arm. Out of the flames forged a broad sword tall enough for the embroidered hilt to reach her neck.

Natalya's sword.

A swarm of black billowed out from behind the Cathedral. Phantoms. Natalya blessed the edge of her now-famous blade in the snow before flipping it around, readying herself. That was when the reporter started running. The video shook before cutting off entirely.

Was that how Belle remembered her: as a knight slaying dragons? Maybe it hurt to even think of her at all.

I thought of Lake, who would cry at night when she thought I was sleeping, and Chae Rin, who would find a way to disappear whenever anyone even mentioned the word "family."

Shutting my laptop, I laid my head on my pillow. None of us were really talking about it: the loss, the loneliness, and the pain. Why wasn't there anything I could do?

Lake cursed the rain, which had destroyed our chances of having an outdoor shoot. Apparently it was the only way to be photographed in Paris. *Teen Vogue* had us indoors instead, their lavish sets ready for photographs. But styling came first.

I'd never been poked and prodded and *manhandled* the way the hair and makeup team did to me. At one point, I literally had two different flat irons ravaging my hair while a perfect stranger assessed the damage my lack of skin-care maintenance had done to my pores.

"Okay." The makeup artist stood up and waved for her assistant.

"We need some BB cream, stat. Get me one of the deeper sand shades."

They decided not to straighten my hair too much. If this would be my formal introduction to a potential fan base, they'd want me to stay as much myself as possible. They teased out my curls instead and pinned them over my shoulder.

Lake was a pro in her styling chair, flipping through a magazine as they sewed in hair extensions, giving her a long black ponytail reaching down her back.

She paused at a page, drawing it close to her face.

"Ugh!" She smacked it. "Jo's talking about me again!"

Chae Rin, who'd let them cut her hair shoulder-length and dye it red, twitched an eyelid as they applied some deep shadow. "Who?"

"Jo! Jo Matthews! You know, from my old group?"

The lead singer of Girls by Day. Lake showed us the magazine page. The group had hit a set back after Lake had left to train in Finland, but after formally kicking her out of the group and replacing two of the members, they'd rebranded themselves. They were now four teenage bad-girl "hood rats" known only as GBD. Needless to say, their teenybopper looks didn't quite work with the heavy chains and bandanas, but Jo, one of the two original members, certainly tried to pull it off in the picture.

"She's spreading gross rumors about me!" cried Lake. "She said I flirted with the producers during the show. I was *thirteen*. Do you believe this?" Lake crumpled the magazine in her hands and threw it onto Chae Rin's lap. "Why does she keep talking about me? God, it's like she's been obsessed with me ever since we auditioned."

"How Shakespearean." Chae Rin flipped through the magazine.

"She was so evil to me when they first put the group together. Kept making fun of my last name and calling me Nala from *The Lion*

King, that horrid cow." Lake straightened up in her chair, her chin high with regality. "Well, we'll show them, eh? And after, we can get back to . . . you know."

The Natalya thing. I snuck a glance at Belle on the other side of Lake. She'd remained silent throughout the beautification process, not even looking at us as the stylists worked on their canvas. GBD at least maintained the illusion of teamwork.

Then again, Belle hadn't seemed right since last night. I was amazed at how skillfully the makeup artists had covered up the deep, dark circles underneath her eyes, but the cream sheen did nothing to conceal her far-off, barely lucid gaze. Quietly, I looked away from her.

The first set had a school feel. Desks, chalkboard, and us, dressed in pale gray private school uniforms. The director must have had a fetish.

"The theme of the spread is secret identities," said the director as they set up the lighting equipment. "One minute you're regular schoolgirls, and the next you're sexy, cool, stylish phantom-killing femme fatales: the two sides of our new team of warrior princesses."

"What cheese," Chae Rin grumbled. "Let's just get this over with."

Weirdly, it didn't take long for me to get uncomfortably familiar with the hot flash of white lights. Off set, the photographer barked orders: "Belle, raise your chin. Chae Rin, sling your blazer over your shoulder—yes, like that. Lake, perfect, perfect! Keep giving me neck. Maia . . . give me *something*!"

Apparently I had a natural tendency to lose any and all signs of having a soul once the cameras started flashing.

Eventually, they switched to the femme fatale set. I hated wobbling around in pin-thin heels, but at least they didn't stuff me into those ridiculous chafing leather pants Chae Rin wore. My *skirt* was leather, though, pulled up high on my waist. I had to admit, it did look pretty cool with the black platforms and the black lace top. My hair was loose over my face, strands of it sticking to my apple-red lipstick.

"Girls, think strength! Strength!"

As the cameras flashed, I thought of Rhys waiting in the lobby with a book his hands. A shy wish crept inside me, but it was gone with the next flash.

The interview came next; some staff brought over a few chairs. A boxy-looking woman from the magazine came right to the set with a tablet in her hands, her blond hair cropped to her chin, curving like a fishbowl. Lake must have seen me fidget, because she gave me a soft nudge.

"Don't be nervous," Lake said. "This is the easy part."

Wishful thinking.

"Lake, there've been whispers that you're far more interested in being a celebrity than fighting to protect the rest of humanity. Do you have anything to say to your detractors?"

Lake blinked. The interviewer, Lydia Klein, had started off asking us the usual teen magazine fluff: what we looked for in partners, what kind of music we listened to, and other meaningless garbage. Thanks to Lake's quick car-ride tutorial, I had my fake answers ready-made, but this was a turn none of us had expected.

Though clearly taken aback, Lake kept her smile strapped to her face like a weapon. "Well," she said, "when you're in the public eye, people *are* going to have negative things to say about you. But I think a lot of people get me wrong. And, to be honest, I think, especially when you're a girl, people expect you to be perfect right from the beginning. A perfect role model. Like you're not allowed to have . . . *flaws*. Weaknesses."

As Lake's smile faltered, I had to grit my teeth to banish the uncomfortable twinge of guilt needling me from the inside. It wasn't too long ago, after all, that I was spending my evenings on the internet crucifying Lake—and Chae Rin—for committing the unforgivable sin of not reaching my impossible standards of what Effigies were supposed to be. Now, as I sat listening to Lake, I'd never felt more stupid.

For just a moment, Lake stared down at her toes before gathering herself again. "So no, it's not that I'm more interested in being a celebrity."

"But doesn't your insistence on being referred to as your stage name imply the contrary?"

Lake balked. "What's wrong with using my stage name?"

"Well, I would expect that after leaving behind your old girl group you would have started going by your real name, Victoria Soh . . . Soyo . . ."

"Soyinka." Lake sounded out each syllable clearly. "Are you serious right now?"

To Lake's chagrin, Lydia's response was to laugh. Things just went downhill from there.

"Let's switch gears here. Chae Rin, you've been doing so well these days, staying out of trouble. Good for you!"

"Thanks," Chae Rin answered without a hint of sincerity. "Your approval means everything to me."

"A few months ago, your father pleaded with the public to be patient with you, but we never see your mother. And, when asked, she never mentions you. Is it for privacy's sake? Or is there something in that relationship your fans should know?"

Chae Rin's eyes narrowed to slits, the muscles in her jaw shifting as she struggled to keep her expression calm. "Maybe you should switch gears again."

"I hope you don't take this personally." Lydia sat back in her chair and crossed her legs. "These questions were voted in by our readers. But if you'd like, I could move on to you, Maia."

Uh-oh. I squirmed. "O-okay."

"It's well-known now that you lost your family in that tragic, hor-rific fire."

Apparently so. Chae Rin shifted her weight to the other side of her chair. Lake solemnly lowered her head.

"How do you think your painful experiences have readied you for the dangerous work of being an Effigy?"

I didn't even know where to start. I looked to the other girls for help.

"Aren't you in the least bit worried? I mean, you're the successor of the great Natalya Filipova. How do you plan on filling those shoes?"

"She doesn't."

Devastatingly, it was Belle who'd spoken. I shrank in my seat, and Lake started to protest, but Belle wasn't finished.

"Maia is her own person," Belle said. "She's not Natalya. Being an Effigy is a sacred duty, and she was chosen by fate. That alone makes her worthy."

Worthy. My heart swelled with pride. It was all I needed to hear. Shutting my eyes, I smiled.

"It's the same for all of us. We were all chosen. Chosen . . . for this."

They were strong words, but with very little strength in them. Belle had said them without resolve or emotion. I looked at her again, my eyes narrowing as they fell upon the almost-imperceptible arch of Belle's lips—the unmistakable beginning of a cynical smirk that van-ished as quickly as it'd appeared. The girl who'd spent so many years of her life fighting nightmares made flesh looked suddenly worn in her chair, her arms limp at her sides, lifeless despite the elegant beauty she wore effortlessly like a mask.

"We were chosen." She stared at Lydia pointedly. "Chosen to fight . . . until we die."

Teen Vogue wanted some solo shots of us, but a few minutes in, Belle left the building, citing fresh air as her primary goal. That was twenty minutes ago.

"She's long gone," muttered Chae Rin, getting up for her shot.

Hopefully not, since she was up next.

"I'll go look for her," I offered when the director started swearing. I found Rhys, still in the lobby, halfway through James Joyce. The book shut the moment he saw me.

"Oh, uh . . ." I'd forgotten I was still dressed up. I didn't know what to say as he stared at me, placing his book aside and rising to his feet. I tugged at my elbow-length lace gloves, which were suddenly hot against my skin. "D-do you know where Belle went?"

"She left a few minutes ago. Hasn't come back." He jerked his head toward the door. "I figured she needed some air. She's probably still out there."

"Oh, okay. They want her in there, so I thought I'd go get her."

"Take this." Catching my hand, Rhys gingerly placed a dark blue umbrella in it. "Don't get wet."

I wasn't used to seeing Rhys's face flush at the sight of me. Tucking a strand of hair behind my ears, I nodded quickly in thanks and ran out of the room.

With careful steps so as to not break my ankles, I descended the stairs. Down the hallway and past the front desk. The open air hit me the moment I crossed the threshold, fresh and heavy with rain. Definitely a welcome change from the stuffy studio. I breathed it in.

Rumbling motors and obnoxious car horns, sparks of conversations carried by the wind, and in the distance, the faint wail of ambulance sirens. The sounds of the city challenged the never-ending rattling of rainfall. If I didn't want to piss off the production team I'd have to be careful not to get rained on—that is, if it was even possible for them to be any more irritated than they already were.

Damn it, Belle, where are you?

I scanned the wet streets, watching people shuffle in and out of the clothing boutiques and cafés. Outside the liquor store a few buildings down, a few men who'd gathered to smoke turned in my direction. My face. My face was exposed. *Crap.* I turned. It was a bad idea to draw a crowd here.

Draw a *crowd.* I almost laughed. Being an Effigy, I was technically "famous" now, or something, but it was still bizarre to think about it. Being recognized, being *noticed,* by random strangers on the street. It excited me about as much as it made me feel awkward and uncomfortable—well, more so.

Hiding behind my umbrella, I quickly started off again, darting down the narrow sidewalk until finally I found Belle in a nearby alleyway.

Well . . . the girl leaning against the brick wall, holding a bottle of booze not-so-skillfully hidden inside a brown paper bag, certainly *looked* like Belle. There couldn't have been another beautiful blonde running around Paris in a neo-Victorian assassin-inspired couture outfit.

I took a hesitant step forward. "B-Belle?"

Belle's eyes had been closed, her umbrella shielding her from the runoff from the roof. At the sound of her name, they fluttered open. "Oh, it's you."

I stared at the paper bag. "Belle . . . what are you doing here?"

Belle spared me a casual glance. "I told you, I needed air."

"Have you . . . have you been *drinking*?"

"Looks like."

I watched, incredulous, as Belle took another sip from the bottle. "Belle, where did you even get that thing?"

Belle shrugged. "You know those PAs, always as scared as they are eager. I had to make sure they'd stay quiet about it, of course, but then, I can be pretty persuasive. Why? Feeling peckish?" Belle held out her arm, offering it to her. "There's some left."

Neither of us spoke. Nothing but the pattering rain interrupted the silence between us. Belle's eyes were glazed and sunken. Despite her steady grip on her umbrella, she carelessly shifted it at an angle just wide enough for the rain to begin splattering against part of her skirt. She didn't even flinch.

"Belle . . . ." My fingers twitched as cold rain splashed onto them. "I don't know what's going on, but we need to get back inside. You're getting wet. You've still got some solo shots to do, you know."

"I know."

"So—"

"You don't need me there."

I batted the hair from my eyes impatiently. "Obviously we do. They want solo pics of the whole team, so—"

Belle's laughter was quiet, but chilling. It came out in short staccatos that still managed to overcome the rain. I wasn't even sure if I'd ever actually heard Belle laugh before. I didn't like it.

"Team. *Team.*" Belle stared at the bottle in her hands, the brown bag wet and tearing from the rain. "I went from fighting by Natalya's side to being in a 'team' with a group of incompetent little girls. I think this is what they call a cosmic joke, yes? Maybe I'm being punished for something."

My body tensed as Belle's laughter rang in my ears.

"Fine." Belle pushed off the wall. "Let's just finish this whole side-show, shall we?"

"No."

Belle's heels stopped against the wet pavement. "Pardon?"

I swallowed. "You don't get to . . ." My fingers went cold. "You don't get to talk that kind of shit and just leave. Not before you apologize."

"Apologize." Belle cocked her head, amused. "But did I lie about any of it?"

"Incompetent little girls?"

"Not too long ago you almost burned down a house filled with children."

My free hand balled into a fist.

"Or did you forget, Maia?"

"No," I whispered. The umbrella quivered in my other hand. "No, I haven't. But that doesn't mean you get to . . ." I shook my head. "You know what? I get it. I get that I'm not Natalya. I get that you don't give a shit about me, and you obviously look down on the other two, but that doesn't mean you get to just erase everything. Everything we've done."

I remembered the terror pulsing through me as I faced Saul in Argentina. Lake flying up to catch me, Chae Rin skewering phantoms while half-conscious. I remembered how hard we'd struggled against him. The four of us together.

"We're not Natalya," I hissed. "But we *try*. We've been trying this whole time."

"And why do you try?" Belle looked drained, her face somehow sallow and pale despite the makeup.

"Huh?" What bothered me most was that Belle seemed

genuinely curious. My lips readied a snarl. "I really hope that's the booze talking."

"Don't be so dramatic," Belle said. "It's just a question. Despite everything you've seen, everything you've lived through, you wear the mantle of 'Effigy' as if it's a Girl Scout badge pinned to your chest. Like a little idiot. I just find it interesting. Funny, actually. Why? Why do you try? What's the point?" Belle studied my face as if she'd find the answers written there. "Is it because you want to be like Natalya? Or, because you idolize me, do you want to take her place? Or maybe you're just a masochist? A fool? Do you even know?"

This wasn't Belle. It couldn't be Belle, the girl I'd waited for at Lincoln Center, desperate for an autograph, a nod, anything to acknowledge my existence. It couldn't be.

"I just wanted to be like you," I said in nearly a whisper. "A hero."

"I already told you." Belle became scarily quiet. "None of us are heroes."

"June didn't think so." I was losing my grip on my umbrella. As rain trickled down my forehead, eyeliner streamed down my face and my curls soaked against my cheeks. "June, my sister. She was bullied, you know. Really bad."

The rain dripped off my gloves as I clasped my hands together, fighting against the tide of memories. I couldn't remember if I'd ever spoken about June so freely to anyone. It was terrifying, like desperately clutching a fluttering secret against your chest, protecting it from the outside world. I felt naked, exposed, but the words flowed anyway.

"She was a geek with a bad stutter," I said. "One day she rubbed a few kids the wrong way. I don't even remember how it started, but . . ." I shrugged. "It went on for a long time. I escaped the brunt of it because I kept out of everyone's way, and June . . . She cut her hair to make sure nobody would mistake the two of us. It was hard. But you guys." I pointed at her. "The Effigies. You and Natalya especially. You made her feel strong. You made *me* feel strong. Like we could . . . I don't know." I let out a bitter chuckle. "But in the end, I couldn't do a damn thing for her."

I didn't dare look at Belle, too terrified of the expression I might find staring back at me. Mentioning June brought up a torrent of emotions thrashing about inside me, heating my skin and flushing my face even in the cold, heavy air. There was so much I wanted to say, and I knew I'd never be able to articulate it all in exactly the way I wanted. A frustrating feeling, to say the least. But Belle surely understood. She had to.

"I guess that's why I try," I said finally. "I'm an Effigy now. And if June were in my place, she'd 'try' too. Try to be like you guys. *That's* what you and Natalya gave her."

There was a silence. I could hear the rain draining into the sewers. Belle took several gulps from her bottle and wiped her mouth clean with the back of her hand.

"Well, then." Belle let out a deep breath. "I guess she was a little idiot too."

I couldn't stop myself. I raised my hand, but Belle caught the slap with ease.

"Let me go!" Tears stung my eyes as I struggled against her. "How could you? How could you just . . ." I bit my lip so hard I thought I tasted blood. "Who the hell do you think you are?"

"Wake up, Maia," Belle hissed in my ear. "This isn't a fairy tale. I asked you last night what our job was. Do you remember?"

"To save people!"

"To fight phantoms. We answer to the Sect alone." Belle's glare was colder than ever. "We are chosen. Chosen to fight. Until we die.

Even Natalya couldn't escape that. Even though she was strong, she died like everyone else." Her voice hitched. "She *died*."

"Natalya was *killed*!"

"What does it matter?" Belle inhaled a haggard breath. "She was *nothing*. She gave up her entire life—for *everyone*—and in the end, her death was nothing more than a loose strand for the Sect to brush under the rug. And then you pop up. *You*." Her hand trembled as it squeezed my wrist tighter. "And it's like none of it even mattered, because, well, here you are! The cycle continues. So who cares? What's the point of any of it? What's the point of all the death and suffering? Do you understand, Maia? We're not heroes. We're not *anything*."

And she flung me to the ground. I hit the pavement hard with a grunt.

"We fight and we die. That's why we're alive. That's why we breathe. That's why we exist. That's just how it is. So don't bore me with any more sob stories about your dead relatives." Chucking her bottle away, Belle straightened the sleeves of her coat. "This is reality. And if you can't accept that, then get off the battlefield."

I rolled onto my side, the tears falling freely.

24

ON THAT HUMID SEPTEMBER DAY MONTHS
ago, as Belle strode out of Lincoln Center and into the swarm of
paparazzi waiting for her, I wondered what she thought of me standing there with a poster and a dream. A dream that started out as
whimsy only to explode into an aching wish, fanned by the fires that
had taken my family.

A wish to become strong. Like Belle.

Strong enough that I would never lose anyone again.

In the dirty Paris alleyway, my knuckles bled on the pavement, my
body soaked and shaking in the rain. "I'm so sorry, June. . . ."

The shoot was finally over; fixing up me and Belle stretched the
ordeal out longer, but by nightfall, we were finally London bound. I
for one couldn't have been happier.

"What?" In the hotel lobby, Rhys barked into his phone. "There's
no jet available?" A pause. "Yes, I know there've been a lot of missions
lately. *Yes*, I *realize* Sect jets aren't for my own personal use, but this
isn't—"

With a frustrated groan, Rhys clicked off his cell phone, but he flashed the four of us a smile when he turned. "You don't mind flying coach, do you?"

Except there were no available flights to London until tomorrow afternoon, and Sibyl wanted me back at the facility immediately to resume my lessons, so we decided to take the train instead. Slower, but it would get us there before the end of the day.

We took the seven forty-five train. Lake gave me an extra pair of shades to veil my face as we traveled through the station. It was to hide my identity, of course, though after the day I'd had, I was all too eager to hide my sickly skin and sunken, red eyes, too.

The train took after an older design, all brass and beautiful wood-work with several long cars connected in succession. There were two entrances into each car: one at the front for public seating, and one at the back for the private area.

We'd paid for the two compartments in the private area to avoid being bombarded by the public. Being known as a "celebrity" would definitely take some getting used to, but Uncle Nathan probably had it worse; who knew what kind of nonsense he was dealing with now that everyone knew he shared his genetics with an Effigy? I'd been checking the news, scouring the internet—he wasn't taking any inter-views, but that didn't mean they weren't hounding him. As we stepped inside the first car, my hands instinctively went to the phone in my pocket, but I knew I couldn't dial.

The back entrance took us into a narrow hallway, on either side of which were the two private compartments, parallel to each other. A door sectioned off the public and private areas, and beyond the com-partments at the end of the car was an exit.

Rhys nudged me. "Hey, look outside."

As the private entrance closed behind me, Rhys pointed at its window. Through it, I could see the spigots in the tracks starting to spark with a faint blue energy that ran down the length of the rails. On each side of the railroad spanned rows of tall poles, each one bending at a right angle to join with its pair. The blue current zipped through each metal bar. It was antiphantom technology. It was creating some sort of field around the train. Protecting us.

"Like in Quebec, remember? It's a variation of electromagnetic armor," Rhys explained. "The tracks send out a signal too. Their functioning's dependent on each other, and they go for about thirty-mile sections each, so if one part of the section gets damaged, the whole APD system's down for that stretch." When I stared at him, he blushed. "I was into trains as a kid."

The train started moving. Though Rhys took the compartment on the right, Lake pulled me into the other one, sliding the door shut once I was inside. Chae Rin was already inside, fiddling with a touch screen screwed into the wall. I didn't ask what it was for.

"After what happened yesterday, we have to talk about Natalya." Lake sat down on the bench. "I hereby declare this a totally full-on emergency meeting."

As Lake rummaged through her bag, Chae Rin leaned in to the corner next to the open window, her now-auburn hair tossed about by the wind. "Not sure what's to discuss," she said. "That guy from the Sect tried to kill Maia. Obviously something dirty's going on in there."

"We need to plan our next move." Lake pulled the cigarette box out of the plastic bag she'd stuffed into her travel bag.

Chae Rin raised an eyebrow. "You put the box in a grocery bag?"

"Of course I did! As if I'd let something that dirty touch my stuff." Setting down her travel bag, she placed the box on the table and lifted the lid. "Chae Rin told me about the letter, Maia. You think it was written by one of Saul's personalities?"

The ravaged doll held my gaze, with its dirt-caked face and the twisted threads where its button eyes should have been. "Alice. I think Alice might have been the one attacking those cities. Nick, the other personality . . . when we interrogated him he seemed so . . ." I searched for the word. "Helpless. Scared. Desperate to talk to Marian. Well, they both want to talk to her."

"Really? But from the letter it seems like Alice wanted Marian's ghost to bugger off or something." Lake sighed. "This is really a lot to take in."

Chae Rin shut the lid. "So then what's our next move?"

"The museum." Lake turned to me. "You said Natalya got inside a secret room in some museum, right? And hid that note for Belle in a book?"

"Yeah."

"Well, until you scry for more clues, we're going to have to take that as our next lead, though I have no idea how to come up with an excuse to get there. Maia still has training."

Chae Rin shrugged as she fiddled with the monitor in the corner. Nothing but rolling hills and yet more rolling hills crossed the screen. "So we lie low until Maia's done."

"Training typically takes two years."

"*You* ditched."

Lake glared at her. "Will you quit bringing that up? Anyway, I already played the photo shoot card, so we'll just have to think of something else. But we should keep this to ourselves."

"Yeah." Chae Rin turned the box around with a finger. "Because the Sect is evil."

"Not *evil*," said Lake with an annoyed sigh. "There's no way of telling who in the Sect is involved in this. Could just be that nutter Vasily. Without proper evidence, we can't just go around accusing an entire international organization and its thousands of members."

I nodded, but in truth I was only half listening. My gaze slid to the door.

"You know, this would be a lot easier if Slayer Barbie would deign to lend us a hand." In all her blunt glory, Chae Rin had taken the words right out of my mouth. "Where is she, anyway?"

"I don't think she'll be much interested anyway."

I finally told them what happened in the alleyway earlier that day. As Lake covered her mouth, Chae Rin folded her arms.

"God, I am so tired of her constant emo ice-bitch act. Like, people die, get over it." Chae Rin must have noticed the change in my expression, because she shrank into her corner. "I mean, obviously I didn't mean it like that. You know what I mean, right?"

She turned to Lake for help, who sighed and gripped my hand, a bit like my mother would have when she was alive.

"We fight until we die," Lake said, after letting go. "Maybe that's true. I think that's why the phantoms really scare me. To be honest, I . . ." She smiled sadly. "I don't want to die."

I needed air.

"Sorry," I said, standing.

"Where are you going?" Lake asked.

"Just keep going without me." I left.

For a moment, I stood in the hallway, wondering where I could go. I needed to clear my head, but Belle was already outside. I could see her through the back exit's window. Venturing into the public seating area wasn't a good idea either. It would just give people an excuse to write more blog posts about me.

That only left . . .

Nervously I spied the door to Rhys's private compartment. I

couldn't. Could I? Would it be weird? I wrung my hands, endlessly debating with myself until the door opened.

"Maia?" Rhys blinked. "You okay?"

"Uh . . ." I stared at my toes. "Can I come in?"

"'Course."

I appreciated the casual tone, though I wouldn't have minded if he'd sounded a bit more eager, at least so I'd feel less like a little kid annoying her older brother. I gingerly sat on the bench opposite him, as if the slightest contact would break it in half. Hopefully, he didn't notice how straight my back was, how stiff my limbs. Then again, it wasn't exactly hard to miss.

I opened and closed my fingers against my jeans as we sat in silence. Trying to avoid his eyes, I looked out the window. The train's APD signal reached far enough to keep the phantoms at a comfortable distance, but I knew if I squinted I'd be able to see their silhouettes, trampling, flying, thrashing about behind the green hills as the train traveled the countryside.

"See this monitor?" Rhys asked suddenly, pointing at the touch screen on the wall. "They have them in the public area too. You can pick any angle outside the train and zoom in. If you zoom enough, you'd probably be able to see a few phantoms out there."

Apparently, just like at Le Cirque de Minuit, seeing phantoms served as part of the entertainment.

I would never understand people's fascination with monsters.

"Wanna try?"

"No."

As he smiled, the tension in my body started slipping away.

Rhys took a sip of his coffee. "Anyway, you wanted to talk?"

Did I? I wasn't even one hundred percent sure why I'd come inside in the first place.

"You haven't looked well since the shoot." Rhys wasn't wrong. "Something happen?"

Something. Everything. With a heavy sigh, I told him the truth, but unlike Lake and Chae Rin, the news didn't seem to surprise Rhys at all.

"She's angry," he said, his expression solemn. "She's always been a little angry, but ever since Natalya died . . . well, you remember how she was when you first met her."

Yep. Our totally un-awkward meeting at La Charte. That should have been the first hint that something was seriously wrong. Even for Belle, she was way colder than I'd expected. Cruel. I should have paid attention.

"This job isn't easy. Not for Effigies . . . and not for agents." Rhys set his mug down on the table. Gripping it with both hands, he stared into its dark contents. "Sometimes the Sect can feel like a tide you can't fight against. Especially when you've been raised with them, raised doing this. They ask so much of you, and you give so much until the sacrifice just feels natural. Like a foregone conclusion."

I laid my head against the seat.

"Sometimes," Rhys continued, "you feel like your life is just a chip in their pile and they can play it however they want. To Belle, I'm sure Natalya's death is just another example of that."

He became silent.

Belle was grieving. Like me. She'd lost something. "I wish things were different for all of us. I wish Natalya hadn't died. I wish I had my family back." My voice cracked. "I wish . . ."

I stopped when I noticed Rhys hunch over and bury his head in his hands.

"Rhys?" After sitting up, I leaned in and touched his arm. "Are you okay?"

Once he raised his head and gazed at me helplessly, I could see it:

a flicker of something deep and painful in his dark eyes. Words yet unformed, desperate to be voiced.

"Maia."

I drew back. "What's wrong?"

It was getting dark outside. Lights dotted the protective poles lining the railroad tracks. Light and shadow passed across Rhys's face as the train's steady rhythm murmured beneath us.

"I'm sorry."

He'd said it so quietly, so weakly, that I couldn't be sure what he was apologizing for. But soon his expression hardened. Straightening his back, he drew in a deep, shaky breath.

"Maia. There's something I need to tell you."

There was a light but unusual rumbling underneath us. We swayed on our bench as tremors surged throughout the compartment.

"What was that?" I looked around. "Oh god, is it phantoms? It's not phantoms, is it?"

Rhys smiled. "Exactly what you'd want to hear from an Effigy."

I grinned sheepishly. It wasn't until a few seconds had passed that I realized the train was slowing down.

"No, seriously, Rhys, what's going on? Are we stopping?"

Before he could say anything, a deep voice echoed through the PA system. "Ladies and gentlemen, we're experiencing some technical issues. We've started braking procedure. Please be patient while we work to fix the problem. Thank you."

Rhys stood. "I'm going to go find out what's going on."

"Wait!" As he began sliding off the bench, I jumped to my feet too. "What were you going to tell—"

The door shut.

Rhys hadn't been gone a few seconds when Chae Rin and Lake slipped inside the compartment.

"Guys," I said, "do you know what's happening out there?"

Chae Rin plunked down next to Lake, who had the plastic bag in her hands. "No idea," she said, "but there's something you should see."

Lake brought out the cigarette box. Flinging open the lid, she reached inside and drew out a tiny shard of some kind of jewel.

Wait.

"Is that what I think it is?" I leaned in for a better look. The shard was a white pearl-like stone, but it was the familiar swirl of black at the center that gave its identity away.

"Yep." Chae Rin shut the lid of the box. "It's *that* stone. Same one from Saul's ring. Same one from the ring I gave my boss. The one that can control phantoms."

"It's much smaller, though." Lake weighed it in her palm. "I almost didn't see it. It's like it broke off of a bigger piece."

I dragged the box closer and pulled out the letter, holding it delicately in my hands as I read. "I will reshape the world," I whispered. Alice's words.

Then it dawned on me.

"Guys," I asked. "Where are the rings?"

Chae Rin and Lake exchanged glances. "Aren't they somewhere in London HQ?" Lake said, but from the look on her face she didn't seem sure.

Brooklyn. Moscow. Buenos Aires. They still didn't know how Saul had managed to disable the central antiphantom devices of those cities.

One time, Uncle Nathan took me on a tour of the Municipal Defense Control Center so I could see where he worked. Dragged me, actually. It was a huge building with plenty of complicated-looking computers with the sole function to keep New York's Needle online.

Saul was in the hotel room with us when the Needle shut off.

He definitely had inside help. But how extensive? Natalya was murdered to keep Saul's secret hidden. Hell, I was almost killed myself. As the train finally crawled to a jerky stop, I thought back to Saul's calculating grin, unwavering even in the midst of an interrogation, while he spoke of his ring.

Safe? Well, I suppose that depends on who has it now.

"Um, guys?" Lake's naturally sweet tone had risen by several pitches as she peered outside the window. "Is . . . the train's APD off?"

Everything faded to silence. One beat. Two. Nothing inside me wanted to peer out the window, and yet I did anyway, wordlessly as if in a trance.

I couldn't see it: the soft, faded blue current running down tracks and up the poles, a symbol of the armor protecting us from the terror outside. It was gone.

No, no, no, no, no. I was on my feet, a tight pressure building in my chest. Chae Rin clicked the monitor in the corner of our compartment. It was dark outside now. We wouldn't be able to see much no matter how furiously Chae Rin searched through the angles.

I hoped, anyway.

Pointlessly.

"Oh my god." Chae Rin's hand fell from the monitor.

The three of us stared at the screen, awestruck by the gaping hole in the tracks in front the train. It'd been blown apart, right down to the bolts.

I couldn't breathe. That was the rumble we'd felt earlier. An explosion? But—

"Where the hell is Belle?" Rhys burst into our compartment, his knuckles drained of blood as he gripped his cell phone. "Where *is* she?"

Static noise spat from his cell phone, but every once in a while a weak, wheezing voice broke through. It didn't take long to figure out the words it moaned:

"... gone ... Saul's gone. ... Warn everyone. ... He's coming for you. ..."

Pushing past Rhys, I bolted out of the compartment and, after sliding open the door to the public area, I ran through the narrow hall. It didn't matter that passengers were staring, pointing, mouthing my name. I needed to get to the conductor. They needed to know before it was too late.

But it was already too late.

I stopped. My hands gripped the seat of the old man beside me. I could see him on the monitor standing in front of the train. In front of the explosion he'd made.

Saul.

Whatever terrible glee I was used to seeing in his eyes had vanished. This was a somber Saul, his familiar malice replaced by a quiet determination that was just as frightening.

And even from where I stood in the train, even with the sound turned off, I could still understand the word that passed his lips. The name he uttered.

"Marian."

25

I BUMPED INTO RHYS AS I WHIPPED AROUND.

"Rhys," I cried. "It's Saul! We have to get people out!"

"What's going on?" Lake's eyes glazed as she wandered down the hall, lost as a child. "Why . . . why is *he* here?" She had to grab on to a seat to stay on her feet.

"What the hell is going on?" A young man stood, his tablet flopping out of his lap, taking his earphones with it. "What's wrong with the tracks?"

"Just sit down," Rhys ordered.

"Why aren't we moving?" A young woman pressed her child to her chest, her arm shaking. "What happened to the lights?"

I just kept tugging Rhys's sleeve. "We have to get them out!"

"We can't." Rhys slid past a pair of empty seats to peer out the window through the blinds. "We're on a tall, very steep hill in the middle of nowhere. We're not anywhere near an antiphantom signal. This train's APD was our only protection." He turned to me, making very sure to keep his voice low. "Going out there would be suicide."

"Is it any worse than staying in here?"

"Neither is a particularly good option."

"*Regarde!*" A teenage boy stood on his seat cushion, pointing to the back of the train. "Belle*! Belle est ici! Incroyable. Dieu merci!*"

Belle had just reentered the cabin, pushed along by Chae Rin. She took one grim look at the monitor and curled her hands into fists. "Saul."

I looked at the monitor and saw that the conductor and two members of the crew had stepped outside to talk to Saul. "No," I hissed under my breath. "Get away from him!"

It was too late. At first the passengers fell silent, confused, perhaps, as they watched the conductor and his men crumple to the ground. It wasn't until a man started screaming that the rest of them followed, climbing out of their seats, pouring into the hall, clambering over one another to escape.

"Calm down!" I could barely hear Rhys's voice over the pandemonium. "Hey! Don't go out there!"

A few passengers had already fled through the back of the train car, chancing the dangerous night.

"No! There are phantoms out there!"

Lake's words paralyzed the crowd, and for a moment we all stared at each other, the realization stunning us into terrified silence. It was a short young woman who spoke first, reaching for Belle.

"It's okay," she said. She had to crane her neck to look at up at Belle, her trembling fingers clasped around the fabric of the Effigy's blouse. "Belle's here. The Effigies are here. We'll be okay! Right?"

"That's right!" cried a passenger.

"Belle's here!"

"Belle's a hero. Everything's okay!" A few more babbled their relief in French.

But something must have snapped in Belle when she looked into the young woman's eyes. "No." She shook her head, backing away. "I'm not . . . don't . . . Please don't count on me."

Pushing through the crowd, Belle fled outside.

It hit me all in one instant: anger. No, rage. Rage so hot it left no room for anything else. I barreled after her, squeezing through the crowd to get to her.

I found Belle outside the train car bent over the metal railings she clutched for dear life.

"I'm not." Belle's chest heaved as she rasped the words. "I'm not that. I can't."

Seeing her like that, so desperate, so small . . . Suddenly, whatever rage had been building in me gave way to a vast cavern of despair. My limbs felt cold and heavy, my knees weak. Everything was coming apart, but I couldn't approach Belle, couldn't take a single step toward the idol crumbling in front of me.

Shoving me aside, Chae Rin pulled Belle around and punched her, hard, in the face. Belle crashed against the railing, slumping to the ground. But she was lucky. She was still conscious. Chae Rin must have held herself back, though I could already see the swelling around Belle's eyes.

"Effigies heal." Chae Rin pulled Belle up by her collar. "And people die. What, you think you're the only one who's ever lost somebody?"

Her voice echoed into the night. Belle gritted her teeth, but couldn't look the younger girl in the eyes.

"This is bigger than you." Chae Rin shook her. "This is bigger than Natalya. This is bigger than us. Look around you. Look where we are."

Lake had just come outside, quiet as a cat. She stayed close to the door, anxiously watching the night.

"We have to do something," I said.

"And you, too!" Letting Belle drop to the ground, Chae Rin pointed at Lake, shivering by the door. "Stop shaking! We have to do this together."

But Lake wasn't the only one. I could hear the quiet tremor in Chae Rin's voice.

"The four of us." Chae Rin straightened up. "We have to do this together."

It was a command and a plea at the same time. I took Lake's hand and squeezed it gently, like Lake would have done, like Lake *had* done for me not too long ago.

The phantom came at us from nowhere, quick as a thief out of the darkness.

It was so fast I thought it was a missile at first. Screeching, it rocketed its long body between the cars with a crash, so close Belle had to jump out of the way to avoid being taken with the railing.

We ducked, shielding ourselves from the destroyed metal hurtling through the air. Screaming. People were screaming, in that car and the next.

Saul's siege had begun.

I ran inside the car to find passengers shrieking and gripping each other as they cowered in their seats.

The phantoms rose out from the floor. First smoke, then bone, then flesh, all incomplete, seeping inside from the metal, linking and twisting into a shape I knew all too well. Saul's wolves.

"Get down!" Rhys ducked down just as two phantoms jumped at him. With the swiftness of an experienced fighter, he pulled two long knives from the holsters strapped around his legs and clicked them on. A hazy blue electricity zipped down the blades, giving them an extra, serrated point, which he promptly jammed through a wolf's head.

"Help! Oh god, *help!*"

"Oh my god!"

I couldn't tell who was shrieking what in the pleas and whimpers surrounding me. People were already beginning to squeeze through the windows.

"Stop!" I tried to get to them, but a phantom reached me first. Grunting, I grabbed a man's briefcase to shield myself from the snapping jaw. The force of the impact shoved me onto the lap of the briefcase owner, his paper files flying into the air.

"I can't take this!" The man shook his head. "No, no! I have to get out of here!"

Shoving me away, he opened his window and dove, headfirst, outside.

"No, wait!" But I couldn't stop him. I watched, frozen in horror as his frail body tumbled down the steep hill with the others, tumbling into the many waiting tentacles of a rotting phantom at its foot. I'd known that phantoms could take many forms. I'd known that they took the appearance of beasts and ancient monsters, but this one . . . I'd never in my life thought that I would see something so grotesque. Its head, round and pulsating, split in two, sharp, twisted teeth frothing as it snared wayward passengers. A horror movie made flesh.

Somewhere, Lake was screaming.

I had no time to watch the fate of the man whose briefcase I'd stolen. Another wolf leapt at me. I rolled over the top of the seat, blocking its jaws with the briefcase.

"S-someone help me!" I cried, bucking under its weight.

A blade pierced the wolf's head, pinning it to the side of the wall. Belle's sword. I backed away quickly as Belle grabbed the hilt, pulling it out with one tug, letting the phantom slide to the ground.

Outside, another phantom torpedoed toward us from across the countryside, its long body flying fast through the night air. I braced myself for the collision, but it never came. The hill shuddered beneath us and the phantom collided with a wall of earth instead.

The impact shook the train car. I tumbled back, grabbing on to my seat to keep myself steady. I could see the wall of earth crumbling and the phantom's broken head falling with the dirt and soil.

"Chae Rin!" I climbed onto the seat. "Where is she?"

"The roof." Belle flipped her sword. "And if she's not careful, she'll level this entire hill."

"E-everyone!" Lake. She was at the back of the train car, blood dripping down her gorgeous face. "Clear the way!"

Rhys and I did what we could to get the passengers into the seats while Belle slashed and hacked the wolves still leaping at her.

"Out of the way!" Lake bellowed one more time and lifted her arms. Belle had just dived into the seats as a torrent of wind barreled through the hall, so sharp and fast it almost looked like a blade, dissecting phantoms and slicing through the floor. Breathing heavily, Lake fell to her knees just as I heard another crash. Chae Rin was practically terra-forming the landscape, but the car was already unsteady on the rails.

It started tipping.

"Damn it!" After grabbing hold of an armrest, Rhys looked around, holding a little girl in the crook of his bloodied arm. "Maia? Maia?"

He was calling out to me, frantically, wildly, but the second I tried to answer, gravity flung me to the floor. With my cheek pressed against a forgotten sneaker between the seats, I tapped around with a sweaty hand, too shocked by the shifting gravity to fully register the pool of blood beneath my palms.

We were going off the rails.

"Victoria!"

I managed to hear Belle scream even in the midst of the chaos.

Lake? Did something happen to her?

The car continued to tip under the weight of passengers colliding against the wall.

Then the train car froze. Something stopped the momentum; I could feel the sheer force of it whipping against the walls from the outside. My own voice joined the confused gasps and whimpers as I pulled myself onto my knees and looked out the window.

Lake. She was sliding down the hill, stopping the train car by summoning a violent torrent of wind. With her other hand she gripped Chae Rin's arm.

Chae Rin? She must have fallen off the train.

But Lake couldn't focus on the car, Chae Rin, and herself at the same time. She continued to slide back, unable to stop—sliding and sliding toward the monstrous phantom at the foot of the hill.

"Lake!" The blood drained from my face. *"Lake!"*

With a final burst of power, Lake managed to push the car back onto the train tracks at the very moment the phantom's tendril caught her around her ankle. She and Chae Rin both shrieked as it dragged them down.

I could barely breathe. The ground rumbled. I pressed a hand against the window, frantic. Chae Rin broke open a fault beneath the hill phantom, sucking it deep into the earth, but the suction was taking them with it. I tried to climb out the window to help, but a fresh wave of screams drew my attention toward the front of the car.

Saul. He'd finally made his appearance, his wolves growling at his feet.

They rushed toward me. I jumped into the hallway, pushing a

little boy out of the way before the phantom could reach him. After kicking one phantom in the face, I caught the knife that Rhys tossed to me and jammed it into its skull while Belle and Rhys hacked their way to Saul.

"Guys!"

Was that Lake's voice? I turned. She and Chae Rin were safe. I inhaled, relieved to see Lake's foot finding the window. Chae Rin hopped through first, but the moment our eyes met, Chae Rin's face twisted with shock.

"Maia, watch out!"

Saul's phantom came from behind. I'd barely had time to turn before I felt a rough hand push me into an empty seat. Rhys cried out in pain.

"Rhys!" I lifted myself off the seat, horrified to see the blood gushing from his chest.

Belle hopped across the seats to get to him, throwing her sword, piercing the phantom before it could gnaw off his flesh, but I was the one who caught him as he fell to the ground.

"Ow," he said. An obvious understatement. He was shaking.

There was so much blood. So much. I pressed against the wound to stop it from flowing, but there was just too much. It drenched my hands, soaked my jeans. Rhys's blood. Rhys's *blood*.

"I'm sorry." I swallowed a gasp as his blood spilled over my fingers. "I'm sorry."

Rhys's eyelids fluttered as he stared up at me, his lips twitching as he struggled for breath. "Maia . . ."

"Marian."

I could feel him. Saul. His breath raised the hairs on the back of my neck.

"I need you to come with me," he said.

"No." I gripped Rhys's knife, ready.

Rhys fought against pain and tried to heave himself off the floor, gasping for air as his body jerked and spasmed. He wouldn't reach me. Saul moved too fast, lifting me up by my collar. With an almost unsettling gentleness, he touched the crook of my neck, and in the next second, I disappeared with him.

26

I COULDN'T FEEL MY LIMBS.

What I could feel was my body slamming against the grass and the cold prickling against my skin. When I tried to move my arms and legs, it was if the nerves were attached to nothing. With my eyelids stuck shut, I couldn't even be sure I still had them.

My head spun with the fury of an amusement ride, and my short, desperate breaths were the only proof I still had lungs. Saul was used to disappearing, but for me it was like being pulled apart from the inside, parts of me ripping out as Saul dragged my body in and out of the space-time continuum. Only after the spinning stopped was I able to feel my hand still gripping Rhys's knife.

With great effort, I pried my eyelids apart. Clutching the ground, I pushed myself up, dirt building beneath my fingernails. It was still dark. Where was I? I couldn't see anything but fields and hills under the waxing moon. Where had Saul taken me?

Grunting, I twisted my body around, only to gasp. *Belle?*

What was she doing here? The last I remembered, the battle princess was jumping across seats to get to me. Somehow, Belle must have disappeared and reappeared with me, but she was in just as bad shape. Clutching her stomach, Belle lay on her back, writhing on the ground. Whatever flash of foolish hope Belle's appearance might have sparked within me vanished just as quickly. She was a mess, and so was I. Neither of us were in any shape to fight.

And fighting was exactly what we'd need to do.

I heard his groaning first before I turned and saw him: Saul, stumbling toward the train.

Train?

I pulled myself to my knees and squinted, my eyes adjusting to the night. It was the train. *Our* train. It was still on the rails at the top of the steep hill, not even that far away. If I could just gather enough strength to blitz Saul from behind, maybe I could drag Belle back with me.

A cold breeze laden with specks of snow brushed past my ears, gathering in Belle's hands. She was re-forming her sword, determined to fight despite the fact that she could barely move. It was too risky. If I could feel the shift in the air and the sudden drop in temperature, Saul would too.

I was right. Through sheer will alone, Belle managed to struggle to her feet, but the moment she tightened her grip on her sword's hilt, long, vine-like limbs cracked through the ground beneath her. With lightning speed, they whipped around her, holding her in place. The phantom they belonged to remained hidden deep in the soil.

One limb clasped her wrist and squeezed so tightly, her fingers trembled apart. The sword clattered to the ground before disintegrating into the air.

"I have nothing against you," said Saul. My body seized as he spoke. "I truly don't. I didn't know you'd grab hold of me the way you did. I'm sorry I took you with me. But this must be between Marian and myself alone."

Saul had changed. His posture was rigid and professional, his demeanor quiet and forthright. Even his eyes were different. He looked at us almost apologetically before turning back to the train. Maybe that was why it took me a few seconds to realize that his accent had changed as well, to a sharp, cool British lilt.

Nick. He was Nick now.

He faced the train, his legs shaking beneath him, his ragged pants and simple white shirt billowing in the wind along with his pale silver hair, now loose from its binds. He lifted both his arms, not easily, but with a sweeping, grand gesture that reminded me of Moses raising his staff to part the Red Sea. But it wasn't the sea that rose.

Phantoms. Long-bodied serpents, a class I knew too well now. They appeared from the other side of the train, arching their torsos over the track. Each car shook violently as the bodies collided against the metal. For a horrifying, dizzying second I thought the flesh, bone, and shadow would crush the train, but the phantoms only coiled around it, trapping the passengers inside. It was a relief, but not much of one.

And then . . . the phantoms shuddered, their bones shifting and *freezing*. For a second, I thought Belle was behind it, but Belle could barely move, restrained by phantoms and still fighting off the effects of Saul's transportation. She'd probably used up her last bit of strength summoning her sword. In the condition she was in, it'd be a miracle if she could even manage to make a snowflake.

So then what was happening to the phantoms? Why did their bodies shiver and harden? And the sheet of ice sliding up their entire length encasing them in a pallid sheen . . . what the hell *was* that?

It was Saul who answered my unspoken question. "I've learned much over the decades. Too much." Lowering his arms, he turned to me. I could see the strain on his flushed face. "Petrification. It's an ability all phantoms have. To become impenetrable. It should keep your friends from following us here."

Feebly, Belle struggled against her binds. "What are you—!"

A tendril whipped around her mouth, silencing her.

"Like I said." Saul began toward me. "This is between Marian and me."

My whole body was crumbling. I managed to stand, placing myself between them, but the moment I felt steady on my feet, Saul pushed me back down.

"I'm sorry," he said. "I'll discuss everything with you later. I promise."

He pulled something from his pocket and continued toward Belle. I could see only the tips sticking out from inside his fists, but I didn't have to wonder for long. Belle gasped as Saul jammed the device in her neck.

The inoculation gun . . . But that was a Sect device. Saul had felt the sting when I'd jammed it into him in Argentina. Now it was Belle wincing in pain.

I was on my own.

I looked up at him as he approached, a quiet rage burning my skin from the inside. "You gonna jam that thing in me, too?"

"And return the favor? No. That would be counterintuitive." He sheathed it in his pocket, pausing when he saw me inching away from him. "I just want to talk."

"About *what*?" I cried. "What do you want from me? Why did you come to Brooklyn? Why did you follow me here? How did you even escape? What are you . . . ?" I tried to swallow, but my throat was so dry. "What are you going to do with me?"

Saul knelt beside me. It was the same Saul who'd attacked those cities and besieged the train, and I was still terrified. But his manner had become soft and careful. He maintained a respectful distance, watching over me with silent concern.

Concern. No. It was a lie. It had to be. He was trying to sneak himself through the barbed wire I'd erected between us. He wouldn't win. When he touched my hand and tried to pull me up, I yanked it away and scrambled back, my heart hammering against my chest. The fact that this made him look so sad *infuriated* me.

He had no right.

"I know I deserve this, but I don't have much time," said Saul. "Maybe it was the drugs they sedated us with. They affected Alice much more than they did me, but she'll be back. She can probably still hear us. I can hear sometimes too. I heard you . . . I heard you say my name in Brooklyn." He shook his head. "But she always comes back. And when she does, she'll be far less kind to you."

Stooping down, he grabbed me by the upper arm, yanked me to my feet, and dragged me toward the train, ignoring my whimpers.

"Your name is Maia, isn't it?" He didn't look at me as he tugged me along. "Maia, I need you to do something for me." He finally stopped, holding my wrist so I wouldn't go anywhere. As if I could; my legs still felt like jelly slopping beneath me. "I need you to find her. Marian. There's something I need to ask her."

"You keep saying that," I spat. "But you never tell me why."

Saul shook his head. "Some things are better left—"

"Tell me why, Saul."

I could feel his hand tremble against my skin.

"Please don't call me that," he begged. Actually begged. "That's the name she chose for us once she took my body. A king from the Old Testament who united god's chosen. So wonderfully brazen. But Alice was always like that."

Even his smirk held no life in it. The bitterness was clear on his face.

"I have control now, but I don't know for how long. I can't even remember the last time I felt my own heartbeat."

As if he couldn't help himself, he pressed his free hand against his chest, breathing deeply.

I watched him. "Who . . . are you?"

I could feel the pressure of his fingers against my pulse. "Nick. Call me Nick."

"You're over a hundred years old." My eyes traveled down his body, still as hard and fit as a young man barely out of his teens. "How?"

"1871," he answered solemnly. "The third of June. A year after Marian died. It was the day I became one of the accursed."

I frowned. "Accursed?"

"Like you. I was called to this life after Alice passed, just as you were called after the death of the one they called the Matryoshka Princess."

The Effigy line. But he spoke only of Alice. Maybe she was the only one, the only Effigy whispering and plotting in his head.

"Each of us has our curse. You and your fire. And her." He jerked his head at Belle, now limp in her binds. "The span of my life is just one part of mine. I couldn't even die with her."

His tilted his head away from me, and for a moment his long hair veiled his expression.

"I'll ask again." It took every bit of control I had to keep my voice calm. "What do you want from me? Why do you need me to find Marian?"

"Because she knows where it is." He drew me in close, and I had to crane my neck to look up at him. "The rest of the stone from which these rings were made."

He lifted his left hand. I saw the ring shining there, its pearl stone glinting in the starlight. Sibyl had told us the ring was safe, and maybe she had even believed it. Just as Saul couldn't have escaped from the London facility by himself, he couldn't have gotten the ring back either. Not without help. My hunch was right, not that it mattered much now.

"That's what Alice believes, anyway. It's her hypothesis. But we need Marian to confirm it."

"So you're working with Alice." I laughed coldly. "And here I thought you were a bit less of an asshole than she was."

"I'm not her," he hissed quickly. "I'm not. It's just that we have the same goal."

"Which is?"

Saul's face softened in the question's wake, his lips parting as he eased into the anguish that had suddenly taken him. "A wish," he whispered. "It's all for a wish."

I remembered. He'd asked me before, in Argentina. . . . No, it was Alice who'd asked as she'd pinned me against the window with Nick's body.

Maia, isn't there something you want more than anything?

"It's the ring, Maia," said Saul, very quietly. "The ring will grant my wish."

"No way," I whispered, shaking my head. "It's not possible."

"Look around you," he said. "A lot of things are possible in this terrible world we live in."

"A wish. The ring can grant wishes." My head was spinning.

"The stone. I don't know all of the details. Alice keeps many things hidden away from me. But we both want the same thing. We both have something we desperately wish for. But this ring isn't enough. I need the rest of the stone."

"I don't understand. You're crazy." I trembled. "You're crazy, Saul!"

"Call me Nick," he pleaded. "My name is Nick." A sob escaped his lips. *"Please."*

"Who the hell do you think you are, *asking* something from me?

You killed them. Not her. Not Alice. You!" I looked back at the train still captive under the weight of Saul's monsters. "You!"

"I have no choice but to kill." His face hardened. "They had to die. Otherwise, how can it grant my wish?"

When my gaze shifted to the ring again, my eyes widened, then narrowed. "No."

"The ring controls phantoms. The more people we sacrifice to them, the more potent the ring becomes. The more powerful."

Death powered the stone. The realization was almost too much to handle.

Now that I thought of it, the ring's stone wasn't as white as it was before. The swirl of darkness inside had flowered, filling more space since the time I'd seen it last.

"All those cities," I whispered. "All those people you murdered. To what? Juice up your ring so you can get . . . *your wish granted*?"

His face creased into an ugly grimace. "Everyone has one. Or are you trying to tell me you don't?"

I didn't want to think of them, but when I closed my eyes I could see my family's faces so clearly my teeth clenched from the pain of it.

"Everyone does. Myself. Alice. The difference between Alice's wish and mine is that mine won't break apart the world. If I can make mine first—"

"You'd still be a selfish asshole."

"But at least I'd have Marian by my side."

The name sounded dark and lonesome on his tongue.

"That's it?" The words were hoarse in my throat. "You just want your girlfriend back?"

"No, that's *not* all." Saul raised his hand. "I could just as easily have brought Marian back with this. It has more than enough power." He turned it over. "After all, parts of Marian are inside of you. To come back, all she needs to do is take your body, the way Alice took mine. I could use the ring to draw her from the depths of you, to force her to the forefront of your mind. But it would be a waste. My wish is bigger than this. And you can call her on your own."

He twisted my arm back, forcing me to my knees. Pain shot through my body, searing my nerves. I cried out as Saul leaned in from behind me. "I don't need Marian to take your body, not yet. I just want you to find her, to ask her where the rest of the stone is. Do it. Do it quickly."

"I can't." I downed the air in shuddering gasps.

"Do it now."

"I—I have to be calm. I have to be calm. At peace . . ."

"Do it, Maia. Find Marian. Do it, or I swear to the heavens I will have them all killed."

My head snapped up. The train. They were all still inside. The passengers, Lake and Chae Rin, and Rhys. My eyes swelled with tears. He was still hurt badly, his chest drowning in blood because of me. Because he risked his own life to protect me.

I tasted the tears on my lips, sucking in drops as I rasped. This wasn't fair. None of this was fair, and I wished none of it had happened. I just wanted to go home.

But I didn't have a choice.

"Okay." I set my teeth, my hair spilling over my face. "Just give me time."

He let me go. "Normally, time would be the one thing I have."

I tried my best to silence my jackhammering heart, but to do it I had to forget everything and everyone. There wasn't any room for error. If I didn't calm myself, didn't find that place deep within myself the way Belle'd taught me to, I'd never see any of them again. How much blood was on my hands already?

Blood. My heart gave a jolt, but I banished the pain. The fear, too. Like a sharp vine, it crept up my insides, threatening me, but I couldn't let it take me. Not this time. Clenching my teeth, I forced it away too.

How would I even reach Marian? The consciousness of the last Effigy was always the freshest. The rest were tangled together in knots, according to Belle. How could I find the one I needed?

Closing my eyes, I squeezed my hands into fists against my lap and shut everything out. Everything but the hardness of the ground against my knees. I inhaled deeply. Once, twice. Again. Again.

Please, I begged them, the girls who'd left shards of themselves inside me. *Help me.*

Belle was right. I had been here before. I remembered the white stream, the heavy mist blanketing the world around me.

And the door. The farther I walked through the thick fog, the clearer it became. Red, just as Belle had said. Connected to nothing, it stood upright on its own.

The stream reached just past my ankles, but it wasn't cold. Belle had gotten that part wrong, or maybe she'd just experienced it differently. For me it was burning hot. Though I expected it to scorch my skin, it didn't hurt at all. The heat became part of me, rising through my legs, warming my body. I could breathe again. The pain in my limbs and joints had vanished too. If only I could hide in this strange place forever.

I trudged through the crystal white waters, the door looming larger with each step. It was magnificent. It belonged in a palace with its golden rims, its woodwork crafted as if for kings.

And like the door to a palace, it was guarded.

"Natalya . . ."

I knew Natalya was tall, but now, as I stood in front of her, the legendary Effigy towered above me. Yes, this was Natalya. Too many times had I seen those eyes, always fierce, always proud, whether in the heat of battle or in the middle of an interview. Her black hair, cut close to her skull, still fluttered from whatever breeze passed through this place. And in her scar-covered hands was the broadsword she'd made famous during her years with the Sect. The edge of its blade disappeared into the white stream as she gripped it proudly.

The beautiful and noble soldier Natalya Filipova.

But she was not the one I was looking for.

"We meet at last."

Natalya's voice shook me to the core. Every word she spoke swelled with the contours of her Russian accent, still prominent despite her perfect English.

Every word she spoke.

Natalya Filipova was speaking.

Speaking to *me*.

My body went rigid as fear suddenly gripped me.

"Don't be afraid." Natalya's tone was soft despite its strength. "I know why you're here. I've seen everything. Through you."

I wrapped my arms around myself. The very idea that parts of Natalya, and parts of so many other girls, were living on inside me made me feel so alien, as if fate had snatched my humanity from me the day it called me to be an Effigy.

Maybe it had.

"You know who Marian is, right?" If I had more time, I'd have made sure my first words to Natalya were more meaningful, full of praise and respect.

"No. Not fully. I . . . I died before I could discover everything."

I was so used to seeing Natalya strong, but now the Effigy's lips curled into something probably meant to be a snarl before she thought better of it. Natalya looked truly crestfallen as she lowered her head, peering at her own reflection in the stream.

The pain was still fresh. The pain of dying.

"Natalya . . . how *did* you die?"

I hadn't meant to ask, but the moment I did, Natalya's eyes were on me.

"Are you sure you want to know?" There was something wild in her eyes, something hidden, even with the rest of her calm. "But then, it would help, wouldn't it?" Natalya nodded. "Yes, it *would* help you. To get to Marian, you'll need to see it, after all. You'll need to see *all* our most difficult memories."

Our. The Effigies'. Despite the heat, I shivered.

"I can show you my death." Natalya's hands tightened around the round pommel of her sword. "In fact, I *want* to show you. You should know what happened."

The corner of Natalya's lips crept up into the faintest of smiles. She was smiling at me. And yet I stepped back, my hands cold. Why? Why was it so unsettling? There was something Natalya wasn't telling me, something screaming in the silence.

"Are you prepared to watch me die, Maia Finley?"

My knees buckled beneath the overbearing weight of Natalya's expectant stare. I knew I couldn't say no.

"Show me."

Natalya stepped aside. The door crept open on its own.

It was dark. My eyes couldn't adjust at first. But once they did, I could see the armchair. . . . Yes, I could *see* Natalya's armchair this time. It wasn't like before. This time, I stood across the living room of Natalya's apartment inside my own body. Not only could I see the armchair, I could see Natalya in it. The pop art on the wall. The scotch-filled decanter on the table, red lipstick staining the rims of glasses. The bottles of alcohol. All of it Natalya's.

I saw everything clearly this time. I could see Natalya's hand clasping her throat, her lips sputtering, but the words unable to form.

No. I didn't want to see it after all. Now that Natalya's body was crumpling to the floor, now that she was clawing at the rug in a desperate attempt to stay alive, I couldn't bear to see her die. Covering my eyes with a whimper, I turned.

"I'm sorry," came the voice from across the room. The voice that stopped my heart. "I'm so sorry."

The ticking seconds slowed until they faded from existence entirely. My arms fell limp at my sides. *Don't turn around*, I ordered myself, tears stinging my eyes. *Don't you do it*. But my legs were shifting rebelliously from under me.

I didn't want to see. I couldn't tell if the desperate breaths I heard were mine or Natalya's, but it didn't matter. My body would give out soon. I knew it. My legs would crumple the moment I turned, the *moment* I turned and—

And saw Rhys standing over Natalya.

I fell back and hit my head against the table, the pain sharply real. But it couldn't be. Nothing about this horrific memory could be real.

It was a lie.

Natalya was lying to me.

Natalya was lying; she was trying to trick me!

That must have been the hidden meaning behind her smile. Yeah. That must have been it! That vile . . . that sickening . . . How *could* she? How could . . . ?

The gasps and the wails were definitely mine. I cried the way I hadn't in so long, my hands wrapped around myself as I shook on the floor.

"No! No, no!" I covered my ears to block out Rhys's repeated apologies. It was all a lie, all a lie. "You're lying to me!" I was on my knees. "You're *lying* to me! Natalya! Where are you? I said, where are you? Why are you lying to me? *Answer me!*"

And then Natalya was in front of me. I could only see her grim face in front of mine.

"It's over," my hero said before my mind shattered.

27

I OPENED MY EYES. MY HANDS. I STARED AT them, opening and closing my fingers as if for the first time. This new flesh . . . like a freshly pressed blanket, it enveloped me with love. This curling hair, this shade of skin, these shorter legs that had yet to be trained. Fascinating. Truly. I took it in.

And then I stood.

"Did you find her?" A voice. Which voice? "Maia, did you find Marian?"

I turned. Ah, yes, I'd seen him before. The man they'd called a terror. The man who'd brought cities to their knees. I recognized his high cheekbones first, the delicate lashes, the hard jaw and thin lips, the impossible silver locks framing his face.

Saul.

I remembered, but it was the girl behind him that drew my attention: Belle. Like a rag doll in a child's hand, she dangled helplessly, held in place by many long, spindly limbs. A phantom, most likely. Belle had been caught.

How disappointing.

I went to free her anyway.

"Wait!" Saul. He was persistent. Out of the corner of my vision, I could see his wide eyes narrowing as I passed by without a word. "I said *wait*." He grabbed my wrist. "I asked you a question."

I stayed silent.

"Did you find Marian? What did she tell you?" He tightened his grip, the desperation in his voice so laughably, pathetically clear. "Please. What did she tell you?"

Swiftly, I pulled my arm out of his grip and grabbed his wrist instead.

Then I broke it.

He cried out in pain like the child he was as I grabbed the collar of his shirt and pushed him back. He flew through the air, but I'd already turned before I could see him land. I heard the crash instead.

Strange. My movements weren't as quick as I'd expected. Then again, I hadn't had a body for such a long time, and this body was so woefully weak. So much potential buried inside it, and the girl had barely managed to pick at the surface. It was regrettable, but Maia had been given her chance. I would simply have to train it myself.

Belle lifted her head, the pain of it apparent on her face, and looked at me with narrowed, wondering eyes. She must have already noticed the change in the way the girl carried herself, the newfound strength in her stride. But there would be time to explain things later.

I held out my hand and flames came with it. Belle's eyes widened from beyond the haze of the flicking fires as the sword's hilt materialized in my grip. A new grip, but the same sword. My sword.

Its name passed silently from Belle's lips.

Zhar-Ptitsa.

I ran through the flames. A few swift cuts was all it took to free

Belle, the remains of flesh and bone falling to the ground like I'd seen so many times before. But I knew it wouldn't be that simple.

As expected, the ground rumbled beneath us.

Pushing Belle out of harm's way, I jumped back just in time for the phantom to burst from the ground, infuriated. I readied my sword, flipping it into position. I could have simply burned it away, but it had been too long. I needed the practice.

The phantom reminded me of an octopus, its monstrous jaws snapping as it waddled toward me with the limbs it had left. It took only a few seconds. Aiming for its head, I planted a foot in the wide gap between his sharp teeth and, boosting myself up, slit its skull before it could snap its jaw shut. As I landed lightly on the ground, it slumped to the side behind me, its head split in two.

Both Belle and Saul stared at me, one in amazement, the other in fury.

"Who are you?" Belle limped toward me, clutching her side. "Why . . . why do you have that sword?"

She already knew the answer. It was there in her tear-filled blue eyes. *Yes, Belle, trust your intuition.*

Still, for now, I ignored her. There was a train in the distance. Phantoms had petrified around it, their flesh hardening into something bone and crystal. I needed to free the passengers before I could attend to anything else. Belle looked too weak to fight, so it would have to be me. I would use my flames, but how should I engage the phantoms without harming the hostages?

It was Saul who solved the query for me. Blood dripped from his hand as he tightened a fist, and with a flick of his head the hard casing around the phantoms' long, snakelike bodies crumbled like a shedding second skin. They barreled toward me.

"You're not thinking," I said in a voice too young and innocent for me to ever get used to. "You still need me to find your Marian, don't you?"

Indeed Saul wasn't thinking. His lips pulled up over his clenched teeth as the phantoms zipped by him, one after another.

I burned one of them, setting its body aflame and rolling out of the way as it zipped by me, howling. I cut off the head of another, jumping atop its torso and riding it as it crashed to the ground. Then I ran for the others.

"This can't be possible!" Saul yelled as four remaining phantoms converged on me at once. "Stop!" His wails drifted atop the shrieks of phantoms as I set fire to their rotted hearts. "I said stop!"

The last remaining phantom broke away, heading for Belle instead. She was paralyzed. She could only drop to her knees as it tore toward her.

I wasted no time. I tossed the sword with expert aim, piercing its neck just as it lifted its terrible elongated head. It crashed a short distance from Belle, who remained on the ground, her disbelieving eyes fixed on me. The sword disappeared; I willed it away, only to summon it once more to my hand when it came time to face Saul.

I relished the familiar heat of the leather hilt against my palm. *Yes, exquisite.* How I longed for this: to breathe air again, to feel the breeze on my face and the muscles in my legs and arms burning with acid as I worked them. There were no sensations in the world of the white stream, but here in the world of the living, my heart beat again, its steady rhythm pounding my chest.

I was alive. I was alive again.

A tear budded in the corner of my eye as I began toward Saul. After all, it was because of him that I had died in the first place. I simply had to finish him off. Then I would pick up where I'd left off. I could start my life again.

No.

I stopped, my foot cemented to the ground. It wouldn't budge, no matter how hard I tried to move it.

This is my body. Mine.

"Maia," I hissed.

This is my *body.* The voice grew louder as the girl crawled out from the grave of her own mind. *Get out.*

"No . . ." My sword fell from my grip and dissipated into the air, my arms frozen in place. "You fool, it's almost finished."

Get out! I said get out!

It was a tug-of-war between two minds, but with only parts of mine still intact, I was fighting a losing battle. It was as if I was sinking deeper and deeper into the abyss. The force pulled me down, away from the flesh, and back toward the darkness.

"Not again," I whispered. "Please, not again." My lips trembled. "Don't make me go back. . . ."

I was gone in the next second.

I woke up on the ground feeling like crap, with my body ridiculously sore and my muscles burning fire. I'd only just raised my head when I saw Saul darting toward me.

"Natalya, look out!" cried Belle.

I was too slow to evade him, but before he could reach me, the earth shifted and broke, swallowing Saul in a pit. Chae Rin. And it was Lake who carried her from the train, the two girls flying through the air to reach me. Thank god.

"Maia!" Once she touched down behind me, Lake ran to my side, yanking me up by the arm. "Are you okay? What the hell happened?"

"Watch out!" Chae Rin shoved Lake aside, using the momentum to boost herself back. Saul had appeared behind her, the blade he swung just managing to slice stray hairs from Lake's ponytail. It was Rhys's blade. He must have found it in the grass.

My body froze. *Rhys.*

Rhys.

The blood drained from my face, and for a moment the world fell to nothingness. It was precisely the opportunity Saul had been looking for.

"Maia!"

I wasn't even sure who'd yelled my name. My body couldn't move fast enough. Saul was behind me, Rhys's blade against my neck.

"Step aside." With his free arm he hooked me by the waist, my back flat against his hard chest. I couldn't even flinch from the sting of his blade, taut against my neck.

Chae Rin and Lake exchanged glances. Each girl looked as if she was fighting with herself, but eventually they acquiesced, stepping back.

"You really don't understand everything that I've been through, do you?" His hot breath brushed the back of my ear. "I never asked for any of this. You have no idea."

"Oh, poor genocidal maniac. Are you kidding me right now?" Chae Rin looked utterly disgusted. "Why don't you can the speech, asshole, because nobody gives a crap."

As Lake shot Chae Rin a frantic look, Saul laughed. "Maybe. Maybe I don't deserve redemption. But I've already come this far, and I've suffered more than enough, to the point where I thought death would be a kindness. But you won't understand. Not until you know what it's like to be trapped in your mind."

But I did know. I'd just experienced the hell of it. It was like watching the world through a foggy window of a cold, dark cellar. Alone. Terrified. I knew what it felt like to have hope ripped away with each movement your body made without your command. After having known that infinite despair, I couldn't imagine living for over a century in my own body without being able to feel my heartbeat. But Nick had. Even if he'd begun his life as a normal boy, the experience had changed him. Shattered him. It wasn't hard to see why.

And yet . . .

"I don't care," I said carefully, because every shift of my jaw risked my throat being cut. A thin trickle of blood was already dribbling down my neck. "You killed people. You killed them. And they didn't want to die."

I thought back to the funeral, to the three caskets lowered into the ground one by one. I thought of Uncle Nathan, his hand squeezing my shoulder as if begging me not to follow.

"I won't forgive you." My whole body tensed. Fury, first a low murmur, billowed and swelled, burning through the exhaustion in my bones, shooting to the tips of my fingers. *"Ever."*

The flames emerged from my entire body, shattering the knife against my throat, scorching Saul's skin. It emerged from the fire, the weapon I'd summoned before. It rested in my hands now, the smooth oak handle, the long blade curving into a sickle. I'd called it once out of fear. Now it stood as a manifestation of my anger.

I didn't let myself think. Shutting my eyes, I swiveled around and swung the scythe. I felt the blade slice through flesh, the resistance of Saul's body reverberating up the pole and through my arms, jolting my eyes open.

Saul staggered back, screaming. Tears leaked from his eyes as he gripped his stomach, tortured by the pain. I was terrified, but I wasn't finished. Not yet. The scythe was heavier than I'd expected, but I managed to lift it above my head. Before Saul could react, I brought it down, taking his hand, and his ring with it.

The screaming was too much for me to handle. Shocked, I stepped back. All the fury vanished in an instant, and my flames and my weapon vanished with it.

I looked at him. And Saul—no, Nick—looked at me too. A boy whose life had been taken from him had decided to take life in return. Because of that alone he had no right to look so hurt, so betrayed as his blood stained the grass.

He tried to open his mouth to speak, but with the blood draining quickly from his body, he could only move his lips, his eyelids fluttering. He used the last bit of strength he had to disappear one last time. To where, I didn't know, but he was gone. That was all that mattered.

I dropped to my knees, totally and utterly exhausted.

"Maia!" Lake ran to me. "Oh my god!" Kneeling next to me, she grabbed my shoulders. "Are you okay? Here, look at me."

My mouth quirked into a little smile as Lake squished my face and rotated it every which way, looking for bruises. "I'm okay, Lake. Just tired."

"You're more than okay." Chae Rin playfully nudged me in the back with her knee, laughing as I rested against her legs. "That was pretty badass, kid. When did you learn to do that?"

I had no idea. My mind was floating away from me as the weariness annexed my body, weighing my limbs. It was lucky Chae Rin was behind me, because I could barely keep my head up.

"It was Natalya who opened the way for her," Belle said.

I hadn't even noticed Belle rising to her feet. She still looked unsteady on them as she trudged across the grassy field. Her chest rose and fell at erratic intervals. Though she wasn't fully recovered yet, she reached us nonetheless.

But Belle wasn't interested in us at all.

Lake sat on the ground, watching with the rest of us as Belle stooped down and slid the ring off of Saul's hand. "Belle?"

"The stone is darker now." Belle placed it in her palm, eyeing it strangely. "Saul killed so many people. For this." Pinching the metal, she held it close to her face, squinting as she peered into the pearl. "He must have been happy every time the darkness spread."

"What are you babbling about?" Chae Rin's leg shifted against my back.

"That's right," Belle said. "You weren't here when he explained it. The ring controls phantoms, and when the phantoms take lives, their deaths strengthen the power of the stone." Belle was very quiet. "So that it can grant wishes."

Silence stretched between us.

"Sounds daffy." Lake laughed nervously, quieting down when she realized no one was laughing with her.

"It does." Belle sucked in a breath. "But I wonder."

She looked at me, and immediately I understood. Belle didn't have to say a word. She'd just seen her come back, after all. Natalya. For me, it felt like that moment had lasted hours, days, decades. But for Belle it had gone by in an instant. Too quickly.

Saul had already told us that the ring was enough to bring back Marian, to force her consciousness permanently into the driver's seat of my body. Surely it would be enough for Natalya too. Belle had to have been thinking it.

I knew how it felt. How many times had I called out for June during those long, terrifying minutes I'd spent trapped inside my own body? How many wishes had I uttered deep inside my heart?

Truthfully, I wouldn't have blamed Belle if she decided to sacrifice my life for Natalya's. But no matter what, I couldn't die yet.

I wasn't the only Finley left. That was reason enough.

"Please . . ." The tear rolled down my chin, mingling with the bloodstains on my neck. "Please don't hurt me, Belle. . . ."

Simple words. Weak. Desperate.

The ring fell from Belle's hands. It was like she'd finally awoken. Whatever had possessed her left with a violent shudder, and she crumpled to the ground. In the pool of blood Saul left behind, Belle laid her head in her hands and cried.

28

"AGENT LANGLEY, AS ACTING DIRECTOR OF the European Division of the Sect and head of the London head-quarters facility, don't you feel even the slightest bit of responsibility for the escape of the international terrorist known as 'Saul'?"

"Considering it's the Sect's responsibility to deal with issues of international security as it pertains to the phantoms, do you believe that more coordination and cooperation with the world's leading governments would have led to a different result?"

"What do you say to the growing number of detractors who claim now, more than ever, that the Greenwich Accords should be repealed?"

Sibyl had nerves of steel. I didn't know how she did it. Despite the vitriol spewed at her from the venomous fangs of the press, she stood at the podium with the hardened, almost defiant confidence of a woman who'd seen and handled much worse.

Back at London HQ, Lake, Chae Rin, and I watched the press conference on TV from inside Cheryl's office. We only just got back to London earlier this morning, and considering I'd had my body snatched, my mind broken, and my life almost snuffed out countless times, I was hoping Cheryl would have at least given us the day off before summoning us. Nope.

As we watched Sibyl respond to questions without giving any legitimate answers, Chae Rin shook her head. "It is cold as ice in there."

"Well, unfortunately, letting Saul escape is kind of a huge deal." Cheryl set the controller on the TV and sat at her desk. "Colossal, if you haven't noticed."

"I dunno, Maia got him pretty good," said Lake. "He's probably dead."

"He still got away. And Effigies heal. And we have no idea what he's going to do next." Taking off her glasses, Cheryl rubbed her eyes. "It's literally the mother of all disasters. How did this happen?"

Back at the press conference, a short, bald reporter raised his pen. "Do you even know the whereabouts of Saul now? Do you have any leads?"

That may have been the first time Sibyl showed any signs of annoyance. She sighed. "I've answered this, Richard, and yes, it's still classified."

"Actually, I believe I can provide some insight into these matters."

The murmurs and flashing lights from the crowd intensified as Bartholomäus Blackwell joined Sibyl on the podium.

Cheryl shoved her glasses back onto her face, too shocked to notice when they slid back down her nose. "Blackwell? What . . . ?"

"What's wrong?" Chae Rin shrugged. "He's the representative of the Council, isn't he?"

"The bloody Duchess of York doesn't answer questions concerning matters of British national security, does she?" Apparently, Cheryl's cockney accent slipped through only when she wanted to hit someone. With a shaky exhale, she placed it back in its cage and continued. "He's more of a diplomat than anything else. He's just the face of the Council."

His face, right now, seemed almost gleeful as he motioned for Sibyl to step aside. It was only too obvious that the woman was trying very hard to maintain her poker face, clenching her jaw, probably so she didn't say anything fit for a scandalous sound bite. Blackwell may have been somewhat ceremonial, but as the official representative of the Council he outranked her; he must have, because Sibyl stepped aside, just as he asked.

"All your questions are understandable, of course. The matter of the international terrorist known as 'Saul' has not been handled to the best of the Sect's ability. This I admit."

Blackwell's red lips and pale skin made him look almost vampiric standing on the podium. Though his suit was professional, I could see why Sibyl didn't want him to take over. While Sibyl had kept her expression neutral, he wore an almost mocking grin, just as he had when he'd assessed me in the Cathedral.

"As for how Saul escaped, we already have the culprit in custody."

"And who is that culprit?" a woman asked him from the crowd.

Blackwell smiled. "His name is Agent Vasily Volkov, though he was aided by members of the London facility's Research and Development department."

As Lake gasped, I sat up in my chair. "Vasily?"

"Dear god." Cheryl buried her face in her hands.

As the crowd erupted, Sibyl shot for the podium. I could tell she was hissing something, but Blackwell put up a hand to stop her.

"Well, this whole press conference just went down the pan real quick," said Lake.

"He's insane." Cheryl shook his head. "Telling the crowd that it was Sect personnel who let him go? Is he *trying* to turn *everyone* against us?"

Vasily. I thought of his fox grin and shuddered. But then Vasily only followed orders. He'd said so himself. If Vasily was willing to cut off a ringmaster's finger for the ring, if he was willing to kill me to keep me from discovering Alice and Nick's secrets, and if he was willing to set Saul free, it was only because someone had ordered him to.

I narrowed my eyes as I watched Blackwell slide his hands into his pockets.

Once the press conference ended, the television news pundits began their discussion. The three of us were, needless to say, a little worried by Cheryl's bloodshot eyes, so Lake granted her the mercy of changing the channel.

BREAKING: LONDON REACTS
TO THE PHANTOM TRAIN ATTACK

"The . . . *phantom* train?" Chae Rin raised an eyebrow. "Is this about us?"

It was. BBC reporters had gone throughout London to interview surviving passengers from last night's attack, along with their families, and really anyone they could snag off the street. I still wasn't used to it: being talked about, having people know who, and what, I was. Squirming in my seat, I prepared for the worst.

"It was terrifying, man, but those girls, they saved us. They were seriously brilliant."

I didn't even recognize the guy speaking. The only face stitched into my mind after the attack, cruelly, and maybe permanently, was the man whose briefcase I'd taken. I could still see the terror in his eyes as he slid down the hill.

But this guy was different, as was the teenage girl who told the story of how Lake pushed the train car back onto the tracks when it was just about topple down the hill.

"I wasn't in that car. I was in the next one. We were fine for the most part—the phantoms didn't attack us, but I saw some of the stuff happening outside from the monitors."

She jittered as she spoke. She was probably still wired from the residual terror in her system, but it was clear there was something else there, beyond the fright.

"They saved us," she said. "The Effigies saved our lives."

It was a refrain repeated throughout the interviews. And no matter how intently I stared at the screen, it just couldn't sink in.

"Interesting." Cheryl swept her hair out of her face and leaned in, watching closely. "I know Sibyl hasn't had a chance to tell you, but you guys really did do a good job out there."

As Cheryl pulled a tablet out of her drawer and started clicking, Lake looked at us, still unsure.

"We couldn't bring Saul back." She wrung her hands. "And honestly, a lot of people . . ."

Died. A lot of people died. None of us could forget that.

"Battles have casualties, Victoria," said Cheryl. "You can't save everyone. As an Effigy, you should know that now. Lucky for us, it seems your popularity's on the rise regardless."

Cheryl fell silent as she read off her device, her lips widening into a grin.

"You've got fans," she said, the screen reflecting in her glasses. "Lots of them. This is perfect." Cheryl set down the tablet. "You know, maybe you were on to something with the whole PR thing, Lake."

Lake looked as confused as the rest of us. "What do you mean?"

"You said it before, didn't you? The Sect needs a face. And not Blackwell's." Cheryl spat his name. "We need friendlier faces. Ones the general public can get behind and support. Yeah." Cheryl sat back in her seat, letting her chair rotate on its axis. "We need to reassure them that, despite any little problems here and there, the Sect is doing things right."

Chae Rin grabbed a magazine from the table next to her, waving it. "And you're going to, what, have us do more photo shoots?" Making a disgusted noise, she threw it back on the table. "No way. The last one was bad enough."

"Obviously we can't have you get too commercial," said Cheryl. "Otherwise you'll lose your value as soldiers. But you can't deny that the four of you working together can boost morale and support for the Sect. You're a package: like the Seattle Siege Dolls, but better."

It was Cheryl's turn to sound like a car salesman. Even Lake was disturbed.

"Lake," Cheryl said, making her jolt. "You explained it so well last time."

Lake raised her eyebrows. "Uh, well, yeah, but I was just trying to get you to—"

Chae Rin kicked her from her seat, silencing her.

"Unfortunately, we don't have a choice." Cheryl eyed the television wearily. "I'm sure Sibyl would agree." She gave a decisive nod. "So that's it, then. I'll let you guys fill Belle in on the details." She paused. "Where *is* Belle, anyway?"

At the sound of her name, I lifted my head.

"Actually, I dunno." Lake turned to the door. "Last I saw her, I was about to go take a shower. She was gone by the time I got out."

"This is so typical." Chae Rin shook her head while tapping her fingers on the armrest. "I am sick and tired of the special treatment she gets. You want us to be some kind of four-girl super squad, you should fix that first."

"At any rate, we should get going," I said quietly.

Cheryl looked at us. "Get going?"

Lake nodded. "We were going to visit the hospital before you called us here. We talked about it with Belle earlier, but I'm totally not surprised she ditched us." Lake turned to us. "You guys ready?"

No. But I couldn't tell them why. Gathering what courage I had left, I rose to my feet and, after a quick nod to Cheryl, followed them out the door.

Rhys had been admitted to a private hospital. He was okay, the EMTs had assured us before they'd whisked him off in the ambulance. But he'd need time to heal.

I stood in front of Rhys's hospital room, paid for not by the Sect, but by his own mysterious family. From what I could tell, none of the members were here. Nobody was here but me, Lake, and Chae Rin. The others stayed behind me, watching anxiously as I rested a hand against the closed door. Twisting a knob had never been so difficult.

"Chae, maybe we should let Maia go in first," said Lake.

Chae Rin agreed. I wished she hadn't.

"That might be a good idea," Chae Rin said. "Let us know when you're done, kid."

I couldn't do this alone, but in some ways it would have been impossible to go in with anyone else. My shoulders slumped, as limp and heavy as the rest of me, but I sucked in a breath and walked inside anyway.

Rhys was asleep in his hospital bed. That in itself was a little miracle. Shutting the door quietly behind me, I approached him, the heels of my shoes clicking off time with the steady rhythm of his heart monitor.

Broken ribs, lacerations, concussion. I could rattle off every detail of his diagnosis because I'd memorized it all. And I could handle it all because of the reassurance the rise and fall of his chest gave me. Seeing him alive filled me with a groundswell of relief, and yet my heart was still hammering against my chest. And my hand . . . it still shook as it reached out for him. I didn't know whether it would find his cheek or his neck first.

No. I withdrew it quickly, squeezing it into a fist. Whatever Natalya had shown me was a lie. Belle had said it herself: A dead Effigy could take the mind of the living only if the latter's mind became greatly unsettled. And Lake had told me once that scrying could be unreliable. Natalya had simply shown me a nightmare to slip into my body. That was all there was to it.

I could still remember Natalya's joy as she tried out her new body. Her desperation to stay. I almost couldn't blame her. Natalya hadn't wanted to die that day.

But it wasn't Rhys who'd killed her.

My eyes followed the battle scars down his chest, faded on his sculpted arms. He'd spent years steadily collecting those scars. His whole life. One whole life devoted to the Sect, devoted to risking his life.

And following their orders.

His eyelashes fluttered. Shocked, I leapt to my feet and rushed to the door without a word. The moment I opened it, I nearly jumped out of my skin from the sudden fright.

"Belle?"

At first glance, Belle looked refined in her fitted jeans and wool sweater, her blond hair twisted into a perfectly plaited French braid.

But it was obvious Belle hadn't slept. Her dulled eyes were red and sunken, her icy beauty as tarnished as dirtied snow. It wasn't just from fatigue.

Belle licked her cracked lips before speaking. "I came . . . to see if Aidan was okay."

My heart gave a violent jerk. Without thinking, I swiftly stepped out of the room and closed the door. "He's sleeping," I said quickly. "You shouldn't go in there."

As Belle nodded, a nervous wave of heat rushed up my head. I could feel beads of sweat already starting to form at my hairline. I had to calm down. I'd already made up my mind, after all: Rhys hadn't done anything wrong.

Like murder Belle's hero.

Hiding my trembling hands behind my back, I leaned against the door.

"In any case . . ." Belle was unable to look at me. "I'm glad . . . glad I found you here."

Belle's gaze settled on the ground. It was the behavior of a girl whose confidence had been shattered. It wasn't the Belle I knew . . . but then, if the past few days were any indication, I clearly never really knew Belle at all.

"I'm sorry." The pain in Belle's whisper was also etched across her face. "I was wrong about everything."

Not even Chae Rin responded to that, though it would have been easier. Each of us stood solemn and silent in the empty hospital hallway.

"But you were right about Natalya," she continued. Saying her name seemed to return a little strength to her. "Someone killed her. And her death is connected to Saul, to Nick, and to Alice. I have to know everything. There has to be more to this. Maia . . . you'll help me, won't you?"

Though I opened my mouth, I couldn't find a sound to come with it.

"*We'll* help you." Lake hesitated before finally patting Belle's shoulder. I could tell Lake didn't know whether Belle would welcome the gesture or turn her into a Popsicle, but she took the risk anyway. "Especially since the Sect is clearly involved."

"I agree," Chae Rin said. "We should definitely stick together on this. Maia?"

They were all looking at me. It was like being in gym class, frozen to the spot while holding the basketball that had just been passed to you. My throat closed. Getting to the bottom of Natalya's death meant opening the very doors I wanted to keep shut. But they were right. Saul was gone, and who knew how many members of the Sect were involved in his antics? Even if I was allowed to go home today, I'd still be haunted by the knowledge of it.

"Yes," I said. "I'll help you."

"There they are. They're right over there!"

I just barely saw the nurse's sheepish expression and outstretched finger before the reporters swarmed the hallway.

We turned to run for it, but the press was already blocking the only exits.

"What the hell?" Chae Rin groaned.

"Nothing for it," Lake said. "We're just going to have to go through." After nudging me, Lake offered me her elbow. "Come on! So nobody gets lost!"

This was my life now. Cameras and flashes. Blood and death. And somehow it all seemed to go hand in hand.

We didn't have a choice. The flood hit. Reporters screeched questions at us from every angle, red-faced and desperate for the story.

"Do you know the whereabouts of the terrorist—"

"What do you think of the support you've been getting from—"

"How long will it be before you—"

I took a breath and nodded to the other girls. Then, linking arms, we disappeared into the crowd together.

ACKNOWLEDGMENTS

Tons of thanks to my agent, Natalie Lakosil, and former editor, Michael Strother, for believing in this book and reading through countless drafts; to Sarah McCabe and the Simon Pulse team for cheering me on; and especially to my family, who remain my original cheerleaders. I also want to send a special shout-out to my oldest brother, David, who heard this idea and kept encouraging me before anyone knew who the Effigies were.

ABOUT THE AUTHOR

SARAH RAUGHLEY grew up in Southern Ontario writing stories about freakish little girls with powers because she secretly wanted to be one. She is a huge fangirl of anything from manga to sci-fi/fantasy TV to Japanese role-playing games, but at book signings she will swear up and down that she was inspired by Jane Austen. On top of being a young adult writer, Sarah is currently completing a PhD in English, because the sight of blood makes her queasy (which crossed medical school off the list).